FROM LUKOV WITH LOVE

MARIANA ZAPATA

Editing by HOT TREE EDITING

Cover by Letitia Hasser at RBA DESIGNS

Formatting by INDIE FORMATTING

To my best friend and the best person I know,
My mom
The real chingona.

CHAPTER 1

2016

By the time I'd busted my ass five times in a row, I figured it was time to call it quits.

At least for the day.

My butt cheeks could handle another two hours' worth of falls tomorrow. They might have to if I didn't figure out what I was doing wrong, damn it. This was the second day in a row I hadn't been able to land a damn jump.

Rolling over onto the cheek I'd fallen on the least amount of times, I blew out a breath of frustration, managed to keep the "son of a bitch" I really wanted to scream inside my mouth, and tilted my head all the way back to make faces at the ceiling, figuring out almost immediately that decision was a fucking mistake. Because I knew what was hanging from the ceiling of the dome-shaped facility. For the most part, it was the same thing I'd been seeing for the last thirteen years.

Banners.

Banners hanging from the rafters.

Banners with the same jackass's name on all of them.

IVAN LUKOV. IVAN LUKOV. IVAN LUKOV.

And more IVAN LUKOV.

There were other names on there right alongside his—the other miserable souls he'd partnered up with over the years—but it was his that stood out. Not because his last name was the same last name as one of my favorite people in the world, but because his first name reminded me of Satan. I was pretty sure his parents had adopted him straight out of Hell.

But at that moment, nothing else mattered but those hanging tapestries.

Five different blue banners proclaiming each of the national championships he'd won. Two red banners for every world championship. Two butter yellow banners for every gold medal. One silver banner to commemorate the single silver medal for a world championship sitting in the trophy case at the entrance to the facility.

Ugh. Overachiever. Ass. Jerk.

And thank fuck there weren't banners for every Cup or other competition he'd won along the years too, otherwise the entire ceiling would have been covered in colors, and I would have been throwing up daily.

All these banners... and none of them had my name on them. Not one single one. No matter how hard I had tried, how hard I had trained, nothing. Because no one ever remembers second place, unless you're Ivan Lukov. And I was no Ivan.

Jealousy I had no right to feel, but couldn't exactly ignore, pierced right through my sternum, and I hated it. *I fucking hated it.* Worrying about what other people were doing was a waste of time and energy; I'd learned that as a kid when other girls had nicer costumes and newer skates than me. Being jealous and bitter was what people who didn't have anything better to do, did. I knew that. No one did anything with their lives if they spent it comparing themselves to other people. I knew that too.

And I never wanted to be that person. Especially not over that jackass. I'd take my three seconds of jealousy shit to the grave with me before I ever told anyone what those banners did to me.

It was with that reminder that I rolled onto my knees to quit looking at those stupid-ass pieces of cloth.

Slapping my hands on the ice, I grunted as I got my feet under me—balancing on my blades was second nature—and finally got up. *Again*. For the fifth fucking time in less than fifteen minutes. My left hip bone, butt cheek, and thigh were aching, and they were only going to hurt worse tomorrow.

"Fucking shit," I muttered under my breath so that none of the younger girls skating around me would hear. The last thing I needed was for one of them to tell on me to management. *Again*. Little snitches. Like they didn't hear the f-bomb watching television, walking down the street, or going to school.

Brushing off the ice coating my side from my last fall, I took a steadying breath and reeled in the frustration flaring through my body at everything—at myself, my body, my situation, my life, the other girls I couldn't fucking curse around—at today in general. From waking up late to not being able to land a jump that morning either, to spilling coffee down my shirt at work *twice*, opening my car door and having it almost break my kneecap, and then this second session of shitty training....

It was easy to forget that in the grand scheme of life, not being able to land a jump I'd been doing for ten years didn't mean anything. It was just an off day. *Another* off day. It wasn't unheard of. There was always something worse that could and *would* happen, someday, some time. It was easy to take things for granted when you thought you had everything.

But it was when you started taking the most basic things for granted that life decided to teach you that you're an ungrateful idiot.

And today, the thing I was taking for granted were landing triple Salchows, a jump I'd been doing for years. They weren't the easiest jump in figure skating—the jump consisted of three rotations that started while skating backward on the back inside edge of the blade of your skate before takeoff, and then required a landing on the back outside edge of the blade of the opposite foot you took off from—but it definitely wasn't anywhere near being the hardest. Under normal circumstances, they were second nature to me.

But not today or yesterday apparently.

Scrubbing my eyelids with the backs of my hands, I took a deep breath in and let another slow one out, rolling my shoulders in the process and telling myself I needed to calm down and just go home. There was always tomorrow.

And it wasn't like I was going to be competing any time soon, the practical but asshole part of my brain reminded me.

Just like it did every single time I thought about that awesome fact, my stomach clenched in pure anger... and something that felt awfully close to despair.

And just like every time it happened, I shoved both those emotions way, way, *way* down, so far down I couldn't see them or touch them or smell them. *They were pointless.* I knew that. Absolutely pointless.

I wasn't giving up.

With another inhale and exhale as I subconsciously rubbed the ass cheek hurting the worst for forgiveness, I looked around the rink one last time for the day. Taking in the girls so much younger than me, still taking advantage of the session going on at the moment, I held back a frown. There were three that were about my age, but the others were all in their teens. Maybe they weren't that good—at least not as good as I'd been at their ages—but still. *They had their entire lives ahead of them.* Only in figure skating, and maybe gymnastics, could you be considered ancient at twenty-six years old.

Yeah, I needed to get home and lay on the couch with some television to get over this shit day. Nothing good ever came out of me throwing my own ass a pity party. Nothing.

It didn't take more than a couple of seconds to weave my way through and around the other people on the ice, paying just enough attention to not crash into anyone before making it to the short wall surrounding the rink. In the same place I'd always left my skate guards, I grabbed the pieces of plastic and slipped them over the four-millimeter wide blades attached to my white boots right before stepping onto solid ground.

I tried to ignore that tight feeling bubbling around in my chest that was more than likely mostly frustration at falling so much today, but maybe wasn't.

I wasn't about to believe my chances were high that I was wasting my time still hitting the Lukov Ice and Sports Complex twice a day to workout in hopes of someday competing again because the idea of just giving up seemed like a total waste of the last sixteen years of my life. Like I hadn't basically given up my childhood for nothing. Like I hadn't sacrificed relationships and normal human experiences for a dream I'd had that had once been so huge, nothing and no one could have taken it away from me.

Like my dream of winning a gold medal... of at least winning a world championship, even a national championship... hadn't been broken down into tiny, confetti-sized pieces that I was still clinging onto even though some part of me realized all it did was hurt me more than help me.

Nope.

It wasn't any of those ideas and possibilities that made my stomach hurt almost daily and made me nauseous right then and there.

I needed to chill out. Or maybe masturbate. Something had to help.

Shaking off that crappy feeling in my gut, I made my way around the rink and continued on down the hall that led toward the changing rooms, taking in the crowd. There were already parents and kids hanging around the rink, getting ready for evening classes; the same classes I'd started with at nine years old before moving on to small groups and then private lessons with Galina. The good old days.

I kept my head down to avoid making eye contact with anyone and kept on going, passing other people who went out of their way to avoid my gaze too. But it wasn't until I was going down the hall toward where my things were, that I spotted a group of four teenage girls standing around, pretending to stretch. Pretending because you couldn't get a proper stretch in if you were busy running your mouth.

At least that's what I'd been taught.

"Hi, Jasmine!" one of them greeted, a nice girl who, as far as I could remember, had always gone out of her way to be friendly to me.

"Hi, Jasmine," the girl beside her said too.

I couldn't help but nod at them, even as I counted down the time it would take me to go home, either make something to eat or microwave something my mom had made, and probably sit on my ass and watch TV. Maybe if practice had gone better, I'd want to do something else, like go for a run or even go to my sister's house, but... it wasn't going to happen.

"Have a good practice," I mumbled at the two friendly girls, flashing a glance at the other two standing across from them, silently. They looked familiar. There was a class for intermediate skaters starting soon that I figured they were enrolled in. I had no reason to pay attention to them.

"Thanks, you too!" the first girl who had talked to me squawked out before slamming her mouth closed and turning a shade of red I'd only seen on one person in the past: my sister.

The smile that came over my mouth was genuine and unexpected—because the girl made me think of Squirt—and I dug my shoulder into the swinging door of the changing room. I'd barely taken a step in, shoulder still holding the door open, when I heard, "I don't know why you get so excited seeing her. She might have been a good singles skater, but she always choked, and her pairs career was nothing to talk about."

And... I stopped. Right there. Halfway in the door. And I did something I knew was a bad idea: I listened.

Eavesdropping never worked out for anybody, but I did it anyway.

"Mary McDonald is a better pairs skater—"

They went there.

Breathe, Jasmine. Breathe. Shut up and breathe. Think about what you're going to say. Think about how far you've come. Think about—

"—otherwise, Paul wouldn't have teamed up with her this last season," the girl finished.

Assault was against the law. But was it extra illegal to hit a teenager?

Breathe. Think. Be nicer.

I was old enough to know better. I knew that. I was old enough to not get offended by some teenage twat who probably hadn't even gone through puberty yet, but...

Well, my pairs career was a sore spot for me. And by sore

spot, I meant a bleeding blister that refused to heal. Mary McDonald and Paul The Piece of Shit Asshole I Would Burn Alive? I'd watched just enough of the Brady Bunch late at night when I couldn't sleep to totally get Jan's beef with Marcia. I would have hated her ass too. Just like I hated Mary McDonald's ass.

"Have you seen all the videos there are online of her? My mom says she's got a bad attitude and that's why she never won; the judges don't like her," the other girl attempted to whisper but basically failed because I could hear her clear as day.

I didn't need to do this. I didn't need to do anything. They were still kids, I tried to tell myself. They didn't know the whole story. They didn't even know part of the story. Most people didn't, and they never would. I'd accepted it and gotten over it.

But then one of them kept on talking, and I knew I wouldn't be able to shut the hell up and let them assume their bullshit. There's only so much a person can take on a good day, and today hadn't been a good one to begin with.

"My mom said the only reason she still trains here is because she's friends with Karina Lukov, but supposedly her and Ivan don't get along—"

I was *this* fucking close to snorting. Ivan and I not getting along? Is that what they were calling it? *Okay.*

"She's kind of a bitch."

"Nobody was surprised she couldn't get another partner after Paul left her."

And there it was.

Maybe if they wouldn't have said the P-name again I could have been the bigger person, but fuck it, I was five foot three and I wasn't built to be that person ever.

Before I could stop myself, I turned around and peeked my

head out the door to find the four girls right where they'd been a moment ago. "What did you just say?" I asked, slowly, keeping the *you talentless fuckers are never going to do shit* to myself at least. I made sure to look right at the two that hadn't said hi to me, whose heads pretty much snapped in my direction in horror the moment I started talking.

"I... I... I...," one of them stuttered while the other looked like she was about to crap her leotard and tights. Good. I hoped she did. And I hoped it had a diarrhea-like texture so it would go everywhere.

I stared at each one of them for what felt like a minute each, watching their faces turn bright red and getting just a little a kick out of it... but not as much as I normally could have if I wasn't already pissed off at myself more than them. Raising my eyebrows, I tilted my head in the direction of the hall-like tunnel I'd just taken from the rink to the changing rooms and smiled a smile that wasn't one at all. "That's what I thought. You should get to practice before you're late."

Somehow, I kept from adding "fuckers" to the end. Some days I deserved a medal for being so patient with idiots. If only they had a competition for that, I could have won.

Chances were that I'd never see two people move so fast ever again unless I watched the sprinters in the Olympics. The two nice girls looked slightly horrified but shot me quick uneasy smiles before following after the other two, whispering God knows what to each other.

Girls like those shitty two were the reasons why I'd stopped trying to make friends with other figure skaters early on. Mini fuckers. I raised my middle finger at the retreating bodies down the hall, but it didn't really make me feel any better.

I needed to snap out of it. I really, really did.

I finished making my way into the changing room and

dropped onto one of the benches in front of the row of lockers mine was located in; the ache in my hip and thigh had gotten stronger on the walk over. I'd taken falls a lot harder and more painful than the ones today but, despite knowing that, you never exactly "got used" to the pain; when it happened regularly, you made yourself get over it faster. And the reality of it was, I wasn't training the way I used to, I couldn't—not when I didn't have a partner to practice with and didn't have a coach correcting me for hours each day—so my body had forgotten what it could take.

It was just another shitty sign that time and life kept going even when I didn't want it to.

Stretching my legs out ahead of me, I ignored the handful of older teenage girls already clustered on the opposite side of the room furthest from the door, getting dressed and fiddling with their boots, talking as they did it. They didn't look at me, and I didn't do more than glance at them out of the corner of my eye. Undoing my laces, I thought about showering for all of a second before deciding that was going to be too much work when I could wait twenty minutes until I got home so I could change and shower there in my full-sized bathroom. I took my right white skate off, and then gingerly pulled off the nude-colored bandage that covered my ankle and a couple inches above it.

"*Oh my God!*" one of the teenagers pretty much shrieked from the other side of the room, making it impossible for me to zone her out. "*You're not joking, are you?*"

"*No!*" someone else responded as I unlaced my left skate, trying hard to ignore the girls.

"*Seriously?*" another voice, or maybe it was the same one from the beginning, piped up. I couldn't tell. It wasn't like I was trying to listen to them.

"*Seriously!*"

"*Seriously?*"

"*Seriously!*"

I rolled my eyes and kept trying to ignore them.

"*No!*"

"*Yes!*"

"*No!*"

"*Yes!*"

Yeah. I couldn't ignore shit. Had I ever been that annoying? That girly?

No way.

"*Where did you hear that?*"

I was in the middle of putting in the code to my combination lock on my locker when there was a chorus of noises that had me glancing over my shoulder to glare at the girls. One of them literally looked like she was on speed, she was baring her teeth, and her hands were hanging out right at chest level as she clapped her palms together. Another girl had her fingers knitted together, palms joined in front of her mouth, and she might have been shaking.

What in the hell was wrong with them two?

"*Hear it? I saw him walk in with Coach Lee.*"

Ugh.

Of course. Who the hell else would they be talking about?

I didn't bother sighing or even rolling my eyes as I turned back to my locker and pulled my gym bag out, unzipping it the moment I set it on the bench beside me so I could dig out my phone, keys, flip-flops, and a tiny bar of Hershey's I kept in there for days like today. I took off the wrapper and stuffed that thing in my mouth before grabbing my phone. The green light on the screen blinked, telling me I had unread messages. Unlocking it, I glanced over my shoulder to see the girls there still squawking and making it seem like they were on the verge of having a heart attack over The Asswipe. Ignoring them, I took my time reading through the group chat messages I had missed while practicing.

Jojo: I want to go to the movies tonight. Anyone in?
Tali: Depends. What movie?
Mom: Ben and I will go with you, baby.
Seb: No. I've got a date tonight.
Seb: James doesn't want to go with you? I don't blame him.
Jojo: The new Marvel movie.
Jojo: Seb, I hope you get an STD tonight.
Tali: Marvel? No thanks.
Tali: I hope you get an STD too, Seb.
Mom: WOULD YOU ALL BE NICE TO EACH OTHER?
Seb: All of you can eat shit except for Mom.
Rubes: I'd go with you but Aaron's not feeling well.
Jojo: I know you would, Squirt. Love you. Next time.
Jojo: Mom, let's go. 7:30 work?
Jojo: Seb- [emoji of a middle finger]
Jojo: Jas, you in?

I looked up as the girls in the changing room made noises I wasn't sure I was capable of, wondering what the hell was going on with them. Jesus Christ, it wasn't like Ivan didn't train here five days a week for the last million years. Seeing him wasn't that exciting. I would rather watch paint dry.

Scrunching up my bright pink-colored toenails, I took them in and purposely ignored the bruise I had right alongside my smallest toe and the start of a blister I had beside my big toe from the seam of a new brand of tights I'd worn the day before.

"*What is he doing here?*" the teenagers kept going, reminding me that I needed to get out of the room as quickly as possible. I'd already reached my limit for how much I could handle today.

Glancing back at my phone, I tried to decide what to do. Go home and watch a movie or suck it up and go to the movies with my brother, mom, and Ben—or as the rest of us called him in secret, number four?

I would rather go home and not hang out in a crowded movie theater on the weekend, but....

My hand fisted for a second before I typed up a response.

I'll go, but I need food first. Going home now.

Then I smiled and added another message.

Seb, I third you getting an STD. Aim for gonorrhea this time.

Setting my phone between my legs in the meantime, I grabbed my car keys from the pocket of my bag and snagged my flip-flops, then carefully set each of my skates into a custom protective case lined with a faux-fur over thin memory foam that my brother Jonathan and his husband had bought me years ago. I zipped my bag back up, slid my feet into my sandals, and got to my feet with a sigh that made my chest feel tight.

Today hadn't been the best, but it would get better, I told myself.

It had to.

The good thing was, I didn't have work tomorrow, and I didn't usually come skate on Sundays either. My mom would probably make pancakes for breakfast, and I was supposed to go to the zoo with my brother and niece since he was picking her up for the day. I'd missed enough moments in her life because of figure skating. Now that I had more time, I was trying to make up for it. It was better for me to look at it like that than get hung up on why I had more time on my hands. I was trying to be more positive. I just wasn't that good at it yet.

"I don't know," one of the girls said. *"But he usually doesn't come in for a month or two after the end of the season, and it's been what? A week since Worlds?"*

"I wonder if he split up with Mindy."

"Why would he do that?"

"I don't know. Why did he split up with any of the rest of them before her?"

I'd already known from the moment one of them said Coach Lee's name whom they were still talking about. There was only one man left at the LC—what most of us called the Lukov Ice and Sports Complex, or the Lukov Complex for short—that these girls would give a crap about. It was the same guy everyone gave a shit about. Everyone except me at least. And anyone else with a brain. Ivan Lukov.

Or as I liked to call him, to his face especially—the son of Satan.

"All I said was that I saw him. I don't know what he's doing here," a voice said.

"He never comes over randomly, Stacy. Come on. Put two and two together."

"Oh my God, are he and Mindy splitting up?"

"If they are, I wonder who he'll skate with."

"It could be anybody."

"Shoot, I'd pay to partner with him," a girl said.

"You don't even know anything about pairs, stupid," another girl said, snorting. I wasn't actively listening, but my brain continued stringing together the pieces of their comments as they went in one ear and out the other.

"How hard could it be?" the other voice rattled off proudly. *"He's got the greatest butt in the country, and he wins with everyone. Sounds like a walk in the park to me."*

I rolled my eyes again, especially at the butt part. The last thing that idiot ever needed to hear was someone compliment it. But, she had missed the most relevant parts of Ivan. How he was the figure skating world's sweetheart-slash-dreamboat. The World Skating Union's poster boy for pairs skating. Hell, for skating in general, really. "Skating royalty" as some called him. "A prodigy" people had used when he'd been a teenager.

He was the man whose family owned the center I had trained at for over a decade.

The brother to one of my only friends.

The man who had not once said a kind word to me in over ten years. That's how I knew him. As the ass who I'd seen daily for years and had only ever bickered to me over the dumbest shit from time to time. The person I couldn't have a conversation with without it ending in one of us insulting the other.

Yeah... I didn't get why he was at the Lukov Complex barely a week after he'd won his third world championship, days after the season had ended—when he should have been resting or vacationing. At least that was what he'd done every year for as long as I could remember.

Did I care he was around? Nah. If I really wanted to know what was happening, I could just ask Karina. I just didn't. There was no need to.

Because it wasn't like Ivan and I were going to compete against each other anytime soon... or ever again, if things continued the way they were going.

And something told me, even if I didn't want to believe it—never, ever, ever—as I stood there in the same changing room I'd been using for more than half my life, that that was the case: that I might be done. After so long, after so many months of being by myself... my dream might be over.

And I had not a single fucking thing to show for it.

CHAPTER 2

"*Did you hear the news?*"

I gave the laces on my boot an extra tight squeeze in the changing room before looping the ends into a knot tight enough to survive the next hour. I didn't need to turn around to know there were two teenage girls down the bench from me in front of their lockers. They were there every morning, usually farting around. They could have had more time on the ice if they didn't talk, but whatever. I wasn't the one paying for their ice time. If they'd had my mom for their own, she would've gotten them out of that standing-around habit real quick.

"*My mom told me last night,*" the taller of the two said as she got to her feet.

I stood up and kept my attention forward, rolling back my shoulders even though I'd already spent an hour warming up and stretching. Maybe I wasn't skating six or seven hours a day like I used to—when stretching for at least an hour was absolutely necessary—but old habits died hard. And suffering for days or weeks from a pulled muscle wasn't worth the hour I'd save from skipping my warm-up.

"*She said she overheard someone say that they think he's retiring because he's had so many problems with his partners.*"

Now that caught my attention.

He. Retiring. Problems.

It had pretty much been a miracle that I'd graduated from high school on time, but even I knew who they had to be talking about. Ivan. Who the hell else? Other than a few younger boys, and the three years that Paul had spent training at the Lukov Ice and Sports Complex with me, there was no other "he" that anyone here would talk about. There were a couple of teenage boys, but none of them had the potential to go very far, if anybody gave a shit about my opinion. Not that they did.

"*Maybe if he retires he'll go into coaching,*" one of the girls said. "*I wouldn't mind him yelling at me all day.*"

I *almost* laughed. Ivan retiring? No way. There was no chance in hell he'd retire at twenty-nine, especially not while he was still killing it. Months ago, he'd won a US championship. And a month before that, he'd taken second place in the Major Prix final.

Why the hell was I even paying attention anyway?

I didn't care what he did. His life was his business. We all had to quit sometime. And the less I had to look at his annoying face, the better.

Deciding that I didn't need to be distracted starting the first of only two hours I had in the day to practice—especially not being distracted over Ivan of all people—I made my way out of the changing room, leaving the two teenagers in there to waste their own time gossiping. This early in the morning, there were six people on the ice, like usual. I didn't come in as early as I had before—there wasn't a point—but every face, I'd been seeing for years.

Some more than others.

Galina was already sitting on one of the bleachers outside the rink with her thermos of coffee that I knew from experience was so thick it looked and tasted like tar. With her favorite red scarf wound around her neck and ears, she had on a sweater I'd seen at least a hundred times in the past and what looked like a shawl on top of it. I'd swear she'd started adding an item of clothing to what she wore every year. When she had first plucked me out of lessons almost fourteen years ago, she had been fine in just a long sleeved shirt and a shawl, now she probably would have frozen to death.

Fourteen years was longer than some of these girls had been alive.

"Good morning," I said in the choppy Russian I'd picked up from her over the years.

"Hello, *yozik*," she greeted me, her eyes darting toward the ice for a brief moment before returning to me with a face that was the same as it had been when I'd been twelve, all weathered and fierce, like her skin was made of bulletproof material. "Your weekend, it was good?"

I nodded, briefly reminiscing on how I'd gone to the zoo with my brother and niece and then gone to his condo afterward for pizza—two things I couldn't remember ever doing in the past, the pizza part included. "Did you have a good one?" I asked the woman who taught me so many things I could never give her credit for.

The dimples she rarely showed came out. She had a face I knew so well I could describe it to a sketch artist perfectly if she ever came missing. Round, thin eyebrows, almond-shaped eyes, a thin mouth, a scar on her chin from taking a partner's blade to the face back in her competing days, another scar at her temple from smacking her head on the ice. Not that she would ever go missing. Any kidnapper would probably release her within an hour. "I saw my grandchild."

I thought about the dates for a second before it clicked. "It was his birthday, right?"

She nodded, her gaze moving toward the rink again in the direction of what I knew was the figure skater she'd been working with since I'd left her to start skating pairs four years ago. Well, I hadn't wanted to leave her but... it didn't matter. It didn't make me jealous anymore to think of how quickly she'd replaced me. But sometimes, especially lately, it bothered me. Just a little. Just enough.

I'd never let her know that. "Did you finally buy him skates?" I asked.

My old coach tipped her head to the side and shrugged a shoulder, the gray eyes, which had stared me down countless times, still settled on the ice. "Yes. Used skates and video game. I waited. He's almost same age you were. Little later, but still good."

She'd finally done it. I remembered when he'd been born —before we'd split—and how we'd talked about him figure skating when he was old enough. It had only been a matter of time. We both knew that. Her own children hadn't made it out of the junior level, but it hadn't mattered.

But thinking about him, her grandson, just starting made me feel... almost homesick, remembering how much fun figure skating had been back then. Back before the bone-crushing pressure, the drama, and the fucking critics. Back before I'd learned the shitty taste of disappointment. Figure skating had always made me feel invincible. But more than anything, back then, it had made me feel amazing. I hadn't known it was possible to feel like you could fly. To be so strong. To be so beautiful. To be good at something. Especially something that I cared about. Because I hadn't known that contorting body parts and twisting and turning them into shapes that shouldn't have been possible could be so impressive. It had made me feel special to go as fast as I could around the oval shape, that I would have no idea until years later, would change my life.

Galina's chuckle snapped me out of my funk. At least for a moment.

"One day, you coach him," she offered with a snort, like she was imagining me treating him the way she had treated me, and it made her laugh.

I snickered at the memories of all the hundreds of times she had smacked me on the back of the head throughout those ten years we were together. Some people wouldn't have been able to handle her brand of tough love, but I'd secretly loved it. I'd thrived with it. My mom always said that if anyone gave me an inch, I'd take a mile.

And the last thing Galina Petrov would ever do is give up a single centimeter.

But this wasn't the first time she'd mentioned the idea of me coaching. Over the last few months, when things had become... more desperate, when my hope of finding another partner began to shrivel up, she'd started dropping the possibility on me when we'd talk, not subtly or swiftly at all. Just *Jasmine, you coach. Yes?*

But I still wasn't ready for that. Coaching felt like giving up, and... I wasn't ready. Not yet. *Not fucking yet.*

But maybe it's time? Some nagging, whiney voice in my head whispered at the same time, making my stomach clench.

Almost as if she could sense what was going on in my head, she made another snorting sound. "I have things to do. Practice your jumps. You aren't committing, you are too much in your head, that's why you have been falling. Remember seven years ago," she said, her attention still on the ice. "Stop thinking. You know what to do."

I hadn't thought she'd noticed me struggling since she was busy coaching someone else.

But I focused on her words, remembering exactly what time period she was talking about. She was right. I had been nineteen. That had been the worst season of my singles career, back when I hadn't had a partner and skated all by myself; that season had been the catalyst for the next three seasons that had led me down the path to pairs, to skating with a partner. I'd been in my head too much, overthought *everything*, and... well, if I'd made a mistake transitioning from singles, it was too late to regret it at this point.

Life was about choices, and I had made mine.

I nodded and swallowed back that old shame at the memory of that horrible season I still thought about when I was by myself and feeling more pitiful than usual. "That's what I was worried about. I'm gonna go work on them. I'll see you later, Lina," I said to my old coach, fiddling with the bracelet on my wrist for a moment before dropping my hands and shaking them both out.

Galina's eyes quickly moved over my face before she dipped her chin gravely and turned her attention back to the rink, shouting something in her deeply accented voice about going into a jump too slowly.

Taking off my skate guards and setting them in their usual spot, I stepped out on the ice and focused.

I could do this.

~

EXACTLY AN HOUR LATER, I WAS AS SWEATY AND AS TIRED AS I'D been back when I'd have a three-hour session. I was getting soft, damn it. I'd ended up doing a few jump combinations—a sequence or at least one jump followed immediately by another, sometimes two more jumps—but my heart hadn't really been in it. I'd landed them, but only barely, wobbling and fighting to stick each one while trying my hardest to focus on them and only them at the same time.

Galina was right. I was distracted, but I couldn't figure out what exactly was distracting me. Maybe I really did need to rub one out real quick or go for a run or *something*. Anything to clear my head, or at least this funky feeling that had been following me around like a ghost.

I made it back to the changing rooms, only slightly frustrated to find a plain yellow Post-It note on the door of my locker. I didn't think anything of it. A month ago, the general manager for the LC had left me a similar note, asking me to go to her office. All she'd wanted was to offer me a job coaching beginner lessons. *Again.* Why she thought I'd be a good candidate for teaching young girls—practically babies—I had no idea, but I'd told her I wasn't interested.

So when I picked the note off the locker and slowly read **Jasmine, come to the GM office before you go**, twice, just to make sure I read it correctly, I didn't think much of it except the fact that whatever the GM wanted from me was going to have to be quick because I had to get to work. I had my days timed to the minute. I had lists with my schedules just about everywhere—on my phone, on sheets of paper in my car, in my bags, in my room, on the fridge—so I wouldn't forget or get flustered. Being organized, prepared, and constantly keeping track of time to be punctual were important to me. As it was, I was going to need to skip sitting under the hot water and putting on makeup to get to work in time, unless I let my boss know.

Pulling my phone out of my bag the moment I had my locker unlocked, I typed up a message, thanking spellcheck like I always did for existing and making my life easier, and sent it to my mom. She always had her phone on her.

Me: The LC GM wants to talk. Can you call Matty and tell him I'm running a little late but will be there asap?

She responded immediately.

Mom: What did you do?

I rolled my eyes and typed a response. **Nothing**

Mom: Then why are you going to the office?
Mom: Did you call someone's mom a dirty whore again?

Of course she'd never forget that. No one did.

Then there was the fact that I hadn't told her about the three other times the GM had asked me into her office to try and talk me into coaching.

Me: I don't know. Maybe my check last week bounced.

That was a joke. She knew better than anyone how much LC fees cost. She'd paid for them for over a decade.

Me: No. I haven't called anyone's mom a dirty whore again, but that other dirty whore deserved it.

Knowing she would reply almost immediately, I set my phone back into my locker and decided I could text her back in a minute. Rushing through my shower after putting my things up, I slipped into my underwear, jeans, collared shirt, socks, and the best looking comfortable shoes I was able to afford, in record time. By the time I was done with that, I checked my phone again and found my mom had replied.

Mom: You need money?
Mom: She did deserve it.
Mom: Shoved anybody lately?

It killed me inside that she still asked me if I needed money. Like I hadn't taken enough of hers over the years, month after month. Failed season after failed season.

At least I wasn't asking her for it anymore.

Me: I'm okay with money. Thanks.
Me: I have not shoved anyone again.
Mom: You sure?
Me: Yes, I'm sure. I would know if I did.
Mom: Positive?
Me: Yes
Mom: It's okay if you did. Some people need it.
Mom: Even I've wanted to punch you sometimes. It happens.

I couldn't help but laugh.

Me: Me too
Mom: You've wanted to punch me in the throat?
Me: There is no right answer to that question.
Mom: Ha ha ha ha.
Me: I never did it. OK?

Zipping up my bag, I gripped the handle, fisted my keys, and walked out of there as fast as possible, basically jogging down one hall and then another to head toward the part of the building where the business offices were located. I was going to have to eat the egg white sandwich I'd left in my lunch bag in my car as I drove. Just as I made it to the door, I typed up another message to be on the safe side, ignoring my misspellings, which I usually didn't.

Me: For real ma. Can you call n tell him?
Mom: YES
Me: Thank u
Mom: Love you.
Mom: Tell me if you need money.

My throat tightened for a moment, but I didn't text anything back. I wouldn't tell her even if I did. Not anymore. At least not if I could help it, and the truth was, I'd turn to stripping if it ever got to that point again. She'd done enough.

Holding in a sigh, I knocked on the door of the general manager's office, thinking that I really wanted whatever conversation was about to happen to last all of ten minutes so that I wouldn't be too late to work. I didn't want to take advantage of my mom's closest friend being lenient with me.

I turned the knob the second I heard a voice inside the office shout, "Come in!"

Let's get this over with, I thought, opening the door.

The problem in that moment was that I'd never been a fan of surprises. Ever. Not even when I was little. I had always liked to know what I was getting myself into. Needless to say, no one had ever thrown me a surprise birthday party. The one time my grandpa had tried to pull that off, my mom had told me in advance and made me swear I'd act surprised. I had.

I'd been ready to face the general manager, a woman named Georgina that I'd always gotten along with. I'd overheard some people call her a hard-ass, but to me, she was just strong willed and didn't take shit from people because she didn't have to.

So, I was pretty much shocked as hell when the first person I spotted sitting in the office wasn't Georgina, but a familiar, fifty-something woman with a bun that was so neat, the only other times I'd seen one so perfect was during competitions.

And I was even more surprised when I saw the second person in the office, just sitting there on the other side of the desk.

My third surprise came in the shape of the realization that there was no general manager in sight.

Just... them.

Ivan Lukov and the woman who had spent the last eleven years training him.

Someone who I couldn't have a conversation with without arguing, and the other who had said maybe twenty words to me over the course of those eleven years.

What in the hell is going on? I wondered, before settling my gaze on the other woman, trying to figure out if I'd misread the note on my locker. I hadn't... had I? I had taken my time. I had read it twice. I didn't usually butcher reading things any more.

"I was looking for Georgina," I explained, trying to ignore the instant frustration in my stomach at the possibility I'd misread the words on the Post It. I hated messing up. *Hated it.* Screwing up in front of them made it even worse, damn it. "Do you know where she's at?" I ground out, still thinking about the note.

The woman smiled easily, not at all like I'd interrupted something important and not even a little like I was someone she had basically ignored for years, and it immediately put me even more on edge. She had never smiled at me before. Actually, I didn't think I'd ever seen her smile, period. "Come in," she said, that smile still holding strong. "I left the note on your locker, not Georgina."

I'd feel relieved later that I hadn't misread the words, but at that point, I was too busy wondering why the hell I was standing there and why she had sent me that note.... And why the hell Ivan was sitting there not saying anything.

As if reading my mind, the woman's smile grew wider, like she was trying to reassure me, but it did the opposite. "Sit down, Jasmine," she said in a tone that reminded me she'd coached the idiot to my left through two world championships. The problem was, she wasn't my coach, and I didn't like people telling me what to do, even when they had a right to. She also hadn't been particularly nice to me either. She hadn't been rude, but she hadn't been kind either.

I mean, I understood. That didn't mean I was going to forget about it though.

For two years, I'd been in the same competitions Ivan had. I was competitive, and so were they. It was easier to want to beat someone that you weren't friendly with. But that didn't explain the years before that, back when I'd skated by myself and had nothing to do with him. Back when she could have been friendly with me... but hadn't. Not that I'd wanted her to or needed her to, but still.

So, she shouldn't have been surprised when all I did was raise my eyebrows at her.

Apparently, she decided that raising her eyebrows right back at me was the best way to respond. "Please?" she offered, almost sounding sweet.

I didn't trust her tone, or her.

I couldn't help but sweep my gaze in the direction of the chairs across from her. There were only two, and one of them was occupied by Ivan, who I hadn't seen since he'd left for

Boston before Worlds. Those long legs of his were stretched out straight, those feet that I'd seen more in skates than in regular shoes were tucked beneath the desk his coach had taken over. But it wasn't the lazy way he was sitting there with his arms crossed over his chest showcasing those lean pecs and leaner torso, or the navy blue turtleneck bringing to life the almost pale skin over the face that the other girls at the facility went nuts over, that caught my attention for the longest amount of time.

It was his gray-blue eyes totally zoned in on me that made me pause. I never forgot how intense the color was, but it always took me off guard anyway. I never forgot how long the black eyelashes surrounding them were either.

Then there was everything else around those eyes.

Ugh.

So many girls went nuts over his face, over his hair, over his eyes, over his figure skating, over his arms, his long legs, the way he breathed, the toothpaste he used.... It was annoying. Even my brother called him a pretty boy—he called my sister's husband a pretty boy too, but that wasn't the point. If that wasn't enough, girls worshipped the broad shoulders that helped him hold his partners a full arm's length above his head with one foot balanced on the narrow slice of metal called a blade. I'd overheard women swoon over a butt I didn't need to look at to know had to be a perfect example of a bubble butt—tight buns were pretty much mandatory in this sport.

And if he had a best feature, those creepy eyes would have been it.

But he didn't. The devil didn't have any redeeming qualities.

I stared at him, and that evil pretty-boy face stared back at me. He didn't look anywhere other than my face. He didn't frown or smile or anything.

And that shit put me on edge.

He just... looked. With his mouth shut. And his hands—and fingers—tucked into his armpits.

If I had been anyone else, he would have made me uneasy with that gaze. But I wasn't his groupie. I knew him well enough to not be distracted by the bodysuit he wore over his natural form. He worked hard, so he was good. He wasn't a unicorn. He definitely wasn't a Pegasus. He didn't impress me.

Plus, I had been there when his mom ripped him a new one once years ago for talking back to her, so there was that, too.

"What's this about?" I asked slowly, staring at Ivan's semifamiliar face for another second before finally dragging my gaze back to Coach Lee, who was almost hunched over the desk, if someone with her posture was capable of hunching, elbows firmly planted, the thin, dark slashes of her eyebrows still high in interest. She was just as pretty as she'd been back when she competed. I had watched videos of her back in the 80s when she'd been the national champion.

"It's nothing bad, I promise," the older woman answered carefully, like she could still pick up on my uneasiness. She gestured toward the chair beside Ivan's. "Can you take a seat?"

Bad things happened when someone asked you to take a seat. Especially one next to Ivan. So, that wasn't happening. "I'm fine," I said, my voice sounding as weird as I felt.

What was going on? I couldn't be getting kicked out of the facility. I hadn't done anything.

Unless those shit kids from the weekend had tattled on me. Damn it.

"Jasmine, all we need is two minutes," Coach Lee said slowly, still motioning toward the chair.

Yeah, this shit wasn't adding up, and it was only getting worse. Two minutes? You couldn't do anything well in two minutes. I brushed my teeth for longer than two minutes twice a day.

I didn't move. They had tattled on me. Those little fuckers—

Confirming that I wasn't hiding my thoughts at all, Coach Lee sighed from her spot behind the desk. I didn't miss the way her eyes slid toward Ivan briefly before returning to me. In a navy suit jacket and a crisp white shirt, she looked more like a lawyer than the figure skater she had been and the coach she currently was. The woman shifted in her seat and sat up straight, her lips pursing together for a moment before she spoke again. "I'll get to the point then. How set are you on being retired?"

How set was I on being retired? Was that what everyone thought I was? Fucking retired?

It wasn't like I'd chosen not to have a partner and miss an entire season, but... whatever. *Whatever.* My blood pressure did something weird it had never done before, but I decided to ignore it and the r-word at least for now and chose to focus on the most important part of what had just come out of her mouth. "Why are you asking?" I asked slowly, still worried. Just a little.

I should have called Karina.

In a straightforward move I could appreciate at any other time, the other woman didn't beat around the bush. And that's what surprised the hell out of me even more than I'd already been, because I wasn't expecting the sentence that came out of her mouth. It would have been just about the last thing I'd ever expect to hear out of her. Shit, it was the last thing I would ever expect out of *anyone's* mouth.

"We want you to be Ivan's next partner," the woman said. Just. Like. That.

Just like that.

There were moments in life where you asked yourself if you did drugs without realizing it. Like maybe someone had put some LSD in your drink and didn't tell you. Or maybe you thought you took a pain reliever—and didn't remember—but it was really PCP.

That right there, standing in the general manager's office at the LC, was that moment for me. All I could do was blink. Then do it some more.

Because *what the fucking fuck?*

"If you're ready to come back out of retirement, that is," the woman continued on, using that r-word one more time, like I wasn't standing there wondering who could have spiked my water with hallucinogenic drugs, *because there's no way this shit was happening.* There was no way these words were actually coming out of Coach Lee's mouth.

No fucking way.

I had to have misheard her or just completely missed a giant part of the conversation somehow because…

Because.

Me and Ivan? Partnering? There was no way. No chance. They had to be full of shit.

…right?

CHAPTER 3

I DIDN'T LIKE BEING SCARED—WHO THE HELL DOES OTHER THAN people who love the shit out of creepy movies?—but the truth was, there wasn't a whole lot that could have that effect on me. Spiders, flying roaches, mice, the dark, clowns, heights, carbs, gaining weight, death... none of that freaked me out. I could kill spiders, roaches, and mice. I could turn on a light in the dark. Unless he was a big-ass clown, chances were, I could kick his ass. I was strong for my size and had taken a few self-defense classes with my sister over the years. Heights did nothing for me. Carbs were great, and if I gained weight, I knew how to lose it. And we were all going to die at some point. None of that fazed me. Not even a little bit.

The things that kept me up at night weren't physical.

Worrying about being a failure and a disappointment weren't things you could just fix. They were just there. All the time. And if there was a way to work on them, I hadn't learned how to yet.

I could probably count on one hand the number of times I'd been freaked out in my life, and every single one of those times revolved around figure skating. Once was the third time

I gave myself a concussion. My doctor at the time had told my mom that she should consider making me give up figure skating—and I'd genuinely thought for a while she would force me to call it quits. I could remember the two concussions following that one, and being worried that she would put her foot down and say that was it, that I wasn't going to risk all the repercussions that came from continued brain trauma. She hadn't.

And the other times when my mouth had tasted like cotton and my stomach had tightened and churned... I wasn't going to think about those moments more than I needed to.

But that was it. My dad thought it was funny to say that I only had two emotions: indifferent and pissed off. It wasn't true, but he didn't know me well enough to be aware of that.

But as I stood there wondering if I was either dreaming this, on drugs, or if this was actually fucking real—and entertaining the idea that it *was*, that I wasn't on some hallucinogenic drug—I felt a little scared. I didn't want to ask if this was real... because what if it wasn't? What if it was some screwed-up kind of joke?

I hated feeling so insecure.

I *really* hated being scared that the answer I was looking for was one I probably would have sold my soul for.

But my mom had told me once that regret was worse than fear. I hadn't understood it then, but I did now.

It was with that thought that I made myself ask the question that a big part of me didn't want to know the answer to, just in case it wasn't what I wanted to hear. "Partner for what?" I asked slowly to be sure, trying to rack my brain for what the hell I could partner up with him for in this screwed-up dream I was having that seemed to be real. Fucking Pictionary?

The man I'd watched grow up from a distance that was

sometimes too close, rolled those ice blue eyes. And just like every other time he rolled his eyes, I narrowed mine in return.

"To skate pairs," he answered like "duh." Like he was *asking* to get smacked. "What did you think? For square dancing?"

I blinked.

"Vanya!" Coach Lee hissed, and out of the corner of my eye, I might have seen her slap her palm across her forehead.

But I wasn't sure because I was too busy staring at the smart-ass in the seat and telling myself, *Don't do it, Jasmine. Be better. Shut your mouth...*

But then a smaller voice I knew really well whispered, *At least until you figure out what they really want from you.* Because this couldn't be it. Not really.

"What?" Ivan asked, still looking right at me, the only change to his nearly blank face being the hint of a baby smirk on his mouth.

"We talked about this," his coach said, shaking her head, and if I'd turned to look at her, I would have seen I wasn't the only one glaring. I was too busy telling myself to be a better person though.

But that comment snapped me out of it, and I turned my attention to the other woman and kept my narrowed gaze on her. "What did you talk about?" I asked slowly. I could take whatever she said. Good or bad. I had survived all kinds of things being said to me, I reminded myself. And when my stomach didn't turn or clench at the reminder of those worse things, I felt better.

Her gaze flicked to mine before she shot the idiot in the chair a frustrated look. "He wasn't supposed to run his mouth until I talked to you about everything."

I drew out the one word. "Why?"

The other woman let out a long breath in pure exasperation—I was familiar with that sound—and her eyes went back to the man on the chair as she answered, "Because we're trying to get you to join the team, not remind you why you wouldn't want to."

I blinked. Again.

And then I couldn't help but twist my head to smirk at the ass in the office chair. His own baby smirk hadn't gone anywhere and didn't go anywhere even as he took in me making a face at him.

Dumbass, I mouthed before I could stop myself and remember to be better.

Meatball, he mouthed back.

That wiped the smirk off my face real quick, just like it always did.

"*All right*," Coach Lee said with a short huff of a laugh that wasn't funny at all as I stood there, eyes locked on the demon in the chair, mad at myself for letting him get to me. "Let's back up here a moment. Jasmine, please ignore you-know-who over there. He wasn't supposed to open his mouth and ruin this *important conversation he knew we were having*."

It took everything in me to slide my gaze back to the other woman instead of focusing on the person to my left.

Coach Lee gave me a smile I might have called desperate on anyone else. She kept right on going. "Ivan and I would like for you to be his new partner." Her eyebrows went up, that weird smile I didn't trust stayed on her face. "If you're interested."

Ivan and I would like for you to be his new partner.

If you're interested.

They—these two people that looked and sounded like Coach Lee and Ivan—wanted *me* to be his new partner?

Me.

This was a fucking joke, wasn't it?

For one split second, I thought Karina had something to

do with this, but then I decided *no way*. It had been over a month since the last time we'd spoken. And she knew me too well to try and do something like this. Especially not with this Lukov of all people.

But this was a joke... right? Ivan and me? Me and Ivan? Just a month ago, he had asked me if I was ever going to go through puberty. And in reply, I had told him I'd go through it when his balls decided to drop.

All because we had both tried to get on the ice at the same time. She had been there. Coach Lee had overheard us. I knew it.

"I don't understand," I told both of them, slowly, totally confused, a little annoyed, and not sure who the hell I should be looking at, or what the hell I should even be doing, because this didn't make any sense. Not even a little bit.

I didn't miss how the two people in the room gave each other a look I couldn't pick apart before Coach Lee asked, her expression almost tight, "What is it you don't understand?"

That there were a thousand other people they could go to, most of them younger than me, which in this sport was what everyone was looking for. There was no logical reason to *ask me...* other than the fact I was better than any of those other girls. At least technically, and by technically I meant jumps and spins, the two things I did best. But sometimes being able to jump the highest and spin the fastest wasn't enough. Program components scores—skating skills, transitions, performance and execution, choreography and interpretation —were just as important to a total score.

And I had never done so well at those things. People had blamed my choreographer. My coaches for choosing bad music. Me for "not having a soul" and not being "artistic enough" and "not having any feel." My ex and I for not having that "oneness" factor. Me for not trusting him enough. And maybe all of those things had been a huge part of why I hadn't done well.

That and me choking.

So.

I swallowed down the bitterness—at least for now—and took my time glancing at both of these people that I knew but didn't. "You want me to try out to be *his*"—I hooked my thumb in the direction of where Ivan sat to make sure we were definitely on the same page—"partner?" I blinked again and sucked in a breath through my nose to calm my blood pressure. "Me?"

The other woman nodded. No hesitation. No side glances. Just a clean, crisp nod.

"Why?" It sounded more like an accusation than a question, but what the hell was I going to do? Act like this was nothing?

Ivan snorted as he shifted in the chair he was sitting in, drawing his extended legs in until they were flat on the carpeted floor. One of his knees jiggled. "You want an explanation?"

Don't flip him off. Don't flip him off. Don't do it, Jasmine.

I wasn't. I wouldn't.

Don't do it.

"Yeah," I told him dryly, but a lot nicer than he deserved and would have usually gotten, as this feeling of uneasiness covered my entire body. Sometimes things really were too good to be true. I would never forget that. I couldn't. "Why?" I asked again, not about to back down until we got this shit sorted.

Neither one of them said a word. Or maybe I was just being impatient because I kept talking before either of them did. "We all know there are younger skaters out there you can ask," I added, because what would be the damage if this was exactly what I thought it was? AKA total bullshit. A trick. A nightmare. One of the most asshole-ish things anyone had ever done to me... if it wasn't real.

And what the hell was going on with my blood pressure? I felt sick all of a sudden. Tracing my bracelet with the fingers of my opposite hand, I swallowed and looked at both of these basic strangers, trying to keep my voice steady, my emotions in check. "I want to know why you're asking me. Besides there being girls five years younger than me you could ask, there are some with more experience in pairs. You both know why I haven't been able to find another partner," I spit out before I could stop myself, leaving the "why" out in the open like a ticking time bomb set up specifically for me.

The answering silence said they were aware of all that. How could they not? Years ago, I'd earned a shitty reputation, and I hadn't been able to shake it off, no matter what I did. It hadn't been my fault people only repeated the parts they wanted to hear instead of the entire story.

She's difficult to work with, Paul had said, for anyone who gave a shit about pairs skating to read.

Maybe things would have been different if I'd explained every single one of my actions every time they happened, but I hadn't. And I didn't regret it. I didn't care what other people thought about me.

At least until it had come back to bite me on the ass.

But it was too late now. All I had left was to own it. And I did.

I had shoved some speed skater dickwad once for grabbing my ass, and I was the bad guy.

I had called one of my rink mate's mom a whore once after she'd made a comment about my mom *having to be great at blow jobs* for having a husband twenty years younger than her, but *I* was the rude asshole.

I was difficult because I gave a shit. But how the hell could I not give one when this sport was what I woke up every morning excited for?

Little things built up, and up, and up until my sarcasm—until everything that came out of my mouth—was taken as a rude comment. My mom had always warned me that some people would always be eager to believe the worst. That was the unfortunate and shit truth.

But I knew who I was and what I did. I couldn't find it in me to regret it. At least most of the time. Maybe life would have been a lot easier if I'd had my sister's sweetness or my mom's personality, but I didn't and I never would.

You are who you are in life, and you either live that time trying to bend yourself to make other people happy, or... you don't.

And I sure as hell had better things to do with my time.

I just wanted to make sure, if this was what I thought it was, that I was walking into it with my eyes open. I'd never close my eyes again and expect the best. Especially not when this involved the same person, who after every competition in my singles days, wrote out all the mistakes I'd done in my programs—the pieces I competed with, one short, the other longer and called a free skate—and made sure I knew why the hell I had lost. Like a fucking dick.

"Are you that desperate?" I asked the man directly, meeting those gray-blue eyes, totally on. My words were rude, but I didn't care. I wanted the truth. "No one else wants to pair up with you now?"

Those glacier-like eyes didn't look away. That muscular, long body didn't flinch. He didn't even make a face like he normally would have pretty much every time I opened my mouth and directed words at him.

In that way that only someone who was so sure of himself,

so sure of his talents, of his place in the world, in the fact that he was the one in a position of power, Ivan just met my gaze like he was measuring me too in return. And then the asshole I knew came out.

"You know what that's like, don't you?"

This mother—

"Vanya," Coach Lee damn near shouted, shaking her head like a mom scolding her toddler for just saying what was on his brain. "I'm sorry, Jasmine—"

Under normal circumstances, I would have mouthed *I'm gonna kick your fucking ass* but managed not to. Just barely. Instead, I stared at that clear face with its perfect bone structure... and imagined myself wrapping my hands around his neck and squeezed the shit out of it. I wouldn't even be able to tell anyone about the amount of restraint I was showing, because they wouldn't believe me.

Maybe I was growing up.

Then I stared at him a second longer and thought, *I'm going to spit in his mouth the first chance I get,* and decided maybe the growing-up thing was a stretch. Luckily, all I decided to say was, "I do know what that's like, shitface."

Coach Lee muttered something under her breath that I didn't hear clearly, but when she didn't tell me not to talk to Ivan like that, I kept going.

"Actually, Satan"—his nostrils flared, and I didn't miss that —"all I want is to know if you're coming to me because no one else wants to deal with you—because that doesn't make sense, so don't think I'm stupid and don't know that—or if there's some other ulterior motive I'm not getting." Like him making this the meanest, early April Fool's joke in history. I might actually finally kill him if it was.

Coach Lee let out another sigh that drew my gaze to her. She was shaking her head and honestly looked like she wanted to pull her hair out, which was an expression I had never ever seen on her face before, and it made me nervous. She was probably realizing the truth: Ivan and I were like oil and water. We didn't mix. Not unless we didn't speak to each other, but even then there were dirty looks and middle fingers exchanged. More than a handful of dinners at his parents' house had gone down that way.

But after a moment that stretched the nauseous feeling in my stomach to almost the breaking point, Coach Lee set her shoulders. Glancing up at the ceiling, she nodded, like it was more for herself than for my benefit, before finally saying, "I'm going to trust that this stays in this room."

Ivan made a noise that she ignored, but I was too busy taking in the fact that she wasn't telling me not to call Ivan Satan or shitface to care.

I snapped out of it and focused. "I don't have anyone else to tell," I told her, and it was the truth. I was good with secrets. I was really good with secrets.

The other woman dipped her chin and settled her gaze on me before going on. "We—"

The idiot in the seat made another noise before sitting up straight and cutting her off. "There's no one else."

I blinked.

He kept going. "This would only be for a year—"

Wait.

A year?

Son of a *bitch*, I'd known this was too good to be true. I'd *known* it.

"Mindy is taking... the season off," the black-haired man explained, his tone tight and a little annoyed as he referred to the same partner he'd had for the last three seasons. "I need a partner for the time being."

Of course. *Of course*. I tipped my chin up to look at the

ceiling and shook my head, feeling that blunt tip of disappointment jab me right in the gut, reminding me it was always there, just waiting for the perfect moment to say it never went anywhere.

Because it didn't.

I couldn't think of the last time I hadn't felt disappointed in something—mostly myself.

Damn it. I should have known better. Why else would he be coming to me? To be his permanent partner? Of course not.

God, I was so lame. Even if I had just considered the possibility for a second... I was an idiot. I knew better. Good shit like this didn't happen to me. It never had.

"Jasmine." Coach Lee's voice was calm, but I didn't look over. "This would be a great opportunity for you—"

I should just go. What the hell was the point of me still being here, just eating up time so I got to work later and later? *Stupid, stupid, stupid Jasmine.*

"—You would gain more experience. You'd be competing with the reigning national and world champion," she kept going, throwing words out that I was mostly ignoring.

Maybe it was time for me to hang up my skates now. What better sign did I need? God, I was an idiot.

Damn it. Damn it, damn it, damn it.

"*Jasmine,*" Coach Lee said, almost sweetly, almost, just *almost* kindly. "You could possibly win a championship or at least a Cup—"

And that had me tipping my chin down to look at her.

She raised an eyebrow, as if she'd known that would get my attention, and for good reason. "You could easily find a partner after that. I could help. Ivan could help."

I ignored the part about Ivan helping me find a partner, because I highly doubted that shit would ever happen, but —*but*—what I didn't ignore was the rest of it.

A championship. Fuck it, *a Cup.* Any Cup.

I hadn't actually won one since my junior days before I'd moved into the senior level, which was where I was at now and had been for years.

Then there was the other thing: Coach Lee helping me find a partner.

But mostly: *a fucking championship.* Or at least the chance of it, the real possibility of it. *Hope.*

It was like a stranger offering a little kid candy if they got into their car, and I was the dumbass little kid. Except instead of candy, this woman and this ass-face were waving the two things I wanted more than anything right in front of me. It was enough to get me to stop thinking and keep my mouth shut.

"It might seem like a great endeavor, but with a lot of hard work, we think it would work," the woman went on, her gaze straightforward. "I don't see how it couldn't, if I'm going to be totally honest. Ivan hasn't had a bad year in almost a decade."

Wait.

Reality set in, and I made myself think of what she was really saying and assuming.

We were supposed to win a championship in less than a year?

Forget the fact that she said Ivan hadn't had a bad year in forever, where I'd had so many bad years, it was like I sucked it all up for him.

She was saying we were supposed to win a championship in less than a year.

Shit. Most new pairs teams took a season off to learn how one another skated, to work on technical elements—everything from jumps to lifts to throws—until they did them together seamlessly... and even then, things could be rough after twelve months. Pairs skating was about unity, about trust, timing, anticipation, and synchronization. It was about two people almost becoming one, but still somehow maintaining their individuality.

And what they were asking for was something we only had months to do—to perfect—before choreography would have to be learned and then mastered. *Months* to do what would normally take a year or more.

The damn near impossible. That's what they wanted.

"You want a championship, don't you?" came Ivan's question, like a shank straight into my chest.

I glanced at him sitting there in his slacks and a thick sweater, the hair that was longer at the top and faded at the sides styled perfectly back, the bone structure that was in thanks to generations of selective breeding making him look every bit like the trust fund baby he was, and I swallowed around the lump in my throat that felt like the size of a grapefruit... if it was covered in nails.

Did I want the one thing I'd sacrificed most of my life for?

Did I want the opportunity to keep going? To have a future? To finally make my family proud?

Of course I did. I wanted it so bad that my palms were getting sweaty, and I had to sneak them behind my back so that neither one of them could see me wiping them on my work pants. They didn't need to know how bad my need was.

But *fuck.*

One year for the one thing I wanted more than anything. For a championship. For the thing my mom had nearly gone bankrupt for, for the thing my whole family had always dreamed of for me. What I had always expected of myself but had always failed at.

And now, for a year, I could team up with this asshole, someone who could give me the best chance I'd ever had at getting what I had started to believe was lost.

But...

Reality and facts.

It wasn't for sure we would win. There weren't any promises that, even if we did win something—anything—I would get a partner of my own. There weren't any assurances things would work out. I had been lucky in my career that I hadn't been injured regularly, but it had happened, and sometimes those injuries were season-enders.

Plus, I could only begin to imagine all the work we would have to put in to be ready. Plans that would interfere with other plans I'd made that I couldn't back out on because I had made promises. And I took my promises seriously.

"We want it to be an easy transition. It's business. Mindy likes to keep her private life private. Ivan does as well," she said, like I didn't know that. Karina didn't even have a Picturegram account, and her Facebook was under a fake name.

"Our focus would be on the sport," Coach Lee took her time explaining, watching me carefully as I stood there trying to process everything and mostly failing at it. "With you, Jasmine, it would look good that you've been training at the same facility as Ivan for years. You're a friend of the family as well. You're a known face in this business, and you're talented. You have the experience under your belt to compete at this level without having to start from the beginning, which we can't afford to do with this time limit. We can work with what you bring." She paused, glanced at Ivan, and threw out one last thing. "The age difference between both of you also helps. I feel very strongly that you would make a good partner for Ivan."

Ah.

The age difference. My twenty-six to Ivan's nearly thirty. She had a point I hadn't thought about. It would look strange if this grown-ass man paired up with a teenager. That would probably actually hurt him more than it helped.

Then there was her comment about them being able to "work" with what I could bring to this partnership, but I'd think about that later. Much later. When I wasn't standing there, the center of attention, feeling like my world had just been kicked out from under me at the same time as it seemed like I'd been given it back.

It would be a lot of work. There were no promises. I had a life outside of here that I'd slowly built up, even though I hadn't necessarily wanted to, a life I was still building up and couldn't just ignore.

These were all facts.

But...

I had to think. Think first, talk later, or something like that, right? I'd already learned the problems that could come with running my mouth before I realized what was coming out of it.

I took a deep breath through my nose and then asked the first thing that came to mind. "Your sponsors would be okay with me?" Because they could try and recruit me all they wanted, but if the sponsors said no, it would be for nothing. It wasn't like I'd had more than a handful of sponsors on and off my entire career, if I didn't include all the dresses my sister made me for me, which was all of them. I still got my skates for free, but I knew how it worked for the people who won, the figure skaters the masses adored. It wasn't like Ivan needed the help financially, but they were still a real and necessary thing.

The sponsors and the ASF, the American Skating Federation, could hate us together, and I wasn't about to let them build up this opportunity for me and then have them rip it out from under me.

Coach Lee shrugged almost immediately. "It wouldn't be an issue. People can and have come back from worse, Jasmine."

Why did that comment make me feel like a drug addict?

She kept going before I could think about her word choice any more. "You can fix an image. That wouldn't be a problem. With the right decisions, it would work out fine. We would just have to have you... on board for the changes we'd need to make."

Her last sentence had claws. She was admitting there was something wrong with me, but it wasn't like I didn't know that. Still, it was one thing for me to acknowledge I had issues, but it was another thing for her to.

"Changes like what?" I asked, taking my time with my words as I glanced between her and Ivan for hints. Because if they told me I needed a makeover, or that I'd have to start kissing babies... or becoming some fake-ass that made it seem like she was made out of ice and was up for sainthood... it wasn't going to happen. Ever. I'd tried being an ice princess once when I'd been too young to know any better. Prim, proper, angelic, and sweet. It had lasted about thirty minutes. Now, I was too old to pretend to be this perfect little beauty queen who didn't cuss and shitted rainbows for breakfast, all for people to like me.

Coach Lee tipped her head to the side. "Nothing serious. We can talk about it later."

Later? "Let's talk about it now." Because I wasn't going to think about anything before I knew what I was getting myself into.

The other woman scrunched her nose before making a noise. "I don't know. I would just be throwing things out—"

"Okay."

Her eyes went to the side for a second before moving back to me. "Okay." Her shrug almost looked uncomfortable. "Maybe you could smile more."

I blinked at her and thought I might have heard Ivan snort, but I wasn't sure.

"You could do photo shoots together, a gala or two. Your social media presence needs work, but being more active, even if it's posting a picture of your life off the ice every once in a while, would make a big difference."

She wanted us to do all this when we'd only be paired up for a year? Was she fucking kidding me?

Then it hit me.

An almost sickening feeling made the back of my neck itch when I finally processed her social media request. I'd once had different accounts, but I'd ended up deleting all of them once I'd started losing sleep. *I should tell her that*, I thought, even as my head told me nothing good would come of posting pictures of myself online.

I should probably also admit to her that I was going to need... extra help. But I couldn't. Not if it meant I would lose this opportunity, which it might.

This was my chance. More than likely my last one.

I could be safe. Couldn't I? I could watch what I posted. Be more careful. I could be smart about it if things started happening again. Especially if this opportunity was real and mine.

I could record our sessions so I could practice them more later on by myself. I'd done it before. My mom and siblings would help if I asked. I could be more focused and make Ivan skate everything first once we got to doing choreography. I could figure it out. I could make it work without telling them.

Anything was possible... wasn't it? I was strong, smart, and wasn't scared to work.

Just fail.

So, I kept my fucking mouth shut.

"We're not going to ask you to change anything major,

Jasmine. I swear to you right now, that won't be the case. I just need to know you're on board for doing whatever is best for the team. This is going to be a lot of work for all of us, but it's doable."

I'd do anything for the sake of winning. Even start up another social media account if I had to. I'd lie, cheat, and steal... to a certain extent.

I mean, I wouldn't beat up a competitor or take steroids or give Ivan a blow job, but everything else I'd probably be game for if this chance was real. From the look on Coach Lee's face and the almost pained expression on Ivan's... I was starting to think it was.

Ivan was the most successful and highly decorated pairs skater in the last two decades. I hadn't even been able to move on to the Major Prix Final the last season I'd competed and nationals had gone terrible. My ex and I had gotten fifth and sixth place in both competitions we'd been in.

This was a better opportunity than any I had ever hoped for after I'd been left partnerless.

"Are you interested?" the other woman asked, her expression and tone cool and even, like this wasn't in a way exactly what I wanted.

Was I interested? Duh.

It was just everything else I couldn't ignore.

Every pairs skater in the world knew you had to trust your partner completely. A female pairs skater—*especially* the female—pretty much put her life in the hands of her partner every single day. I didn't need to tell Coach Lee or Ivan that. Trust was the foundation for every partnership. Whether it was trust that someone might hate you, but they wanted to win badly enough that they wouldn't jeopardize the chance, or that straight, pure trust that you gave away to people who earned it and could only hope it didn't backfire on you.

But I wanted to win. I wanted *this*. I'd always wanted it. I'd bled for it, cried for it, bruised for it, had broken bones, had concussions, pulled just about every muscle in my body, never made friends, never went to a single school anything, never loved anyone, ignored my family, all for *this*. For this love that was greater than just about everything and anything I had ever known. For this sport that had given me the confidence to know I could get up after every fall I'd ever take.

A year ago... six months ago... this would have been the answer to every prayer in my life.

I glanced between both of them, torn between getting excited at this chance, even if it was with the reincarnated version of Lucifer—that's how bad I wanted it, that I was willing not to factor that in. But like my mom said when we were kids and didn't want to eat whatever she'd made for dinner, beggars can't be choosers—and still, *still* I couldn't help but worry that this was some kind of fucked-up ploy that they were playing. It wouldn't be unheard of. It really wouldn't. Some people in this world didn't care what or who they hurt to get what they wanted.

I couldn't handle being used. Not again. I wouldn't say it, but I'd give them everything in me if they gave me this chance. *Everything.*

But...

I'd made commitments. Compromises and promises I didn't want to go back on. As much as I wanted to say yes! Yes! Yes! I needed to think about it. Not everything was about me, and it had taken me a long, long time to come to terms with that.

I still was.

"If this is some kind of trick, or if you're going to try and use me to make a point with another skater you're interested in"—I wasn't going to get excited. I didn't trust these two people to not be playing with me, regardless that they were saying otherwise—"don't even think about it." Ivan should already know I'd kill him. Hell, his sister would kill him if he did this to me.

There was a pause in the room, and I didn't know what it meant. Guilt? Or acknowledgment that it was a shitty thing that I even had to bring it up?

"No," Coach Lee said after a moment so full, it left the room with this heavy sensation I couldn't pick apart. "That isn't it. This isn't a trick. We want you to do it, Jasmine."

If my heart gave a little pinch at her saying they wanted me to do something, I wasn't going to focus on it.

I looked at the man sitting in front of the desk, quiet, so freaking quiet and watchful... and I wondered what had made his other partner decide to take a year off. Maybe she was getting married. Maybe someone was sick. Maybe she couldn't stand his ass and needed a break. I wished I had her phone number so I could just text her and ask. She had always been nice.

"You can take a picture if you're going to stare," Ivan said dryly, leaning back against his chair.

I rolled my eyes and glanced over at Coach Lee to hopefully keep me from saying anything to the shitface before I ruined this opportunity. I could save it up for later.

Luckily, Coach Lee rolled her eyes too, like she wasn't surprised by his dumbass comment and focused on me, the strain on her face saying she was trying to keep this professional. "You don't have to give us an answer right now. You can have some time to think about it, but we do need one sooner than later. Time is ticking, and if you're both going to compete next season, we need every minute we can get to get ready."

~

"WHAT'S UP YOUR ASS?" MY BROTHER JONATHAN ASKED, NOT even five minutes after I'd sat down beside him with a plate of our mom's chicken parmesan. It was something that a year ago I wouldn't have been able to eat unless it'd been my once a week cheat meal. Now, almost every day had a cheat meal. All of my pants—and bras and underwear and shirts—showed that reality. My damn boobs had gone up a full cup size, not that that meant much. My mom had cursed all of her girls with mosquito bites for tits; the greatest ass-et—literally— passed down through our genes were our butts. My slightly larger boobs and even bigger ass were one of the only benefits of toning down my training in competitive figure skating. Going from skating six or seven hours a day to two was a giant difference.

And now... well, now I might be getting back to that point. Maybe.

It had almost been twelve hours since my meeting, and I hadn't reached a decision.

If, and that was a big *if*, I said yes to Coach Lee and Ivan's proposal, I'd be saying goodbye to the bag of M&Ms I'd been eating three times a week. It was a sacrifice I'd willingly make though. *If I did it.*

But I was getting ahead of myself. Maybe I'd sleep on it like I'd promised Coach Lee and decide I didn't want to risk everything again for just a *possibility.* I needed to consider and weigh every option. I hadn't been able to stop thinking about it. Not during work, not afterward during my second workout session, and not during the Pilates class I still took once a week.

I hadn't been surprised when I'd pulled into the driveway to find a familiar car parked on the street half an hour ago. My family came over whenever they wanted; it wasn't limited to just weekends or holidays. With two older brothers and two older sisters, someone was always over. My brothers and sisters randomly showed up for dinner, even though they had all moved out years ago, leaving me alone with my room-mates... AKA my mom and her husband.

My mom, my brother Jonathan, and his husband, James, were all in the living room when I walked in.

The first thing any of them said to me was, "Go shower!"

I gave my brother the middle finger because he'd been the one to yell about the shower, and kept my words to myself as I jogged up the stairs and headed toward my room. It didn't take me long to gather clothes, shower, and get dressed—all the while thinking about the conversation I'd had in the office before the most distracted day of work I'd had since I'd found out my last partner had ditched me.

I made it back downstairs to find my family in the kitchen, filling plates with whatever Mom had made for dinner. I gave each of them a kiss on the cheek, and in return got an annoying wet kiss from my brother, a peck from his husband, and a slap on the butt from my mom, before I started scooping food onto a plate.

Trying my best not to constantly think about Satan and his coach, I had loaded my plate up with a portion of noodles and chicken parm before I took a stool around the kitchen island we were all eating at. The only time the dining room was ever used was if it was a holiday. I'd only gotten about three bites in, chewing slowly, when my brother asked the question I should have seen coming. I'd been too quiet, and that didn't happen often.

Before I could think of what the hell to tell them, my mom made a noise as she made her way around the island, one hand holding a plate, her other hand holding a glass of wine so big, she had to have poured at least half a bottle inside of it.

"Damn, Mom. You should have just brought the bottle

over instead of dirtying a glass." I snickered as she set the glass down more carefully than she'd probably ever set me down as a baby.

She rolled her eyes as she put her plate down beside it. "Mind your own business. I've had a long day, and it's good for the heart."

I snorted and raised my eyebrows as I finally got a chance to take in her clothes: skinny jeans I'm pretty sure were mine and a bright red blouse I thought I could remember my sister wearing before she'd moved out.

"*Anyway*, Grumpy. What's up your butt? Did you get in trouble at the LC?" she asked as she took a seat, oblivious to the looks I was giving her for "borrowing" my clothes.

She had sent me a message halfway through the day asking how the meeting had gone. I hadn't responded. I hadn't even given myself a chance to think about whether I wanted to tell them anything about my offer or not. It wasn't like I lied regularly. I didn't. But... what if it didn't work out? What if I got them excited for no reason? I'd let them down enough over the years.

Yeah, that thought was a shard of glass right down the windpipe.

Drawing my gaze away from the woman who got hit on more in a week than I had in my entire life, I focused back down on my plate, twirling the tines of my fork into the noodles with a shrug. "Nothing," I answered too quickly, immediately aware that I'd screwed up by saying that.

There were three different scoffs around the island. I didn't need to look up to know they were all sharing a look with each other like they thought I was full of shit—which I was—but it was my brother that finally snorted. "Damn, Jas, you didn't even *try* to pull that lie off."

I made a face at my food before looking at him and

bringing the middle finger closest to Jonathan up to my face and pretending to rub at my inner eye with it.

The only member of my family that sort of looked like me with his kind of tan skin, black hair, and dark eyes, stuck his tongue out. Thirty-two years old and he stuck his tongue out at me. What a little bitch.

"We might have believed you if you hadn't said 'nothing.' Now we know you're lying," our mom egged him on. "*You not telling us when something is bothering you?*" She pretty much snorted, her attention down on the chicken she was cutting into pieces. "Ha! Since when have you done that?"

This was what I got for making them my best friends over the years. Other than Karina, who I spoke to less and less over the last few years, and a couple of other people I didn't mind, my family was it for me. My mom said I had serious trust issues, but honestly, the more people I met, the more I didn't want to meet more.

"You okay, Jas?" James, my brother's much better half for the last ten-ish years, give or take, asked, his tone worried.

Moving my fork tines in the noodles some more, I looked over at the most handsome man I had ever seen in my life and nodded my head. With dark hair, the clearest hazel eyes, and his skin color a shade of honey brown that didn't give anyone a single clue about his heritage, he could have dated anyone. Anyone. Literally. I'd seen straight men check him out countless times. If he had decided to be a model, it would have been over for every other male model in the world. Even my sister, who was all about women 24/7, three hundred and sixty-five days out of the year, had said before she'd marry him if he asked. *I* would marry him even if he didn't ask. He was the nicest man, good looking, successful, and down-to-earth. We all loved him.

He loved us back, but not the same way he loved my brother Jojo.

People liked to say love was blind, but there was no way love could be *that* blind. I'd stopped trying to figure out my brother Jonathan and James's relationship a long time ago. How he'd ended up with the biggest idiot in the family, I didn't get. My brother had giant Dumbo ears and a gap between his two front teeth that my mom had claimed was so adorable his whole life, he'd never bothered getting braces. I'd had a little bit of an overbite and ended up with braces for three years.

Not that I was hung up over it or anything.

"I'm good. Don't listen to them," I said to James, sounding distracted enough that I knew I was messing up again. So I tried to change the subject and chose the most obvious one: my mom's husband, who should have been at the table with us... but wasn't. "Where's Ben at, Mom?"

"He's out with his friends," the redheaded woman who had given birth to me, explained quickly before raising her gaze and aiming her fork in my direction. "Don't change the subject. What's wrong with you?"

Of course that didn't work.

I just barely held back a groan as I shoveled a piece of chicken into my mouth and chewed slowly before answering, "I'm fine. I'm just... thinking about stuff, and it's putting me in a bad mood."

My brother snickered beside me. "You? In a bad mood? *No.*"

I reached over before he knew what was happening and pinched him on the puny thing he called a biceps.

"Oww," he cried, yanking his arm away and cradling it.

I tried to do it again, but he flailed his elbow to keep me from being able to.

"Mom! Look at her!" my brother whined, gesturing toward

me like there was someone else attacking him. "James, help me!"

"Snitch," I whispered, still trying to pinch him. "Bitch."

His husband laughed but didn't choose sides. No wonder I liked him so much.

"Quit hurting your brother," Mom said for probably the thousandth time in my entire life.

When he moved his hands to block me around the area of his waist, I reached up, quick, quick, quick and flicked him on the neck before he turned his mouth to try and bite me. "Momma's boy," I whispered, snatching my hand back.

He tipped his head from side to side with a smirk, mocking me like he always had when Mom took his side. She always did. The suck-up was her favorite, even though she'd never admit it, but the rest of us knew the truth. I loved both my brothers, but I got why my mom loved him the most. If you ignored the similarities between him and Pluto, he always put a smile on someone's face. Those giant ears had that effect on people.

"Baby girl, even I know something's up with you just from the way you're talking. What's wrong?" my brother's husband asked, leaning forward over the table with an expression so full of concern, it made me feel guiltier than anything my mom or Jojo could have said.

I wanted to tell them.

But...

I could, and probably always would, clearly remember how my brother had cried angry tears when we first found out I'd been left without a partner. My mom would never admit she'd been devastated, but I knew her too well to not see the signs. I'd seen the same signs after every marriage before her current one had failed, when she knew her life was changed forever and there was no going back to the way things were before.

Right after I'd quit training to compete—because you couldn't exactly practice a lot of elements in pairs skating by yourself, and I'd been totally aware of how slim my hopes were in women's singles—I had emotionally turned into myself majorly. The right term might have been depression, but I didn't want to think about it. It wasn't the first time it had happened; I was a sore loser.

It hadn't been a secret how heartsick seeing my dream slipping away had made me... how angry and hurt and upset I'd been. How angry and hurt and upset I still was. Honestly, part of me worried I would never get over it. I held grudges like a motherfucker. But my family had all ridden this ride with me, year after year, one up and five downs, over and over again.

Most importantly, they had all been there for me in the aftermath of me slowly trying to build up this new life I had outside of the rink, from forcing me to do little things like eating dinner with my family while all I wanted was to hole up in my room alone, to threatening me into going out with them, and guilt-tripping me into doing things I hadn't made time for before. They had done that over and over again until it had begun to feel like second nature. All those things I hadn't done enough of in the past, but could once I told my mom she wasn't going to have to keep paying the astronomical fees that came with coaching because I didn't have one anymore. He had ditched me too.

It was one thing for me to be sad and heartbroken, but I didn't want them to feel that way too. Never again. Not if I could prevent it.

And I still wasn't sure what I was going to do.

The selfish part of me wanted to do it. Duh.

But the other part of me, that tiny part that didn't want to be a selfish shit, didn't want to let these people down by turning into the person I'd been before. The one who was never around. The one who everyone thought didn't care... probably because I hadn't cared enough to.

Then there was the whole part of me not being sure I could handle things not working out... as much as that made me a pussy.

And the whole it-being-Ivan this deal was with.

Ivan. Ugh. I wanted it that bad that I wasn't immediately saying no to the possibility of spending most of my days with him of all people. This was what my life had come to. Possibly spending time with that arrogant dipshit.

I really had no idea what to do, damn it.

So, for that moment... I lied. "I think it's just my period on the way."

"Ahh," was Jonathan's response, because girls being on their periods was old news after sharing a bathroom with three sisters for the first eighteen years of his life.

My mom, on the other hand, squinted a little, watching me for two moments too long. So long that I thought she was going to call me out on my shit, but right as I assumed that, she shrugged and then dropped another bomb. "So, is it true Lukov and his partner split up?"

I blinked, not sure why I was surprised.

She always knew everyone's business. Someway, somehow.

It was James, my brother's husband, who sucked in a loud breath first. That's how long he'd been with Jonathan, that the name meant something. I could remember a time, many, many years ago when James hadn't known a single thing about figure skating. But now he'd been a member of the family long enough that he knew more about the sport than I'd bet he'd ever imagined he would.

"He got rid of his partner?" Jonathan perked up, shoving his glasses up his nose, like this was the best gossip he'd heard in a while.

Mom raised her eyebrows and nodded. "From what I heard, it happened a few days ago."

I made sure to shove a big piece of chicken into my mouth so that I wouldn't make a face that said *that's not what happened.*

Luckily, my nosey-ass brother gasped. "Hadn't they just paired up a few years ago?" Jojo asked, aiming the question at our mom because he knew she had all the gossip.

"Uh-huh. The partner before her fell twice at the Major Prix final. They won a bronze, but with this girl he won a national title and worlds with."

The Major Prix. Worlds. Nationals. They were three of the most prestigious competitions in the figure skating world, and only he could screw up that much in a competition and still win something. That should have reassured me that I'd be making a good choice if I accepted his offer, but all it did was make me resentful toward myself for fucking up so much that I had nothing.

"Karina didn't tell you anything about it?" My mom turned her attention to me.

I made sure I still had chicken in my mouth while I shook my head and said with a mouthful, "She's still in Mexico." They knew she was in school.

"E-mail her and find out," she urged.

I frowned. "You e-mail her and ask."

Mom snorted like *bring it on.* "I will."

"I always forget Karina is his sister," James noted, leaning across the table. "Is he just as good looking up close, in person?"

I snickered. "No."

Jojo snorted out, "Uh-huh," but the tone put me on edge and had me glancing in his direction to find him leaning into James's shoulder. He pretended like he was trying to whisper, but the idiot looked right at me as he added, "Jasmine used to always flirt with him. You should have seen it."

I gagged on the chicken I hadn't swallowed yet before coughing out, "The hell did you just say?"

His "ha!" made me get my middle finger ready. "Don't even pretend. You used to always come home talking about him," the five-foot-seven-inch man who had always been a perfect balance between a supportive older brother and an annoying pain in the ass with boundary issues claimed. "You had a thing for him. We all knew." He looked at James and raised his eyebrows. "We knew."

Was he fucking with me? He was fucking with me, wasn't he? Me flirting with Ivan? *Ivan?*

"No," I told him calmly, only because if I said it too aggressively they would cry bullshit. I knew how they worked. "I did not flirt with him." And just so James knew, I emphasized it. "Ever."

Mom made a noise that basically said, "Well."

I swung my gaze toward her and shook my head. "No. No, I didn't. He's all right looking"—I only said that because, if I said he wasn't my type, they would assume I was trying to hide something, and I wasn't. "—but it was never like that. Not even a little bit. He's kind of a jerk. His sister and I are friends. That's it."

"He wasn't a jerk," my mom interjected. "He's always very polite. He's very good with his fans. He seems like a very nice boy." She slid me a look. "And you did like him."

A nice boy? What the hell were they on?

Yeah, everyone did love him, and they all thought the world of him. Handsome, talented Ivan Lukov, who had won the world over as a cute, winking, cocky teenager. He knew how to play the game. I would give him that. But *I had never liked him*. Not ever. "Nope, no I didn't," I argued, shaking my head in disbelief they would be trying to claim that kind of crap. Were they for real? "You're imagining shit. We say a sentence to each other once a month, and it's always sarcastic and a little mean."

"Some people might consider that foreplay—" my brother started to say before I cut him off.

I made a horrible noise again, still shaking my head. "Hell no—"

Jonathan burst out laughing. "Why's your face turning red then, Jas?" he asked, slapping his palm over the top of my head and giving it a shake before I could jerk it out of the way.

"Shut your mouth," I said to Jojo, thinking of a dozen different comebacks and knowing I couldn't use any of them because they would all come out way too defensive and make me look guilty. Or, worse, I'd tell them about the offer I'd been given that morning. "I didn't like him though. I don't know why you two would ever even think that."

Mom snickered. "It's okay to admit you used to have a crush on him. There are plenty of girls around the world who have. I might have even had a little crush on him back in the day—"

Forgetting we were on opposite teams, Jojo and I both gagged.

Mom groaned. "Oh, stop. I didn't even mean it like that!"

Of course the woman who was married to a man not even ten years older than me would have to clarify that comment. Mom wasn't just a cougar, she was The Cougar. All other cougars hailed to her.

"I'm going to pretend you just didn't say that so I can sleep tonight, Ma," Jojo muttered with a borderline sick look on his face before he physically shook it off. Then he elbowed me. "You did used to talk about him a lot, Jas."

I blinked. "I was like seventeen, and it was only because he'd been an asshole."

Mom opened her mouth, but I kept going.

"No, no. He was. I swear he was. Y'all never heard him, but it happened, he just made sure not to ever get caught. Karina knows."

"What did he do to you?" James asked, the only one who seemed to still be on my side. At least because he wasn't denying my claim and sounded interested to actually hear the facts.

I was going to give them too, because the last thing I wanted was for Mom and Jonathan to keep assuming that crazy shit. Especially with what *might* happen. Maybe. Possibly.

So, I told them.

SHIT HIT THE FAN THE DAY IVAN LUKOV WORE THE UGLIEST costume I'd ever seen in my life up to that point.

I had been sixteen back then, and Ivan had just turned twenty. I remembered that because it had always amazed me that he wasn't even four years older than me but already so much further ahead in his career. He had already won multiple championships as a junior with his longtime partner before going into the senior level at seventeen. At twenty, people had already been shitting themselves all over him for years. Little did I know, nothing would change over the next decade.

By that point, his sister and I had already been friends for a few years. I'd already spent the night at her house more than a handful of times. She had already spent the night at my house more than a handful of times. Ivan had just been that family member I saw on her birthdays and randomly at her house when he'd drop by to visit. He'd never really *said* anything to me directly up until then, apart from shooting me reluctant expressions that existed because his parents expected him to have good manners.

So, on that day years ago, when he'd skated out on the ice as I was stretching on the floor, I hadn't been able to hide my horror, and I didn't even bother trying. What he had been wearing resembled something the Chiquita Banana lady would have worn. Frills, yellow, red, green... there'd even been a flower somewhere in there, and these awful yellow pants that made his legs look like genuine bananas in his boy-man body back then.

That costume was the worst. The absolute worst. I'd worn some leotards my sister had made me that had been... experimental, but I hadn't wanted to hurt her feelings so I'd put them on anyway.

But what I wore had nothing on what the hell he'd been wearing that day.

Ivan had then started skating with his partner, some girl that he'd skated with for years before then but hadn't lasted much longer after that. Bethany something. Whatever she had been wearing hadn't been anywhere near as bad as his costume though. I'd seen their program in bits and pieces when I wasn't busy; I'd heard the music that would go along with it too, obviously. But I hadn't seen the costumes until then. It was like watching someone break dance to Mozart. It didn't make sense. And in my mind, the train wreck he'd been wearing had taken away from the piece he and his partner were performing, which wasn't exactly a mambo.

I'd blame that for being the reason I opened my big mouth

that day. I thought he'd be doing a disservice to his routine. So, I thought I was doing him a solid by saying something.

I know for sure I hadn't thought about what I was doing before I went up to him as he'd been getting off the ice following the end of his practice, clipping his skate guards on to the blade below his black boots. And in that moment, I told the boy-man who had said zero to me before that, "You should really change your costume."

He hadn't even blinked as he'd turned his head to look at me and asked, in the one and only polite sentence that he had ever and would ever direct at me, "Excuse me?"

Maybe I could blame my mom or even my siblings for not stressing enough that I needed to shut up and keep my opinions to myself. Because of all the things I could have said to soften my words, I didn't pick any of them. "It's ugly," was exactly what had come out of my mouth.

Not "*It takes away from your lines and the height in your jumps.*" Not "*It's a little too bright.*"

I didn't say any of those things to make my comment less asshole-ish.

Then to let him know that it wasn't *just* horrific, I'd added, "It's butt ugly."

And everything changed after that.

The twenty-year-old had blinked at me like it was his first time seeing me, which it *wasn't,* and then reared back. He spit out in a low, low voice from that boy-man body, "It's not *my* costume you should be worried about."

I remember my first thought: *bitch.*

But before I could say a word, those black eyebrows, which were a complete opposite of his sister's light brown ones, had inched their way up his smooth forehead in this way that reminded me of the way that other girls looked at me sometimes... like I was less than them because I didn't wear the same fancy clothes and brand-new skates they did. My mom couldn't afford that stuff, and she had always avoided asking my dad for money if it was possible... but I'd always thought it had been more about her being worried he wouldn't give her the money because it was for figure skating and not just because he was being cheap. I would have skated in my underwear back then as long as I had ice time. Not having fancy clothes hadn't been an issue once she had explained to me that it was all she could afford.

But the thing was, no one had ever made me feel bad about not wearing designer dresses and costumes. At least to my face. Behind my back was a different story. You couldn't hide a person's expressions or eye movement. You couldn't shut off your ears from hearing what people thought they were whispering, but really weren't. Back then, other girls hadn't liked me because I was competitive and sometimes had a bad attitude when things didn't go the way I wanted them to.

I'd reared back just like he had, thinking about my sister who had made me my costume—this plain but pretty light blue leotard with rhinestones along the neckline and sleeves —and got pissed. And I'd said the only thing that came to mind, "I'm just telling you the truth. It looks dumb."

His cheeks had turned a shade darker than the normal near-peach they were. It wasn't a blush or anything close to it, but for him, I think now it was basically the same thing. Ivan Lukov had leaned toward me and hissed a warning that would follow me for the next couple years, "Watch yourself, runt," before he'd gone off toward the changing rooms or wherever the hell he went.

Two weeks later, in his mambo outfit, he'd won his first US National Championship in pairs. People had talked a lot of shit about his costume, but even as gaudy as it was, it hadn't been enough to shadow his talent. He'd deserved to win. Even if he'd hurt the eyes of the people who'd watched.

One week after that, on his first day back at the LC, while I'd been feeling pretty bad about what I'd said and Karina had been no help in telling me what I could do to fix it because she had thought what I'd done was hilarious, Ivan went out of his way to talk to me. And by talk, I really meant mutter in passing, "You might as well quit now. You're too old to get anywhere."

Me with the big mouth had been too shocked by what he'd said to have time to form a comeback before he'd skated away.

I'd thought about his words all that day because the honesty in them had hurt my feelings and made me angry at the same time. It had been hard back then to not compare myself to the girls who had been skating since they were three and were more advanced than I was, even if Galina had told me I was naturally gifted and that if I worked hard enough I could be better than them one day soon.

But I didn't tell anyone what he'd said. No one else needed that idea in their heads.

I didn't say anything until a month later, when this asshole had gone out of his way to ask me to my face after practice, "Is that leotard supposed to be a size too small or...?" For no damn reason.

That time, I did get out, "You bitch," before he'd disappeared.

And the rest... was history.

BY THE TIME I FINISHED TELLING THE ONLY PARTS OF THE STORY they needed to hear, my brother had his head tossed back and snorted. "You're such a drama queen."

If I'd had anything other than noodles left on my plate, I would have flicked them at him. "What?"

"You're a drama queen," the third biggest drama queen in the family after our mom and oldest sister, claimed. "You said he gave you hell, but none of that sounded like hell. He was messing with you," he explained, shaking his head. "We give you more shit than that in an hour."

I blinked because he had a point. But it was different because we were family. Giving each other shit was pretty much mandatory.

My friend's brother, my rink mate, giving me hell... was not.

"Yeah, Grumpy. That doesn't sound so bad," my mom piped in.

Fucking traitors. "He told me once I needed to lose weight before my blades gave out on me!"

What did all three people sitting around the kitchen island do? They laughed. They laughed their asses off.

"You were chunky back then," my fucking brother cackled, his face turning red.

I reached toward him again to try and pinch him, but he lunged away, practically falling into James's lap.

"Why didn't I ever think of telling you that?" Jonathan kept going, almost on the verge of crying-laughing from his body language as he draped himself over his husband, even further away from me. I'd seen him do it enough to recognize the signs.

"I can't believe y'all," I said, not sure why the hell they still managed to surprise me. "He told me once before a competition, 'Break a leg. Literally.'"

Repeating another rude thing he'd said to me did nothing to convince my family Ivan had been a jerk; all it did was make them laugh harder. Even James, who was the nicest, lost the battle. I couldn't believe it... but I probably should.

"He's been calling me Meatball for years," I said, almost feeling my eyelid start to twitch at that fucking nickname that drove me insane no matter how much I told myself to get over it. Sticks and stones could break your bones, but I didn't let people's words hurt me.

Usually.

They were all choking though. All three of them.

"Jasmine, honey," James croaked out, his palm covering his eyes as he had his meltdown. "What I want to know is—what did you say back to him?"

I thought about slamming my mouth closed and not saying anything, but if anyone in the world knew me, it was these people—and my other brother and sisters. God, how the hell could I work with Ivan after ten years of this history we had? His own coach made him keep his mouth closed so that he wouldn't be tempted to say something that might get me to deny their offer.

We'd probably throw down into a fistfight after a week. If we even made it that long. It was honestly only a matter of time. We'd been building up to it over the years.

I had a lot to think about.

"Stuff," was all I went with, purposely not thinking about all the shit I'd said back to him.

"What kind of stuff?" James asked, his tan face turning red as he pinched the tip of his nose.

I looked at him out of the corner of my eye and gave him a little smile he didn't see as I repeated myself. "Stuff."

James laughed and barely managed to get out, "All right. I'll let it go for now. You two don't talk shit to each other anymore though?"

I blinked. "We still do. I called him Satan today."

"Jasmine!" my mom hissed before she fell over onto the empty stool beside her, laughing.

I smiled so hard my cheeks hurt... at least until I remembered what I was keeping from them.

Was I willing to wake up before the sun was out to train for six or seven hours a day with the same man who had asked me if I'd been cast as Ugly Betty? With the intention to win a championship?

I wasn't sure.

CHAPTER 4

I WASN'T THAT SURPRISED THAT I SLEPT LIKE TOTAL SHIT that night.

I could have blamed the coffee I'd had after dinner—I didn't usually drink caffeine in the afternoon or later because it made me crash, and I needed all the energy I had to get through the rest of my day—but it hadn't been the coffee's fault.

It had been my mom's. And Coach Lee's. But mostly my mom's.

But that's what would happen when she dropped a bomb on me I should have seen coming, but hadn't. Since when the hell had I ever been able to pull something over on her, and why had I expected I was going to be able to do it now?

It was when she came to sit beside me on the couch after my brother and his husband had left, with her slinging her arm over my shoulder, that I knew without a doubt, I hadn't hidden shit from her. We were pretty affectionate in my family... if you could call giving each other bruises, wedgies, and playing pranks affection... but we weren't the type to constantly hug and kiss, unless someone needed it. The last time I'd randomly hugged my oldest brother, he'd asked if I was going to jail or dying.

So that night, when Mom hugged me to her side on the couch and squeezed my knee, I accepted that I made the same mistake most people made with her: I'd underestimated her. My brothers and sisters knew me really well, their significant others did too—I wasn't that complicated—but no one knew me the way Mom did. My sister Ruby was close, but still not on her level. I doubted anyone would ever be.

"Tell me what's wrong, Grumpy," she said, calling me by the nickname she'd given me when I was four. "You've been so quiet tonight."

"Mom, I talked half of dinner," I said, eyes trained on the *Unsolved Mysteries* rerun on the television, and shook my head, not trusting myself to look her in the face and keep my dilemma to myself.

She rested her head against mine after setting down a normal-sized glass of red wine on the coffee table, pretty much falling on top of me, like she was expecting me to hold her up. "*Yeah*, to your brother and James. You barely said three words to me; you didn't even tell me what happened at your meeting. You think I don't know when something is off with you?" she accused, sounding insulted.

She had me there.

Mom squeezed my shoulder again. "Just because I didn't say anything in front of Jojo and James doesn't mean I didn't notice." She gave me one more squeeze before whispering like a total creep, "I know *everything*."

That finally made me snort and glance at her out of the corner of my eye. I'd swear, she hadn't aged a day in the last fifteen years. It was like time slowed for her. Preserving her. That, or she'd scored herself a wish with a genie a long time ago and was going to be immortal, or something pretty fucking close to it.

I stretched my legs out to rest my heels on the coffee table and wrinkled my nose, still looking away from her as I muttered, "Okay, 1-800-PSYCHIC."

She snuggled herself closer into my side the same way she always did when she was being a pain, and I leaned away just a little to mess with her. "*Tell me what's wrong with you*," she insisted directly into my ear, her voice deceptively soft—and fake as fuck. Her breath, which smelled liked straight-up wine, wafted into my nostrils. "I'll give you a milk chocolate covered cherry from my Valentine's Day stash...."

Not even a chocolate covered cherry would get me to open my mouth. I leaned away from her even further, but she just followed me, hitting clinger level 100 as she threw a thigh over mine. "Good lord, lady, do you want me to just hook up a wine IV to your arm from now on? One of those wine connoisseurs could probably guess the years the wine was bottled from how strong your breath is."

She ignored me and hugged me even closer. "The sooner you talk to me, the sooner I'll leave you alone," my mom tried to bribe me.

I couldn't help but snort. Like anything was ever that easy with her. "You don't even believe yourself when you say that, you know?"

That had her huffing and retreating all of an inch. "Give me a break and spill the beans. You're going to tell me at some point anyway," she let me know, which was the truth.

But...

There were only so many failures I could carry on my shoulders... and most days it felt like I'd hit my max a year ago.

My mom was the one I wanted to protect the most,

because she'd been the one to singlehandedly pay for everything while I'd grown up because my dad had thought it was a waste of money, and *"isn't there something else Jasmine can do?"* he'd always ask, not knowing she usually had him on speakerphone and my nosey ass was always listening. By the time he'd come around, my mom had told him we didn't need or want his support... even if it meant there were years where she was constantly behind on bills. Years where looking back on it, I wasn't sure how the hell she managed to make everything work; how she'd been able to keep a roof over our heads, pay the bills, and keep us fed.

I wasn't sure I would have been able to do the same. But she'd done it for me. And the only way I'd ever been able to pay her back was by "winning" a couple of second place spots.

I'd never been able to win after I'd moved into the senior level and no one really knew why except for me.

She deserved better, and I wished I could have given her that.

"Jasmineeeee," Mom playfully whined beside my ear as she snuggled closer to me, ignoring my squawk as she did it. "Just tell me. I know you want to. I won't tell anyone. *Promise.*"

"No," I scoffed, obviously full of shit and knowing she was aware of it. "And you're a liar."

"I'm a liar?" she had the balls to ask like she honestly believed her own bullshit about keeping something to herself. I had a big mouth, but I had gotten it from somewhere: her.

"I'm not the one promising to keep a secret," I insisted with a side glance, trying to give myself some more time to think about what I could say before digging myself into a deeper hole.

Should I tell her? She already knew I was hiding something.

I knew I had her when she made a noise, knowing she was

what she was: a big, fat liar. "Fine, but I'll only tell... one person. Deal?"

"Who?"

She paused. That's how many people she usually blabbed to. *She had to choose.* God. "Ben."

Her husband, Number Four. I could only see her red hair out of the corner of my eye, but I knew that was as good as I was going to get. She wasn't about to let this go. Especially not now that I made it known that I knew she was full of crap.

I sighed. Now or never, right? "I don't want you to get excited—"

"*Oh my God,*" she practically exhaled, telling me it was too late.

I rolled my eyes and turned my entire body to the side so I could give her a look. "No, Mom. No. Don't get excited. I wasn't even going to say anything—"

"*Tell me,*" she whispered in a throaty voice that almost made her sound like a possessed kid in a scary movie.

I blinked. "If you promise you'll never make that voice again."

My mom groaned and went back to doing her best spider monkey impersonation by smothering me with her arms. "Fine. I promise. Tell me."

"I...." I paused and slid her a look, trying to pick my words so I could explain what was happening in the most calm, possible way. "Okay. *But don't get excited.*"

"I already said I wouldn't," she said, but she didn't even believe it herself.

"I had a meeting—"

"I know. You told me. For what?"

I sighed, shooting her a look she couldn't see, which I was grateful for because she might smack me if she had. I wasn't even sure why I'd thought I could keep it to myself. There were only about a handful of things I had ever not told her about and managed to still keep to myself. "Remember Coach Lee?"

Her body stilled. "Yes."

"Coach Lee asked if I wanted to partner up with Ivan for next season."

Silence.

She said nothing. Not one single thing. It might have been the first time she'd ever not said something.

I wiggled the shoulder she had her head on, taking in the fact that she still wasn't moving around or saying anything. "I thought I still had a few years left until you got to that age where you start randomly falling asleep."

"I should have left you at the fire station," she threw back without missing a beat, her head not moving from its spot on my shoulder.

Then, she didn't say anything else.

What the hell was up with that?

"Why aren't you saying anything?" I tipped my head just enough to the side so I could see the top of her head. I wasn't tall, only five foot three, but my mom was even shorter at an even five feet tall that I was pretty sure she was exaggerating.

"I'm thinking," she answered, honestly sounding distracted.

God help me. "What are you thinking?"

She still didn't move. "About what you just said, Grumpy. You dropped that on me like I was ready for it, and I wasn't. I thought you were finally going to tell me they offered you a coaching position at the LC."

I made a face even though she couldn't see me. How did she know about the coaching position? And why hadn't she said something before?

As if sensing my confusion, she pulled herself upright and

angled her body so she could face me. We were pretty much polar opposites of each other, except that our faces were shaped the same, we weren't tall, and we both had freckles. She had long red hair that had just enough orange in it to look natural, her skin was basically pale, she was slim, beautiful, bossy but likable, smart, lovable... and I was none of those things. I wasn't ugly, but I wasn't my mom and sisters. And the rest... well, I wasn't any of those things either, except bossy sometimes.

The point was: she wasn't excited or overjoyed at this opportunity. Half an hour ago, I would have bet my life she'd be all over it.

But she wasn't. And I didn't get why.

"Well?" I drew the word out.

Those dark blue eyes that reminded me of the sapphire in *Titanic* narrowed, and my mom's mouth screwed to the side.

I narrowed my eyes at her, screwing my mouth to the side too. "What? Say something."

She squinted one eye at me.

"I thought you would've been excited. What is it?" I asked before a thought barged into my head so unexpectedly it almost stole my breath away. Did she—

I couldn't say it. Couldn't think it. I didn't want to.

But I had to.

Ignoring that awful, uneasy feeling in my belly, I blinked one more time, steeling myself for her response—I could handle it, I would handle it—as I asked in a steady voice I could be proud of even while my hands got clammy, "You don't think I can do it anymore?"

Sometimes I regretted how brutally honest my mom and I were with each other. She might mince her words for my older sister, Squirt, and every once in a while she might try and word things more pleasantly for the rest of my siblings, but with me, she never had. At least not as far as I could remember.

If she said yes—

Her head snapped up so sharply, it eased the ache that had instantly built in my chest at the idea that she didn't think I could do it anymore. "Don't fish for compliments. You're better than that." She rolled her eyes. "Of course you can do it. Nobody's better than you, don't act like you don't know that. Sheesh."

I hadn't realized I was holding my breath.

"*What I'm thinking*," she emphasized, still squinting that one and only eye, "is that I'm not sure if it's a good idea."

Umm....

It was my turn to squint at her. "Why?"

She eyed me back. "You said they asked you to be his partner for next season... what does that mean?"

"It means, just for a season."

That timeless face scrunched up in confusion. "Why only a season?"

I shrugged. "I don't know. All they told me was that Mindy was going to take the season off." She had always been pretty decent to me. I hoped she was okay.

My mom's facial expression didn't change. "So, what happens after that?"

Of course she'd ask. I just barely held in a sigh and picked the most promising part of what I would get from a partnership with Ivan. "They said they'd help me find another partner."

Her silence was so stiff and fucking weird I couldn't help but stare at my mom, trying to figure out what she was thinking.

Luckily, she didn't make me wait long. "Have you talked to Karina about it?"

"No. I haven't talked to her in a month." And it wasn't like I was going to call her to ask her about her brother. What kind of shit would that be? We never talked about Ivan. Plus, we didn't talk as much as we used to before she'd started college and got busy with school. We still liked each other and cared about each other, but... sometimes life split people up. It had nothing to do with caring about someone less. It just happened. And it wasn't her fault I hadn't been as busy as I was used to. Before that, I hadn't really noticed much how we'd grown apart.

My mom hummed, and her mouth twisted to the opposite side like she was still in deep thought.

I watched her carefully, ignoring the weird feeling in my belly. "You don't think I should do it?"

She glanced at me and tipped her head to the side, hesitating for a moment. "It's not that I don't think you should do it, but I want to make sure they're not taking advantage of you."

What?

"I barely made it last year without getting arrested, Grumpy. I don't think I can handle keeping my hands to myself if somebody else screws around on you," she explained, like it was the most natural thing in the world.

I blinked. "You were just defending him two hours ago."

She rolled her eyes. "That was before I heard he might be your partner."

How did that make any sense?

Then it was her turn to blink. "What I want to know is why you didn't automatically agree to it."

All I could do was answer with one word. "Because."

"Because what?"

I shrugged the shoulder closest to her. I didn't want to tell her my worry about not winning and everything that would come from it, so I kept that part to myself. "I'm working more hours for Matty now, Mom. I've made plans with Jojo to go to the gym twice a week even though he half-asses every workout. I've made plans with Sebastian. I'm going out rock climbing with Tali once every other week. I don't want to just back out on them. I don't want them to think they don't mean enough to me." Especially not when they already assumed I was a flake who didn't care about them, when it was the total opposite.

Mom's forehead scrunched up, and her face was a little too watchful. "Is that it?"

I lifted my shoulder again, the lies and the truths clotting up my throat, trying to pour out of my mouth.

She didn't look like she totally believed me, but she didn't make another comment, when she normally would have. "So, you're worried about the time aspect of it?"

I swallowed. "I don't want to go back on my word. I've done it enough." I hadn't realized how much I missed them—my siblings, her—but I did. I had. It was just easy not to think about what you didn't have when you had your mind on other things.

A small, sad smile crossed her mouth, but she knew better than to try and baby or coo at me. But the words that came out of her mouth next went totally against the expression on her face. "That sounds like a bunch of BS to me, Grumps, but okay. We can focus on one thing at a time for now."

I narrowed my eyes at her.

"Talk to Matty about your hours. You weren't working that many before and he was surviving. Talk to your brothers and your sister. If you start training again, you can still spend time with them, Jasmine. All they want is to be with you, it doesn't matter what you do together."

My stomach clenched in frustration, but probably mostly guilt at her words.

"They don't each need six hours a week from you. They don't even need three. Just some. Not even every week either, I bet."

I grit my teeth to keep from wincing, but I wasn't sure it worked.

She knew what I was thinking and feeling but didn't give a shit because she kept going. "You can have a life outside of figure skating. You can do anything you want, you know that. You just have to make it work."

How many times had she said those exact same words to me in the past? A hundred? Thousand?

I swallowed but didn't shift my gaze. "What are you trying to say?"

She slid me another look. "You know what I'm trying to say. You can do whatever you want in this life, Jasmine. But I want you to be happy. I want you to be appreciated."

My nose started to sting, but I couldn't help but hang on to the caution in her voice. "So you don't think I should do it?"

The woman who had gone to every single competition she'd ever been able to afford, who had always made sure I had a ride to every lesson I'd ever needed to take, who had cheered me on even when I sucked, cocked her head to the side and raised up a shoulder. "I think you should do it, but I don't think you should sell yourself short. There's no one else he could ask that's better than you. Even if it's only for a year. He's not doing you a favor by asking. You're doing him the favor. And if he's dumb enough to screw this up somehow—" She smiled. "—I'll be your alibi if something happens to that fancy car of his. I know what it looks like."

I didn't want to smile at her offer, but I couldn't help it.

My mom's face softened, and she touched my cheek with her fingertips. "I know you miss it."

Miss it? This swell of emotion, or some shit awfully close to it, made my throat close up, and just like that, I wanted to cry. Me. Wanting to cry. It had been a long time since I'd thought about doing that.

I more than missed it—competing. Figure skating in general, for a purpose. For the last year, I'd felt like a part of me had been ripped away without my consent one night while I hadn't been expecting it. And since then, every night, it was like I waited for it to be returned to me. But it hadn't been.

And my eyes must have agreed with how much I missed it because they started to burn as I sat there. And if my voice cracked, neither one of us paid attention to it, and I told her the truth that she didn't need to hear, "I've missed it so much."

That beautiful face fell, and her fingertips turned into her palms as she cupped my cheek. "I want my normal, happy grumpy old woman back," she said carefully. "So if he tries to do something like that son of a whore...." Mom hooked a thumb out and brought it up to her neck, dragging an imaginary line across it, her smile as weak as the coffee Ben made.

I smiled at her as one tiny tear welled up in my right eye, but fortunately the bastard didn't jump out and shame me. My voice did sound watery though as I practically croaked, "Have you been watching *The Godfather* again?"

She raised her red-blonde eyebrows and smiled her creepy, crazy woman smile she usually only brought out around her exes. "What do I always tell you?"

"If you've got it, flaunt it?"

She rolled her eyes. "Besides that. We always do what we gotta do in this family. You've always tried harder at everything than any of the rest of your brothers and sisters combined, and I never wanted that for you, but it's never stopped you from anything. I'd tell you, '*no, don't jump on the bed*,' and you'd wrap a sheet around your neck to jump off the roof instead. Maybe you make terrible decisions sometimes—"

I sniffed. "Rude."

She kept on going, reaching out to take my hand. "But you've always jumped right back up after a fall. You don't know anything else. Things don't always work out the way we want them to, but no girl of mine, especially not you, is a quitter," she said to me. "And whatever else happens, you're more than this sport. Understand me?"

And what was there for me to say after that? Nothing. We'd sat there for another half hour before she begged off, claiming she needed her beauty sleep, leaving me to dwell on everything we had talked about and everything we hadn't.

But one thing was for certain: my mom hadn't raised me to be a quitter.

I had a serious fucking decision to make.

So instead of sleeping, I tried to think through all the pros and cons of Coach Lee and Ivan's proposal while I lay in bed that night.

What I came up with as pros were: I'd get to compete again. Obviously. My partner would be someone who didn't just have a real chance of winning, but someone who probably wanted it just as much as I did. Even if I didn't get another chance to continue after our year was up, it would be the best fighting chance I'd ever have. But if I did manage to snag a partner after this was over....

A shiver had run down my spine at the possibility.

When I tried to think of cons, I couldn't come up with a single one besides my pride getting injured if we didn't win. That I might not get a partner at the end. That I would be left with nothing.

But what the hell did I have now anyway?

What did I have to be proud of? Failing? Getting second place? Getting remembered for being dumped?

Nothing else about the situation worried me. Not all the work I'd have to put in to learn the way Ivan moved and the way he held, and the speed and length of each glide of his blades on the ice. I wasn't worried about all the falls I'd probably take until we figured out how to work with each other doing lifts and throws—which were exactly what they sounded like, when a male partner threw his partner across the ice with the expectation she'd do some rotations and land on her own. I was also okay with having to watch my diet again. Sure, I loved the hell out of cheese and chocolate and not having bruises and being sore daily, but there was something I loved more. Much more.

Plus, maybe this time, maybe, if I was really good, I could figure out how to balance having a tiny personal life with the huge job I'd have ahead of me. Everything in life required a sacrifice. Being able to see my niece more often just meant that instead of going home and doing my best impersonation of a beached whale every chance I had, I could go see her instead for an hour.

I could make it work.

When you want something bad enough, you can always make it happen.

Waking up before the sun rose, I got dressed and followed my usual morning routine perfectly. I didn't know if Lee or Ivan would be at the rink so early, but if they were... then I'd talk to them. I thought about writing my friend an e-mail but didn't bother. It wasn't like she would tell me not to partner up with him.

I ate my first breakfast, made my second breakfast and lunch, ran through my list to make sure I'd done everything I needed to do, and collected my things for the day before getting into the car. When I got in, I hooked my phone up to listen to one of my playlists, keeping my nerves nice and even on the drive to the rink. In the lot, there were only eight other cars, including a shiny black Tesla I knew had to belong to Ivan because no one else could afford one, and a gold-colored Mercedes that I recognized as Coach Lee's.

But when I went inside, I didn't find them in the general manager's office. So, I decided to go about my routine like I was used to, finding my little spot of quiet on the side of the rink furthest from the changing rooms. Forty minutes of solid stretching and then twenty minutes of practicing my jumps on solid ground, I eyed the clean, barely used ice. And I felt this weight lift off my chest; it was the same effect the rink always had on me.

I could look for them after my morning skate.

I'D BEEN ON THE ICE FOR FORTY-FIVE MINUTES WHEN I NOTICED the two well-dressed figures sitting in the stands, watching.

Watching me specifically.

Watching me go through the same section of the only short program I could remember from my singles days, more than likely because the two minutes and fifty seconds of choreography had been my favorite. For me, memorizing programs—one of the two routines you perfected and then competed with each season—was hard enough. I had to rely on muscle memory more than actually *thinking* about what I was doing, which meant I had to do every move and sequence over and over and over again because my mind might struggle with what was next, but my muscles wouldn't. Not after enough repetitions.

My old coach, Galina, used to say that specific program I

was doing was a jump extravaganza. It was one hard jump after another; I hadn't wanted to hold back. Sure, I'd never done the program perfectly, but if I had, it would have been magical. I'd been too stubborn to listen to her when she said the routine was too difficult and that I wasn't consistent enough when it mattered.

But like my mom had always said, usually shaking her head or rolling her eyes as she did it, I "came out doing things the hard way" because I'd decided to come out of her feet first. And ever since, nothing had ever been easy for me.

But it was fine. Challenges were only hard if you went into them expecting not to succeed.

So, when I spotted Ivan Lukov because of his gray pullover sweater and that hair the shade of the purest black—which he probably spent fifteen minutes styling every day until every strand was perfect—and the much shorter, equally dark-haired woman beside him, I kept going. I turned my body around to skate backward so I could go into a triple Lutz, one of the hardest jumps I could do, mostly because you had to counter-rotate your body in the opposite direction of how you went into it. It was my favorite, even though I realized it was a huge factor in all my back pain over the years. Your body didn't want to turn in a different direction than the rest of it. It was awkward and hard, especially when you had to go into it as fast as possible.

I hadn't been able to land anything for days, but on that day, *thank God, halle-fucking-lujah*, at that moment, I landed it as good as I ever did. That was the thing about figure skating: it was all about muscle memory, and the only way to make your body memorize anything was to do it thousands of times. Not hundreds. Thousands. Then, once you did that, you had to make it look effortless when it was anything but. And that triple Lutz I had worked on twice as much as any other jump because I'd been determined to make it my bitch, and I had. I'd been able to do a decent triple Axel on a good day, and had landed quads in practice when I attempted them in practice for the hell of it, but the 3L—what we called the triple Lutz—that's what I had focused all of my energy on in my singles days. It was one beautiful thing that no one could take away from me. Or do as well, I thought.

Even though I realized it was stupid to cut my time short because I'd already paid for it, I decided to go ahead and get this next conversation over with. I didn't want to get to work late if I didn't have to.

Work. Shit.

I was going to need to talk to my mom's longtime friend about my hours again. Not that it would be a problem, but I hated bailing on him after I'd made a commitment to work more, months ago. He would understand and even be over-joyed, but it still made me feel like a flake. Plus, I was going to need the money. I was going to have to figure it out. More money and less hours. That wasn't going to be easy.

With my heart still racing from the series of jumps I'd just done in the routine before the 3L, I skated toward the exit of the rink, passing by the other skaters on the ice but keeping my attention mostly downward as I did it. It wasn't until I got to the wall right beside the opening in it that I looked up and found Galina leaning over the edge a few feet away, her eyes intent on me.

I dipped my chin at her.

After a moment, she nodded back at me, a strange expression on her face that I couldn't remember seeing before. She looked really thoughtful. Maybe even sad.

Huh.

Putting my skate guards on, I grabbed my bottle of water too and asked myself if I was sure—really, really sure—this was what I wanted. If I wanted to get back into this world with a partner who more than likely didn't accept mistakes any better than I did. A partner that I couldn't talk to without bickering with. A world with people judging every single tiny thing about me. A world with zero guarantees. I was going to have to work harder than I ever had before to get this to work in a season. Was I ready for it?

I sure as fuck was.

My mom had been right. There were very few things worse than regret. And I would definitely regret not taking this chance—even if it meant stretching myself thin—more than I would taking it and getting nothing out of it.

Plus, I'd never been that much of a little bitch before. Ten years ago, I wouldn't have even thought twice about jumping into this opportunity, even if I got nothing out of it. Now... well, burns leave scars sometimes, and I wouldn't forget it.

With adrenaline pumping through my veins, and still slightly out of breath, I made my way over to the part of the stands where Ivan and Coach Lee were still sitting. They weren't even trying to be discreet with their stares. One last chance to make sure they knew what they were getting? Probably.

My hands didn't shake, and my knees didn't feel weak as I approached them; it was only my breathing that was choppy and irregular, but my stomach gave this roll of nerves I wasn't used to and sure as hell would never admit to.

"I hope you don't mind we came to see you," Coach Lee started the conversation while I was still feet away from them, confirming my suspicions.

I shook my head as my gaze briefly slipped in Ivan's direction, taking in that cool but somehow still smug face, before just as quickly glancing back at the other woman. I couldn't screw this up by opening my mouth and arguing with him. At least not yet.

"Not at all," I told her. I understood why they did it. I would have done the same. "Morning."

The corners of her mouth slipped up at the edges just enough to be a fraction of a smile. "Morning."

Ivan didn't say shit.

Good. Maybe he was doing the same thing I was: keeping his mouth shut so we could get through this as painlessly as possible. That reassured me more than I would have liked, because if he wasn't arguing with me, maybe he did want to be my partner.

Okay, *want* was the wrong word to use. Need might have been more like it. Whatever.

I had no idea what the situation was, and honestly, I didn't give a shit. All I cared about was this opportunity. I wasn't about to screw it up for myself.

Getting to her feet and putting her at an inch shorter than me, Coach Lee crossed her arms over her chest and said something I wasn't expecting. "Your triple Lutz is beautiful. Your height, your speed, the amount of ice you cover, and your technique... I forgot that was your signature move until you did it. It's perfect, Jasmine, really. You should be proud of it." Her smile turned into a grin. "It reminds me of Ivan's."

I ignored the part about Ivan and focused on the rest. I was proud of it. I didn't say that though. I'd torn that jump apart to perfect it. I'd watched and re-watched the best figure skaters doing it to see what it was that made it so spectacular, so I could do it too. There were even hours of footage at home of me doing it over and over again, just so I could see how to improve what I was doing. My mom had wanted to kill me back then for forcing her to record the same thing over and over again for hours and days. And once I had figured it out, she'd tried to take all the credit for it.

"When did you do that last combination? I don't remember it from any competition," she said, thoughtfully. "I didn't think Paul was very good at Lutzes...."

He hadn't been. And I told her she was right. "It's from an old short program from my singles days," I explained.

Both her eyebrows went up at the same time like "ah." "That's a shame," she said. "You'll have to tell me one day the story behind you switching from singles to pairs. I was always curious about it."

And it was that comment that made me shrug and say, easy and smooth, "It's not that interesting of a story, but one day."

It was the "one day" that had her eyes widening. "You're sure?"

Was I? Was I really?

I looked at her, and only her, and said, "I have a few questions, and a few stipulations."

"Stipulations?" Ivan drawled out the question from where he was on the bench, all lazy and in that snobby voice that said he didn't think I was in any position to bargain.

Wrong.

I glanced at him for all of a second then moved my gaze back to his coach before I said something stupid. "Nothing crazy." I used the same words she had used on me the day before when she had basically said I was going to have to agree to not be stubborn to making changes.

Coach Lee slid a look toward Ivan that I didn't absorb before agreeing. "Would you like to talk here or should I see if the office is open?"

I didn't need to glance around to know we had privacy. "We can do it here and save time."

The other woman raised her eyebrows but nodded.

I moved my left hand to my right wrist without thinking about it, spinning my bracelet for moral support. *I could do this.* I could make everything work.

I had to try.

Ivan might be an amazing skater, but I had worked just as hard as he had. Maybe for not as long as him, because I hadn't started skating before I was three years old, but in all the ways that mattered, I had done almost everything I could. He wasn't doing me a favor. This was going to be an equal partnership or it wasn't going to be anything. I wasn't going to accept less.

"What's on your mind?" Coach Lee finally asked.

I spun the bracelet on my wrist again. *I can do anything*, I reminded myself. Then I started. "I want to make sure that you won't be asking me to do a makeover and start kissing babies in public if I agree to be Ivan's partner."

There.

I was pretty sure her cheek twitched, but her expression was so neutral, I might have imagined it. "No kissing babies and no makeovers. That's not an issue. What else?"

I could really start to like this woman and her directness. So I kept going. "You can't get rid of me before the year is over."

Out of the corner of my eye, I could see Ivan shifting around from his spot on the bench, but I still didn't look at him. Instead, I watched the woman I was practically doing business with, our mediator. She didn't flinch at my demand, but her eyebrow did do this quirk thing that she couldn't smooth out fast enough.

"Why would you think we would terminate the agreement before the year is up?" she asked slowly.

That time I did glance at Ivan. On purpose. Then I pointed at him with the thumb closest to him so that there wasn't any confusion. "Because I'm not sure how he and I are going to get along."

He scoffed and opened his mouth like he was about to argue, but I didn't let him.

"I'm just trying to cover my bases. I know how I am, and I know how he is too." I called him a "he" because even though I was looking at him, I was really speaking to Lee. "If something is my fault, I'll work at it until I fix it. I promise you that, but if it's his fault...."

He changed his posture from sitting in that relaxed position to leaning forward, spreading his knees and planting his elbows on them. His pale blue eyes were so intense it was like they were trying to bore a hole right into me. The tip of his tongue was poking at the inside of his cheek. He'd made that face at me enough times in the past for me to recognize it.

He was giving me a death glare.

Good.

It would have been weird if he'd pretended like everything was fine and dandy.

"If it's Ivan's fault..." I glanced at him that time. "*Yours*," I emphasized because *he* needed to get that he wasn't perfect and that he and his coach couldn't blame me for everything. "I trust that you'll bust your ass not to make the same mistake again either. If something is wrong, we'll both work at it. We both agree to do whatever we have to do to make this work."

Because I was still looking in his direction, I could see his jaw move from one side to the other the entire time I talked, and I could feel the argument hanging in the air.

"All I want is to make sure the responsibility is split evenly between us. We're a team or we aren't. I won't be treated like the redheaded step-kid. This can't be just The Ivan Show."

"The Ivan Show?" he echoed, still giving me his death glare.

I shrugged a shoulder, feeling my nose beginning to wrinkle in a sneer that I only barely wrangled in before it turned into a full one. I dragged my gaze back to Coach Lee just barely. "And when the year is over, I want your word that you'll both find me another partner. Not just help me find one, but actually find me one." I swallowed and said, "That's all I want. I'll do just about anything you ask, but I want those two things, and I want to be sure it isn't debatable."

There was a beat of silence.

I didn't need to look to know they were both looking at me and not at each other.

Andddd. Why the hell were they taking so long to say yes? I wasn't asking for that much.

Was I?

Standing there, looking at both of them, I asked what felt like the most important question of my life because I just wanted to get it over with. Either we were doing this or we weren't. I wasn't good with anticipation. I wasn't patient. "Do we have a deal?"

There was another pause, and Coach Lee finally glanced in Ivan's direction for what must have been half a minute at least before she made an amused noise. Her mouth twisted to the side and then back. She took her time moving her attention back to me, and then blinked.

And I thought, *we don't have a deal.*

And my stomach sank.

And for the first time in forever, I thought I was going to throw up and I wanted to kick my own ass.

"Fine," came the unexpected reply straight out of Ivan's mouth, not looking at all like he was excited to do it... and still watching me carefully. Still not making a face. Not looking at all like this was a major decision when it was the total opposite for me.

But I didn't let his little bitch face distract me from what the hell had just happened.

He'd agreed.

He had agreed.

Holy fuck.

I was going to compete again.

Once, when I was younger on vacation, I'd gone with my brother to the beach and we'd decided to go cliff diving. I remember jumping in from a spot so high, my mom would have killed me if she'd seen it. Even my brother had chickened out at the last minute. But I hadn't.

I hadn't been expecting how far under the water I would go when I dove in. I'd had to hold my breath for so long as I kicked and kicked and kicked to reach the surface, it had felt like I'd never make it. For maybe half a second, I had thought I was going to drown. But when I reached the surface, I would probably always remember what it was like to take that first breath of air. To take that first breath of air and think *I had done it.*

Sometimes it's easy to take something so essential to your existence for granted.

More than ever, I understood it then as I stood there, taking turns looking between Coach Lee and Ivan and feeling... feeling like I was supposed to be feeling. Like I was alive again. Like I was *right*.

But...

There was one more thing that I hadn't taken into consideration while I'd been worried about everything else. Something that was just as important as the other two things. Maybe even more.

It was a deal breaker. A deal breaker that my pride didn't want to even factor but had to. I was trying to be an adult. "There's one more thing." I swallowed and fought back the temptation to keep my mouth shut. "How much are coaching and choreography fees going to be?"

I wasn't going to ask my mom to contribute as much as she used to. But I also had a vague idea how much Ivan paid his choreographers. I had called one once and gotten pissed off when he told me his rates.

I was already cringing on the inside, expecting the worst. There was no way Coach Lee was cheap either. My past two coaches hadn't been the most expensive, but they hadn't been the cheapest either, because they coached other figure skaters at the same time at different levels in their careers.

So when Ivan blinked at me and Coach Lee said nothing, my thoughts went straight to *shit*.

I was going to have to ask them to let me defer my payment until the season was over so I could sell a kidney. Fuck it, I could wear a wig and strip. I didn't have any birth-marks to give me away.

"Ivan will cover coaching and choreography fees, but you'll be responsible for travel and your wardrobe," the other woman said after a moment too long.

The muscles at my shoulders went tight, my gaze went to Ivan, and I asked him, when I knew better, "You will?"

Those gray-blue eyes lazily blinked before he said, "You can pay for half if you want."

I wasn't that prideful.

So I blinked right back at him. "Nope."

He straightened in his seat, that face, which had been on a lip balm commercial once, stayed perfectly even. "You're sure?" he asked, that annoying tone prickling at his words.

"I'm sure."

"Positive?"

This bitch. I narrowed my eyes. "Positive."

"I don't mind splitting it," he kept going, the corner of his mouth coming up into a baby smirk I was way too familiar with.

I ground down on my molars. "Nope," I repeated myself.

"Because we—"

"*Okay*," Coach Lee butted in, shaking her head. "I think I'm going to need a raise to deal with both of you."

That had both of us turning our heads toward her.

"I'm fine. It's him," I said at the same time Ivan said, "It's her fault."

The older woman shook her head some more, giving us both expressions that said she was already fed up with our shit. "You're both professionals and mostly adults—"

Mostly an adult?

It was just because I didn't know Coach Lee well enough yet that I kept the scoff in my mouth.

"This is going to be a lot of work, and both of you are aware of that. This bickering thing you have going on, save it for the evenings when we're done if you can't get past it. We don't have time to waste," she said, using that tone my mom used when she was fed up with our shit.

I kept my mouth shut.

Ivan didn't.

"I'm professional," he muttered.

The other woman just stared at him. "We talked about this."

He gave her a look, and she gave him one right back.

I almost smiled... until I took in what they were saying... and what they weren't. What the hell had they talked about? How we always argued and needed to get past it if we were going to partner up? Because that would actually make a lot of sense. It was one of my biggest worries, but I knew I could keep it to myself.

At least most of the time.

The woman turned her head to look at me. "Jasmine, will that be a problem?"

I didn't trust myself to look at Ivan, so I kept my gaze on my new coach. God, that felt weird to even think that. "Save it for afterward. I can do that." It would probably be harder than actually practicing so much, but I could do it.

"Ivan?"

If he glanced at me or didn't, I had no idea, all I heard was what was basically a grumbled, "Yes."

"Constructive criticisms won't be a problem either," the other woman kept going, telling us, not asking.

No shit, we could handle constructive criticism—

"From each other," she finished.

That time I did glance at Ivan, but he was already looking at me, his eyelids slit like he was thinking the same thing I was. We could already barely talk to each other. We hardly were, because we both knew what happened when we opened our mouths and aimed them at each other.

But...

I was trying to be better, and I would be. I wasn't going to let my mouth ruin anything for me. Much less my pride. I told them I'd do anything for this, and I would.

Even if it meant dealing with this jackass.

So I nodded, because what else was I going to do? Ruin something that in the future might give me everything I wanted? Possibly lead to other great things? I wasn't that dumb.

"Fine," came the bit off response from the only male nearby.

"Good, I'm glad that's settled now before we go any further."

I glanced at Ivan again, but he'd beat me to it. He was already looking at me....

And I didn't like it.

Stop looking at me, I mouthed.

No, he mouthed back.

Coach Lee sighed. "Excellent. Lip whatever you want to each other as long as I don't have to hear it."

I swear on my life he smacked his lips together.

I wanted to smack him.

Then he opened his mouth to talk. "You're going to need to get a physical before we start."

What? Was he for real? I was in prime fucking health—

Shut up, Jasmine. It isn't a big deal. And maybe I wasn't exactly in my prime, but none of my injuries would pop up in a physical.

I shut up and dipped my chin down like *okay, uh-huh.* What was a little checkup when I'd have this opportunity again? Nothing, that's what.

"We need to make sure you don't have any pre-existing conditions that you aren't telling us about that might come up later on," he continued on, slowly, still making a face like this entire conversation—and situation—was costing him.

The smart-ass crept up my throat, not going anywhere, especially not after his hand went up to his check and his middle finger scratched at the tip of his nose. Ass. "That's what I figured you wanted when you said you wanted a physical, not to get my weight or cholesterol levels," I muttered, stopping myself before I said anything more aggressive.

It was his turn to be a smart-ass apparently. "Speaking of your weight—"

No he didn't.

Coach Lee cleared her throat just as I'd started to raise my hand to point at him. With my middle finger. "*All right,*" she said tightly. "Let's focus. We just talked about this. We'll have an agreement drawn up that you'll need to sign, Jasmine.

Other than that, practice will be six days a week, twice a day. Will that be a problem?"

It took every ounce of self-control in me to tear my gaze away from the idiot who had been just about to say something about my weight. I could feel my nostrils flare as I swallowed and focused back on the woman. "It's not a problem." She didn't need to tell me we needed all the training we could get in with less than six months before the start of the next season. "What times?" I asked, my hand twirling my bracelet.

It was Ivan that answered as he shifted around on the bench. "Four hours at four in the morning at the LC, and a three hour workout at one in the afternoon."

Shit.

That would only leave me four hours to work and that was going to be cutting it close, but I couldn't quit. I wouldn't. Maybe I could pick up a shift here or there too on my day off. I'd make it work. Somehow.

I managed to nod before I caught on to something he said. "You said at the LC. Are there going to be more practices somewhere else?"

Coach Lee didn't even try to hide the glance she cast in Ivan's direction. A glance that again put me on edge. I hated secrets and secret looks. I wanted to ask what those faces were for but decided to wait. Patience. I could be patient. If I tried really hard.

Luckily, she didn't make me wait long. "You understand we've discussed your strengths and weaknesses before we asked you to join the team?"

"Yeah." Did I like that they had talked about me? No. But it was part of it, and I couldn't hold it against them. Before I'd gotten to this point of desperation, I would have done the same.

"You're a strong athlete, Jasmine," she started to say, and I made sure I had my armor on so I could handle whatever non-compliment was going to eventually come out of her mouth. That's what coaches did. They tore apart all the things you were bad at and helped you try to fix them. At least that was the goal. "I've always thought you had an amazing amount of potential—"

A "but" was about to come out of her mouth. I could feel it. There was always a "but" when someone paid you a compliment.

Maybe it was just me.

I kept my face even, but it was a little harder than I would have wanted it to be.

"But there are things you can work on to take it to the next level, specifically your showmanship. I've spoken to Galina in the past, and she confirmed that you didn't have a heavy amount of training in ballet. I think your skating would really benefit from it."

When the hell had she spoken to Galina?

"We want you to take some one-on-one training with the instructor Ivan has used in the past to tweak a few bad habits—"

Bad habits?

"—and work on improving what's already good but could be better. Apart from that, you will be taking lessons with Ivan at the same time. There's always room for improvement. I'm sure you're familiar with that."

Was she saying that just to make me feel better about basically telling me that I had none of the grace that came from having a serious background in ballet? It wasn't like I didn't know that Ivan did. Karina had only taken figure skating lessons up until she was fourteen—which was how we had met—but she had focused on dance before and afterward. Plus, there was something really elegant and graceful about

Ivan's movements that could only come from a ballet instructor with a drill sergeant's heart. He'd had the money. He could afford someone to teach him everything he needed to know.

My mom had been able to afford two group lessons a week for an hour each, so that's what I had done for years. I wasn't going to apologize for it. And I'd said I would do whatever I needed to make this work. So, all I said was, "Okay."

The corners of Coach Lee's mouth tightened for a moment before her expression went back to normal. "Good. I'll call tomorrow and see what's available so you can pick the times that work for you on your schedule. Ivan attends Monday and Saturday mornings from nine until eleven. Will that be a problem?"

It was, but I would have to make it work. I was going to end up quitting my job and stripping. Jesus Christ. "No, not a problem." My stomach hurt for a moment, but I shoved it aside and focused on what was important. "I also take a Pilates class once a week to work on my flexibility. I'm planning on still taking it."

"Good, keep doing that," the woman replied with a slow nod.

I tried to put all my thoughts in order. "What do you want the season to look like?" I asked.

It was Ivan that answered. "We'll do the Discovery Series, the Major Prix, nationals, and worlds." He blinked. "We can skip the rest."

I did the math in my head and swallowed back the nerves at the realization that would be seven different events we would be competing in. At least. Two or three competitions in the Discovery Series. Three in the Major Prix, if we made it to the final. Then one each for nationals and worlds.

Money. Money. Money. And more money.

But I didn't even care. All the more chances to win.

Or fail, that negative-ass voice in my head whispered until I shoved it away. I needed to stop thinking that way. It hadn't done me any good ever before, and it never would. I couldn't get psyched out so early.

"Okay," I got out with another nod, feeling this tightness in my chest that I didn't love.

Coach Lee dipped her own chin down. "Now that that's all sorted, can you start tomorrow?"

Tomorrow? Fuck.

I was too worried about my voice being all high and pitchy and giving away how overwhelmed I was at what was happening, that I decided to keep my mouth shut and nod again. I was going to need to talk to my boss today. *Holy shit.*

"Is that it then? You don't want me to do a tryout?" I asked, just to be sure.

"That's it," she confirmed. The expression on Coach Lee's face wasn't exactly a smile, but she looked... pleased. She extended her hand out in my direction, and I took it. "Good. Tomorrow we get to work then. I'll schedule your physical today and let you know where to go and what time."

"Tomorrow," I agreed on an exhale, feeling this weight lift off my chest for all of a second before crashing back down. Feeling heavy, I pulled my hand back to my side and turned to where Ivan had been sitting the entire time. He hadn't moved. His elbows were still on his knees, hands hanging loosely between his legs, and his attention was still on me. That long, blunt line of his jaw was set firmly, and it was an expression I'd seen enough.

I had a feeling it was one I was going to keep on seeing a whole lot of over the next year.

The next year. Shit.

I had told Coach Lee we could get past this, or at least put up with each other, and I wasn't about to back down or take my word back. I wasn't going to screw this up for myself. I could be the better person... and thinking about it like that put a smile on my face.

Hesitating for just a moment, I extended my hand out toward him.

And it hovered there. For a second. For two seconds. For three seconds.

Three more seconds and I was going to slap him in the face.

Ivan was watching me in return as he stood up, going up to that full height that put him at an inch shy of being a foot taller than me... and he slipped his hand into mine for the first time ever.

His eyes met mine, and I knew what he was thinking because I was thinking the same thing.

Once—just once—years ago, I'd fallen badly after a jump. He had been on the rink with me at the same time. I'd been lying there on the ice, blinking up at the rafters, trying to catch my breath because even my brain had hurt after hitting the ice so hard. This bitch had skated up to me for some reason. And he'd stretched his hand out toward me, looking down at me with a smirk on his face.

I hadn't been thinking. All I'd seen was a hand reaching out toward me, so I'd tried to take it. Like an idiot.

My fingers had probably been inches away from Ivan's when he'd snatched his hand back, smirked even wider, and left me there. On the ice. Just like that.

Bitch.

So he could only blame himself when it took me a minute to close my fingers around his, giving him a look the whole time, expecting the worst. But nothing happened. His palm was cold and wide, and his fingers were longer than I'd expected. In all the years we'd gravitated around each other, we'd never touched except for the one Thanksgiving I'd spent at his family's house and he'd sat beside me and had taken my hand during their prayer. We spent the whole three minutes squeezing each other's hands as hard as we could, at least until Karina had kicked him under the table, probably seeing my fingertips going white.

If he was expecting me to say something, he was going to be waiting forever because there was nothing I needed to say to him. Okay, maybe I just didn't trust myself not to say something stupid before we were too deep into this to go back. Apparently, there was nothing he needed to say to me either. Fine by me.

That was the good thing about figure skating. You didn't have to talk to do it.

Ivan gave my fingers a hard squeeze.

And I squeezed his as hard as I could right back.

CHAPTER 5

I'D FORGOTTEN HOW MUCH IT HURT TO GET DROPPED.

"Are you all right?" came Coach Lee's voice from... somewhere.

I had my eyes closed as I lay there, thankful for the fact that someone had decided at some point in history that the world needed cushioned mats. Because if it weren't for cushioned mats—even if they were only an inch thick—I probably would have broken three times as many bones as I had in my life.

But still.

Fuck.

I tried to take a breath, but from the sting of it, my lungs were still in shock from Ivan's hands slipping—or whatever the fuck had happened—resulting in me falling from close to eight or nine feet in the air and landing right on my goddamn back.

Fuck.

"I'm fine," I half whispered, half wheezed out, trying to take another inhale but only being able to take a baby-sized one that wasn't anywhere near enough.

Gulping, I tried to take another breath and only managed half of one before my spine went "*Not yet, sucker.*" Dragging my bare heels across the mats, I planted my feet on the floor and attempted to take another breath, a little more successful that time. The good thing was: my ribs weren't broken. The other good thing was: at least he'd dropped me on here and not the ice, which felt like the equivalent of cement when you hit it.

I swallowed again, took another breath, and when that went well, I reminded myself this was nothing. Not really, at least.

I opened my eyes and immediately spotted the big hand that had held me high above the floor—the big hand that had wobbled and dropped me—extended in my direction.

For a second, I thought about taking the hand offering me help, but then remembered the other time he'd done the same thing. I shook my head and rolled up onto my butt on my own. "I'm fine," I muttered, only wincing with my entire face as I did it.

"You need a minute?" Coach Lee asked from her spot off the mats as I shifted onto my knees and slowly climbed up onto my feet, taking a couple more breaths that only slightly made my back ache. I was going to feel it tomorrow for sure.

"I'm fine. Let's do it again." I waved her off as I tipped my head back and took another breath to catch the one the fall had taken from me. When my breathing was back under control and I was ready to go, I turned to face my brand-new partner of all of four hours.

Four hours.

We'd spent that morning doing basics, and I meant the most basic of basics. I hadn't slept well the night before, mostly because of the anticipation of what was coming the next morning—our first practice—but when I woke up, I'd been ready.

When we'd met up beside the rink at four in the morning, I'd already had a black L on the top of my left hand and a red R on my right hand; I'd warmed up on my own and so had he. Coach Lee had started us off skating laps side by side... for hours. All to find our rhythm together. His legs were longer than mine, but we both listened to Coach Lee's corrections, kept our mouths shut, and it had worked out. I didn't even think we looked at each other's faces, we were so busy focusing on our feet... and only a couple of times did I have to glance at my hands.

And when she'd told us to hold hands and do it all over again, we did it. Then we just did it over and over again, holding hands and not holding hands until we got it right. Baby steps, but they were important. These were all things we should have figured out if we'd done a tryout.

So when we got to the rink that afternoon after I'd gone to work—and explained to my boss that I was going to have to work less hours from here on out—Coach Lee had told us we'd start off working on lifts on the mats, I'd been pretty pumped to move forward a little more.

At least until his hold got weird as he had me in a carry lift —his hands on the spot between my lower stomach and right above my groin, his arms locked straight above his six-foot-two head, while I had my legs together and extended, back arched and head held high. I'd done it a thousand times before with my ex-partner.

But just like I'd forgotten how much it hurt to fall, I forgot how every lifting partner had a different way they liked to hold. Or so I'd been told. I had only had one partner in my short and shit pairs career.

Maybe I weighed more than Ivan's last partner.

"Let me see where you're putting your hands, Ivan," Coach Lee called out. "Then push up as slow as you can do it, so I can see Jasmine's movement too."

Nodding, I made myself look up at Ivan after I got into position directly in front of him. In his fitted and tapered gray sweatpants and a T-shirt so white it might have been brand new, his hair was combed and parted in that perfect way it always was, he looked more like he was about to do a modeling shoot for sweatpants than to actually work out.

With his chin to his throat, he looked down at me with those almost clear gray-blue eyes and nodded at me like "*let's do it.*" We hadn't said anything to each other so far. We hadn't even mouthed anything either.

Yet.

I dropped my chin to my throat too, to tell him "*let's do it.*" So we did. His hands went into position in a place that I hadn't let very many guys touch me, and we went into it.

I knew the second he had me at about his head level that something was wrong, and I needed to figure out what it was.

"What is it?" Coach Lee asked, like she read my mind.

"His palm is weird," I told her immediately, trying not to squirm too much before I ended up on the floor again.

"There's nothing wrong with me," Ivan claimed from under me, sounding just as insulted as I figured he would.

I rolled my eyes. I had promised I wouldn't talk shit, that didn't mean I couldn't roll my eyes, especially not when he couldn't see me.

"I don't know what it is. I think his hands are bigger—" I started to tell Coach Lee before the man under me made a snickering sound that had me rolling my eyes again. "It feels strange." The lift went as high as it could possibly go, and I was in the same position I'd been in when he'd let me fall. I sucked in my stomach and grit my teeth, tensing my biceps as

I tried to move the weight around a little on my palms and fingers. I could do this.

"I know what I'm doing," came the idiot under me.

"I'll get used to it," I told Coach Lee, pretending like I didn't hear Ivan.

"Put her down and do it again," the other woman said.

And Ivan did, lowering me to the ground a lot faster and not as carefully as he could have. Fucker. I glared up at him, but he was too busy looking at Coach Lee to notice.

We did it again.

Again and again and again.

That was all we did for the next three hours, the entrance into the lift one time after another and after another, until it stopped feeling so different... and my arms—and Ivan's—were shaking with exhaustion. My shoulders were sore, and I couldn't imagine what his had to feel like. But neither one of us complained or asked for a break.

By the time four o'clock rolled around, ab muscles I'd forgotten I had were exhausted, and I was 90 percent sure I'd have a giant bruise on my stomach the next day.

"One more time and we'll call it a day," Coach said from the spot she'd taken sitting cross-legged on the mat a few feet away from the circle of space Ivan and I had been working in. We hadn't even gotten to the point where he was walking with me over his head yet; we were still just doing the same lift.

I didn't look up as I took a step back before leaning forward at the same time Ivan's hands went into position. And he raised me, a little more swiftly even though I knew he had to be tired, a little easier and consistent. It lasted all of twenty seconds before I was back on my feet, biting back a grimace at the ache coming from my abs. I was going to need to apply the arnica ointment in my bag the second after I showered so I wouldn't be dying tomorrow.

"Ice your stomach tonight, Jasmine. We can't afford you being in pain," Coach Lee called out almost immediately after I landed on both feet. I looked at her and gave a nod. "Good work today."

Was it? Part of me thought it would have gone better, or at least faster, but it wasn't like I had anything or anyone else to compare to. I wasn't going to let myself get overwhelmed. One step at a time. I knew that. One small step at a time, to build another step and another until we had an entire staircase.

"Rest, ice what you need to ice, and I'll see you both tomorrow," the other woman called out. I already knew from experience that she had her younger figure skaters she usually focused on once Ivan's season was done. I watched her as she turned around and then was gone.

Okay.

I didn't want to stand around talking either.

Raising my eyebrows to myself, I headed toward where I'd kicked off my shoes and socks. The silence in the huge room was weird; it was one of a couple of different practice spaces set up at the LC that any skater was free to use. Bending at the waist, I grabbed both socks and slipped each one on, noticing I had a chip in my hot pink nail polish on my big toe. Maybe tonight I could redo them if bending over didn't make me tear up. The color never lasted longer than a couple of days at a time, and they especially wouldn't with this new training schedule, but I liked having them painted. I liked getting pedicures more than doing them myself, but that wasn't going to be happening again.

At least not for a year.

I'd just straightened to slip my feet into my shoes when I heard a deep sigh from behind.

I pretended like I didn't hear him.

But I couldn't pretend not to hear him when he said in that

voice that was somewhere between deep and baritone, "We need to work on your trusting me if you want me to help you find another partner when this is over next year."

And... I paused with my hands filled with shoelaces and glanced over my shoulder to find Ivan standing where he'd been the last time I'd seen him: barefoot on the middle of the mats; except this time, his hands were on his hips and his attention was focused on me. "What?" I asked, frowning.

The muscle along Ivan's jawbone twitched. "We. Need. To. Work. On. You. Trusting. Me. If. You. Want. Me. To. Help. You. Find. Another. Partner," the smart-ass repeated himself.

I blinked, and then if my eye started twitching, it wasn't intentional. Lee was gone, wasn't she? We had only talked about watching our words during practice. Right? "I. Know. How. To. Listen. The. First. Time," I replied, taking my time just like he had. "I. Want. To. Know. What. You. Mean. By. That."

"I. Mean. You. Need. To. Trust. Me. Or. This. Will. Never. Work."

This son of a bitch. *Calm down, Jasmine. Talk to him normally. Be the better person.*

But I couldn't. "Are you threatening me?"

It was his turn to blink. His turn for his eyebrows to go up. His turn to shrug a shoulder.

"It's been a day and you're already threatening not to help me?" I asked him, taking my time with each word.

"All I'm saying is that this isn't going to go well unless you trust me, and even you know that," he said.

My eye was twitching, and I swear to God my fingers ached with the need to pull on someone's hair. "You dropped me."

"Once, and it's not going to be the last time. You know that," was his excuse.

I blinked at him. I did know that. I didn't expect anything different.

But...

It was still him that had let me fall.

Ivan blinked. "I didn't do it on purpose." Yeah, I didn't exactly believe him, and he must have expected that because he shook his head, those slim nostrils on that perfectly straight nose flared, and he repeated himself. "I didn't."

I didn't say anything.

"I'm not going to risk hurting you," he tried to say before his cheek went tight. "Not while you're my partner."

"That's real reassuring."

His cheek twitched.

"I trust you enough," I said, *liar, liar, liar* tickling at the base of my throat. "I'm just not used to the way you hold, that's all." And it was hard to trust someone I'd called a shitface for years, but....

The tip of his tongue went to the inside of his cheek, and those ice blue eyes narrowed on me. Did everything about him have to be immaculate all the damn time? "You're the worst liar, you know that?" he asked.

"You're a shitty liar," I said before I could stop myself.

He shook his head, and I noticed not a single one of his pitch-black hairs moved. "You said you would do whatever needed to be done so we could win, didn't you?"

I nodded slowly.

He raised an eyebrow. "So, I'm telling you what's wrong, and you need to fix it."

Oh my God. "It's been one day, and I told you what's wrong. Your hand placement is weird."

"My *hand placement* isn't weird."

"It is," I repeated myself.

He blinked. "No one else has ever complained."

I blinked back. "No one else has probably had the balls to complain," I told him. "I'll get used to it. I'm sure you're doing it right—"

"I am. Want to go look at the trophies in the case on the way out?" the ass asked.

I blew out a breath and gave my wrist a shake... because it was a little achy, not because I wanted to punch him already. Nope. "Do you admire them on the way in and out every day? Polish them up every Sunday? Give them a little kiss?"

Ivan's mouth opened and then closed.

I smiled. "I'll get used to it."

He blinked. "It's not you getting used to it that's the problem. You don't trust me. I can feel it."

"I trust you not to drop me on purpose," I said slowly, not liking where this was going. "I think you'd want to figure this out as soon as possible. You wouldn't want to waste time."

"No shit, Sherlock," he said slowly, instantly drawing a line up my spine.

"Look, Satan, how do you expect me to trust you in like the six hours we've been practicing?" I snapped before I could stop.

That drew that freaky, joyous smile I'd only seen on his face when we were bickering. "I knew it."

"No shit, Sherlock. I know you're not going to drop me on purpose, but what do you want me to do? We don't like each other. I'm constantly expecting you to not watch out for me, no matter what I tell myself."

He raised an eyebrow, and I didn't miss how he didn't argue the fact we didn't like each other. Ass. "You need to. Lee thinks we can do this in a year, and I know I can do it in a year—"

I rolled my eyes because I was pretty sure he thought he could do or master anything in that time.

Okay, maybe I thought the same thing about myself, but it was different. I wasn't a prick for no reason and only to one person.

"—but we need to get over this, and we need to do it soon. You're hesitating because you don't trust me because of that idiot before me, so what do you want from me? Or what do you need from me so we can get there?"

That time, it was my turn to blink, because who the fuck was this person? *What do you need from me?* What the fuck? And why was he bringing up Paul?

Him catching me off guard must have been on my face because he sighed. "I don't have all day."

Oh *God.* "Neither do I." I didn't say "shit face," but I thought it. "Look, I don't know. I told you, my head knows you won't drop me on purpose, but the rest of me doesn't trust it. A week ago, I wouldn't have trusted you to catch me doing a trust fall. I don't know how to fix that."

Ivan blinked. "You aren't my first new partner, and this is only for a year, so let's figure it out. You want my word?"

"Notice how you didn't say you would've caught me doing a trust fall."

"I wouldn't have."

I fucking *knew* it.

"That was then, this is now, Meatball. You want my word I won't purposely let you get hurt?"

I almost laughed. "Your word? You remember all the other words you've told me over the years?"

That jaw of his went hard, making his perfectly sculpted face look tight.

"That's what I thought."

"What do you want me to do? Lee's going to ask what I did to fix this, and I want to tell her I did everything I needed to. Tell me."

Tell him?

I slid a look to the side before sliding it back to him. "Tell me something embarrassing."

He didn't even hesitate. "No."

I would have smiled if this was someone other than him. "Uh-huh. Who's the one with the trust issues now, jackass?" I shook my head. "Don't worry about it. I'll get over it. Everything will be fine. I need this more than you do. I'll figure it out, and everything will be fine."

It had to.

"Fine."

I glanced back down and finished tying my shoelace before getting to my feet. God, I really was going to need to ice myself tonight. Maybe even do a whole ice bath. *Fuck.* I didn't miss those.

Rolling back my shoulders, which I hadn't realized were so tight, I glanced at Ivan, who had moved at some point and was busy sliding his feet into what looked like slipper boots.

Whatever. I wanted to get home.

I took a step toward the door and hesitated. We were partners now. For a year. I could be better. I would be. So, I glanced over my shoulder and called out, "See ya."

I didn't even add a name to the end of it. That had to mean something.

I waited all of maybe two seconds before I realized he wasn't going to respond—ass—and headed toward the door, telling myself that it didn't matter he didn't say anything. What the hell else was I expecting? Him to actually be friendly? I knew what this was and what this wasn't.

He'd said it already. One year. That was all we were going to have together.

And he wanted it bad enough to talk to me about what was wrong so we could fix it.

At least I could trust him enough to know I could always rely on him to make the best business decision.

Did I trust him? Hell no. At least not enough. But for what mattered, yes.

Pulling up the waistband of my leggings, which had gotten stretched out from practice, I rolled my shoulders, sucked in my stomach to see if it was really as sore as I thought it was—and it was—and decided I might as well drop by the convenience store and pick up two bags of ice. Ice baths were pretty much torture, and there were very few things I hated more than them, but... I was going to hate being in pain even more. I just needed to woman up and handle it.

But still, my bones already hurt just thinking about it.

With a shiver racing up my spine that made me feel like a little bitch, I made my way down the hall as quickly as I could. The faster I got home, the better. I could still squeeze in movie night with my mom and Ben.

No one had really batted too many eyelashes at us this morning when we'd skated together, but I figured it was only because everyone in the mornings was too focused on themselves to care. It was the other people, the ones in the afternoon, that would talk.

And if I hadn't already told my mom about the situation, she would have definitely found out somehow.

I wasn't going to tell my brothers or sisters in advance, mostly because I liked it when they all lost their shit over things and threw tantrums. It made me laugh. And it made me happy that they cared.

Continuing to roll my shoulders back in place as I walked, I turned down another hall and stopped. Because down the hall by the doors was one figure I knew too well and another that was familiar but not as much. It was Galina and the girl she had replaced me with, and from her body language, I could tell Galina was aggravated. I'd done it enough to her over the years to know exactly what it looked like.

And from the way the girl was rubbing at her cheeks, I could tell she was crying.

She had never made me cry, but I could see how she'd do it to other people who didn't understand.

Continuing down the hall, wishing I'd brought my bag with me so I could find my headphones and put them on and pretend I couldn't hear them, I could see and hear Galina talking to the younger girl in a hushed voice that only let me catch onto bits and pieces of her Russian accent. Something about expectations, goals, and not giving up.

I'd probably gotten halfway down the hall when both of them turned around to look at me.

"*Yozik*," my former coach greeted me with a tight nod.

"Galina," I said back to her before flicking my gaze over to the other girl and giving her a nod that probably resembled the older woman's exactly. "Latasha."

"Hello," the younger girl greeted me, looking like she was holding her breath as she ducked her head. Maybe so I couldn't see her eyes and know she was upset at getting scolded for whatever.

She couldn't know I didn't care, and I wasn't going to tell her.

"Congratulations on the new partner," Galina said. "I'm happy for you. It was only matter of time, I always knew."

And that had me almost stumbling.

She was happy and she always knew? What did she always know?

"Your triple Lutzes will look beautiful together," she kept going, and I could only look at her like I didn't know her at all.

Where the fuck were all these compliments coming from and why?

"How many times you work on them?" Galina asked, her question pointless because she damn well knew how much I had worked on them. She'd been there. I had told her about all the times my mom had helped me film them so I could see what they looked like.

But I didn't need to ask why she was asking me this. We'd been together too long for me not to know how her brain worked and what the purpose was. It was to make some kind of point to the younger girl.

"Five thousand times?" I told her with a shrug, because I could only guess. Numbers weren't my strong point, and I'd lost count after a while.

"Did you cry doing it?"

Now she knew I damn well never cried, and as much as I didn't want to upset this girl more than she already was by bringing that up, I wasn't going to lie either. So all I did was shake my head, because actually saying the words felt too brutal. I changed the subject before Galina could keep asking me things that would only make the other girl upset. "Lina, can I ask you something in private?"

The older woman cocked her head to the side, like she was thinking about it, and gave me another of her decisive nods.

When I walked a little further down the hall, she followed after me and stopped at the same time I did. I jumped right into it. "What did Nancy Lee ask you about me?"

Her expression didn't change, like she wasn't surprised I was asking her. And she shouldn't be. She knew I'd never had a problem asking questions. "If I thought you were done. That's what she asked."

I blinked.

"If you listened. If you worked hard. If I would coach you again," she kept going, that hard-as-steel face focused on mine. "I say yes. I said you were meant to have a partner. You have the shoulders. The arms. It was me that didn't follow you. I said to her you were the best I ever taught—"

I blinked.

"—you only live in that head too much, *yozik*. You know this. You care too much. You know this too. I tell her all this too. Nobody deserves a chance like Jasmine, I say." Her gaze was intent on mine as she finished. "I also tell her you and Ivan will kill each other if you talk too much."

She....

"You are welcome. You will not make me regret this, yes?"

She....

I swallowed. And before I could get another word out, Galina slapped me on the back of the head like she had a thousand times before and said, "I have things to do. We talk later."

CHAPTER 6

I MADE IT THREE DAYS BEFORE THE TEXT MESSAGES STARTED ONE afternoon while I was trying to finish warming up before our afternoon session. I had gotten to the LC later than usual and had gone straight to the training room, praising Jesus that I'd decided to change my clothes before leaving the diner once I'd seen what time it was and had remembered lunchtime traffic was a real thing. I was in the middle of stretching my hips when my phone beeped from where I'd left it on top of my bag. I took it out and snickered immediately at the message after taking my time with it.

Jojo: WHAT THE FUCK JASMINE

I didn't need to ask what my brother was what-the-fucking over. It had only been a matter of time. It was really hard to keep a secret in my family, and the only reason why my mom and Ben—who was the only person other than her who knew —had kept their mouths closed was because they had both agreed it would be more fun to piss off my siblings by not saying anything and letting them find out the hard way I was going to be competing again.

Life was all about the little things.

So, I'd slipped my phone back into my bag and kept stretching, not bothering to respond because it would just make him more mad.

Twenty minutes later, while I was still busy stretching, I pulled my phone out and wasn't surprised more messages appeared.

Jojo: WHY WOULD YOU NOT TELL ME

Jojo: HOW COULD YOU DO THIS TO ME

Jojo: DID THE REST OF YOU KEEP THIS FROM ME

Tali: What happened? What did she not tell you?

Tali: OH MY GOD, Jasmine, did you get knocked up?

Tali: I swear, if you got knocked up, I'm going to beat the hell out of you. We talked about contraception when you hit puberty.

Sebastian: Jasmine's pregnant?

Rubes: She's not pregnant.

Rubes: What happened, Jojo?

Jojo: MOM DID YOU KNOW ABOUT THIS

Tali: Would you just tell us what you're talking about?

Jojo: JASMINE IS SKATING WITH IVAN LUKOV

Jojo: And I found out by going on Picturegram. Someone at the rink posted a picture of them in one of the training rooms. They were doing lifts.

Jojo: JASMINE I SWEAR TO GOD YOU BETTER EXPLAIN EVERYTHING RIGHT NOW

Tali: ARE YOU KIDDING ME? IS THIS TRUE?

Tali: JASMINE

Tali: JASMINE

Tali: JASMINE

Jojo: I'm going on Lukov's website right now to confirm this
Rubes: I just called Mom but she isn't answering the phone
Tali: She knew about this. WHO ELSE KNEW?
Sebastian: I didn't. And quit texting Jas's name over and over again. It's annoying. She's skating again. Good job, Jas. Happy for you.
Jojo: ^^ You're such a vibe kill
Sebastian: No, I'm just not flipping my shit because she got a new partner.
Jojo: SHE DIDN'T TELL US FIRST THO. What is the point of being related if we didn't get the scoop before everybody else?
Jojo: I FOUND OUT ON PICTUREGRAM
Sebastian: She doesn't like you. I wouldn't tell you either.
Tali: I can't find anything about it online.
Jojo: JASMINE
Tali: JASMINE
Jojo: JASMINE
Tali: JASMINE
Tali: Tell us everything or I'm coming over to Mom's today.
Sebastian: You're annoying. Muting this until I get out of work.
Jojo: Party pooper
Tali: Party pooper
Jojo: Jinx
Tali: Jinx
Sebastian: Annoying

I smiled to myself as I read through the messages slowly, rubbing the palm of my hand over the top of each of my hands. I didn't need to look down to know that the red R and black L I'd been reapplying every day, were still there. I hadn't really been scrubbing my hands that hard. It was probably going to be months until I could wash them off completely. I had thought about just settling for forming my fingers into L-shapes to tell me which side was what, but it took too long, so Sharpie colors and letters it was going to be... for a while.

I typed out a reply, because knowing them, if I didn't, the next time I looked at my phone, I'd have an endless column of JASMINE on there until they heard from me.

That didn't mean my response had to be what they wanted.

Me: Who is Ivan Lukov?

"What are you smiling at, Meatball?"

My shoulders went tense for a second before I reminded myself that this idiot wasn't worth getting all riled up over. At least not where he could see me react. He didn't deserve that. Setting my phone next to my knee, I glanced around to see that Coach Lee wasn't in the room. Huh. I leaned forward, back straight, soles of my socked feet pressed together. I didn't even give him the benefit of glancing over as he lowered himself beside me for some reason.

"Just checking out pictures of you naked." I leaned into a stretch even more as my palms walked me forward until my forehead hovered just an inch above the floor. "I needed a laugh."

His "Hmm" made me smile into the mat, and thankfully he couldn't see it. "You know what I look at when I need a laugh?"

The smile on my face immediately disappeared. I didn't reply to his dumbass question.

"Videos of your programs with what's-his-face," he answered his own question.

Ass. I turned my head to the side just a little so I could peek at where he was sitting beside me. "I have a video bookmarked of you falling doing a death spiral at the Cup of Russia last year."

He tried to hide his hiss, but I recognized it immediately. I couldn't help but smile again. I turned my head back to where it was and shared my smile with the mats. But I should have expected him to have a comeback almost immediately. "You watched that live at home, huh?"

I turned my head to glare over at where he was sitting a few feet away, his legs extended straight out. His head was turned toward me. Of course it was. He was always fucking looking at me, trying to get a reaction. "I was. Did they give you anything for coming in fourth that day or...?"

He didn't miss a beat. "They didn't have anything to give me for fourth place. They said something about how they ran out of ribbons after you decided to switch over to pairs."

I blinked.

He blinked.

Be better. Be better. Be better.

"Always a bridesmaid, never a bride," he muttered.

"This next year isn't going to come fast enough," I whispered more to myself but a little to him too because why the fuck not?

The corners of his mouth quirked into a smug smile that *really* made my palm itch. "I'm going to count down the days, Meatball. Believe me. One year, and I'll probably pay someone to take you so I can get rid of you."

Something ugly and maybe even hurt bubbled up in my chest for all of a second before I squashed it. One year. I knew it. He knew it. That had been part of it. It wasn't a surprise. "In a year, I'll pull my voodoo doll of you out of its box and go back to sticking needles into your black heart."

His eyelids hung low over his eyes. "The one I have of you is still sitting on my nightstand."

"I hope your hair falls out."

He blinked. "I hope—"

"*What is wrong with both of you?*" Coach Lee hissed from behind us. I tipped my head over a little more to catch her shaking her head as she stood between us, watching us with almost a horrified expression on her face. "I'm a few minutes late and you...." She closed her eyes and shook her head before reopening them. "You know what? Ignore me. I told you not to talk about each other during practice, but you can do whatever you want as long as we aren't training."

Neither one of us said a word, but our eyes met.

And I mouthed *you suck.*

And he whispered back with his pale pink mouth, *you suck more.*

There was another sigh, but it sounded even more resigned. "My eyes work. I can read your lips. Both of them."

I didn't *ignore* Coach Lee, but all I'd promised was not to *say* anything. So I didn't worry about it when I moved my lips at Ivan again. *Eat shit.*

His tongue tapped at the inside of his cheek. Then he opened his mouth. *I'm looking at it.*

"Whatever we have to do to make this work, *remember*?" Coach Lee emphasized, obviously still watching us.

Ivan and I were both staring at each other as we muttered, "Uh-huh."

WHATEVER WE HAVE TO DO WERE INFAMOUS WORDS TO LIVE BY.

It wasn't like I was going to regret them but...

Goddamn.

It was going to be close.

"Again!"

"Again!"

"*Again!*"

"No! *Again!*"

If I never heard the word "again" in my life, I would be totally fine with it. Totally fucking fine. Because starting over from what felt like scratch—it wasn't really scratch but it seemed like it—was a giant pain in the ass.

Mostly because it was Ivan I was doing this with. Ivan, who I could tell was getting just as aggravated.

It wasn't until Coach Lee dropped her head back and sighed at the ceiling that she finally changed her words. "Okay, that's it for the day. Your speeds stopped getting better half an hour ago, and your timing has only slightly improved. We're wasting time at this point. It isn't going to get any better." She shot us both a look that was pretty damn accusing, like she didn't understand why we were running out of energy.

I wasn't used to this anymore. This basic exhaustive shit that I hadn't done since I'd first gotten paired up with The Piece of Shit four years ago.

Fuck me.

Despite the ice bath I'd been taking every night for the last week, everything still hurt. My ribs. My entire abdomen. My shoulders. My wrists. My quads. My back.

The only thing that didn't hurt was my ass, and that was only because my butt cheeks hadn't become unused to falling on them. That, and one of them had less nerves still working than the other one did. I was pretty sure I'd killed those nerves while I was trying to work on my 3Ls—my triple Lutzes—back in the day.

I'd been icing my lower back multiple times a day, icing my knees, my hips... everything. It was only a matter of time, I knew that, until I got used to it again. At least I sure as hell hoped so. There was a reason the younger girls quit figure skating before they were legal. Your body's ability to recuperate took longer and longer every year you got older, and the fact that I'd done more damage to it in twenty-six years than most people would do in double that amount, didn't help.

Her fingertips were rubbing at the bridge of her nose when she sighed and said in a low voice, "Let's go over a few things before this afternoon, since we still have time."

Was she in a bad mood or...?

"Let's meet in the office in fifteen," Coach Lee called out, huffing in exasperation as she turned around and walked away.

Yeah, I wasn't imagining it.

I mean, I didn't think practice had gone *that* bad. It hadn't been the best one yet, but it hadn't been the worst either. Things had gotten better with every day that went on.

Ivan's demeanor hadn't changed, and neither had mine. We didn't talk to each other unless we were talking to Coach Lee at the same time. We didn't argue when she gave us instructions or when one of us gave the other a pointer....

It took everything in me to keep my mouth shut, and I bet it took him the same amount of effort too.

But we did it. Because we had to.

That and she hadn't left us alone again.

"Well then," I muttered to myself, rubbing at my hip bone with the palm of my hand to ease the ache there from the position I'd been holding doing camelback spins—where you pretty much contorted your body to form a tear drop shape by pulling the heel of your boot toward the back of your head. It had been a hell of a lot easier when I'd been sixteen. Now... it was harder, and that was bullshit.

Without waiting for Ivan, or even turning around to look

at what he was doing at that point, I skated to the exit to the rink, put my skate guards on, and then headed toward the changing rooms so I could get dressed and get this meeting over with. Maybe I'd get out of here earlier than normal and could squeeze in another table at work. I made it to my locker, ignored the icon blinking on my phone until later, rubbed myself down with a baby wipe like I'd been having to do every day now that I didn't have time to shower, got dressed, and put on just enough makeup to look decent.

It didn't take me long at all to get ready, but by the time I was done, only ten minutes had passed. What she wanted to talk about, I had no clue, but I wasn't going to worry about it. Whatever it was, I'd deal.

Hauling ass down the three different hallways it took to get to the right side of the building, I found the GMs office easily. Knocking on the door, I waited until I heard Coach Lee's familiar voice call out, "Come in!"

I went in and found that she was alone inside, her cell pressed to her hear. She held up her index finger, and I nodded, taking a seat in the chair closest to the wall.

"*This isn't what I asked for,*" the other woman said quietly into the phone, her hand going to cover her face as her voice got even lower to whisper.

Shit, I could tell when someone needed privacy. Digging through my bag, I pulled out my cell phone and took a look at the screen. I had new messages. A group one to be specific. It was from **Dad, Jojo, Tali + 2.** The one and only other group chat I had. The one that was used the least amount, one that had my dad in it and not my mom. I almost thought about ignoring it until later, but when Coach Lee's voice got even quieter, I opened it anyway.

The first message was from him.

Dad: I bought my ticket to come visit in September.
Rubes: Yay!
Jojo: What days?
Rubes: You can stay with us.
Dad: OK.
Dad: 15-22
Rubes: Hopefully Jasmine will be here.
Dad: Where is she going?
Jojo: She has a new partner.
Dad: I thought she quit?
Jojo: No...
Rubes: Jasmine wouldn't quit, Dad. You know that. Sometimes she has competitions in September. I'll find out.

He thought I quit.

I shook my head and let out a breath before turning my screen off and tossing my phone back into my bag.

He really thought I quit. Of course he would. The last time I had spoken to him, three months ago, I had specifically told him that I was still training... and he had asked, "*Why? You don't have a partner anymore.*"

"Are you all right?" Coach Lee asked, drawing me out of my thoughts.

Swallowing back my frustration and what I was pretty sure was bitterness that I wasn't going to double check, I lifted my head and nodded at the other woman. "I'm fine." Because I was.

She raised her eyebrows, her face drawn and tired looking. More tired looking than I had ever seen it in the years I'd sneaked glances over in her direction. "Okay," was all she said with another sigh that said she was anything but.

And even though I kind of didn't want to, I couldn't help but ask, sounding how I felt, hesitant as hell, "Are you... okay?"

Her dark eyes flashed upward in surprise before shifting to the side for one moment then coming back to me with a nod of her chin. "Yes," she lied.

I blinked.

The sigh that came out of her was totally unexpected before she shook her head. "Personal life. Don't worry about it."

Yeah, I knew what "don't worry about it" usually meant.

I didn't want to worry about it, I sure as hell didn't want to talk about it, but I wasn't a punk. "We can talk about it." I spun my bracelet around my wrist and eyed her, secretly hoping she wouldn't want to. I was the last person in the world to give anyone advice or know what to say in uncomfortable situations. "If you want."

Her snort—and her smile—caught me totally by surprise. "Oh, Jasmine, that's sweet, but it's fine. I'm all right."

Me? Sweet?

She snorted again, her smile growing just a little wider. "Don't look like I'm insulting you. I appreciate you asking. I wasn't expecting it is all," she said carefully, wiping a hand across her brow. Then she raised her eyebrows. "Let's talk about you instead, deal?"

Shit.

"Nothing bad," Coach Lee added, like she could tell I didn't want to necessarily do that, but knew I had to.

I nodded at her.

She stopped smiling as she leaned into the desk, planting her elbow on it. "First thing, have you opened new social media accounts?"

Fuck me. Of course she'd start there. "No," I answered her honestly, this weird, almost nauseous feeling lining my stomach for a moment before I shoved that shit back down. I would be fine. Everything would be fine. It would. "I haven't made time for it yet. I will this weekend."

The older woman nodded, but there was something hesitant in her expression. "Can I ask you something?"

I hated when people asked me that, but it wasn't like I could tell her no.

"Why'd you delete your accounts to begin with? I used to follow you on your Picturegram account. You had a good amount of followers on there. Your Facebook page was popular too, but you deleted both of them at the same time," she went on, her expression watchful.

Damn it.

"That was what? Almost two years ago? You got rid of it while you were still with Paul," she added like I didn't know that. Like I hadn't been the one to go on there and personally cancel those accounts. I didn't have a publicist or a team of people working behind the scenes of my life. It was just me. And sometimes my sister got on there.

At least it had been my sister until I'd told her to stop because I'd been worried she would catch on to what was going on. She'd freaked out enough the first time I got a creepy message. If she'd seen the rest of them, it would have gotten worse. Maybe my family had never been super overprotective of me, but they had it in them to be. I just didn't want it or need it. They had better things to do.

And I didn't want to tell Coach Lee about it either but...

Did I want to start this relationship off by being a fucking liar?

Damn it. I knew the answer. I just didn't like it.

"I had a situation with a... fan," I told her, making a face at using the f-word because it should have been more along the lines of "creepy ass stalker." "It was uncomfortable, and I ended up cancelling my accounts because they were distracting me too much."

Her forehead had wrinkled and then gotten even more wrinkled the more I spoke.

Shit.

"Did you go to the police?" she finally asked, her forehead still lined.

"There were never any actual threats to me, so there wasn't anything they would do," I told her honestly, feeling like an idiot. "Everything was online." There I did lie, somewhat. When I had first gone to the police, it had been true, but it hadn't stayed that way.

Her expression still didn't change at all, but there was something about it—maybe her eyes—that made her look more thoughtful than she had before. "You'll tell me if there's a problem?"

I lifted a shoulder and made my face do the closest thing to a smile it could make when it didn't feel genuine.

Her forehead flattened, and the corners of her mouth twitched just a little. "I can appreciate you not lying to me. At least keep me in the loop if things pick up again. I would rather you be comfortable and safe than being harassed, understand?"

I was going to take that as her telling me she would rather I not have an account than have one where I got sent videos of someone jerking off to pictures I'd posted of myself.

I nodded at Coach Lee, shoving the memory of *that* away.

She didn't look like she believed me exactly, but she didn't call me out on it. "Let me think about it some more, but for now, post basic things around the LC. Once a day is best, make sure they're good, quality photos. In a few weeks, start to mix the content up. Ivan and I were talking—"

When the hell did they talk? On the phone? I had never

seen them whispering to each other or anything.

"—and after what you've just said, I think it might be a good idea if we set up an account dedicated to the two of you."

I blinked at the t-word. "For...?" We were only in this for a year together. I blinked again. "Why?"

Her expression almost made me feel like an idiot. "The more fans like you, the more they'll root for you, the easier it'll be to get donations to hopefully cover the rest of your expenses, Jasmine. If you need the assistance—"

I made a face.

"—or even if you don't," she threw in, probably seeing my expression, "you might want to think about starting one of those online fundraising pages to cover your other expenses."

Right. Like that would go well. I could name the people who would donate, and I was related to all of them. I was used to it, but the last thing my rep needed was for people to laugh over no one giving a shit about me.

No fucking thanks. Stripping or the kidney black market it would be.

When I didn't say anything, she went on. "It's also a good idea for you two to do a few interviews together in the near future. I was thinking we should invite a reporter or two to the facility and get some footage of you both practicing. We can spin the story nicely. Two rinkmates coming together. It would look great."

Me and Ivan doing an interview together? Uh....

"A unified front," she kept going. "Knowing each other for so long and then coming back together—"

I choked.

A unified front? Knowing each other for so long? There was a video of us from a couple of years ago that was supposed to have been a recording of another skater's practice, but it had caught me telling Ivan to suck my dick after he told me the only way I was going to get better at a spin I'd been working on was to be reincarnated. But the mic hadn't picked up that part. Just what I'd said, because that was my luck.

I wasn't exactly the most book-smart person in the world, but I wasn't dumb. So I knew there was something about the tone of her voice and the way she was speaking that I didn't like. And I wasn't wrong.

I blinked at her. "Are you trying to make it seem like we're dating?"

She pursed her lips together for a moment. "No. Not dating—"

Uh....

"More like... you're very friendly with each other. As in you respect and like each other—"

Oh God.

"The more unified the better—"

What?

"People would eat it up," she finished off, her face calm and even.

The blank stare I was aiming her way must have said exactly what I thought because she raised her eyebrows in a way that I didn't appreciate.

"We just don't need it to look like you can barely stand each other. Do you understand me?"

I didn't move from my spot as I said carefully, "You want me to act like we're all giggly and cuddly and friendly."

She sighed the same way Galina used to, but I didn't focus on that at all. "No, that's not what I'm saying. Respect and admiration—"

"I don't admire him."

She squeezed her eyes closed for a moment, and I'd bet my life she was praying for patience. "You can act like it."

"He doesn't admire me either."

"He can act like it too. But it's important, and he knows that. You can't glare at each other. You act when you're on the ice, and I'm sure those emotions will translate well in the choreography that's put together in a couple of months. I'm not worried about that. We'll find the right musical compositions to flatter your chemistry. You've also both been doing great during practice, and I'm very proud of you—"

For not killing each other? Good God. That's what my life had come to? People being proud of me for keeping my mouth shut?

"But you both need to keep it going even outside of the rink, at least where other people can see... and read your lips." She slid me a look.

All I could do was sit there and blink. Realistically, I knew she wasn't asking for something outrageous or even unheard of. She didn't want us at each other's throats was what she was trying to say.

But what it felt like was something completely different.

It felt like she was asking me to pretend to love him or something. And I felt a whole lot of things for Ivan Lukov, but love was nowhere in the top one thousand words I would have used. Nope.

In the way she had been showing me lately of being able to read my body language and face, Coach Lee sighed and gave me another tiny smile that had exasperation around the edges. "Jasmine, I'm an atheist. I don't believe in miracles. I'm not asking you for anything I don't think you're both capable of."

I didn't say a word. I was an idiot for not seeing this coming. I really was. I could admit it. Why the hell I hadn't thought that we'd have to put our best behavior pants on in front of public eyes was beyond me.

I was a really shitty actress. And I hated lies.

And I hated even more that we were having to have this conversation to begin with.

Pushing down hard on my temple with my index and middle finger, I let out a slow breath that wasn't at all like me. The question hovered on my lips and in my heart, and I didn't *want* an answer, but I needed it. "Is my reputation that bad that we have to do this?"

"No one denies that you're a world-class figure skater, Jasmine—"

Here we go.

"—but there are these small worries about things in the past that we want to improve as much as possible to help us all out. You understand."

That was the fucked-up part. I did understand. I understood completely.

My reputation was that bad that people thought the only way to salvage it was to have the little doll of the figure skating world be my friend. That if he could like me, everyone else could too. Because if he didn't, then there was something wrong with me.

There wasn't anything wrong with me. I stood up for myself. I stood up for other people. I didn't take shit from others. Was that so wrong? Even Jonathan, my brother, had told me once years ago that if I were a man, no one would think twice about it. People would think I was some kind of asshole hero with a heart of gold.

"You don't have to act it up over the top." She made a face that said that if I did, no one would complain. I got it. "But be friendly with each other. Be a team. Keep the comments between the two of you and out of the spotlight."

The door creaking open kept me from saying anything else. Then the pure black head of hair peeked out around the slot in the doorway and a face I was growing more and more familiar with by the second appeared. "I had to sign a few autographs," he apologized before coming inside and closing the door behind him, before pausing and glancing between the two of us like he didn't know what to think.

Of course he would be signing autographs at the same facility he trained at almost daily. It was only because Coach Lee was right there that I didn't open my mouth and say something sarcastic about him paying people to ask him for his signature.

But I managed to push that out of my head and focus on Lee's words. "Did you know about this?" I asked him, my voice sounding weird and even a little hoarse to my ears.

Those intense blue eyes went from Coach Lee to me to back to her, and he replied, making a face at me for some reason, "What?"

"Us acting like we're dating," I snapped, shooting a look at Coach Lee, who was making her own face like I was overexaggerating.

"I didn't say to act like you're dating—" she started to explain before Ivan cut her off.

"We're supposed to act like we're dating?" Ivan stood there, his eyes bouncing back and forth between Coach Lee and me so fast I knew there was no way he'd heard about this. His frown helped too.

"Fine, more like we're 'best friends'." Somewhere in the back of my mind, I realized I was totally blowing this out of proportion and stealing the reins of acting like a drama queen... but not really caring at the same time.

"No. Not even best friends, I would settle for just friends," the other woman tried to clarify.

"That respect and admire each other," I muttered.

Ivan said nothing for once in his life.

"You don't have to... kiss... or anything like that. Just... be friendly, smile at each other, don't act like... like... you think the other has cooties," she offered, as if that was better. I was going to ignore the fact she'd used the word cooties to describe what we thought of each other. I thought he was the devil, or at least an immediate family member to him... or her; I didn't think Ivan had cooties.

I was staring at her with my mouth slightly open, and I wasn't sure if Ivan was or not, but I didn't care.

The other woman gave Ivan a look I wasn't sure what to do with. It was... frustrated? Angry? "You're both going to act like this is impossible?"

Ivan blinked.

Then I blinked too.

"It'll be good for both of you, and you know that."

That was debatable.

My mind was racing. Had he acted all buddy-buddy with the rest of his partners before? I couldn't remember. Paul and I had been a little affectionate with each other, but not anywhere near as much as other pairs partners were. And at least half the time, I didn't look at him like I wanted to kill him, I thought. But Ivan and the partners before me? I really couldn't be sure; I didn't think so, though. Then again, I hadn't paid that much attention to them because I was always so focused on his annoying ass.

Out of the corner of my eye, I watched Ivan raise his hand and cup the back of his head with it, but I was too busy taking in the expression Coach Lee was shooting him to really absorb his actions at first.

Her face was turning pink... and was she giving him big eyes?

"Ivan," the woman said, slowly, carefully, another message hiding in his name alone.

He blinked. Those long, sweeping black eyelashes hung

down over his eyes, and I could see the hard breath in and out of his throat and chest.

Something told me there was something wrong about this. The way they were looking at each other... I couldn't figure it out but....

"Sure," he huffed unexpectedly, shooting me a look I almost missed that seemed like I was putting him out and making him do something he would rather not.

"Sure?" I croaked.

He nodded, looking pissed off. "Yeah. Sure. I can do it."

"What the fu—" I closed my mouth and pressed my lips together. *Think. Think, Jasmine.* I had given them my word.

"It's not the best idea I've ever heard, but we should do it," Ivan muttered. Then he looked in my direction and his forehead scrunched up. "It's only a year before I get rid of you."

Motherfucker.

Coach Lee groaned, but I barely heard it over the need for me to call him a little bitch.

He sighed and tipped his head up toward the ceiling. "I can fake a smile," he went on as I leaned over in my seat and planted the tip of my elbow onto the armrest. "She doesn't have to marry me or have my kid... right, Lee? Or did I miss that?"

That had me rolling back to sit up straight so I could glare at him. "I wouldn't have your kid if you paid me a million dollars."

Something strange happened to his cheek before his facial features went completely smooth. "I'm not asking you to. It isn't that big of a deal. I can do it." Those dark, thick eyebrows of his went up just half an inch, max. "You can't do something so small?" he asked, and I swore he was purposefully trying to egg me on.

If that throwdown wasn't enough to calm me down and get

my thoughts in order, I didn't know what was. Of course there was nothing he could do that I couldn't do better. Except a quad—a jump with four revolutions—but that was beside the point. I wasn't about to let evil think they were better than I was. So I kept my voice nice and even as I tried to explain, "I can do it, but I'm just not good at pretending, all right?"

Neither one of them said a word.

"I'm not," I reiterated.

They were asking me to be affectionate. All right, maybe not affectionate, but... at least not act like I couldn't stand him. I guess.

Of course I could do it. I just didn't know if I wanted to. I'd never been a good actress. I had never seen a point in pretending to feel something that I didn't, or like someone I couldn't stand. I had dealt with enough shit like that in my life.

"You're not exactly my type, if that helps any," Ivan threw in, forcing me to turn my head slowly to look at him. "I can look at you like I don't hate you."

I blinked. "Good. You're not my type either."

He blinked.

I blinked.

And then Coach Lee let out an uncomfortable noise. "I'm glad neither one of you is each other's type. So, can we agree that you can be nice to each other in public? I have an interview set up for both of you next week."

Ivan shrugged as I stared at him, his own gaze not going anywhere. "I can do it. It's up to her if she can."

Years from then, I'd look back on that moment and see how well they played me. How well Ivan knew me after so long. Because I walked right into that shit. My pride led me there. "Of course I can do it."

And with a clap of her hands, it was settled. "Good. Let's

move on to the next thing."

"The Sports Network wants to have you in their magazine," Coach Lee said, her fingernails scratching at her neck in a way that told me she was anxious.

And she was never anxious.

I glanced at Ivan to find him in his seat with his arms crossed over his chest, looking totally unfazed... until I saw the way he was shaking his foot.

"Okay," I said slowly, still watching Ivan as he sat there, looking *almost* checked out.

But I knew his form of evil too well. He wasn't.

Coach Lee let this small, awkward smile cover her mouth, putting me on edge. "Both of you."

Well, no shit both of us. Why would they only want me when it was Prissy Pants over here that was the most well-known one between us? There was more to this, my gut knew there was.

She was just taking her time telling me for some reason.

So I waited. And I didn't say anything as I stared at her, ready to hear the rest of it.

When Coach Lee's eyes flicked in Ivan's direction, it just confirmed everything. Her voice was higher than usual as she said, "It's for a special issue—"

The idiot in the seat coughed.

"It's highest-selling issue every year—"

Oh.

Oh.

I knew exactly what she was talking about.

But I kept my mouth shut and didn't let her know I knew, because what would the fun in that be when she was nervous and maybe even a little embarrassed to be trying to talk me into something that would require me to get naked? She didn't know I wasn't shy, but she should. I'd strip down right then if I had to. I'd been changing in front of other people since I was a kid starting off in competitions.

"It would be great publicity if you did it—"

I kept on watching her. Kept the blank look on my face too.

"It would only take a morning or an afternoon—"

I nodded that time and did it slowly.

"Possibly a day at the most, but no longer than that," she finished up her pitch with a tight smile.

I blinked at her, looking as innocent as I was capable of. "What's the issue?" I asked her, keeping my tone light.

Her face flushed red, and her gaze moved to Ivan quickly.

"You already know it's for the Anatomy Issue, Meatball, quit being a pain in the ass, dragging it out." Ivan snickered, shaking his head.

There went fucking Meatball again. *Focus. Be better.*

I shot him a bland look and shrugged. "Sorry," I said, only half meaning it.

Her face immediately went into a frown. "You knew?"

"I figured when you were trying extra hard to sell me on it."

She still didn't look happy, but she didn't look mad either, just... surprised. "You're fine with it?"

I raised a shoulder. "All they need to do is take pictures of me in my skates, right?"

Coach Lee blinked. "Yes."

"I get to tape my extra private parts, right?"

She nodded slowly, her face still twisted into an apprehensive expression.

"And it's only the staff that are around?"

She did the same gesture, her expression not going anywhere.

"It's fine with me then," I told her easily. "I know that would be good publicity." Plus, I had always secretly hoped I'd be invited to do it. It was pretty much an honor in a sport with so many talented people.

Coach's eyes narrowed almost suspiciously, and she took her time saying, "Don't take this the wrong way, but I'm having a hard time accepting that you're being so understanding with this."

"I get naked in front of total strangers in the changing rooms," I said. "The people taking the pictures and on the staff have seen better bodies and worse bodies than mine. We all have butt cracks and genitals. I don't see what the big deal is. And it's not like anyone is going to see my nipples or anything." Then I blinked. "Neither one of you needs to be there, right?"

Ivan coughed again, and Coach Lee's face turned bright red. Her sputter could probably be heard around the world as she replied, "Jasmine.... the shoot isn't of you by yourself. They want you and Ivan together."

Me and Ivan together.

Naked.

"It would be great for the two of you to do it," Coach Lee added, trying to put some enthusiasm into her tone, like that would convince me. "Just a quick shoot. Knowing both of you, you'd get it done as fast as possible."

"I'd have to get naked in front of *him*?" I hooked my thumb and pointed it toward the idiot that was smirking from his spot on the seat. I didn't need to glance at him to know he was doing it. I just knew he was.

She nodded.

I didn't even think about it. "No."

Ivan's laugh, this lazy, bright thing that got on my nerves every time I heard it, filled the room. "You said a second ago that you get naked in front of complete strangers."

I shot the idiot in a fleece pullover and navy blue sweatpants a look. "Yeah, *strangers*. Not people I need to see every day." I scoffed. "Not you."

He wrinkled his nose, clearly enjoying the shit out of this. "Yeah, you know me. You know you can trust me—"

I laughed. "*No.*"

"What am I going to do? Take a picture of you and post it on the Internet?" He made a face.

He had a point, but... "No."

"I trust you to not post a picture of me naked," he offered, like that would help.

I shot him another look. "Why would I do that? Nobody wants to see that anyway."

He rolled his eyes and made an exasperated noise in his throat that I had seen and heard him do at least a handful of times over the years when he didn't know what to say in return, AKA I'd won. "I don't get what the big deal is." He changed the subject. "She was worried you would tell us no, but I thought for sure you'd say yes. It's the highest-selling issue."

Fuck me.

Ivan tipped his head to the side and gave me that clear, smug face again. "We made a deal."

Damn it. "I know we made a deal," I hissed, suddenly feeling off.

"We have to do it."

I wanted to lift my hands up to cover my eyes, but I didn't. I wouldn't. But shit. *Shit.* I looked up at the ceiling and let out a breath.

"You know I've seen naked women before, right?" he asked, with what might have been humor or smart-ass in his tone.

I shook my head and kept my gaze upward. How the hell had I gotten into this? And how could I get myself out of it?

It was one thing for a bunch of other girls to see me butt-ass naked.

It was one thing for a total stranger to see me in my birthday suit.

But it was a completely different thing for this man who used to tease me for years about my body to see me without clothes.

I was going to have to look him in the eye for the next year. Listen to him for that time period.

One of the last people in the world I would ever want to be that vulnerable around would be Ivan. He didn't need more ammo for his arsenal. God forbid he make a comment about the size of my ass when I didn't have underwear on. I'd probably try to pull his dick off.

But...

I had given them my word. I was going to do whatever I needed to do to take advantage of this time we were going to have together. And if that meant having to get shit about my small chest or the shape of my belly button or my vagina lips... it was going to be his dick that got ripped off.

Son of a bitch.

"So... yes?" Coach Lee asked, sounding hopeful.

I still wouldn't look at them as the reality of the situation hit me right in the chest. "I don't have a choice, do I?"

"Don't look so pissed. We'll get it done as fast as possible. Holding you up fully clothed is bad enough, I don't want to do it when you're naked."

I didn't hesitate flipping him off, even with my attention on the ceiling. Lowering my gaze, I gave him a mean smile. "I don't want to see your junk either."

The idiot winked. "Aww, it's not junk, Meatball. It's the good stuff."

I gagged.

CHAPTER 7

SPRING/SUMMER

"*WOULD YOU STOP?*" IVAN HISSED AT ME AT THE SAME TIME HE bumped his leg against mine under the table.

"You quit. I'm on my side, you keep your legs together." I hit my knee against his right back, even though I had *told* myself I was going to be good and get through this next hour like a champ.

Because I could.

And I would.

For sure if he hadn't sat next to me.

I wasn't going to be the one to screw up this interview that Coach Lee had set up for us. If anyone was going to do it, it was going to be this jackass beside me. We had done pretty well since our meeting, where Lee had asked us to try and not hate each other and keep our ugly looks and words to when we were in private... or at least not in earshot of anyone else. She still hadn't made the same mistake of leaving us alone either, so there was that.

But today was the day we really had to be on our best behavior. I thought it wouldn't be a problem. I'd survived worse things for sixty minutes

Then Ivan had decided to sit next to me, and I started to doubt myself. I had already been sitting at the bench in the LC's staff break room when he had slid in. We were supposed to be waiting for the journalist or blogger or whoever she was to come over and ask us questions in preparation for the *official* announcement that Ivan and I were now competing together.

Except we weren't supposed to say it was only for a season. Lee had briefed me on that yesterday. *The only people that need to know that is us.*

Great.

Shifting my legs so that the inside of my thighs were pressed together and not touching Satan's so this lady wouldn't walk in in the middle of us arguing, I looked around the empty kitchen area and tried to ignore the heat of Ivan's body not even an inch away.

Then his lower thigh bumped into my knee. *Again.*

"Why are you touching me?" I whispered, barely moving my lips, eyes on the door. I didn't trust myself to look at him.

"You're touching me," was his smart-ass—and stupid—response because he'd been the one to move.

I still didn't glance at him. "Why are you sitting next to me?"

"Because I can."

"You're too close."

"I've been closer to you."

I side-eyed him. "Because you have to be. Go sit over there. Away from me."

He was already watching me with those creepy clear blue eyes. "No."

I blinked, and he blinked right back at me.

Bitch.

"Then move so I can go sit across the table."

"No."

I turned my head to fully get a look at him. His hair was neat and brushed over backward, without one strand out of place. Today he was wearing a sweater I recognized, in a shade of gray so light it was almost white. It made his eyes stand out... if I noticed that kind of thing. "Move," I said.

He repeated himself.

"Move or I'll make you move."

That time, he shook his head.

"Why?"

"Because it'll look better if we're sitting together."

I opened my mouth to tell him he was stupid, but... I closed it.

The corners of his mouth flexed a little, just a little.

I scrunched up my nose and made myself look back at the door. A minute passed. Maybe two.

Where was this lady? We had cut practice short to do this. We had barely started moving forward with training. We were doing side-by-side jumps together, and... it was going great. We moved so similarly, especially with jumps, that there were hardly any corrections for us to make. I could tell Coach Lee was pleased. I knew I was.

Ivan knocked his leg against mine out of the blue once more, making me glance back in his direction. He was making a face at me. "Stop doing that. You're making the whole bench shake."

What the...?

Oh. I hadn't even realized I'd been shaking my knee. I stopped and shoved my hands under my thighs.

Then I started bouncing my heels. Where the hell was this lady? She was definitely late.

A hand came down on top of my knee. "Stop. It," Ivan muttered in that perfectly balanced voice that was deep but not too deep, just perfectly aggravating. "I didn't know you knew how to be nervous."

I stopped bouncing my heels and slid him a look out of the corner of my eye, taking in that flawless complexion. I didn't think I'd ever seen him with a single pimple, whitehead, or blackhead. Ever. Ugh. "I'm not nervous."

He snorted so loud I turned my whole upper body toward him. He was smiling. That lean face with its microscopic pores, high cheekbones, and angular, hard jaw were all lit up. He was smiling, and he hadn't just won a competition, and he wasn't around his family either.

I'd never seen that before.

Who the hell was this person? His leg hit my thigh as he asked, "That's why you won't stop shaking your leg?"

"I'm shaking my leg because we could be practicing right now instead of waiting around," I said, only partially believing my own bullshit. "Why are you in my business anyway? And why are you being so talkative?"

The truth was, I hadn't been able to stop shaking some part of my body from the moment I'd woken up, knowing this interview was coming. I had no problem talking to people, but what I had a problem with was the fact that I had to answer questions and those responses would be recorded and kept forever to be judged and torn apart for the rest of history. While sitting beside Ivan. Ivan who was already getting on my nerves and no one had even started asking us questions.

No pressure.

"You're full of shit," he muttered back, shifting beside me so that his hip pressed against mine.

I glanced back at the door as I said, "You're full of shit."

He made a noise in his throat.

Another minute passed.

Maybe two or three more. And the lady still hadn't shown up.

I was leaving when time was up. I wasn't going to sit around and wait.

"I'll talk if you're worried you'll say something wrong," Ivan said in an almost whisper, like he didn't want us to be overheard either.

I paused for a second at his offer, then scoffed. "I'm not worried."

"You're a liar," he replied immediately.

I couldn't think of a single comeback, damn it. So I settled for, "Shut up."

The laugh that came out of him caught me off guard, and it only made me madder about the entire situation.

"What are you laughing at?" I snapped.

It only made him laugh harder. "At you. Jesus. I've never actually seen you so tense. I didn't think you had it in you."

Pulling my hands out from under my thighs, I set them on top of the table and started tapping my fingertips on it.

"*Relax*, Meatball," Ivan kept on talking, sounding way too amused.

I ignored the Meatball, even though I felt myself wince. "I am relaxed," I lied again.

"Anyone ever told you that you suck at lying? You're not even trying." He snickered.

Rolling my eyes, I kept my gaze on the door and slid my hands back under my thighs. I was just about to start bobbing my ankle up and down when I realized I'd start shaking all over again. It was harder than I would have expected to sit still. "Weren't they supposed to be here at ten?"

"Yeah. It's ten-oh-six. Give them a break," my new partner muttered.

"I have things to do," I explained, only partially lying. "And why isn't Coach Lee in here with us?"

"Because she doesn't need to be?" he replied, trying to make me feel like an idiot with his tone.

Huh.

"What kind of things do you need to go do anyway? Steal blankets from babies for fun?" God, he sounded so amused with himself. Dumbass.

"No, Satan. I don't do that anymore," I told him dryly.

"Push over elderly people using walkers?"

"Ha ha," I replied, gritting out the words as I glanced at the door for like the tenth time.

"So? What are you doing after?"

I glanced at him. "Why do you care?"

"I don't," he replied easily, and something in my chest felt tight. I shoved it away.

"Good, you shouldn't."

"I still want to know."

I glanced at him again, feeling a sneer come over my mouth and nose. "I have to get to work, nosey ass. Is that okay with you?"

His blank expression was confusing. "You have a job?"

"Yeah."

"Why?"

I blinked. "Because things cost money and money doesn't grow on trees?" I offered, still blinking.

"Ha ha," was his dry response as he crossed his arms over his chest and gave me another one of those lazy looks that drove me crazy. "Where do you work at?"

Now *that* genuinely made me laugh. "Yeah, I don't think so."

A hint of what might have been a smile or a smirk crossed his features. "You're not going to tell me?"

"Why? So you can show up at my job and make fun of me?" I asked.

He didn't even try and deny he would do something like that. He just stared at me. I'd swear some muscle in his jaw twitched too.

I raised my eyebrows like *see?* Obviously he did, because he didn't bother arguing over it at all. Instead, his jaw shifted to the side and then back in place before he glanced down at the table, then again at me. "What's your deal anyway?" he asked, shifting even more so that the entire length of his side —thigh, arm, and my shoulder—were lined up alongside his. "It's only an interview."

It was only an interview, like he said.

But it still made me feel *almost* sick.

"I'll only laugh at you a little if you tell me why they freak you out so much," he offered, like that was some sort of consolation. He'd laugh at my fears, but just a little. Oh, okay. "So?" he egged on.

I stared right into those soul-sucking eyes and didn't reply. He blinked, then I blinked right back. That stupid smile-smirk didn't go anywhere, and it was that, that had me hunching over to the side to lightly dig the boniest part of my elbow to the middle of his thigh in a warning.

He didn't flinch or move as I applied pressure. Instead, he lifted his leg to purposely press it against my bone, trying to get a reaction. "It'll be harder to hold you later if I have a bruise on my leg," he tried to threaten me.

"So much harder." I rolled my eyes. "Fuck off. You could do it with bruises all over your thighs."

He laughed, and it caught me off guard again. "Tell me what your deal is before they get here."

"I don't have a deal."

"You have a problem."

"I don't have a problem. I'm fine."

"I've never seen you so squirmy before, and I don't know if it's annoying or kind of cute."

I stared up at him for using the c-word, but nothing on his face confirmed he'd said anything like that to begin with. I didn't think he'd use the c-word on me, at least not that c-word. Cunt, *maybe*. Cute, no way.

"We'll go with annoying," he went on, still leaving that word in the open. "I'm going to keep asking you until you give me an answer."

God. What was with all these people in my life who couldn't and wouldn't take no for an answer? This was the same game my mom played when she wanted something. Actually it was the same game everyone in my family played when they wanted something that I didn't want to give them.

"Meatball."

"You're the annoying one. I hope you know that." I glanced toward the doorframe again. "And don't call me Meatball in front of the reporter person. I don't need anyone else calling me that."

"I won't, if you tell me what's wrong with you."

"You're an idiot."

He let out a little puff of breath from his nose. "I won't. Tell me."

I sighed and rolled my eyes, not feeling like hearing about this the rest of the day—or days—if I refused to. "Look, I don't like the media is all. I don't like most people period. They're always twisting and turning words around to make them controversial. And people eat that shit up. They want the drama. They want to believe all the bad things they hear."

"So?"

Did this bastard just say "*so*" like it wasn't a bad thing? "So, one time I said that I thought the judging system was still not correct, and they turned it around to make it seem like I thought the person that won another event didn't deserve it. I got hate mail for months after that. Another time, I said someone had a beautiful Y-spin, and suddenly they weren't any good at anything other than that," I told him, remembering those two things because they had bothered me for months. And that was just a small fraction of the things that had been twisted and turned until they weren't at all what I thought or said. I hated people for doing that kind of stuff. I really fucking did. God. "And don't get me started on videos."

Ivan didn't say anything for so long, I had to glance at him. His thigh was still against mine, but he was frowning. I thought about shifting my leg away, but fuck it. He was in my space. I wasn't going to give him anymore. His question came so unexpectedly, it surprised me. "So, you never said you thought the WHK Cup was rigged?"

Shit.

Tipping my head to the side, I glanced up at him and shrugged. "No, I said that."

He looked down at me and made a face. "Nothing has been rigged since they changed the scoring system."

I did know that. The scoring system had been changed when I was a kid after things *had* been rigged. What had once been a subjective point-system based on a "perfect" 6.0 score, had been ripped apart and reformed based on a stricter point system where each element was worth a certain amount of points; points that would be deducted if the element wasn't performed well. It wasn't a flawless system, but it was better.

But I'd been mad at the WHK Cup back then, and who the hell could be responsible for what came out when they were pissed as hell? "Your partner landed double-footed and you almost dropped her doing a triple twist. It was rigged." The second sentence was a lie, but the rest of it wasn't. I remembered the incident perfectly.

He snorted, and that time it was him who twisted his entire body to face mine. "It wasn't rigged. Our base score was a lot higher than yours was, and she completed all of her rotations."

I knew that, but I was going to be damned if I admitted that his program had much harder elements in it that equaled a much higher score than what my ex and I had. Plus... we hadn't been perfect. Almost, but not. I probably remembered every single mistake I had ever done in every program ever. Some nights, it kept me up going over everything, even programs from back when I was a teenager. If I hadn't been so cocky or if I had done just a little better.... How different could my life be if I had just lived up to my potential and not fucked up almost every single thing in my life?

"Okay, it wasn't rigged," I agreed, just because I would be more of an idiot if I kept trying to say that it was. By some miracle, I kept myself from smiling. "One of your people just paid off the judges. Whatever you want to call it is fine with me."

Ivan blinked, and I blinked back at him.

The tip of his tongue touched the inside of his cheek, and his face was smooth when he said, "I won that fair and square."

"I won third place that night, and I landed everything fine."

He blinked again. "You landed everything fine, but your choreography was atrocious and you pulled back on your jump sequences after what's-his-face bailed on the 3S in the event before that one. You also looked like a robot, and your partner looked like he was on the verge of throwing up the entire time."

He had a point but....

Ivan shrugged so casually I wanted to backhand him. "Your music sucked too."

The only sucking going on in that moment revolved around me sucking in a breath. "Excuse me. What are you? A musical genius?" I snapped.

He lifted a shoulder. "I have a better ear than you do. Don't get mad. You're either born with it or you aren't."

I would have gaped, but I didn't want him to know that he could get that reaction out of me.

Then he kept going. "You're out of your mind if you think I'm letting you choose the music for any of our programs."

Now that had me turning my whole body on that bench seat to give him this "the fuck did you say" look. My knee was pretty much on top of his thigh as I leaned toward him. It wasn't like I didn't touch him a hundred or three hundred times a day and had for weeks by that point. I could pick him out in a crowd by smell alone, I bet. "What?"

That light pink mouth twitched for the second time that day. "You heard me. Nancy, the choreographers, and I will pick it. It'll be perfect." Then his mouth twitched again. "Trust me."

I had to throw my head back and laugh. "Ha!"

"It's okay, Jasmine. I've always chosen. It's probably more important than the choreography. You want to win, don't you?"

No shit I wanted to win, and honestly, he did have great taste in music. His arrangements always surprised me. They were good, but I wasn't going to admit that. "There's no 'I' in team, you know that?"

The son of a bitch had the nerve to wink. "But there's an 'I' in winning, and if you want to win, you have to listen to me."

I scoffed. Then I laughed, even though I didn't want to.

"That doesn't even make sense, you idiot. And quit doing that thing with your eyes. It's freaking me out."

Those broad shoulders hunched up without the least bit of apology, straining at the seams of his beautiful sweater that I didn't have to touch to know it had to be soft as hell. "Makes sense to me."

"Because you're a dumbass. You're not the boss of me. We're partners. There's no 'I' in partners either."

He winked again. "We can argue about costumes and choreography, but I'm choosing the music."

Sheeeit.

I'd take it, but what was I going to do? Say okay? Really, I didn't care about the music. I'd skate to anything. Now the costumes... "Remember your Chiquita Banana Mambo costume nightmare? I'm sure as hell not letting you choose the costumes without seeing them first. And I already have someone who will make mine."

A muscle in his cheek twitched for all of a second before it stopped, and he ignored my comment about our costumes. "Who's a national champion, world champion and Olympic champion?" he had the nerve to ask.

I reeled back. And then couldn't form a single fucking word. Not one other than one that started with an m, ended with an r and sounded like trucker wucker.

Until this slow smile crept over his mouth.

Then I could. "You're such an annoying *shit*. God, I just want to punch you in the face sometimes. *Who's a champion?* Shut the hell up."

What did he do? How did he respond? He laughed. Ivan Lukov laughed loud.

"You probably paid the judges with your Russian mafia money," I kept going, which earned me another laugh so loud that I almost smiled back at him. When Karina and I were way younger, I had asked her how her parents made so much money that they could live in their giant mansion, and she had said she thought they were in the mafia. They weren't, but it still made me laugh.

"You're such a sore loser," he got out after a moment. "I thought I was bad, but you've got me beat."

"Oh please." I wasn't the one who got rid of partners every time one of them failed.

But I didn't say that.

"You probably sit in your Tesla and cry every time you wrinkle your sweaters."

Ivan barked out another laugh that was pretty much shouted up at the ceiling.

"What are you laughing at? I'm not trying to be funny," I said, watching him lose his shit for the first time in the more than ten years we'd known each other. The most I'd ever seen out of him was a smile or two around his family, specifically Karina.

But that was it.

I hadn't even known he knew how to laugh.... Unless he was doing something shitty, like taking people's souls and stuff.

"Oh, that's nice," a new voice piped up, nearly getting lost into the volume of Ivan being a pain in the ass.

And just like that, he stopped, the sound of his laugh replaced with silence.

We both looked toward the door at the same time. Sure enough, there was a woman standing there at the doorway holding a messenger bag in one hand and a purse in the other. "You don't have to stop on my account," she said, smiling.

I didn't say anything, and neither did Ivan.

She kept her smile on her face. "I'm sorry I'm late," she went on, without offering an explanation.

If she was expecting an "it's okay" out of me, she wasn't getting it. I couldn't stand people that were late. Apparently, Ivan wasn't a fan either, but out of the corner of my eye, I saw him bob his head. "We're ready whenever you are to get started. We both have other engagements and can't stay late."

He had something to do too? Since when? He didn't have a job. I used to think I wouldn't have one either if I had the opportunity to stay at home, but the truth was, I'd probably go apeshit without things to do. I could barely sit still for ten minutes.

But... what the hell did Ivan have to do?

The other woman nodded and began making her way into the break room, clutching a bag in each hand. "I understand, all I need is a minute to get ready," she said as she dropped her messenger bag on the table in between the bench seat that Ivan and I were sitting on and the chairs on the opposite side. She had to be in her mid-thirties, maybe even a little older. I never trusted guessing people's ages because neither one of my parents looked like theirs. "Amanda Moore," she said, thrusting a hand out in my direction first.

"Jasmine," I responded, taking her hand and giving it a shake.

She did the same to Ivan, who said, "Ivan. Pleasure to meet you."

Pleasure to meet you? What a suck-up. But I kept my attention forward on the lady, because as much as I wanted to shoot him a side-look, there was no way I'd be able to hide my "you're full of shit" face.

She gave us both a tight smile before beginning to go through her bag. She pulled out a laptop, a small black device that had to be a recorder, and a small yellow notebook along with a pen. "One minute," she said, as she opened her laptop.

Ivan's leg touched mine underneath the table, but I didn't look at him.

Not too long afterward, after moving things around, the woman gave us a tight smile. "Okay, I'm ready now."

The idiot beside me touched his leg against mine once more. That time, I hit my knee against the side of his thigh at the same time I folded my hands and stuck them between my thighs out of view. I wasn't going to be the one to break. No way. Lee wasn't going to get the chance to give me shit.

"I already thanked Ms. Lee for reaching out to Ice News for the interview, but I wanted to thank both of you myself. When the rumors started coming in that you and Mindy weren't going to skate together, we were wondering who would replace her," the woman named Amanda started, her gaze shifting to Ivan's direction as she spoke to him.

Good. I didn't know what they thought or knew about Ivan's situation besides that they wanted to keep the details under wraps. They could figure that out and deal with it. All I wanted was to compete.

"So," she continued on, glancing down at her notebook for a moment. "I'm going to record this conversation, if that's okay with both of you."

I nodded at the same time Ivan said, "Yes."

The woman beamed. "I have it here that you've been training together at the Lukov Ice Complex for the last four-teen years?" she asked me.

"Yes," we both answered at the same time. Was he trying to answer for me?

She bobbed her head. "And, Ivan, you've been here since it was built twenty-one years ago?"

"Yes. Before that I lived and trained in California," he replied, like he'd answered that question countless times in the past, maybe because he had.

The reporter switched her attention to me. "You've known each other since you started coming here?"

I could do this.

"No," I answered, trying to keep from instantly thinking her questions were dumb. Wasn't it common knowledge that Ivan had been doing this longer than I had? "He was more advanced than I was. We met about a year or two later." She didn't need to know we had "met" at his house instead of the LC.

The woman gave me a little smile. "But you're close friends with the family, aren't you?"

I blinked. How the hell did people know that? "Yes."

"You were in the same classes as—" She paused and glanced at her notebook. "—Karina Lukov, Ivan's sister. Correct?"

I nodded. Unlike Ivan, her parents hadn't put her into figure skating until she was a lot older. She had taken dance classes instead. The only reason they put her into figure skating was because Ivan had won a gold in the junior level and she had wanted to try. You know, since her family already owned an ice rink and all. Why not? I had shaken my head the first time she told me that story.

"How long did that last?" the Amanda woman asked.

Luckily, Ivan decided to answer that question. I didn't want to. I didn't even want Karina being brought up into our conversation. She didn't like having attention on her of any sort, and I respected that. "My sister stopped at fourteen. She decided to pursue other things."

Did his voice sound weird or was it my imagination? Maybe he didn't like talking about her either.

"But you two were best friends?" she asked me.

I nodded again and didn't miss the funny look the woman gave me. Maybe she wanted more than one-word answers and nods, but that's all she was getting, until I had to say more.

"This partnership is a decade in the making then?"

I froze. *Don't look at Ivan. Don't look at Ivan. Don't—*

His knee knocked mine, and it was only because I was familiar with his voice—mostly his smart-ass voice, but whatever—that I noticed how off it sounded, almost choked, a little gravelly... weird. "You can say that," he said slowly in that awkward voice.

I was not going to laugh. I was especially not going to laugh at this idiot. So all I did was nod. Slowly. Very slowly in agreement.

Amanda Moore's eyes slid to my direction to see me agreeing, and a little smile came over her mouth. "I'm sure you've seen the video of you," she pointed at me, "telling Ivan some *things*. There was so much feedback from his fans toward you after that—"

She was bringing that up, wasn't she? Great. Now whoever didn't know about it was going to look it up.

Shit.

"—was that simply both of you playing around then?" she kept going.

I went tense. I was pretty freaking sure that my eyes were almost bugging out of their sockets, and the fact I was pressing my lips together, probably made my face even worse. *Shut up. Don't say anything. Shut the hell up.*

So I nodded. Slowly again. Feeling like I was about to burst from the lying.

Beside me, the idiot, the complete moron, hit his leg against mine again, and he said in that ragged voice that wasn't his at all, "Yes. We play around all the time."

Damn it. *Damn it.* I wasn't going to laugh. I wasn't going to deny. I couldn't.

I had promised Lee that I could do this. That I could pretend we were friends.

"Jasmine is wonderful," Ivan basically choked out, somehow not bursting into flames as he said them. "What a sense of humor."

I had to fist my hand and dig my nails into my palm to keep from reacting. What a shit liar. Oh my God. And he gave me hell for being bad at lying.

I cleared my throat and plastered on a smile that felt like melted rubber as I said, "Ivan is great," I pretty much spit out, going "heh" at the end, as I remembered our conversation not that long ago about having voodoo dolls of each other.

The leg beneath the table hit my knee, and it took all of my self-control to not say a single word, because obviously he was thinking something similar. *Don't laugh. Don't choke. Keep it together. Professional.* United and all that shit.

But the lies must have been evident because the reporter almost immediately frowned and glanced at Ivan—who I had no idea what kind of facial expression he had on his face because I might die if I actually looked at him—and then glanced back at me. "Is there something funny?"

Out of the corner of my eye, I could see Ivan shake his head. "No. Nothing. We respect and admire each other a lot."

Oh my God.

My shoulders shook for the two seconds it took to get them under control.

Respect and admire. Of all the things he could have said, he literally went there. That time, it was me that banged my leg against his beneath the table.

Something, which I was pretty sure was the back of his hand, hit my forearm under it too.

"So much respect and admiration," I ground out, barely holding in a choke as I nodded.

"I've always been a big fan of Jasmine," the idiot continued on.

"Me too," I warbled out, trying to smile again and more than likely looking like a serial killer. "Ivan is a very likable guy."

She gave us both a funny look for a moment before either deciding to let it go, or believing us. I didn't care. "What are your favorite strengths of Jasmine's skating?" the woman asked.

"Oh, you know...."

I didn't even move my knee that time, I just kicked him. Straight-up kicked him in the shin. Not hard, but hard enough.

"She's a tremendous athlete," he finally got out, hitting my forearm again.

"And you, Jasmine, what drew you to want to partner up with Ivan? Other than the fact he's the reigning world champion," she asked.

"What more is there?" I got out with a shrug, taking the easy route, despite her comment rubbing me the wrong way.

"I know you haven't been together very long, but if there was one thing you wanted to say to the other, as a criticism, what would it be?"

I jumped on that real quick because I didn't trust Ivan. "Criticize this guy?" I ground out, tapping my heel against his, lightly as a warning and a reminder. "Oh, there's nothing. Nothing at all. Everything he does is... perfect."

I almost gagged at the effort those words took.

The smile that came over the reporter's face was just about a beam. "That's sweet."

Ivan's heel hit mine.

"And you, Ivan? What about Jasmine?"

It hit it again.

"A criticism? Jasmine is... too nice."

The woman blinked at the same time I did. "Too nice?" she asked, not even offending me because *really?* That's what he was going to go with?

I glanced at him at the same time he was nodding. "Yes. Too nice."

She probably wasn't even expecting the "huh" that came out of her mouth because it came out so swiftly. I looked over at her and blinked. Then she blinked too... like she couldn't believe that had slipped out of her mouth.

Bitch.

Maybe I wasn't the warmest, cuddliest person in the world, but I was nice.

Or as my mom would say, "when I wanted to be." But that was my mom. She had earned my love and deserved it. She could say whatever she wanted to me.

"What do you think about your old partner and Mary McDonald announcing they're competing this season?" she asked out of nowhere.

Just the mention of my "old partner" and then bitch-ass Mary McDonald afterward ruined everything about the day so far. Just like *that.* My whole body tensed.

Then Ivan kicked me. Literally kicked me.

But it snapped me out of it. It only took me a second to get my thoughts together and say, "I don't think anything about it." Maybe I should have said, I wished them luck or the best or something, but I wasn't that good of a person.

"Is it true you haven't spoken to him since your last season together?"

I wasn't going to count the one night I had called him drunk and upset right after he'd ditched me. He hadn't answered, but I had taken advantage of it. I was pretty sure I had called him a weak little pussy bitch, but... I wasn't positive.

All I knew was that I didn't regret anything that had come out of my mouth. Whatever it had been, he deserved.

"No, we haven't."

"Is it true that he sent you a text message to tell you?" she had the nerve to ask about the rumor that had been circling for some reason I didn't understand. I had never brought it up to anyone other than my family, so I knew it hadn't come from me.

Plus, the truth was... he hadn't told me. Period. I'd found out when he'd announced Mary and him were taking the next season off to train together. That's how I'd found out. From an article. Two days after we had started our planned one-month break.

Spineless bitch.

"Can we talk about Jasmine and me instead? I thought Coach Lee had mentioned that we didn't want to talk about our partners in the past," Ivan cut in suddenly, his tone that snooty shit one that I usually hated.

...until then.

The woman's face went pink, and she nodded quickly. "Yes, sure." But she didn't apologize for bringing up a topic that they had already told her not to. I hadn't known they had done that, but I appreciated it. A lot more than I thought. "What are your expectations for the season?" the woman continued with, not missing a beat.

"We're going to do well," Ivan answered, almost immediately. "Better than well."

"What do you mean by that?"

The heat and muscle of his thigh fully rested against mine, but I didn't move. "That means I don't expect this season to go differently than any other season."

The woman's eyes went wide. "You think so?"

I was watching him as he did his slow nod. "I know so."

"You're not taking the season off?"

Little did she know we only had a season together. I didn't have time to spare.

"No."

"You're that confident?" she asked with a smirk of amusement on her face, like she loved his confidence. Ugh.

"Yes," Ivan answered immediately.

She tipped her head to the side like "okay" and glanced at me. "What do you think? Is it possible?"

Maybe normally I would have made a joke, but she had already insulted me more than I deserved. So I didn't. "I think Ivan is one of the best competitors in this sport. I think I've already learned a lot from him, and I'm going to keep learning a lot from him."

Damn, that sounded good. Even I almost believed it.

"But you think it's possible to skip through a learning period?"

"Yes." At least I could hope. But no one ever believed someone who sounded hesitant.

Her eyes narrowed. "Do you think you'll be able to get over the nerves that have plagued you in the past?"

She was back at it again with the condescending shit that fast? Goddamn.

Be better. Be better. Be better. You can do it.

I could do it. I just didn't want to.

"I think that I have a partner I can rely on, so I have less to stress out about," I said slowly, watching her eye to eye as I said it so she knew I wasn't going to pretend like she was being polite when she sure as fuck wasn't.

"So you think your issues in the past are because of—"

Ivan's hand sliced through the hair. "Can we focus on Jasmine and me instead?" He blinked. "Please."

"I didn't—"

"It's my fault," I said quickly. "I shouldn't have said that. I don't know if I'll be able to get over my nerves, but I feel more confident with myself than I have in the past, and I think part of that is because of Ivan's history and record. I'm hoping he'll rub off on me." Bitch.

The woman made a face like she didn't believe me... but glanced back at her questions. "Okay. We can change the subject and move on to something else. What about a twenty-questions-type game?" She flicked her eyes toward Ivan. "If that's agreeable."

I blinked, but beside me Ivan answered, in an almost hesitant voice, "Okay."

"It'll be fun," she added, like she was trying to convince us this wouldn't be torture.

I probably had a different view on what she thought was fun, but okay. As long as the questions didn't involve Paul and his bitch-ass partner, or me being a screwup, I could take it. I nodded.

She smiled. "You haven't been partners together very long, but since you've known each other for a while, it should be fun."

Ivan kicked me.

And I kicked him right back.

Because it was one thing to pretend like we could put up with each other, but it was a totally different thing for us to "know each other."

"Okay," the woman went on, glancing at her laptop.

I snuck a look at Ivan, but he was already watching me.

What the fuck? I mouthed.

The man I'd never even seen get flustered, shrugged. *Guess*, he mouthed back.

"Okay, I've got a good one," she announced, totally oblivious to us wondering how the hell we were about to get through this as she had her eyes on the screen as she typed something. "What is Ivan's favorite color?"

I glanced at Ivan and made a face. "Black," I answered, but mouthed *like your heart.*

He rolled his eyes.

"Is that true?" the other woman asked, moving her gaze from the computer back to us.

"I don't have a favorite color," Ivan answered.

"What is Jasmine's favorite?" she asked.

He glanced at me at the same time the woman looked away, "Red." Then added *like the blood of the children you eat.*

I was not going to laugh.

I was not going to laugh.

Especially not when he looked so pleased with his fucking self. Idiot. Asshole.

Then he had the nerve to wink, and I had to force myself to look back at the woman instead. I kicked him after half a second.

"Did he get it right?" she asked me, glancing over.

I shook my head. "Nope. It's pink."

"Pink?" he croaked beside me.

I glanced at him out of the corner of my eye. "Yeah. Why is that so weird?"

"It's just...." He blinked, then blinked some more. "I don't think I've ever seen you wear pink."

Why the hell would he notice or pay attention to what I wore? I wondered. "I don't. It's still my favorite color though."

His forehead wrinkled, but all he said was "Oh."

Which offended me. "It's kinda fun," I explained, probably a little harshly.

All he said was his "Oh" again.

"Ivan's favorite jump?" the woman continued on.

That was easy. "The triple Lutz."

"That's right," the man beside me agreed.

"Jasmine's favorite?"

Ivan didn't hesitate. "Easy. The 3L."

"Can we expect to see some triple Lutzes in the future?" Amanda asked.

We glanced at each other, and I said, "Yeah," at the same time Ivan said, "Yes."

She nodded as she looked at her screen. "Ivan's favorite food?"

I mouthed *butthole* to him, but actually said, "Escargot" for no reason other than it sounded fancy.

There wasn't a moment for him to hold back a choke. What he also did was hit his leg against mine. "*No.*"

"No?"

"No," he insisted. "Why would you think that? *No.*"

I pressed my lips together and shrugged.

"Pizza."

I glanced at the body beside mine. His sweater was chunky but not that chunky. There was no body fat on him. He was all elegant, rock-solid muscle on long arms and long legs. It wasn't a body that knew pizza.

"Don't look at me like that," he said, using the same tone of voice that I had probably used on him when he didn't believe me that I liked pink.

"What kind of pizza?" I asked, half expecting him to say it was some fat-free shit.

He blinked at me, and I swore for one second that he could read my mind. "Plain old pepperoni."

It was my turn to say "Oh."

And he knew what it meant, because he raised his eyebrows.

"What is Jasmine's favorite food?"

The idiot beside me didn't miss a beat. "Chocolate cake."

How the hell did he know that?

"Is that true?" the other woman asked.

I was trying not to look at him like he was crazy for knowing that, and somehow I managed to nod. He had probably guessed since it was Karina's favorite too.

"If Ivan wasn't a figure skater, what else would he do?"

I had to pause. Ivan not being a figure skater? I couldn't imagine that being a possibility in any alternate universe. From what Karina had told me when we had been teenagers, he'd been skating since he was three. His grandfather had taken him to an ice rink, and it had been love at first sight. It had become his entire life. She had told me once he'd never even had a girlfriend. There had been a couple of girls he'd gone out with back in the day but nothing serious. Not when there was something else he loved more.

I got it. I really did.

Not that I'd ever admit how much we had in common, but I understood. I'd had a couple of short-term boyfriends but nothing serious, and that had been years ago. One of them had been the guy I'd chosen to finally lose my virginity to in the backseat of his SUV when I was nineteen, and the other had been a baseball player that had been like me: way too focused on his career. Every other guy I'd gone out with had all been one date and one date only.

Nothing and nobody would ever come between my dreams and me.

And imagining Ivan not owning the ice wasn't a reality I could picture, because he was the same as I was. Just evil. Well, annoying and evil.

"I can't see him doing anything else," I made myself respond honestly, unfortunately.

Beside me, even he shrugged like he had no idea what else he would do either.

Amanda must have seen that because she then asked, "What about Jasmine?"

There was no hesitation before his reply. "There's nothing else."

"There isn't anything else," I confirmed, letting the reminder that there wasn't a plan B for me, go. I freaked out about that enough. I didn't need to think about that reality more than I already did. I glanced at Ivan to find him looking at me with a smug expression on his stupid, perfect face.

Then the fucker mouthed *the Grim Reaper.*

I didn't even bother rolling my eyes.

"If Ivan could meet one person living or dead, who would it be?" she asked.

I wanted to say Jeffrey Dahmer, but Amanda was looking at me, so instead, I went with "Jesus."

There was a pause and a "Correct."

I kept my smirk to myself. He was so full of shit.

"What about Jasmine?"

I glanced at him, watching as he made a thoughtful expression before answering. "Stephen King."

I didn't wait for the woman to ask me if it was true, and instead frowned as I asked, "Why?"

"He wrote your favorite book."

I blinked.

"Misery."

He wouldn't know I didn't really read. I borrowed audio-books from the library, but that was as crazy as I got. But I couldn't correct him, so all I did was nod and say, "Uh-huh." I'd look it up later or ask my mom's husband. He read a lot.

Amanda had a funny look on her face, but she kept going. "What would Ivan enjoy more, books or magazines?"

"Magazines."

"What about Jasmine?"

Ivan snickered. "Picture books."

I blinked at him, feeling something ugly and defensive in my chest. "Why picture books?" I asked him, the ugliness growing inside of me as I prepared for the worst.

He grinned. "I don't think I've ever seen you read anything. My sister usually reads everything off menus to you."

If I blushed, I had a feeling everything from my belly button up would have been red as fuck at his comment. Karina did always read things off for me. I didn't even have to ask her to do it, she just always had. I didn't feel shame in having her do it because she didn't do it out of pity but because it was faster than me having to take my time and read it.

But I had never noticed that someone else was paying attention, judging me and making his own assumptions for it. He wasn't the first person, but...

I didn't like it. Not at all.

I swallowed and tore my eyes back to Amanda, giving her a tight expression as I shrugged. "I like audio books," I corrected.

"Me too," she agreed quickly.

There was nothing for me to be embarrassed about, I told myself for about the millionth time since I was four. I had come a long way. There was nothing shameful about having a learning disability. Nothing at all. It had taken me a lot of work to get as good as I had at reading... but it still took me too long; that was just the only part that frustrated me. I didn't love reading because it took me too long. I didn't love number sequences either. I learned by listening and by doing. I wasn't stupid.

And I sure as hell didn't like Ivan of all people making a joke about it.

I didn't like it so much that I didn't look at him again after that. Not for the next twenty minutes, when I barely answered with only one word if I could get away with it. I let Ivan direct the conversation and answer almost everything. She stayed away from more questions about my ex and kept it easy.

At one point, Ivan hit his leg against mine twice, but I didn't hit him back. I didn't feel like it.

When the time was over and my phone beeped, telling me the hour we had set aside for the interview was over, Ivan got up, hitting his elbow against mine so I could do the same. And I did. But I didn't glance at him as I did it. And I hated that too.

"It was nice meeting you," Ivan said, shaking her hand.

I just nodded and took her hand too. "Thank you," I muttered, sounding like an asshole, but I didn't even care.

I never expected Karina to ever tell anyone I had trouble with... things. Once, my mom had even suggested that I tell everyone I had a learning disability, but I had told her no. No because I didn't want anyone to pity me. I'd gotten that enough when I was younger and they had figured out why I had such a hard time learning my alphabet, then reading and writing. I had never let my own family baby me over it. My mom used to say I would rather stay up all night than ask anyone for help.

Ivan shuffled out of the bench, and I followed right after him, except when he stopped at the side of the table, I went completely around him and headed toward the door and out. My hand instantly went to my wrist, and I gave my bracelet a spin. *There is nothing to be mad at. He didn't call you dumb. He didn't say you couldn't read.*

He was just messing with you. The same way you were messing with him, and he didn't complain or cry about it. Don't be dumb. Don't be all sensitive and shit. You've heard worse.

And I had.

So why was I so damn mad, and maybe the tiniest bit... hurt?

"Meat—Jasmine," Ivan's familiar voice called out from somewhere behind me.

I didn't stop because I was on a schedule, not because I was running away from him. "I've got to get to work," I replied over my shoulder, not slowing down.

"Hold up a second."

Raising my right hand, taking in the big red R on it; I winced and waved it anyway. "I'll see you this afternoon," I said before turning down the hall leading to the changing room. I darted inside because I really had to get to work, not because I was avoiding whatever the hell was going to come out of Ivan's mouth.

God, I was such a weak shit.

Why hadn't I just talked to him?

Luckily, there was only one other person in the changing room right then, and she and I just glanced at each other, but that was it. Opening my locker, I grabbed my bag and pulled out my clothes for work, deodorant, makeup, and baby wipes. But it was the blinking green light on my cell phone screen that made me pause. I grabbed my phone and unlocked it to find that I had two texts waiting for me.

One was from my dad.

Sent you a msg last week. I'm coming in September. Hope I get to see you.

That weird feeling I'd gotten back in the break room went through my upper body again, but I shoved it all away. I typed in **OK** and hit send, feeling just a little guilty I hadn't sent anything longer. But then I scrolled up and saw that my last message from him had been four months ago, and suddenly, I didn't feel so bad.

Then I checked my next message, and saw it was from my mom.

Good luck with your interview. Don't fidget, make faces, or roll your eyes if there's a camera. Don't cuss either.

That brought a little smile to my face that replaced the ache, and I typed back, **To late…**

Not even thirty seconds later, as I was fishing for my socks and work shoes, my phone vibrated with another message from my mom.

Mom: I don't know you.

CHAPTER 8

"Not that I care, but are you mad at me?"

I had just finished doing a loop around the ice to warm-up following my hour-long stretching session when Ivan skated up beside me, asking his dumbass question.

I didn't even bother glancing at him when I answered. "No."

"No, you're not mad?" he asked.

Out of the corner of my eye, I could see the outline of the white zip-up pullover he had on and the navy blue sweatpants tucked into his black skates. Why did he always have to dress like he gave a shit? Ugh. I was in my usual outfit of faded leggings and faded long-sleeved T-shirt with a couple of holes in it. The good thing about not being tall was that I hadn't grown out of clothes in more than a decade.

"No," I repeated myself.

He didn't say anything for a second as he kept up next to me as I went around to do another loop, gaining a little more speed than I had on the first lazy one. "Anymore?"

Why the hell was he hounding me? He hadn't seen my

face the day before, and I didn't think I had acted like something was wrong.

Had I?

Then I remembered his "not that I care" comment and rolled my eyes at that. "No, I was never mad at you to begin with."

"I didn't do anything for you to get mad at."

"Okay," I answered shortly.

There was a pause. "You weren't mad?"

Had I been mad? No. Had he joked about something I was sensitive about? Yes. It would tell him that he'd caught on to one of the few things I was hung up over, but telling him that might just make him pick on me more.

Because that's what we did, and the only person I could blame was myself. And him. We had built this boat our... working relationship—or whatever the hell else it could be called—was based on.

"Nope," I said. With my eyes still focused forward, I threw his words back at him, "I'd have to care what you think to get mad."

He looked down at me over his shoulder, not responding as we finished another loop around the ice rink, having it completely to ourselves so early. Yesterday afternoon, we had gone straight to business for our afternoon practice. Had I ignored him more than usual? No. I just treated him like I needed to: like we only had a limited time to get our shit together and I needed to make the best out of it.

"This is only for a year," he reminded me suddenly, like I had forgotten.

I didn't even bother rolling my eyes. "I heard you the first time y'all brought it up, numbnuts."

"I'm only making sure you don't forget," he added in that aggravating tone.

"How could I when you remind me every other day?" I snapped before I could stop myself. I needed to stop. I'd known what I was getting myself into.

That had him glancing at me. "Someone's touchy."

I rolled my eyes. "You're bothering me by telling me something I know and haven't forgotten. I'm not being touchy."

"You're being touchy."

"*You're* being touchy."

"All I'm doing is making sure you aren't setting yourself up for disappointment later on," he said, his tone off and strange and rough, and that made me stop skating so I could really get a good look at him.

"What the hell are you talking about?" I frowned, watching as he stopped a moment after I did and turned to face me. I wished he wasn't so much taller than me. It was annoying how he literally had to tip his chin down to look at me.

"You heard me," he said in a tone that made my palm itch.

"What the hell would I have to be disappointed over?" Chances were my eyes were either already bugging out or well on their way to.

And this idiot blinked. "Not getting to partner up with me for longer."

I stared at him, thinking he was joking but knowing with an ego the size of his, he was genuinely telling me the fucked-up thoughts in his head. "I'll be just fine, Lucifer. Don't worry about me. I'm not going to get *that* attached to you. Your personality isn't that awesome."

I wasn't surprised when he genuinely looked offended. "You know, there are a lot of people who would love this opportunity."

"Yeah, and there are a lot of people who would appreciate

this opportunity but know you don't shit out golden eggs, buddy."

His eyelids hung low over his almost transparent blue eyes. "Golden eggs?"

"Yeah, you haven't heard of Mother Goose?"

He fully blinked. "A picture book?"

That wiped my expression clean, at least until I narrowed my eyes at him. "So what if I fucking like picture books and your sister reads out menus to me?" I blurted out, before I could remind myself not to engage in this shit.

Ivan seemed to rear back for a moment before blinking. Then he shook his head. "I knew you were mad. I *knew* it."

Damn it. "I'm not mad, dumbass."

He shook that dark head. "You literally yelled at me fifteen seconds ago."

I blinked, fisting my hand without even realizing it. "Because you get on my nerves."

"Over me talking about you liking picture books. I've said worse things to you and you haven't batted an eyelash, but—"

Was he right? Of course he was. Was I going to admit it? Hell no.

"I'm not mad," I repeated, trying to tell myself to calm down and keep it cool. To not let him get the best of me because it wouldn't be worth it. It wouldn't. Nope.

"You're mad," he insisted.

I slid him a look. "No, I'm not."

"Yes, you are," he kept going, not realizing he was pissing me off more and more... or maybe he did know and he just didn't care. It was Ivan. It could be either. "You aren't the first woman to lie and tell me you're not mad when you really are."

I was going to sock him one of these days, and he was going to deserve it.

But I could only do it when we weren't in public. I couldn't forget that stipulation.

"Don't compare me to your exes," I gritted out.

Something strange came over his face so fast, and was gone just as quickly, that I might have thought I was imagining it. But I wasn't.

Before he could feed me some more bullshit or try to bring up his ex-girlfriends or ex-partners or whoever the fuck else he was referring to, I kept going. "I don't care what you think about me, Ivan. If I did, then this would be a different story, but I don't. There isn't anything you can say to me that would hurt my feelings."

His blink that time was different. Slower. Longer. But it still only lasted about three seconds before his facial expression was back to normal, and he said, "I know you well enough."

"You don't know shit," I clipped.

But this man had never been one to back down, and I doubted he ever would. He stared at me for a moment, taking a deep breath, then letting it back out. "I know you better than you think I do."

It was my turn to take a breath in and out. *It doesn't matter what he thinks*, I told myself. It doesn't matter. I didn't care. I knew what this was for. A year. A possibility to win. A possibility to get a permanent partner afterward.

"No. You don't," I claimed, making sure my exhale was nice and smooth instead of choppy. The last thing I wanted was for him to know he was having any kind of effect on me.

"I leave you both alone for four minutes and you're already arguing," Coach Lee's familiar voice carried out across the ice from her spot by the boards, as she unclipped her skate guards to join us on the ice. "Are you two ever going to get along?"

Ivan said, "Yes" at the same time I said, "No," giving him a dirty-ass look as I said it.

Coach Lee sighed, not even looking up as she did it. "Forget I asked. Let's get started, shall we?"

~

I SHOULD HAVE KNOWN THAT TODAY WOULD BE THE DAY THIS would happen, I thought to myself, as I turned the key in the ignition and heard nothing. Not the choke of the engine trying to turn on. Nothing. Just a click.

"Goddammit," I hissed as I banged my forearms on the steering wheel and hissed out, "Mother-fucking-son-of-a-bitch-ass-whore. *FUCK ME!*"

Why? Why did this have to happen? If I cried, right then I would feel totally justified for doing it.

I was tired. My ankle, wrist, and knees hurt from Ivan dropping me on the fucking ice as we worked on twists—which meant he hurled me straight up into the air, while I tried to do at least three turns at the peak of height, and then he caught me again on the way down. He had only dropped me three times, but it might as well have been a dozen. He'd dropped me twice that amount on the mats, if not more.

All I wanted to do was go home. It was Saturday afternoon, early enough so that no one had arrived at the LC for evening and night lessons, and it was my night off from Pilates and the runs I'd been going on multiple times a week, usually with my brother, who had only just barely begun to forgive me for not telling him about Ivan. It was my night to have dinner without rushing because I needed to get to bed or take an ice bath, or whatever else there was to do.

And all I wanted was to go eat the lasagna and chocolate cake my mom had said she was going to make. I'd been dreaming about her husband's garlic breadsticks for the last two days since she had let me know Saturday was going to be *the day* so I could plan my cheat meal around red meat and cheese.

And I was stuck.

Of course I was going to be stranded.

Drawing my phone out of my bag, I tried to think of who I could call. I had declined roadside assistance on my insurance because it made it more expensive. I could call my oldest brother, but according to our group chat message from earlier, he had left for a trip out of town that morning with some girl he was seeing. Jonathan would tell me to look up what to do on YouTube, and my mom's husband was worthless with cars. My mom, though, would tell me to call my uncle, who had his own mechanic shop and a tow truck.

So...

I looked through my contacts for the right number and hit send. Three rings later, his low voice came up on the other end with, "Baby girl, how's it going?"

I couldn't help but smile. He and my grandpa were the only ones who ever called me things like that. "Hi, Uncle Jeff. I'm alive, you?"

"Still kicking, sweetie."

"I'm sorry to bother you—"

He let out a muffled chuckle. "How many times have I told you you're not a bother? What's going on?"

"My car won't start," I told him immediately. "The engine isn't turning; there's just a click sound. I didn't leave my lights on."

He made a humming noise. "How old is your battery?"

Shit. "I have no idea."

He laughed. "Chances are it's your battery, but I'd like to take a look at it. Your terminals might be corroded, and I could clean them up for you, but I won't know until I take a look. Problem is, I'm in Austin today and tomorrow. Where you at?"

"I'm in the parking lot of the Lukov Complex," I replied.

"Could you leave it there until I get back into town tomorrow?"

Tomorrow.... All I had to do was go for a run, have a stretch, and buy my weekly groceries. I could borrow my mom's car for that. "Yeah, I can leave it here."

"Okay, leave it there. Tomorrow I can meet you, take a look at it, and let you know what's going on, is that all right?"

It was either that or paying a tow truck driver hundreds of dollars, which I needed for other things, to tow my car home or to his shop, which was closed anyway. "It's fine. Thank you. I'm sorry to bother you."

"Girl, what did I just say? You're never a bother. I'll see you tomorrow though, honey. It'll be early evening, so keep that busy schedule open for me. It was about time I dropped by to see your mama anyway. It's been long enough, she needs somebody to remind her she looked like a troll under the bridge before she hit puberty," he laughed.

I smiled. "You're the only one who can do it. She almost beat my ass the last time I told her I thought I saw a wrinkle on her face."

He laughed more. "All right, I'll talk to you tomorrow. Sorry again I can't help you out today."

"It's okay. Bye, Uncle Jeff."

"Bye-bye, Jasmine baby," he said before hanging up.

I felt better as I hung up the phone.

Then remembered I still had to get home.

Fucking shit.

Shoving the door open, I got out of the car and went around to the other side as I decided who would give me the least amount of hell if I asked for a ride. I was opening the passenger door to grab my bag, debating whether Ruby or Tali would be the best option when a car honked. I ignored it as I grabbed my bag and swung it out, closing the door with my hip as the sound of a car honking again made me glance over my shoulder... and regret it.

Because in a black car with sleek lines and the driver-side window rolled down was a face I knew too well.

"Want some candy, little girl?" the idiot asked as he placed a forearm on the door and shoved his black-framed, black-lensed glasses up onto the top of his equally dark hair.

I blinked as I took a step back and let my butt rest against my mustard-colored passenger door of my Subaru. "Not from you," I replied, watching the guy I had tried my best not to talk to all afternoon.

He didn't flinch or make a face, but raised his eyebrows. "Need a ride?"

How the hell did he know I needed a ride?

"I saw you get into your car and start banging on the steering wheel," he went on, like he knew what I was wondering. "I don't have any jumper cables."

Of course he didn't. His car was not even a year old. His car before that had been a midnight blue BMW that couldn't have been more than three years old.

"Get in," he kept going.

"I—"

"I'll give you a ride. Stop overthinking it. You don't even have to pay me."

Oh God. I hated him. I hated him even more when he smiled like he thought he was hilarious.

I could call Jojo or Tali or Ben or James or Ruby. They would come get me. I knew they would. Even if they were already over at my mom's.

"You really want to wait around here for someone to come get you?" he asked, raising his eyebrows again.

He had me there.

But I also didn't want to get into the car with him, so....

"Get in, loser."

And that had me blinking. "Did you just quote—"

"I don't have all day. Let's go. You don't want to wait around, and neither do I," he finished before tipping his head toward his passenger seat.

Shit.

Two other cars had parked in the lot while we'd been arguing, and I could see the families getting out of their vehicles. Did I want to be out there arguing with Ivan while people watched? Maybe. But I had said we would do better and keep going with this façade so....

"Fine," I muttered, fully aware I sounded like an ungrateful ass and only slightly feeling bad about it. I took a step toward his Tesla and then stopped, narrowing my eyes at him. "You promise you won't kill me?"

He grinned. "I promise if I do, it'll be quick and painless."

I did this to myself.

"I'm going to take a picture of your license plate so if my body comes up missing, they'll check your car for my DNA."

"I have bleach," he returned immediately.

Why was he being... it wasn't *nice*, but more... not a total asshole?

I frowned at him as I walked around the back of the car to take a picture of his license plate, because even though I realistically knew that Ivan wasn't actually going to kill me, someone should still know where I was. At least that's exactly what I would tell my sisters to do if they were in my position. You couldn't trust anyone.

Circling back around the front of the car after sending my mom a picture of Ivan's plate number, because if there was anyone who would raise hell to get me back, it was that woman, I got inside the car and set my duffel on the floor, then clipped my seat belt in.

Then, cringing on the inside, I turned to look at Ivan and forced an almost-smile on my face as I slowly murmured, "Thank you," like each word was getting plucked out of my mouth with pliers.

"Don't sound so excited," he replied. Then he smiled. "Which bridge do you live under and how do we get there?"

"I can't stand you."

He snickered as he dropped his sunglasses onto the bridge of his nose and faced forward. "Where to?"

I wrinkled my nose but gave him the directions to start off, watching in silence as he turned one way and then the other before guiding the quiet, beautiful car onto the freeway. I took turns looking out the window, then glancing at the huge screen built into the dashboard, and then looking back at Ivan when I didn't think he could see me. The last thing I wanted was for him to catch me taking in how perfectly shaped his nose was, and how well it fit into the profile of the rest of his bone structure. His jaw was this thing that I'd overheard the older teenage girls babble over. His cheekbones and brow bones were proportionate to the rest of his face. To me, his face reminded me of one that would belong to a prince or something. Royal.

Not that I would ever admit that.

And it wasn't like it mattered when under that pretty face and pretty skin was evil incarnate.

"Take a picture, it lasts longer," Ivan drawled all of a sudden.

I blinked and thought about glancing away but decided that would look even worse. "I will. I think the encyclopedia needs an entry on Assholes and could use your picture as an example."

His right hand let go of the steering wheel and covered a spot over his heart. "Ouch."

I snorted. "Oh please."

He glanced at me with those crazy dark glasses covering his eyes. "What? You don't think you could hurt me?"

"You need a heart for it to hurt."

His hand didn't go anywhere. "Ouch, Jasmine. Really. I have a heart."

"It doesn't count if it's made out of sticks and stones and painted red."

The only corner of his mouth I could see, turned up just a little. "I made it out of clay, Meatball. Give me some credit."

I didn't mean to. I really didn't. But I snickered and turned my face away, like if he couldn't see me doing it, it wasn't actually happening.

"You know, we might be able to get along if we tried," he said after a moment, while I still had my face turned away.

I wanted to look at him... because there was a lot a person's face couldn't hide, especially a face I figured I knew as well as Ivan's... but I made sure to keep my gaze out the window. Because Ivan and me as friends? Why was he bringing it up and asking? I wasn't sure what his motives were. "I don't know about all that," I told him honestly.

There was a pause as he kept driving. "You like my sister."

"But you aren't your sister. Your personalities are totally different." Because they were. Karina was sweet most of the time, but had a backbone that I respected a lot. She didn't take most things seriously, unless she really cared about them. She balanced me out. She was warm and easygoing where I... wasn't.

He hummed but said, "I didn't think you made so many excuses."

Now that had me glancing at him. "I'm not making excuses."

Ivan had his gaze forward as he said, "Sounds like it to me."

"I'm not—" Was I? Shit.

"You always say you can do everything—"

"Because I can." Then I frowned. "Lee only asked us to be nice to each other. We've been... handling it."

He didn't say a word; he just lifted his shoulder like he was egging me on. But why the hell would he do that?

"It'd be easier if you didn't hate me," he added.

I frowned at the windshield. "I don't hate you."

That time he did glance at me, his expression even, but something about it still disbelieving.

"I don't hate you," I repeated, looking at him even though he'd glanced away by then. "Why the hell would you think that?"

"Because you've said, '*I hate you.*'"

I blinked. "That doesn't mean I really hate you. I didn't know you were that sensitive. I don't like you, but I don't hate you-hate you."

His snicker was annoying. "I don't really *care* if you hate me."

That had me rolling my eyes. "*Let's be friends, but I don't care if we are or not, okay,*"

I mocked him, shaking my head because that didn't make any fucking sense at all.

"So?"

He was *still* going with this? "So what?"

"So, yes or no?"

Yes or no? To us being friends when I didn't understand why he would bother to try? When he made it seem like he didn't care whether we were or not? The fuck? Was this how people became friends in real life? I didn't know. How the hell would I? Every friend I had I'd made back when I didn't distrust every person I met.

And Ivan?

"I mean...."

"If you don't think you can do it...." He trailed off with a shrug of those shoulders I'd put my hands on five thousand times in just a couple of months.

If I didn't think I could do it....

Shit.

I watched his face, but nothing about it changed; he just kept looking forward. I felt... off, and weird. "What does it mean if we are? Do we have to do something or...?"

"I don't know," was his brilliant-ass and unexpected response. Because how did he not know? I'd seen him hundreds of times surrounded by people, smiling, hugging, acting like he loved attention and had been born to be the center of it every minute of his life.

But had I seen him actually talk to people before for longer than a few minutes?

Huh.

I wasn't sure I had.

"I'll think about it," I said before I could stop myself.

That had him glancing at me, and if his voice was huskier than normal, I didn't notice it. "Okay," was his response.

What the hell did this all mean? What was I supposed to do? I wasn't the type to hug for no reason, and I didn't have time to hang out or whatever it was that "friends" did. I hadn't lied. I didn't hate him. I hated my ex and a few other people, but I just didn't like Ivan. He was argumentative, arrogant, blunt....

I'd just described myself, hadn't I? Shit.

This was never going to work. This was why I didn't have friends, or more than a couple because—

Then I remembered this was Ivan. Ivan who had the same schedule I did. Ivan who didn't have time either. Or did he? I didn't know what he did when we weren't together.

Could we... be friends? Or at least try to bicker less?

What I really wanted to know was would he even want to?

"This is only for a year," I said, reminding him about something he already damn well knew. They were the same words he'd used on me every time he wanted. The same words he'd literally used on me hours ago just this morning, before practice and ballet.

"I know that," he muttered.

"So what's the point?"

"Fine, forget it," he mumbled, turning the car down onto the street leading to my mom's neighborhood.

"You're the one who brought it up," I muttered in return.

"Well, I changed my mind."

"Well, I don't think you really get to change your mind after you said it."

"I did."

I blinked, not liking how insulted I felt all of a sudden now that he'd "changed" his mind. I didn't even want to be his friend. It would have been the last thing I wanted or expected, but now....

I didn't like him telling me what to do. That had to be it. That's what I was going to tell myself. He didn't get to choose what I did with my life and time more than he already had. "Too bad, shitface. I guess we can try." I might have broken into a sweat just saying that.

He made a noise as he turned the wheel. "You *guess*?"

"Yeah, I guess."

He made a face but said, "I'll think about it."

I scoffed, forcing myself to look forward. "You'll *think*—" I cut myself off as I saw the two-story house coming up on the right. There were three cars I recognized parked in the driveway. Fuck me. "We're here," I said, pointing at the house.

Ivan steered the car to the open spot in front of the house, and the second he did, I rushed to say, "Okay, thanks for bringing me," hand already on the door, my other hand going to the straps of my bag.

I watched him turn off the car more than I actually heard him turn it off.

What the hell was he...?

Ivan raised his eyebrows after turning to me. "Can I use the bathroom?"

CHAPTER 9

I BLINKED.

I blinked, and every single word I had learned over the course of my life stopped existing. Because in that moment, as I sat there on top of butter-smooth leather seats with my hand on the door handle to a car that cost more than most people's homes, I wasn't sure what the hell to say. I wasn't even sure I'd heard him correctly.

"Say what?" I basically croaked for what I was pretty sure was the first time in my life.

The man sitting behind the steering wheel didn't even bother answering my question. What he did was reach to the side... and open his door. Then he said, "Can I use the bathroom?"

He...?

He wanted me to invite him in? Was that what he was seriously fucking asking me? Was he not so subtly telling me he wanted to go inside *my house*? Where my family was? To pee?

I blinked again, the "no" on the tip of my tongue, filling the back of my throat and so large it went down my esophagus too. It was a stupid-ass response, one I knew I was more than likely going to regret, but I gave it anyway. Because: *be better.* "If... you want to."

Ivan's reply was to get out of the car and slam the door closed, all while I still sat there, wondering what the hell had just happened. Then, just as quickly as Ivan had gotten out, I did the same, grabbing all of my things and closing the door as gently as possible. He was already waiting for me halfway up the paved pathway leading to the front door, hands tucked into the pockets of his sweatpants, his black fleece pullover matching his low-profile black tennis shoes perfectly. Mostly though, it annoyed me that he hadn't taken a shower either, and I looked like I needed one while he... didn't.

"Who's here?" the nosey bastard asked.

I slid him a side-look as I walked around him onto the grass to head to the front door, shoving my arm into the opened zipper of my bag to look for my keys. I'd already taken in the cars parked in the long driveway. The Cadillac was James's, my brother's husband. The 4Runner was Tali's, and the Yukon was Squirt's husband's. "My mom, her husband, Ben, my brother and his husband, both my sisters, Aaron, my sister's husband, and their kids."

"Which sister?" he asked.

I eyeballed him again as I slid the key into the lock, wondering on a scale of one to ten how shitty of an idea this was going to be. With my luck, probably a thirty. Because today would be the day that he invited himself inside to use the bathroom.

God help me.

"The redhead or the sweet, quiet one?" he asked, like I didn't know the difference in my sisters.

"Aaron is Ruby's husband; she's the nice one," I replied, my words coming out choppy and stilted because I didn't get when the hell he'd paid enough attention to know my two sisters. It had been years since Ruby, the younger of the two, had gone with me to the rink. Not since she'd been pregnant with their first baby. Tali still tagged along every once in a while to sit there and judge me, but not as often as she used to. And I couldn't remember either one of them ever going to his parents' house to pick me up after I'd hung out with Karina.

"You have another brother, don't you?" he asked, just as I pulled the key out of the lock and went to turn the doorknob.

How the fuck did he know I had another brother? Maybe Karina had mentioned it before. She did used to claim she had a crush on Seb. "My oldest one. Sebastian."

Ivan dipped his chin down before taking a step forward, closer to the door—and me—as I shoved it open. Instantly, I could hear quiet laughter coming from the direction of where the kitchen was.

I was going to regret this. I knew for sure I was going to regret letting him in. But if I told him I didn't want him to come inside, it would just make me look weak or like there was something I was trying to hide from him. Plus, that was kinda mean.

I waved Ivan inside as I stood beside the door and closed it after him. "Let me show you the bathroom," I offered.

He made a face, his attention going in the direction of the laughter. "Shouldn't you go tell them hi first?"

Should I, maybe. Did I want to? No.

"I should tell your mom hello, shouldn't I?"

Oh God.

There was a reason I had never brought a boyfriend over to my house to meet my family. And now... well, now I was going to bring one of the most important people I would ever meet and have a relationship with over to see these psychos, even if it was only for a moment to greet my mom.

Thinking about all the horrible things I had said in front

of my brothers and sisters' old boyfriends and girlfriends over the years was almost enough for me to regret the hell they were more than likely going to pay me back with now.

I wasn't fool enough to think they were going to be on their best behavior because a gold medalist was coming in to say hi.

At least I sure as hell hoped that's all he was doing. From a single sniff, I could tell dinner was well on its way to being done. It smelled so good.

With a shrug, I tipped my head to the side so he would follow me. I passed by the living room and found it almost empty except for Ben, who was standing at the liquor cabinet, filling three different glasses with what looked like gin and tonic. "Hey, Ben," I called out, stopping behind the couch to greet him.

He didn't look back as he closed the bottle in his hand. "Hey, Jas," he whispered, glancing over his shoulder before his eyes hit where I was standing and he stopped talking. His whiskey-colored eyes widened, and I knew he was fully aware of who was standing not even six inches away.

"Why are you whispering?" I asked.

He pointed upstairs. "The kids are napping in our room."

Oh. Deciding to go peek into my mom's room later, I focused on the person beside me. "Ben, this is my partner, Ivan. Ivan, this is my mom's husband, Ben," I introduced them both, not sure what to do with the way Ivan blinked slowly before finally taking a step forward and saying, "Nice to meet you" like a normal, polite human being.

Huh.

I noticed Ben slide his eyes in my direction, giving me a "*what the fuck, Jasmine?*" look before taking Ivan's outstretched hand. "Nice to meet you, too." He paused. "Want a drink?"

"I'm driving, but thanks," he replied easily.

"Let me know if you change your mind," Ben replied, giving me another bug-eyed look.

Ivan nodded at the same time I waved to him so he'd follow me into the kitchen. I recognized my sister's laugh, followed by Jojo saying, "Shut up."

Stepping into the wide doorway of the kitchen, I took in my siblings and their significant others sitting around the island and focused way too hard on something in the middle of it. My mom on the other hand was peeking into one of the double wall ovens and poking something inside. Glancing back at Ivan, I raised my eyebrows at him and then went into the kitchen, expecting him to follow behind me at the same exact time. Jonathan threw his hands in the air a split second before the sound of a few things falling on the granite filled the room.

"No!" my brother hissed at the same time my sister Tali went, "How did you screw that up?"

"You know he sucks at Jenga," I threw in, coming up behind the body I knew belonged to my sister. She turned around just as I touched the top of her head.

"Jasmine," Ruby, my slightly older sister, squealed, her hands moving toward me before stopping halfway between our bodies, like she was hesitating. She always did.

I didn't even sigh; I just wrapped my arms around her and noticed it took her all of a second before she hugged me back.

"I come over all the time, and you never hug me like that," Jojo piped up from his spot across the island.

I was still hugging Ruby when I glanced over at him and said, "Because she's never come into the bathroom while I was showering and dumped a pitcher of ice water on me."

"You're still mad about that?" my brother asked, planting his elbows on the island and smirking so wide his gap-tooth grin came out.

"You did it last week," I reminded him. "And two weeks before that."

"I was only trying to help you—" he started to say before James, who was sitting beside him, elbowed him in the arm, hard enough to get his attention as he rubbed his arm. "What was that for?"

James's eyes were on the spot behind me as he elbowed his significant other again.

Now or never, right? "Ivan gave me a ride home because my car wouldn't start," I explained, watching as all of them, even my mom who was at the oven, all turned to try and look behind me. "Everyone, Ivan. Ivan, this is everyone."

My brother squeaked. James elbowed my brother again. My sister, Tali, blinked. The hand that Ruby had on my lower back jerked. My mom did nothing, and neither did my sister's beautiful blond husband who was sitting in the seat directly to my right.

"Hello," Ivan, who was apparently wearing his polite pants, called out.

It was my mom that replied, "Hello, Ivan," as she came around the island, wiping her hands on the apron she had on over her clothes. "It's nice to see you again."

He replied something I couldn't hear when Ruby's hand on my back moved, and she leaned in to whisper into my ear, "He's so tall and handsome in person."

I glanced at the man beside her, who had turned back around to face the island and begun collecting the wooden blocks that were spread all over the counter. "I'm going to tell Pretty Boy you're eyeing another guy."

She scowled and pulled away. "You're a pain, Jasmine."

I smiled at her and touched the top of her head again. She had been the last of my brothers and sisters to move out, and even though it had been six years since it had happened, I still missed her like it was just yesterday. Even though I was pretty close to Jonathan in our own screwed-up way, it was Ruby that I had always been the closest to. My mom said it was because we were polar opposites and balanced each other out. Like Karina. I always thought it was just because she had the most patience with me, and I had always been really over protective of her despite the fact she was five years older than me.

With the back of my hand, I reached to the right and tapped her husband's shoulder, taking in the baby monitor sitting in front of him on the table. It was one of those fancy video ones.

He peeked over at me in the middle of collecting Jenga pieces and grinned. "Jasmine."

I gave him his own little smile. It was hard not to. "Aaron."

"I've been meaning to tell you how happy I was when Rubes said you got another partner," the man replied in his honey-sweet Louisiana accent. "I knew it would only be a matter of time."

My smile grew a little wider, and I nodded at him, tapping his shoulder one more time to tell him thank you. In return, the man my brother had joked around that he'd sworn he'd seen on the cover of a book before, smiled at me, like it was enough. It had only taken Aaron about five minutes to convince me that he deserved to be my sister's first boyfriend. I'd been prepared to hate his guts. But in those first five minutes after she'd brought him to the house to introduce him to us all—six months before they eloped, and six and a half months before we found out about it—he had asked her to show him all of the cosplay outfits she had made over the years, and I knew she had found a kind, decent man.

If he hadn't been, my mom and I had been ready to whoop his ass one dark, rainy night when he couldn't identify us.

"'Sup, man," my brother, Jonathan, said from close by.

Peeking over my shoulder, I found that Jojo had gotten up from the island and was towering over my mom at her side, hand already shaking Ivan's.

"How's it going," Ivan replied. "Ivan."

Like Jojo didn't know who he was.

"Jonathan," my brother said, sounding totally cool, and not at all like he'd talked about Ivan's "skater butt" in the past. "This is my hubby, James," he continued on, hooking his thumb behind him to point at the island. James waved.

"You're my fourth favorite figure skater," James said, shooting me a wink.

Fourth?

Even Jojo wondered the same thing. "Who's one through three?"

"Jasmine."

"Two and three?"

"Jasmine."

My dead heart gave a little burn of emotion, and if I was the kind of person to blow someone a kiss, I would have done it to him. "I'd push you out of the way if you were about to get run over," I told him and meant it.

He smiled and winked at me again. "I know you would, Jas."

I smiled back at him before glancing at Ivan to see him watching me. I was about to ask him what the hell he was looking at but stopped when I remembered I had agreed to try and be friends with him. What the hell had I been thinking?

"Would you push me out of the way of a car?" Jojo asked.

"No. But I'd pick some pretty flowers for your funeral."

He scowled and stuck his tongue out at me. I stuck mine out right back. His middle finger came up to his face and scratched at the tip of his nose. I brought mine up and rubbed it across my eyebrow.

"Jasmine, come on," my mom moaned. "Not in front of guests."

"But he—" I started to say, pointing at Jonathan before stopping myself and shaking my head.

My brother's "hehe" was really low, but I still heard him.

"Dinner is almost ready. Are you going to shower, Jasmine?" my mom asked just as Tali approached Ivan and introduced herself. At least that's what I assumed when she hugged him.

I was watching them as I nodded, "Uh-huh."

Ivan gave my sister a smile I hadn't seen before... and it made me feel weird. Tali was a younger version of my mom. Beautiful, slim, with that red hair, pale skin, and bone structure that no plastic surgeon in the world could replicate. I couldn't think of a single time I had been out with her and hadn't caught someone staring at her or hitting on her. She was so used to it she didn't even notice it anymore. And I had stopped caring that she was so pretty a long, long time ago.

Some were just better looking than other ones. Maybe I wasn't as pretty as my sister, but I could kick her ass, and that had always made me feel better. But Tali would be the one to help me bury a body... if I ever needed to.

"Go shower then," my mom demanded. "I don't want the lasagna to burn."

I nodded and glanced at Ivan, who was still talking to my sister. "Ivan, I'll show you where the bathroom—"

"Do you want to play this next round of Jenga?" Jonathan asked him while I was still talking.

I blinked.

In the span of that blink, Ivan replied, "Sure."

What?

"Go shower, stinky, so we can eat," Jojo kept going.

Ivan looked over and must have seen the "wtf?" on my face

because that hint of his smirk-smile crept over his cotton candy pink mouth. "Yeah, stinky. Go shower," he echoed like an ass.

"He hasn't showered either," I let them know.

"I don't smell," Ivan said.

"I don't either."

"That's debatable," Tali said on a cough.

I blinked and ignored her because I knew what was going to happen if I didn't take control of the situation. "Ivan, you don't have to stay if you don't want to. I'm sure you have better things to do. I can show you where the bathroom is."

"I'd like to play Jenga," was his reply.

What was I going to do? Tell him no? I was going to regret this. I really was.

"I'll show you were the bathroom is," Jojo offered.

Shit.

"Okay," I mumbled before leaning into Ruby and whispering, "Please make sure nothing bad happens." I heard her laugh and felt her nod. Touching her head again, I gave one last look around the kitchen to see Ivan taking a seat beside James.

Then I got the fuck out of there, brushing by Ben on the way up the stairs like my ass was on fire. I took the fastest shower of my life, imagining all the random awful shit they were probably telling Ivan about me. It would be exactly what I deserved. I got dressed, looking decent for one of the only nights out of the week I had the chance to. Saturday night dinners were my period to be lazy and eat what I wanted to eat.

After rubbing aloe vera lotion into my poor, tired feet, I went down the stairs, straining my ears to listen to what the hell they could be talking about in the kitchen. The problem was, for once, it seemed like they were all whispering or not talking, because I couldn't hear anything clearly.

At least until I made it just to the doorway. Then I heard them all laughing very, very quietly.

"I don't get it, why does that make everyone laugh?" I heard Aaron, Ruby's husband, ask.

It was Jojo who answered. "Have you seen pictures of her before she hit puberty?"

That was all it took for me to know what they were talking about. Bunch of assholes. But I still didn't move.

"No," was the other man's reply.

Someone snorted, and I knew it was Tali. "Jas hit puberty really late. What was she? Like sixteen?"

I had been sixteen, but I wasn't about to confirm it.

But my mom didn't think twice about it.

"Some kids carry around baby weight for a while, you know," Tali kept going, still talking really quietly. "Jas just happened to carry it for sixteen years until puberty hit," she snickered.

"No," Aaron tried to deny, bless his heart.

"Yeah," Tali confirmed. "She was a little chunky."

Jojo snorted. "A little?"

"Aww, now y'all are just being mean," Ruby threw in. "She was so cute."

"She had such a big butt, she hated wearing leotards because they would always give her wedgies," my mom decided to share. "The more we tried to tell her to wear looser fitting clothes, the more she would wear those damn leotards and unitards, even though she was uncomfortable."

There was a snicker that I knew belonged to Ivan. "That sounds like her."

"You have no idea. That girl has always made it a point to do the opposite of what people want from her. She does it on principle. She always has. The only time a 'no' has ever stopped her was when she watched that one movie... what was it called? The hockey one she was obsessed with...."

"*The Mighty Ducks*," Ruby offered.

"*The Mighty Ducks*, right. She begged me to put her into hockey, but there weren't any hockey lessons that allowed girls. I was in the middle of arguing with this one coach to let her try out when she got invited to a birthday party at the Galleria, and the only reason I convinced her to go was because I had told her a lot of hockey players do figure skating to build up their skills."

"I didn't know that," James said.

"Oh God, she watched that movie a million times. I tried throwing the tape into the trash at least once a week, but Mom would always take it back out," Tali groaned.

"Didn't she see you do it once and you guys got into a fight over it?" Ruby asked.

That made me smile, because I could remember that day completely. We had gotten into a fight. I'd been ten. Tali had been eighteen, I think. Luckily for me, she was an extra small person, and it hadn't been so hard to try to beat her up for trying to throw my movie away.

"Yeah. She punched me in the damn nose," my sister replied.

My mom burst out laughing. "You bled so much."

"How can you laugh at me being attacked?" Tali gasped, reminding me she was the second biggest drama queen in the family.

"Your ten-year-old sister punched you in the face. Do you know how hard it was for me to not laugh when it happened? You had it coming. I warned you, she had warned you, but you did it anyway," Mom cackled, sounding like she was proud of me in a fucked-up way.

It made me smile.

"It's bullshit, Mom."

"Oh, be quiet. Ivan, you don't care that a little girl beat up her older sister, do you?" Mom asked.

There was a pause and then, "I'm sure you weren't the first person Jasmine has ever punched. Or the last."

There was another pause, and then Tali added, "No. I wasn't." Then there was a noise that sounded suspiciously like a snort. "She's always been a scrappy little shit. Wasn't she like three when she hit that kid in daycare?"

"I thought she kicked that boy that tried to look up her skirt when she was three?" Jojo asked.

"It was both—" my mom started to say before Ivan laughed.

"What?"

"She got her first warning kicking a boy who pushed her down. Then she got kicked out of that daycare when she socked that same boy when he tried to look up her skirt. To be fair, I'm pretty sure Sebastian told her to do that when the kicking thing happened."

"Then she got detention in kindergarten twice. One girl pulled on her hair, so she pulled her hair right out—"

I recognized James's laughter.

"Then another girl ate her snack, and she threatened to spit in her eye and the teacher overheard," Mom continued. "In first grade, she got suspended for giving a boy a wedgie. Jasmine said it was because he had been picking on another little boy. In second grade, she got detention twice. She spilled milk on—"

And that was enough of that. I'd been a little shit. That shouldn't surprise anyone.

"Okay, Ivan, Aaron, and James don't need to know all the

times I got in trouble when I was little," I said, as I finally came into the kitchen.

My mom had taken a seat between Ivan and Ruby and shot me a huge smile. "I was just getting to the good stuff."

"I wouldn't mind hearing everything else," James piped up with a wink.

I sighed and stopped behind Ruby. "Mom can tell you about ages five through ten next Saturday."

Mom pushed her stool back. "Let's eat, children." Then she glanced at Ivan. "Are you eating with us? It isn't Gold Medal approved, but—" She shrugged. "—it's good."

I should have known Mom would invite him to stay and eat too. Shit.

Ivan seemed to think about it for a moment as I stood there on the brink of praying he would say no, before glancing in my direction and asking, "Are you eating?"

Fuck. "Yes. It's my cheat meal." I wasn't sure why I'd explained that.

Those glacier-colored eyes lingered on my face for a moment. "Okay." Then he turned to my mom. "If you have enough, I'll stay, but if you don't, I understand."

Mom snickered. "We have enough. Don't worry about it." Then it was her turn to pause. "We eat in the kitchen."

Ivan blinked. "Okay."

"That was awkward," Tali mumbled before shoving her stool back and getting up. "I'm ready to eat."

Like we had done it for the last twenty-plus years, plates were grabbed and handed over. Then we filed in line to grab food from the pans Mom and Tali spread out on the counter. I waited in the back for Ivan while he went around the island, and I let him go in front of me.

"I'm not really surprised you were raising hell since daycare," was the first thing he whispered.

I rolled my eyes. "I've had a lot of practice since then."

He raised the eyebrows on that annoying face of his. "I'll keep that in mind next time someone bothers me."

Huh.

Was this us trying to be different? I wasn't sure. "Okay." Then I kicked him in the calf. Gently. Mostly. "Move up the line. I'm starving."

He took a step backward, glancing over his shoulder to see he was directly behind James, who was still in line, before looking back at me and whispering, "You don't care I'm here, do you?"

Yes. I definitely cared. I didn't know what to do with it. With him. With Ivan Lukov who had less than an hour ago said we should try get along for some reason.

After all the things we had said to each other and all the things we had done to each other, this man I thought I knew wanted us to try and be friendly.

I didn't like not knowing what to do or how to react.

But I didn't say any of that shit to him, mostly because my nosey-ass family was around, and I knew at least a couple of them were eavesdropping. Instead, I lied and went with, "I don't care."

He narrowed his eyes. "You're sure?"

I really was a horrible liar. I raised my eyebrows and figured there was no point in trying to play it off. "Would it matter?"

That made his pink mouth curve up at the edges... slightly freaking me out. "Nope."

That's what I thought.

"Your family is funny," he kept going.

"Sure they are."

"You already know mine, it's only fair."

"Fair for what?"

"For us. Being friends."

I didn't even realize my hand had gone to my bracelet, picking at the plate between the links, until the metal dug into the pad of my thumb from how hard I had subconsciously started playing with it. Glancing around, I made sure no one in my family was at least looking at us when I whispered, "I don't get what all this being friends thing means."

He blinked. "What do you mean?"

I didn't look at him as I said, "What it sounds like. I don't know what you're expecting out of me."

"Whatever friends do."

It was my turn to blink. And because no one was looking at us, I kept on telling him the truth, because it wasn't like it was a secret. Or that I was ashamed. Because I wasn't. "I get that. But you know your sister is the only real friend, that I'm not related to, that I've managed to keep over the years." I was proud of it. I didn't have time for other people's bullshit. I thought that was one of my most admirable traits, honestly.

All Ivan did was look at me.

I lifted a shoulder.

Then he blinked again. "Have you talked to her recently?"

I shook my head. "You?"

"No." He turned around and took a step forward just as he made it to the counter. Over his shoulder, he asked, "Did you not tell her we're partners then?"

Shit. "No." I paused. I had assumed he would. "You haven't told her either?"

"No."

"Your parents?"

"They're in Russia. I haven't spoken to them since worlds. Mother has sent me a few picture messages, but that's been all our communication."

Double shit. "I thought you would have told them."

"I thought you would have told Karina."

"I don't talk to her as much as I used to. She's busy with medical school."

I could only manage to see the back of Ivan's head as he nodded, slowly and thoughtfully, like he was thinking the same thing I was. And his next words confirmed it. "She's going to kill us."

Because she was. She sure as fuck was.

"Call her and tell her," I tried to throw it on him.

"You call and tell her," he scoffed, not looking at me.

I poked him in the back. "She's your sister."

"She's your only friend."

"Asshole," I muttered. "Let's flip a coin to see who should do it."

That time he did glance at me. "No."

No. Ass.

"I'm not doing it."

"Me neither."

"Don't be a pussy and do it," I hissed, trying to keep my voice low.

His snicker made me frown. "Sounds like I'm not the only pussy," he returned.

I opened my mouth and closed it. He got me. He fucking got me.

"Question. Do you two ever agree on anything?" Jojo asked, from where he stood a few feet ahead of Ivan, in front of the counter holding a plate piled high with food.

See? Nosey. Eavesdropper.

"No," I answered at the same time Ivan said, "Yes."

The slow smile that crept over my brother's face told me he'd heard everything. Or at least mostly everything. "I wasn't *trying* to listen, but I couldn't help it. If you're both too scared to call Karina, why don't you just video call her while you're here, so she can't get mad, or if she does, it's at both of you at the same time. Eh? Eh?" he offered, like him listening to something that had nothing to do with his life wasn't a big deal.

And it wasn't. I expected no less from him or from anyone else I was related to. I didn't think my dad was nosey, but... I didn't know for sure, and honestly, it didn't matter. He was never around anyway.

What I did focus on was that Jojo had a point. And Ivan must have recognized that he did because he glanced at me and raised his eyebrows. Did I want to worry about Karina getting mad because neither one of us had told her something pretty important? No.

But...

"It's a good idea, if you ask me," Jojo mumbled before walking past us to keep going to the seat he'd left at the island.

Ivan moved forward in the line and immediately got busy scooping food onto his plate when he said, just loud enough for only me to hear, "It's not a bad idea."

"It's not, but don't let him hear you say that. He'll write it down in his journal and bring it up for the next five years if you do."

The tall man in front of me handed me the serving knife for the lasagna. I grabbed the portion I wanted that would fill me up but wouldn't be so much it made me gain ten pounds after watching my diet for the last few weeks. After that, I picked two slices of garlic bread and a small portion of salad because, even though it was a cheat meal, I still needed vegetables.

By the time I turned around, there were only two mismatched stools that didn't have an ass in them, and they were beside each other; Ivan took one and I took the other, sandwiching myself in between him and Ruby. I eyeballed him as he reached for the paper towel roll someone had left in the center of the island. He ripped off one, let his hand hover there for a moment and then ripped another one. Just as I started to cut into my lasagna, something white dropped onto my lap.

It was one of the paper towels.

"I wasn't sure if you could reach them," he whispered, being a smart-ass.

I glanced at him out of the corner of my eye, my hands still above my plate of food.

"You know, because you're short."

Biting the inside of my cheek to keep from physically reacting, I muttered, "Yeah, I know what you meant." But mostly, I looked at the napkin and told myself that he had done something nice for no reason. He hadn't spit in it. I'd watched. But I still didn't know what to do with the gesture other than say, "Thank you," that alone almost hurt. Just almost.

He must have known it because out of the corner of my eye, I saw his upper body turn, and I was pretty sure he raised his eyebrows like he couldn't believe that I'd just said the t-word.

I couldn't believe I had just said the t-word again either. I'd already said it once today. I didn't want to hit my quota.

"So, Ivan, how are practices going?" my mom asked from her spot across the table while I was still trying to figure out what was happening and what I was doing and what Ivan's game plan was for this "friends" shit. "All Jasmine tells me is that they're going well."

Shoving a forkful of lasagna in my mouth, I shot my mom a look. Crybaby. She wanted a report, but there wasn't anything to tell her. She just didn't believe me for some reason. She knew I usually always ended up telling her everything.

"They're going well. We haven't started any choreography yet; we're still trying to get other kinks worked out. We'll more than likely get the choreographers out the first week of June," the man beside me replied easily, his hands resting on each side of his plate, one holding a knife, the other a fork.

There were a few nods around the table, so I bit off a piece of garlic bread and watched my family members to see who was going to continue giving him the third degree. Because that's what this was, and that's what was going to happen. It's what I'd been trying to avoid. It didn't matter that he wasn't my boyfriend; he was just of an important figure in my life, if not even more important. Actually, he was definitely more important than any of those wastes of time.

"That's good," my mom replied when I was halfway done chewing my food. Then she smiled, her face eerily calm and pleasant, and I knew whatever was about to come out of her mouth was going to be something off. I'd swear even Ben beside her must have seen it or sensed it because I was pretty sure he muttered, "Oh no," under his breath.

"Why are you only pairing up with Jasmine for a year?" she asked with that creepy-calm smile.

I snorted, which made the bread in my mouth fly to the back of my throat, and I started choking as Ruby hissed, "Mom!"

I choked some more, the wet grain stuck *right fucking there* in my windpipe or wherever the hell it was and not going anywhere. Something heavy and big slapped me on the back hard, loosening up the bread. Grabbing the paper towel Ivan had just handed me, I spit the clump of food into it and wheezed, then coughed. My eyes watered just as someone shoved a glass of water into my chest, and I took it almost blindly, gulping it down then coughing into my hand some more until I had it under control.

What had to be Ivan's big-ass hand smacked me on the back again, just as hard as he had the first time. "I'm fine," I coughed out.

I wasn't surprised when he gave my back another hard smack.

"You okay?" Ruby asked beside me.

Taking another sip of water, I nodded, blinking away the tears that had popped into them while I'd been choking.

"So?" my mom asked, with that way of hers that didn't surprise me.

"Ahh—" Ivan started to say before I held up my hand and shook my head.

Did I want to hear the answer? As much of a coward as it made me, no, I didn't, at least sure as hell not in front of my family. "Nope, you don't have to answer that." I glanced at my mom and shrugged my shoulders. "No, woman. It's his business."

Mom made the same face she always did when she thought I was being a chicken. Turning her head back to face forward, she decided to go a different route. "How are your parents then, Ivan? I haven't seen them since their Christmas party a few months ago."

"They're visiting family in Moscow, but they're doing great," he answered.

"Your grandfather is doing better? Your mother had mentioned that he'd had a heart attack last fall."

Those wide shoulders went up half an inch. "He's doing better, but he's a stubborn old man who refuses to accept he's in his eighties and has people that run his companies for him now. He isn't supposed to be under stressful situations anymore but—" The warmest smile came over his face, and I didn't know what to do with that either. "—no one can really tell him what to do."

Across the table, I heard Jojo mutter, "We have one of those in the family," which was followed by James turning to him and shaking his head to get him to shut up.

Me, on the other hand, I just let the comment go. We had more than one of those in the family, and he damn well knew it. Starting with the woman asking all the questions.

"Some people don't know how to retire or take it easy, that doesn't surprise me," my mom responded.

Ivan nodded.

"They told me he wanted you to move to Russia," she threw out.

And I stopped the cutting motion I was doing with my knife to take in her words.

Ivan move to Russia? My mom hadn't told me about that.

Then again, why would she? Before all this, there had been no reason for us to bring Ivan up. She knew I wasn't his greatest fan. She also knew he wasn't my biggest fan.

But...

Ivan move to Russia? He'd been born in the United States. His sister had told me the story once years ago, about how her parents had immigrated because of threats against their family because of Karina's grandfather's businesses. The couple hadn't been married that long, but they didn't want their children in danger and decided to start over, far away from one of the wealthiest men in Russia.

Once, and only once, Karina had mentioned how disappointed her grandfather had been that his gold-medal-winning grandson hadn't competed for the country the older man had lived in his entire life. She had brought up how he had tried to bribe Ivan to move and how it hadn't worked. Meanwhile, Karina had laughed and said she would take the money and go if he offered it to her... but he hadn't. Because Karina wasn't a talented athlete who could make her country proud. All she was was a smart person with a big heart who wanted to be a doctor. No big deal.

"He asks me every other year to move," Ivan let her know, his tone unfailingly polite.

But I could tell it sounded off.

And maybe he was the last person in the world that I thought needed to be babied or protected, but if anyone knew what it was like to be forced to talk about something that you would absolutely rather not, it was me. And these people were my family. So, in a move that I wasn't going to overthink, I decided to get them to pay attention to me even though I was more than likely going to regret it.

"We're doing a photo shoot in a couple of days," I dropped vaguely, already regretting trying to be nice.

It was James that asked, "For a website or the paper?"

I shoved another piece of lasagna into my mouth and waited until I'd chewed most of it before replying with, "A magazine."

"Which magazine?" he asked. "I'll make everyone I know buy one."

Everyone he knew? Fuck it. What did I have to be ashamed about? Not a goddamn thing. "TSN," I replied, referring to The Sports Network's magazine.

It was my sister's husband that spoke up next. "Rubes got me a subscription to it for Christmas."

I closed my eye, reminding myself about the same fact that had gotten me to agree to do the shoot in the first place: everyone had butt cheeks. It wasn't like they were going to make me bend over and spread them wide.

But...

"Yeah, you might want to skip the page we'll be on," I said to my brother-in-law, mostly because, while I didn't care if James saw my ass—because he obviously didn't put a lot of weight into looks since he was married to Dumbo—Aaron seeing it felt different to me. Maybe because he was straight. And really, really handsome. And I wasn't sure how Ruby would feel about it.

And like the way that was my mom, she suspiciously asked, "Why's that?"

I shoved some more lasagna into my mouth before telling them all the truth. "Because I'm going to be butt-ass naked, and so is Ivan."

I saw Ivan glance at me, and I thought I might have seen a partial smile come on his face.

"For the Anatomy issue?" Aaron asked, apparently knowing exactly what it would be for.

I nodded at him before biting off another piece of garlic bread.

"That's great, Jas," James piped up after a second. "Do you care if I get it?"

Beside him, my brother snorted. "That pervert won't care."

Oh, here we went. "Just because I'm not a shy little shit, doesn't mean I'm a pervert." Then moving my attention to James, I added, "And no, I don't care. The worst they'll show is my butt...." At least that's what I assumed. There was no way they were going to show my nipples on a magazine. Would they? I thought Coach Lee had confirmed they wouldn't, but now I couldn't remember for sure. I turned to Ivan and asked, "Right?"

"See how she sounds disappointed that the most they'll show on the magazine is her booty?" Jojo asked James, making a face.

I ignored him. Everyone knew my brother, for all the things he was, was very self-conscious. He had scars from an injury back when he'd been a marine. For all I knew, he might have always been a prude, but I wasn't sure. Mom and I thought it was cute he was so conservative, but I sure as hell would never tell him that.

Ivan made a face that told me he wanted to make a joke but was going to keep it to himself. "Do you want them to show more?" the idiot beside me asked.

I blinked at him.

"It's pretty PG-13 from what I've seen," he said. "No one other than the photographer and staff will see... everything."

Besides him.

I wasn't ashamed of my body at all. Maybe I wasn't as lean as I would get closer to competition, but I'd been watching what I ate since we'd gotten into this, and I wasn't embarrassed about what genes I'd been given. I was vain, but not *that* vain.

I still wasn't sure about this idiot beside me seeing me naked regardless of the conversation we'd had weeks ago when Coach Lee had brought it up to me.

"Mom, you're not going to tell her not to do it?" my brother asked.

"Why would I do that?" Mom raised an eyebrow as she took a sip from the giant glass of wine she had pulled out of nowhere like a magician.

"Because." Jojo shrugged. "Your daughter is going to be naked on a magazine where millions of people can see her in her birthday suit."

"So?" was a response that didn't totally surprise me. Mom still wore bikinis, stretch marks and sixty-year-old skin be damned. "What's the problem with that?"

Jojo's dark brown eyes slid from side to side before he said, "She's going to be naked?"

Mom's blink made me wonder if that was what mine looked like. "Don't you get naked?"

Jojo groaned, leaning back against his stool. "Not for millions of people to see and jerk off to!"

Something about his words *clicked*.

And I remembered what would be the problem with "millions of people" seeing me naked.

Shit.

Shit, shit, shit.

"Are you saying there's something wrong with your sister's body?"

"That's not what I'm trying to say."

"If it was Sebastian doing the photo shoot, would you tell me anything?" Mom asked, taking another sip or five of her wine, but I was too busy still thinking about Jojo's comment. About the people I wouldn't want to see me in my birthday suit.

You already said yes, I reminded myself. I had already said yes. What was I going to do? Stop living my life because of some assholes?

No. But I wanted to.

But I couldn't. I shoved my worries aside for later. I didn't need anyone reading my face and noticing I was worried about something I didn't want them to know about.

Jojo sighed, then mumbled, "No."

That had Mom winking. "Then don't be a hypocrite or sexist. The human body is a natural thing. What she's doing isn't going to be sexualized... is it, Ivan?"

Ivan's leg beneath the island hit mine, but he got out, "No, ma'am. It's for art."

"See? It's for art. David is naked. The Venus de Milo is almost naked. In my younger days, I had a boyfriend that was an artist. I sat for him once or twice. Naked as the day I was born, Jojo." She smiled. "Do you think your sister isn't as good as Ivan? You think she doesn't deserve—"

"Oh God. I'm sorry," Jonathan rushed out, shaking his head, like he finally remembered who the hell he was talking to. "I shouldn't have said anything."

"Your sister is a beautiful, strong woman who has done things millions of other people can't do. Her body is honed from thousands of hours of practice. She has nothing to be ashamed of. We all have nipples. I breastfed you and you didn't complain then."

About halfway through, Jojo had started shaking his head quickly like *no, please no*. That's what he got.

"I'm sorry, I said I was sorry. Pretend I didn't say anything...," he said.

"There's nothing to be ashamed of—"

"Mom, I said I'm sorry."

Ivan's leg hit mine again, but I was too busy trying not to laugh at Jojo's facial expression to react.

My mom ignored my brother. "Breasts are natural—"

"I know, Mom. I know they are. I love and respect women. Breasts. I just don't want them in my face—"

"They represent womanhood, beauty—"

I'm pretty sure Jojo started choking. "Mom, please—"

"It's close-minded, sexist mentalities that think just because we have vaginas and breasts that women are the weaker sex—"

"You're not weak. None of you are weak, I swear—"

"Do you know what it's like—"

Ivan's leg hit mine, and I couldn't help but twist my upper body enough to face him, pressing my lips together so that I wouldn't start laughing. Two glassy gray-blue eyes met mine, and it was obvious he was trying not to laugh too. Especially not when my mom went off on how degrading it was to not be seen as an equal.

"Women marched, rallied, and were assaulted to make

your mother and your sister human beings that weren't their husbands' properties." Mom eventually reared back the conversation after a couple of minutes. "If your sister wants to show off her God given body, she can, and I'm not going to stop her, and you're not going to stop her, and nobody is going to stop her."

She then pointed her fork and blinked. "I taught you better than that, Jonathan Arvin."

I almost lost it at her busting out his middle name.

Jojo had tipped his head up minutes ago, and it still hadn't moved as he moaned, "You did. I'm sorry. I'm so sorry."

Mom smirked and shot me a wink that made me laugh. "That's what I thought. We can buy every issue around and make sure it sells out. I'll frame it and put it on the mantle."

I didn't know about all that, but I kept my mouth shut.

Aaron chuckled. "I don't think there's going to be a problem making it sell out. It usually does well."

"See? Everyone appreciates nudity. There's nothing wrong with it. It isn't like you didn't watch pornography when you thought I didn't know."

That had all of us moaning.

"Don't ever say pornography again," I told her, trying to erase that word coming out of my mom's mouth from my memory.

"You be quiet," Mom said. "Jasmine Imelda."

And I kept quiet before she turned it around on me even more and brought up something I'd done or said in the past. On that note, I jumped on the opening to change the subject or risk her going on another rant that I secretly loved but wanted to spare everyone else that wasn't used to it from.

"Do you want to call Karina and spill the beans?" I asked Ivan all of a sudden.

Jojo made a gasping, squeaking sound from across the island, like he was now revived.

Ivan on the other hand, made a weird face like he didn't get why I changed the subject all of a sudden. Maybe he wouldn't give me any credit or realize what I'd done, but it wouldn't be the first time. "Sure?"

His "sures" always felt more like "I guess," but that was just part of him.

I wasn't going to die from cold lasagna and garlic bread, I told myself, eyeing what was left of my food regretfully. Pulling my phone out of my pocket, I set it on the island and went to my contacts icon, finding Karina's name at close to the top; I hit the call button.

"What are you doing?" Mom asked.

"No one has told Karina that Ivan and Jas are partners," my brother replied, setting his fork and knife on top of his plate, following it by lacing his fingers together and shoving his hands under his chin with his elbows propped on the counter, back to normal.

I put the phone on speaker just as it started dialing. Chances were, she might not answer. But chances were she might. I didn't know her schedule anymore. The last time we had talked, she'd called me.

"Call Karina! Call Karina!" Jojo started chanting quietly, followed up by my mom throwing in her voice too.

"Call her!" Tali's nosey ass piped up with her mouth full.

"I am," I whispered, watching the screen as it showed the call was still connecting.

I could see Ivan glance at me, but he didn't say anything.

Just as the phone made one last dialing attempt, one second before it would have given the last beep it needed before I could leave a voice mail...

"Hello?" a panting voice came over the line.

Ivan and I definitely eyed each other then. Why the hell was she breathing like that?

"Jasmine, you there?" Karina's familiar voice came over the line.

"Yeah. Is this a bad time?"

"I was on the treadmill and hopped off as fast as I could," she explained, still breathing hard. "I'm sorry. One second."

My brown eyes met Ivan's blue ones in what I figured was relief that she hadn't been doing other shit that brothers and sisters shouldn't know about.

"Okay, I'm back. Sorry. I had to get some water. What's going on? You finally remembered you used to have a best friend or what?" she teased, still breathing hard.

"You have my number too."

She made a tsking sound. "I've been so busy—"

"Whatever you say. Look, I'm having dinner with my family right now—"

"Am I on speakerphone?"

I paused. "Yes."

Then she paused. "Are you pregnant?"

Across the table, Tali snorted, and I gave her a nasty look. "Why the hell would you think that?"

"Why else would you have me on speakerphone?" she demanded before adding, "And hello, my other family. I miss you all."

"Hi, Karina!" Tali, my mom, and Jojo each called out, with Ruby adding in a lower greeting.

"Hi!" she cried happily before her voice went back to normal. "But, Jas, no kidding, are you pregnant?"

"No," I snapped. "Of course not."

"Oh, blessed Jesus. I thought your life was about to be over. Phew."

"I have five kids," my mom chipped in.

"Not you, Mom," Karina replied, calling my mom the same thing she always had: Mom. "But Jasmine's would. Anyway, why are you calling then if it isn't just to tell your best friend hi and that you haven't forgotten she's alive?"

I rolled my eyes and mouthed to Ivan, *that's your sister.* "I've been busy and forgot to tell you something," I started.

There was a moment before, "Go on."

"So did Ivan from what I learned today."

There was another moment. "Ivan? My brother, Ivan?"

"The only one, genius," I said. "In March, he asked me to pair up with him to be his new partner."

She didn't respond. Not for ten seconds, not for twenty or thirty. It might have even been a whole minute of silence with Ivan and me sharing a look before Karina's loud-ass laugh came through the speaker.

"*Oh my word,*" she pretty much shrieked into the phone.

"Why is she laughing?" I heard Aaron ask Ruby.

My sister shrugged.

"*Ahhh!*" Karina pretty much started screaming her laugh.

"Stop laughing," I called out to her, knowing damn well she was too into it to pay attention to me.

"*You and Ivan?*" she shrieked.

"He's right here," I let her know.

"Hi, Rina," he greeted.

She started laughing her ass off. Again.

"*I can't believe it!*" She began howling all over again.

"Who hurt her to make her this way?" I asked Ivan without even realizing it.

"She was born like that," he replied, his eyes glued to the blank screen.

"This is going better than I thought," James said.

Jojo sighed. "I'm disappointed. I thought she was going to get mad you guys forgot about her."

"*The two most stubborn people I've ever known skating together?*" Karina shrieked. "*BAHAHAHAHA!*"

"You have problems," I said.

"*Please! Please! Tell me someone has recorded your practices together. Ooh! Tell me you're doing a live video of them. I would watch every minute. Give me all your competition dates in advance. It'll be the* Hunger Games *on ice. I'll buy everyone in the family front row seats,*" she cried out, her voice full of laughter.

I rolled my eyes and shook my head. "We're getting..." What? Along? It was a little too soon for that shit. "We're doing fine."

"*This is like my dream come true fourteen years too late.*" There was a break and then more, "*You and Ivan! BAHAHAHA!*"

I wasn't sure why this surprised me... but it did. Of course she would think this was hilarious.

Two years ago, I would have thought the same thing.

Me and Ivan. Having dinner. At my house. With my family. Trying to be friends. Whatever that meant.

But here we were.

And apparently, Karina was eating this shit up.

CHAPTER 10

"I DON'T KNOW IF I WANT TO DO THIS ANYMORE," I SAID TO Coach Lee a week later.

A week after I hadn't been able to stop thinking about all the reasons why doing this was a stupid idea, including but not limited to flashing all my shit at Ivan.

Our one-week long friendship had gone... well. We hadn't said anything insulting to each other in that time period. He had even smiled at me once when I'd agreed with him that we had done something right when Coach Lee had claimed the opposite.

It was fine. Totally fine.

And maybe that was part of the reason why I didn't want him to start teasing me. At least while I didn't have clothes on. I didn't give a shit what the photographer or her staff thought... but Ivan was the only one who had the power to genuinely piss me off.

So there I was, after a full night of stressing out about the shoot. Galina would have said I was antsy, but I wasn't antsy. Just... stressed. About the consequences. Long term and short term. With Ivan and without.

It wasn't like I'd been stoked about doing it in the first place, and if my gut said this was a shitty idea... there was a reason for it. Every time I had ignored my gut feeling before, I'd paid for it.

So...

Coach Lee turned to face me from where we were standing off to the side of the ice at the nearly empty LC. Her face instantly shuttered, and her mouth twisted to the side, but it was the fingers she immediately started wiggling that gave her away. That and the tight smile she forced onto her lips as she nearly croaked, "Is there something I should know?"

Was there something she should know?

Nerves, real nerves, bad nerves that made my insides twist up and my stomach *almost* ache, pretty much took over my entire body, but all I could do was shrug. "I don't know if I want to do this with Ivan after all," I told her. "It's one thing for us to do all our lifts fully clothed, but the more I think about having to do this naked... I don't know," I partially lied.

Because I did know. I knew what might have been the biggest reason. I was hesitating again.

Three days ago, I'd had to start deleting comments and messages from random guys on my Picturegram page. It had only been two comments, but two was too many. They said they would "wreck me" and "tear (my) ass up." Then there had been the private messages, which had been two dick pics and another asking me to post a video of my bare feet. Which then got me thinking about what my brother had said during dinner days before about strangers jerking off to my pictures.

I wasn't a prude, but I also wasn't a fan of living my life, posting pictures of one of my ballet lessons with Ivan that Coach Lee had e-mailed me—for that specific purpose—and then dealing with those kinds of comments and messages. I was no stranger to dicks. But I wanted it to be my choice when

I saw them. I definitely wasn't a fucking fan of remembering when other people had sent me pictures and videos so much worse. Pictures and videos that had made me lose sleep because of how helpless they had made me feel. How dirty.

And that's what had started to happen unless I was exhausted. I had started to lose sleep. More and more sleep.

Until I was here, at this point, stressing over stuff like that happening more and more. I didn't want to see that kind of shit. All I wanted was figure skating. I didn't care about the rest.

But that's not how stuff worked nowadays.

A funny expression came over Coach Lee's face as she took me and my words in. "Did Ivan say something?"

Shit. I hadn't thought this through well enough, had I? The only thing I could do was be vague. Just a little. Just enough. "He always says something, but that's not it."

She narrowed her eyes. "You know what I mean. Did he say anything about doing the shoot with you? Because I'm going to be honest, that doesn't seem like it would bother you."

Was I that obvious? Because she was right, Ivan's comments didn't usually bother me. Aggravate me, yeah. Make me want to kill him, yeah. But bother? Not so much. But being naked in front of someone, especially someone like Ivan who was constantly judging with those clear blue eyes, felt like a power exchange that left me with nothing. He would know something about me so many people didn't. And this person teased me over everything.

"I don't know if I want to stand in front of him naked. That's all. If I did it by myself, it wouldn't be a big deal. Even total strangers, sure, but to do it in front of him when I have to see him all the time, I don't know."

Her hand went up to her eyes, and she pinched the bridge

of her nose, clearly exasperated before finally nodding slowly. "Okay. All right. Let me go talk to him and talk to the photographer and see what we can come up with."

For a moment, I thought about apologizing for changing my mind, but fuck that. I didn't want to show Ivan of all people my naked body. I'd bet nobody else here would want to either. It was my choice. My decision. My body.

I wasn't about to say I was sorry for being an inconvenience, because I wasn't.

But I did feel just a little bad as Coach Lee turned on her heel, rubbing at her neck, and headed where the photographer was standing with Ivan and an assistant, deep in conversation. They had come in early to make a couple of sets on the ice, one with a gray background and another with a white one, surrounded by lights. It was fancy.

I made myself watch as Coach Lee's mouth moved and then watched as Ivan's chin slid forward a moment before his eyes sliced to my direction before focusing back on Lee to listen to whatever else she was saying.

And I couldn't say I was totally surprised when maybe a minute or two later, Ivan began shaking his head, clearly ignoring whatever Lee was saying, and started skating toward me, the knot at his robe the only thing keeping me from seeing more than just a slice of his thighs, calves, and chest as he did it.

"I'm not doing it," I said before he got a word out. "If you want to do it by yourself, go for it. I'll do it by myself too. But I don't want to do it together."

Something tight snapped across his shoulders the second the last sentence was out of my mouth. But it was the way his face went serious, his rectangular jaw tight, mouth pursed and eyebrows heavy, that really became visible.

"I don't want to do it, Ivan, and you're not going to guilt trip me into it, all right? I know it's a big issue, but I don't want to do it with you."

Those pale gray-blue eyes hadn't moved off of me as he slid to a stop at the boards and paused there at the entrance, staring at me like he didn't even know who I was. He was watching me closely as he asked, slowly, drawing out each letter, "Why?"

I didn't even think about it. "Because I don't want to have my tits and vagina in your face." *There*. Done.

The breath he took was so ragged I could see it in his chest. "You were bragging about not being self-conscious a few days ago, and now you're backing out?" he asked, watching me a little too closely. "You'll do it alone but not with me?"

When he said it like that...

"*Yeah*," I agreed, nodding.

"Because of me?"

"Yes, because of you." Friends were honest with each other. He couldn't fault me for that. Maybe I wasn't being completely honest but it was something.

He blinked, still taking me in. "They want us to do it together, not separate."

I shrugged both my shoulders, totally unapologetic. "Well, there's this thing called Photoshop; they can probably blend us in so it looks like we're together," I suggested.

He blinked again, his jaw grinding from side to side.

I just looked at him.

Ivan blinked at me, and I blinked right back.

One of those big, strong hands that could hold my hundred-plus pound ass all by itself over his head drifted to the back of his neck. His jaw twitched again. His breathing slowed. His Adam's apple bobbed. "What did I do that you don't want to do it with me?" he asked slowly. "You talk shit right back. I thought we agreed to be friends." Those eyes drifted across my face, which was covered in makeup that had taken the artist almost an hour to apply. "We had dinner together," he reminded me, as if I'd forgotten he'd spent three hours in my mom's kitchen, playing Jenga with my family, eating lasagna, gobbling down the smallest sliver of chocolate cake while I'd eaten three times the amount because why the hell not.

He'd gotten me a paper towel—maybe because he genuinely thought I couldn't reach across the table, maybe not. He'd driven me home. He'd asked me to be his friend, even though the more I thought about it, the more I figured he wasn't so familiar with what the hell that meant.

Gentle. Be better.

So, I tried. "Ivan, I have to look at you every day. Isn't that reason enough to not want to be naked in front of you?" I asked, keeping my voice as far away from aggressive as possible as I tried to be an adult.

He didn't hesitate. "I don't care if you see me naked."

Shit.

Okay. I was going to have to go at this more directly. "Well, I don't care if the whole world sees me naked either, but I don't want you to see it, all right? Can you respect that?"

"But why?" he asked, honestly sounding confused.

Exasperation, or maybe frustration, hit me hard. Real hard. The last thing I'd expected was for him to want an explanation. "Because. I already told you."

"No, you didn't."

I blinked. "Yes, I did."

"No. You. Didn't."

"Yes. I. Did."

"No. I want you to tell me. What did I do over the last week to make you not want to do this anymore?"

He wasn't going to let this go. I tried not to be a dick. But he wanted an explanation, so I gave it to him. "Ivan, do you think I want you to tease me about skipping puberty after you've seen my tits? Because I don't. Not even a little bit, all right? Is that what you want to hear? That I don't want you looking at me and judging me when I have to see your face all the time? I like myself just fine. I don't want to listen to you make fun of me, of things I can't change. I have little tits. Okay. We both know that. What if you think my nipples are too big, or you think they're too small, or you'll laugh at my stretch marks, or tell me you get where all my weight comes from! My thighs!"

"*What?*"

I shrugged at him again, my stomach giving this uncomfortable roll as I told him more of the tiny truth I was sharing. "I like my body, all right? I don't want you to make me not. I know I'm not...." I shook my head, not finishing the sentence. "I'm good with who I am and what I look like, and I'll trim down a little more before the season starts."

I wasn't sure if I hadn't noticed it gradually happening, or if it happened in the blink of an eye, but at some point, his face had gone pale, and in the next blink, he was off the ice, going around the barrier and standing two feet away from me, looking totally and completely stricken, like I'd stabbed him. "*Jasmine*," he said my name slowly and in almost a hiss, for one of the rare times he didn't call me Meatball. "Come on."

I just looked at him. "No *come on*, Ivan. I hate the fact that I care what you think, okay? You don't need to rub it in. I'm trying... to be friends with you," I tried to make a joke, but it didn't work when nothing about him changed even a little bit.

If anything, Ivan looked surprised. "Jasmine," he repeated my name, his voice low and almost hoarse.

"I'm not doing it," it was my turn to repeat. "Sorry. Nothing you say or do will get me to change my mind, so get out there, tiger, and get your part over with, so I can do mine. I'm sure everything will look fine, and if it doesn't... sorry not sorry." If I could tell him the other half of the truth, he would understand. I knew it.

But I didn't.

Ivan though, didn't get over there. He didn't move. Didn't look away. Ivan just stared down at me, his breathing even, the smooth skin between his pecs clearly visible in the V-shape of the robe he had on. Those blue eyes bounced all over my face, and I hated it. I hated the fact that I'd admitted I wasn't about to strip down because of him, because I didn't want to hear teasing later on about the shape of my barely B-cups or the shape and size of my ass or the million other things he could nitpick. Because there were a lot of them. I wasn't perfect. I wasn't my mom or Tali or Ruby.

"Meatball," he said, still speaking slowly, still not moving. He struggled with a swallow. Struggled with his words, if the strange expression on his face said anything. "I'm just fucking with you when I make fun of you," he claimed, watching me. "You know that, don't you?"

I glanced away and nodded, barely suppressing the urge to roll my eyes. "Yeah, I know you're fucking with me. I can handle it. Sometimes...." God, it pained me to tell him this, but fuck it. "Sometimes, you almost make me laugh. But I don't want to do this with you naked. It feels too personal now. We're too... close."

I heard more than saw him exhale. But what I felt was him taking another step closer to me. "The only reason I give you so much shit is because you were a pain in the ass, and then you were the only one who dished it back to me. You know you're beautiful."

I snickered and rolled my eyes that time, because *come the fuck on*. Really? Now I knew he was trying too hard. Please.

God. "If you think flattering me is going to convince me to do this, you don't know me at all, Lukov."

"Not Lukov. Ivan," he replied easily, his tone so gentle, it made me uncomfortable, because that wasn't what I wanted from him. Much less what I expected from him. "I'm sure you're perfect under there."

I snorted that time, because goddamn, he was laying the bullshit on thick to convince me. Jesus.

But he kept going. "I'm sure there's nothing under your robe that wouldn't give every man here a hard-on. Some of the women too, I bet."

I side-eyed him using the h-word and shook myself out of it. He was full of shit. I knew that. He knew that. Even Coach Lee would have known that if she could hear him now. Who the hell did he think he was talking to? Someone who hadn't known him for over a decade and been the focus of his petty, asshole comments that entire time? Now he was just pissing me off. "Would you shut up? I don't need to hear you saying this, all right?" I snapped.

His hand touched my wrist, and by some miracle, I didn't jerk it out of his reach. "I'm not just saying all this," he said in a tone so quiet, so... I don't know, tender or shit, that it made me uncomfortable. I didn't think anyone had ever spoken to me like that before. Not even James, the nicest guy in the world. Ivan kept going. "I'm just giving you shit when I tell you that you haven't gone through puberty. Come on," he insisted, still using that voice that I didn't know what to do with. What to think of. "I didn't think you were that sensitive."

I blinked. "I'm not that sensitive."

"*Jasmine*," he breathed out, wrapping his fingers around my wrist tightly but not painfully. That dark head of hair and that flawless face that might have had makeup but might have not, dipped closer to me as he asked, "What the hell is going on with you right now?"

"Nothing," I insisted.

"You're full of shit," he claimed. "You know who you are and what you are. I'm not about to fucking tell you and blow up your ego even bigger than it already is, cut me some slack," he almost barked out. "I want to do this shoot with you, not by myself. With you. *As a team.* It'll be great for both of us coming into the season."

"I know who I am and have a big ego, *sure. Okay.* Look, just go get it over with, and I'll go after you. I don't want to talk about this anymore. I don't feel like arguing right now."

The second the two hands landed on my shoulders, I jumped, unexpectedly. And when his mouth lowered to where his lips hovered just over mine, I definitely didn't move either. We were close seven hours a day, six days a week. There were no physical boundaries between each other because there couldn't be.

But this...

This I didn't know what to do with. I couldn't think of the last time anyone had been this close to me.

"I'm being fucking serious," he whispered with all the strength and determination in the world.

I couldn't help but peek up at him, that's how strong and demanding his tone was.

He was looking down at me with that fucking face, looking more serious than I'd ever seen before, even right before competing. "I'd never make fun of you."

I frowned.

He shook my wrist, gently, covering the spot where my bracelet usually was. I'd taken it off and left it in my locker. "I wouldn't when you're naked," he said to me. "And who would make fun of you without clothes on? I bet none of those men out there have ever seen legs and an ass that launch a person in the air like yours do."

I wasn't going to pick at that comment with a stick. Instead, I blinked at him. "Why are you looking at my ass?"

The corners of his pink-pink mouth tilted up the tiniest bit. "Because it's there, in my face all day."

I guess he had a point. It wasn't like I didn't look at his ass from time to time. Because it was there. "Then, don't. Friends don't look at each other's butts."

The way he rolled his eyes did something uncomfortable to my stomach. "Jasmine, this body—these thighs you think I'm going to make fun of you over, and this ass you think the same thing of—are going to win us first place from now on. I wouldn't make fun of it. I wouldn't make fun of *you*. We'll do it like we always do. When we step out on the ice, it's work. It's us focusing, not fucking around."

I held my breath, watching his features as I did it. "I don't believe you."

"That I won't make fun of you?"

"Yes."

There was a pause and then, "Do you want to see me naked first?"

I burst out laughing. Instantly. Without meaning to. It was the last thing I would have wanted to do. "*No!*"

And from the smirk he gave me, he knew it too. "You sure? I have a mole on my thigh that looks like Florida. Maybe you'll find something to make fun of me over, but I don't think so."

I was still laughing, even though I didn't want to—I really didn't want to—as I glanced up at him and shook my head. "God, you're a cocky asshole."

His smile was small. "It's the truth. You can look as hard as you want, and if you find something, go for it, but I work out all the time. I have about... seven percent body fat year round. Looking at myself in the mirror isn't a hardship."

I laughed even harder, but how could I not when he was being like this? This guy I didn't know.

"You can make fun of me, but I would rather you didn't, honestly. I don't like when people say I'm skinny, because I'm not," he said almost gently, and it was my turn to blink.

Who the hell would think this man was skinny? There wasn't a single "skinny" thing about him. I'd seen him work out once, years ago. He'd been bench-pressing twice what I figured his body weight would be. Swimmers and runners had nothing on a body like Ivan's. Absolutely nothing.

Not that I'd ever admit that shit.

The hand on my bare wrist gave it a shake. "Come on, Meatball. You and me. We'll make everybody jealous with our work-of-art asses."

Was this what friendship was like? What it was supposed to be? Him teasing me? Me talking shit back but doing it with a smile on my face? If it was...

If it was, I could do it. I thought. Maybe.

"I hate you," I sighed, peeking at him again because I sucked.

Then he laid it on me real thick, those blue-blue eyes aimed right into my brown ones. "Do it for Paul then. So he can see it and regret he never got to do a naked photo shoot with you for TSN." My wrist got another wiggle. "Or any photo shoot."

And there he had me, proving he knew me better than I expected.

Because goddamn motherfucking Paul. Ugh. *Ugh.*

I didn't want people jacking off to me. But if this was a chance to rub something epic into that asshole's face... it would be worth it. Totally fucking worth it.

"There's my Meatball," he said in almost a whisper, his fingers loosening from around my wrist until they were slipping through mine, holding our hands together like we had done it a thousand times. Because we had. "We're doing this, right? Together? I won't make fun of you, but you can make fun of me a bit?"

I didn't know who the hell was standing in front of me right then. This nice, funny, gentle guy. But I squeezed his hand in mine anyway and nodded. "Yeah, we're doing this together," I grumbled, knowing it was the right thing. Knowing maybe I'd regret some parts of it, but not all of it. At least not if he didn't make a puberty joke.

"That's what I thought," he said, sounding almost cheery as he gave my hand a tug.

And then we were on the ice, in our robes, with makeup on and ready—at least me for sure—and Coach Lee and the photographer immediately stopped talking the second they spotted us skating toward them. She raised her thin, black eyebrows and asked hesitantly, "Did you change your mind?"

I nodded.

"I only want to do this if you're comfortable," the photographer said quickly. "We all have nothing but respect for you and your body, Jasmine. We can work on some angles if you keep your underwear on—"

I shook my head. "It's fine." I wasn't about to say I hadn't wanted to get naked because of Ivan. Much less because of strange assholes that had nothing better to do. Pathetic pieces of shit.

"You sure?" the photographer asked, not sounding at all like she would be put out if I said I wasn't.

But I was. And I said that. "Yeah, I am."

She shrugged. "Okay. Let's start then, if you're both ready."

Ivan squeezed my hand—he hadn't let it go—and said just

loudly enough for me to hear, "I underestimated how cold it was, so you can't make fun of... certain body parts if they're trying to crawl back inside of me to protect themselves...."

I only barely held back a smirk as this feeling of being *right* covered my entire upper body. "I won't make fun of Peter, if you don't make fun of Mary and Maggie. Those two bitches aren't hiding because it's cold. They've been hiding," I said, evenly.

He nodded, but his mouth tipped up a millimeter of an inch. "You know I'm expecting you to have three nipples now, right?"

I rolled my eyes. "And I'm expecting your winky to be an inch long. We're even."

Ivan made a face, his fingers tightening over mine. "Maybe an inch too long." I groaned, but he kept going. "Let's get this over with, yes?"

Neither one of us said anything as we let go of our hands and skated to where the two backdrops had been set up in the center of the rink, the lighting umbrellas on and ready to go. Coach Lee approached us, looking skeptical. "Ready?"

Ivan nodded, and I said, "Ready." Because I was.

It would look good. It would make a point to people I shouldn't have wanted to make a point to, but needed to. It would be worth the other shit.

With a deep breath that I wasn't used to, I let it out and watched as the photographer went behind her camera, nodding at us in encouragement as her assistants got into position. "Whatever you want to do first, we can start there. Any lifts or stationary positions would be great though."

Yeah. Apparently I wasn't going to manage to avoid getting my crotch out of Ivan's face, but there was a reason I waxed regularly.

We were about to get to know each other on a totally new

level, I guessed. *I could do it.* Of course I fucking could. I was strong, smart, and I could do anything, just like my mom had always told me.

"Hand to hand lift?" I asked my partner—my Ivan—as my hands went to the knot at my robe and began undoing it.

"Sure," he responded, almost too easily, his own hands in the same place mine were.

Either he was really trying hard to be nice to me or he was up to something. I wasn't sure. But I doubted he'd do something fucked up in front of cameras, especially after that pep talk.

I thought.

"Whenever you're ready," the photographer called out.

Is it me or do the lights seem to be too bright? I asked myself. Everyone knew the camera added at least ten pounds, but with all these lights, I had a feeling it was going to feel more like twenty. Oh well. Let them judge. I had nothing to prove to people who didn't matter or mean anything to me.

Standing in front of Ivan with my hands still on my robe, ready, I asked him, "You're good to go?"

Already in the zone, he nodded.

It was time to party, I guess.

Undoing the knot at my waist, I got myself under control, scrounged up every ounce of my confidence and dignity and reminded myself that no body was perfect, and hopefully they'd Photoshop the shit out of anything that didn't look right even though they probably wouldn't since the issue was called The Anatomy Issue to begin with. But fuck it. If people wanted to point out a roll if I was bent over, *go for it.* I'd grown up around three of the most beautiful women in the world. I'd accepted a long time ago that I wasn't one of them, and that was okay.

And then I took my robe off.

No one had said anything, but I'd put white cloth tape directly over my nipples, leaving the rest of me free. I mean, they couldn't post pictures of me totally topless, so I hadn't seen what the big deal would be. My bare butt and vagina, I couldn't care less about. We'd all come out of one.

I could do this. I really could.

And then, out of the corner of my eye, I saw the movement of another robe being taken off and handed over, a flash of skin and more skin, just a second before a hand was outstretched to take mine.

Time to get it over with, I thought to myself, and turned around to face Ivan for the first time, maybe, kind of, holding my breath. I raised my eyebrows up at him the second my eyes met his, hoping to God I hadn't suddenly decided to start blushing for the first time in my life, because that would make this real humiliating.

"Fuck," I heard Ivan mutter under his breath as I looked at his face... only to find that his eyes were squeezed closed.

"What?" I snapped.

"Nothing," he snapped back immediately.

"What?" I insisted, trying to figure out why his skin had gotten even paler... and why he wasn't looking at me.

"*Nothing*," he replied, sounding just like the Ivan I knew: a pain in the ass. He shook his head and swallowed. "Let's get this over with."

"Get it over with?" I asked, not feeling at all insulted. Maybe he was the one regretting it now. Oh fucking well. "You're the one who wanted to do it," I reminded him.

"Well, I'm starting to think it was a shitty idea, so let's get it done," he muttered, eyes still closed.

"Prude," I whispered, not getting why he wasn't looking at my face at the very least. He was beginning to make me feel like there was something wrong with me.

So I looked at him. Because he was there.

And I suddenly began regretting doing this again.

Because Ivan's body...

Fuck.

Maybe because I was an athlete—regardless of what other people stupidly thought—I could appreciate all the different forms male athletes held. I'd never been a big fan of male models with their perfectly sculpted tiny muscles that had to be worked on regularly, one at a time. I liked raw strength in all its shapes. I really did.

But Ivan's in particular had been basically painted by a master. The caps of muscle at his shoulders were drawn by pen, the lean, rigid muscles of his forearms and biceps were strong. Then there were his firm pectorals, the flat abs with eight small square shapes at them. The detailed muscles at his hips from all his lifting, and the long, lines of muscle striations at his thighs and calves.

I didn't need to look at his ass to know that it was high and tight.

And I'd be a fucking liar if I said I hadn't glanced at his penis, but like me, he'd decided to cover *something*. That something was hidden by what looked like a nude-colored sock that covered his junk, leaving only trimmed hairs at his groin there.

I wasn't going to bend down to see if I could see his balls.

I glanced all over Ivan again and barely held back a head shake. He was seriously a work of perfection. Honestly. Truly.

But I would die before I told him that, so I needed to stop thinking about it. We needed to get this shit over with.

"Come on then, shy boy, before your balls start receding back into your body too," I told him.

That had him snapping his eyes open to glare at me, his face scrunched up. "Hopefully my hand doesn't slip."

"Hopefully I don't lose my balance and my foot goes up your ass—"

"Okay! All right! Let's start you two," Coach Lee hollered, and I didn't need to look at her to know she was shaking her head.

I blinked at Ivan, as I stood there fucking naked and said, "Come on, Socks. Let's do this. Maybe we'll end up on the cover." And I felt zero nausea or worry as I said it.

CHAPTER 11

I SHOULD HAVE KNOWN SOMETHING WAS GOING ON WHEN I GOT home that evening and found my mom in the kitchen, a plate of food sitting in front of the stool I usually sat at, waiting for me. She hadn't served me dinner in years. I couldn't actually remember if she had ever prepared any of us plates in advance... with the exception of Ruby. It was usually a free-for-all. Mom always said she wasn't our maid, and that we should be grateful she cooked to begin with.

So, I should have known something was up. The problem was that I was exhausted following the photo shoot that took all damn morning. *Don't smile. Look natural. Do that pose again. Can you hold it a little longer? Hold your leg in this awkward, unnatural position for one more minute. Stand there and freeze your ass off. Tilt your head this way—no the other way—and hold it there. Ivan, put your freezing fucking hands on Jasmine's body and hold them there for two minutes.*

Fuck, fuck, and double fuck.

He didn't laugh every time he touched me, and I'd have to suck in a breath because it hurt, but I knew he wanted to.

My nipples were still hard from being on the ice, covered

with only the tiniest pieces of tape, and I was pretty sure my vagina was never going to be warm again. My clit had probably turned into a raisin. I hadn't even glanced at the sock covering Ivan's dick after the first time because it had been cold as hell. I wasn't going to judge a man for what his junk looked like in the cold.

Plus, there had been other things to look at.

Everything north of the Equator and everything south of the Equator. Muscles, muscles, and more beautifully carved muscles. It wasn't exactly difficult, even though every time his hands touched me, I wanted to punch him in the gut.

And once, I'd accidentally caught a glimpse of huge balls dangling between his legs that had for one second, made me wonder what the hell he did with those things in his costumes.

But it was none of my business, so I'd shoved that question aside for later.

The important part was, we'd gotten it done. At the end of the day, that was all that mattered. We had gotten it done, and we hadn't killed each other or made fun of one another. It had just taken way too long. Luckily, I had thought ahead and taken the day off, even though my bank account didn't need that kind of loss. Especially not when we were going to be competing in so many events.

Things hadn't been awkward during our afternoon practice, but I'd be lying if I said I hadn't glanced at his upper body once or twice and not remembered what he looked like without a shirt on. Just as quickly as I'd thought about it, I'd forced myself to stop. Luckily, he hadn't had anywhere near the same amount of trouble; Ivan hadn't actually said anything to me directly during our afternoon practice, even after he'd been so weirdly nice that morning.

"Hi, Grumpy," my mom greeted me the second she heard me come into the kitchen.

"Hi, Mom," I said, coming up behind her to kiss her cheek. I'd already dropped my things off. "How was work?"

She shrugged her thin shoulders as she turned off the water to the sink and reached for a towel to her left. "Fine. Eat before your food gets cold. I stuck it in the microwave when I saw the light in the driveway."

"Thank you," I said, still not paying attention, but turning to take a seat. I dug in to the baked chicken, jasmine rice, sweet potatoes, and side salad like I was going to collapse if I didn't. I'd eaten lunch six hours ago between the shoot and the one hour break we'd taken between it and afternoon practice, but it felt more like a hundred hours since then. Ivan and I had worked on throws and side-by-side spins for three hours, and afterward, I worked out at the LC's gym for three hours, including some high-intensity interval training on the treadmill to get my heart ready for the 180-200 beats per minute it was going to be pumping for close to five minutes during our free skate.

Out of the corner of my eye, I saw my mom take a seat at the island too. When we were both home at the same time, we always ate together, or at least kept the other company. So I didn't think much of it.

Until she looked up, holding a mug of tea to her mouth and ruined my whole day.

My mouth dropped open the instant I got a good look at her face, and I pretty much yelled, "What the hell happened to your face?"

Mom's blink was completely unimpressed.

And I didn't give a shit as I took in the tape over her nose and two puffy, reddish-purple circles around each of her eyes.

And was that her fucking lip busted or was I imagining it?

She didn't say anything as I looked all over her face, a thousand scenarios going through my head at what the hell had happened to her, when I asked, "*Who did that to you?*" I was going to kill somebody. I was going to fucking kill somebody, and I was going to enjoy the hell out of it.

"Calm down," she said easily, like there was no reason in the world for me to flip out over the fact that half her face was bruised.

Of course I ignored her. "What happened to you?"

My mom's blue-blue eyes didn't even move over into my direction as she said, word for word, right before taking another sip of what I knew was tea, "I was in a car accident. Everything is fine."

She was in a car accident and everything was fine.

I blinked at her as she picked up her phone from the counter like everything was no big deal and started reading something on the screen. Me on the other hand, I just sat there and tried to process her words and their meaning... and wasn't able to. Because I understood what an accident was. What I didn't understand was why the hell she hadn't called to tell me about it. Or at least send a fucking text.

"You were in a car accident?" The words were out of my mouth, as slow coming out as they'd been going in for me to process them.

She had been in an accident. My mom had been in an accident and it had been bad enough that she looked like hell. That's what she had said without even looking in my direction to do it.

What. The. Fuck?

My mom still didn't look at me. "It isn't a big deal," she went on. "I have a concussion. They set my nose again. My car was totaled, but the other driver's insurance will cover it because he hit me and there were witnesses." Then, the woman who even with two black eyes didn't look like she'd given birth to five kids, and definitely didn't look like her youngest—me—was twenty-six years old, finally did glance in my direction. My mom was totally unfazed as she pursed her lips in that way I'd become familiar with as a teenager when I'd talk back to her and she'd almost whooped my ass. "Don't tell your brothers or sisters."

Don't tell my—

I grabbed the paper towel sitting beside my plate and held it under my chin as I spit my rice into it—wasting precious food and not giving a shit—as my heart rate and blood pressure racked up so fucking high, so fucking fast, it was a miracle I was just as healthy as I'd ever been in my life at that point... minus some physical stuff... because anyone else would have had a heart attack right then. At least anyone that gave half a shit about another person—and I gave a massive shit about my mom. My heart wasn't supposed to be beating that fast while I was technically resting.

Mom groaned, sitting up straight, just as I set the paper towel beside my plate. "No, *no*. Don't you spit your food out."

I didn't bother thinking about the last time I'd spit my food out; I didn't need to get more pissed off. "*Mom*," I said, my voice higher and squeakier than ever, sounding not at all like me and, maybe, a little like a teenager on the verge of throwing a temper tantrum.

But this wasn't a tantrum. This was my mom being injured and not telling me about it. And not wanting me to tell anyone else about it.

The woman who had practically raised me on her own tipped her head to the side and made her eyes go wide like she was trying to tell me without words that I needed to scale back on the drama. But the thing that *mostly* caught my gaze was the fact that *she didn't even set her mug of tea down* as she basically hissed, "Jasmine. Don't start with me."

"Don't start with you?" I spit back at her, more alert than I'd ever been after a practice. Here I'd been just a minute ago, staring into the stone countertop of the kitchen island, thinking about how badly I wanted to get into the shower and go to bed... not even thinking about practices and figure skating and the future... and now, *now* I was about two seconds away from losing my shit. Just like that.

Because. What. The. Mother. Fuck.

"Don't start with me," she demanded again, taking a sip of her tea, just as easy as can be, like she wasn't telling me to blow off her accident and concussion and broken nose, and that I couldn't tell my siblings about it for whatever reason she had in her head. "I'm fine," she said before I ignored *her don't start with me* BS and leaned forward, blinking at her, like I had the worst dry eyes in the world.

"Why didn't you call and tell me?" I asked, using a tone that would have definitely gotten me grounded ten years ago, as anger twisted my guts. *Why hadn't she?*

My hands had started shaking.

My hands never shook. Never. Not when I was mad over getting screwed by people I had slightly trusted. Not while I was waiting to skate. Not after I skated. Not when I lost. Not when I won. Never.

Mom rolled her eyes and focused on her phone again, trying her best to be dismissive. I knew what she was doing. It wouldn't be the first time. "Jasmine," she said my name just forcefully enough for me not to make another smart-ass comment. "Calm down."

Calm down. *Calm down?*

I opened my mouth, and she shot those blue eyes, the ones I'd be able to pick out of a color wheel with my eyes closed, in my direction once more. "*I'm fine.* Some dumb-dumb stopped paying attention as he exited the freeway and rear-ended me. I crashed into the car in front of mine," she went on, and I *knew* why she had thought about keeping it to herself. "It isn't worth getting worked up over. You don't need to get mad about it. I'm fine. If I could have hidden it from you of all people, I would have.

"Ben already knows. Your brothers and sisters don't need to worry about it either." She made a dismissive snort. "Don't get worked up over me. You have better things to focus on."

My mom didn't want me to get worked up over her because I had *better* things to focus on.

Raising both my hands up toward my face, I pressed the pads of my fingers to my temples and told myself to calm down. I told myself to. I tried to go over all the relaxation techniques I'd learned over the years to deal with my stress and... nope. None of it worked. None of it.

"I don't want you to be distracted by me," Mom insisted.

I swore my ears started to ring. "Did an ambulance have to take you to the hospital?"

She made an annoyed sound. "Yes."

I pressed my fingers deeper into my temples.

"Oh, put your hands down and pull your thong out of your butt," she tried to joke. "*I'm fine.*"

My ears definitely started to ring. For sure.

I couldn't even look at her as I said, my voice sounding lower and hoarser than normal... not even sounding like it belonged to me, "You could have called me, Mom. If it was me in the accident—"

"You wouldn't have called me either," she finished.

"I—" Okay, maybe I wouldn't have either, but that knowledge didn't ease my anger even a little. If anything, it just made me madder. My hands shook so bad, I stretched my fingers long and lifted them up to either side of my face, shaking them. Mad, so fucking mad, I wanted to scream. "That's not the point!"

She sighed. "You had a big day. I didn't want to bother you."

She didn't want to bother me.

My mom didn't want to bother me.

I dropped my hands and tilted my face up to the ceiling, because if I looked at my mom the way I wanted to, she'd probably smack the expression right off. And then I wondered where I'd learned to keep so many secrets. Holy fuck.

"It's only a little concussion and a fractured nose, Grumpy. And don't raise your voice at me," she said for the second time, and for the second time, it had zero effect on my blood pressure. "I know what this year means to you. I want you to take advantage of it. You don't need to worry about me."

I replayed her last sentences in my head, and it nearly exploded. This sickening feeling swelled up from my stomach to make it to the back of my throat.

Maybe I was being dramatic, but I didn't think so. This was my *mom*. My mom. The woman who had taught me by example how to get up every time I was down. She was the strongest woman I knew. The strongest, the smartest, the prettiest, the toughest, the most loyal, the hardest working....

My throated ached. Years ago, she had scared the shit out of us by saying they had found a lump in her breast that ended up being nothing, I'd heard or seen pretty much all of my brothers and sisters cry. I'd just gotten pissed off. And scared. I'd admit it. I'd been terrified for my mom and, as selfish as it was, for me. Because what the hell would I do without her?

Worst of all, I'd been a dick about the entire situation. But I blamed it on being a teenager—and on my mom being the greatest anchor in my life—on why I'd flipped the hell out and tried to blame her, like she could have prevented it somehow. Now... well, now I was pissed again but not at her.

Well, maybe at her, but only because she would have avoided telling me she'd gotten hurt if she could have, and... and because she didn't want to distract me. Didn't want to *bother me*. I balled up my fist, and if my fingernails had been any longer, I probably would have drawn blood.

"Ben met up with me at the hospital," she explained, her voice slowly beginning to edge back into a calm, even tone. "You don't need to get worked up."

All I could do was stare at her.

"I want you focused," she added. "I know how much this means to you. If the accident would have happened three months ago, I would have called you, but you're busy again, Jasmine. I didn't want to take away from it."

Didn't want to take away from it? If she had gotten hurt before I'd started training so hard again, she would have called me but now she wouldn't?

I glanced up at the ceiling and undid my fist, stretching my fingers as wide as possible. I couldn't find the words. I couldn't pick them, choose them, find them, make them up. I was too stuck on her *I know how much this means to you.*

My chest joined my throat in the aching game.

Did she not understand I'd do anything for her? That I loved her and admired her and thought she was the greatest human being in the world? That I had no idea how she had raised five kids with my dad only being in the picture until I was three? That I didn't understand how she could have been married three times before Ben, had her heart broken each time, but somehow she hadn't given up hope and hadn't let any of that stuff jade her?

There were a lot of things I didn't let get to me. There were so many times I fell and hurt myself but kept going. But people had been assholes to me when I was younger, once, maybe a couple of times, making remarks and comments, and that alone had made me give up on strangers.

But my mom never let anything get her down for long.

How could I not think the world of her? How could I not love her, who raised me to think I was invincible, more than anything? How could she believe she wasn't a priority to me?

"You don't have to worry about me," she insisted, casually. "I'll be fine. When Ben and I go to Hawaii in a few weeks, I won't let him take any pictures of my face. That way I have an excuse for us to go again," she said brightly.

But it didn't do shit for me.

This was my fault. This was all my fault. She thought and felt the way she did because I had told her a thousand and a half times how figure skating was what had made me feel special. What had given me purpose. What had made me finally feel like there was something I was good at. What gave me life, what made me happy, what made me strong.

But in reality, it was my mom—my whole family—that had given me the foundation for those things. I knew what all those emotions were because of them. Because of her.

I guessed I had just always assumed she knew.

But maybe I had just been too much of a self-centered prick to come to terms with realizing that until now.

My chest hurt even more, and my throat tightened so much I couldn't swallow as I sat there, taking in the face that I loved with my entire heart. "Mom," was the one and only thing I could get out.

It was right then that her cell's ringtone started blaring. She didn't even say a word to me as she reached for her phone and answered it. "Baby girl," she said immediately, and I knew it was Ruby.

That was the end of that conversation. It was just how my mom worked. She was done when she was done.

And she expected, and for good reason, that if we'd kept talking about it, I probably would have gone on a rant. Under normal circumstances, at least.

This knot in my throat doubled in size as I stared at her as she talked to my sister with a smile on her face like she hadn't just finished telling me being in a car accident was no big deal. Then implied that she wasn't as important to me as she was.

Did I come off that heartless?

Something that felt an awful lot like a tear beaded up in my right eye, but I pressed the tip of a finger against that corner and ignored whether or not there had been some wetness on it, because my throat and my heart ached so bad, they overwhelmed everything else.

I sat there. I sat there and stared at my mom, and wondered what kind of person she really thought I was. I knew she loved me. I knew she wanted me to be happy. I was fully aware she knew all of my strengths and flaws.

But...

Did *she* think I was a selfish piece of shit?

My appetite disappeared, and so did my exhaustion. *Kaput.* Bye. Just like that.

"Oh, baby, you shouldn't be doing that...." My mom trailed off as she shoved her stool backward, gave me a grin that must have hurt her face, and then headed out of the kitchen, to what I could only assume was the living room.

Anger flooded my veins as I sat there with a basically full plate of food below me, the sound of my mom's low laugh just loud enough for me to hear. She was fine, and that's what should matter.

But...

My mom really thought figure skating was more important to me than she was.

I loved it. Of course I loved it. I couldn't breathe without it. I didn't know who I was without it. I didn't know who I would be in the future without it.

But I couldn't breathe without my mom either. And if I'd ever have to choose between both, there wouldn't have been any competition. Not even a little bit.

It was my fault for being a shitty daughter. A shitty person. For not opening my mouth and telling her the things she needed to hear. More I love yous and less sarcasm. For being so heartbroken over Paul leaving me that I didn't appreciate *enough* her and my siblings trying to pull me back into a real life even when I was a moody, angry little bitch.

All they had ever wanted was for me to be happy. For me to win because *that's* what I had wanted. Always.

And I hadn't given them shit. I hadn't made them proud no matter what. I had nothing to show in exchange.

It was my fault for choking. For overthinking. For being obsessive and a little difficult.

The knot in my body tripled, choking me, suffocating me.

God.

I couldn't sit here and act like I was fine when I wasn't. All I'd wanted was to sit at home and relax while eating before I started to wind down, but now... now there was no way I could do that. No fucking way in hell.

I was such an asshole.

God, I was such a fucking asshole, and it was all my fault. If I were a better person, a better athlete, maybe this would all be different. But it wasn't.

I had to do something.

Sliding back my own stool, I almost headed straight

toward the front door, ready to get out, but I paused for a second, wrapped my food in plastic and set it in the fridge.

And then I grabbed my keys, and I was fucking out of there, something that sure tasted like guilt and desperation filling my mouth, making me restless... making me feel like shit.

I didn't know where I was going.

I didn't know what the hell I wanted to do.

But I had to do something, because this... shit... inside of me was growing and growing and growing.

My mom was my best friend, and she thought figure skating was more important to me than she was.

Did everyone I love think that way? Was that the impression I'd left on them?

Figure skating made me the happiest, but it wouldn't mean anywhere near as much to me without my mom and siblings supporting me, giving me shit, caring and loving me even while I was at my worst. When I didn't deserve it.

My throat and eyes burned as I drove, and my mouth went dry as I kept on driving. Before I knew it, before I let myself do more than have my throat ache and my eyes tighten, I pulled my car into the parking lot of the LC. I didn't even realize it until I was there.

Of course I'd go back.

It was the only thing I had other than them. And I sure as hell didn't want to talk to Ruby or Tali or Jojo or Sebastian about any of this. I wasn't ready to feel worse, and that's what would more than likely happen if they tried to console me or tell me it was okay.

Because it wasn't.

I had to make all the sacrifices that had ever been made for me worth it.

And this was the only way I knew how.

In no time at all, I was out and heading toward the front doors, on a mission to go to the changing room. I'd left my bag at home, but I always left my last pair of skates in my locker as backup. I wasn't wearing my favorite clothes to train in either, but... I needed this. I needed this thing that had always taken my mind off everything... even if it was the one thing that destroyed my body and made my whole family think they were second best.

The realization that I shouldn't have left my mom after she'd admitted something so big finally hung in my brain, but... I couldn't go back. What the hell would I say to her? That I was sorry? That I didn't mean to make her think she wasn't important?

The changing room was almost empty by the time I made it inside; there were two girls that were younger than me, but not by much, talking, but I ignored them as I put in my combination and opened my locker. In record time, I'd taken my shoes off, grabbed the extra pair of socks I always left in there, and stuffed my feet into them and my skates, ignoring the fact that I might regret not putting on the bandages I usually wore that protected my skin from the top edge of the boot that was well broken in.

But I needed to burn some energy off. I needed to clear my head. I needed to make this better. Because if I didn't... I didn't know what I would do. Probably feel more of a piece of shit than I already did. If that were even possible.

Ignoring the other girls in the room who were looking in my direction in confusion because I was never at the facility this late, I made my way as fast as I could toward the rink. Luckily, there were only about five other people on the ice at eight in the evening. The younger kids were already home and in bed, and the teenagers were heading there.

But I didn't give a fuck about any of them.

The second my blades touched the ice, I was off, skating so close to the walls, only millimeters separated me from them. I went faster and faster, needing to get this shit out. *Out. Out, out, out.* I needed to remember why this had been worth so much.

I don't know how many times I circled my way around, taking on speed skater speed, and I wasn't sure when I started going into jumps. Jumps I hadn't warmed up for. Jumps that I had no business doing while my body had already gone through a tough practice and I hadn't refueled since. I did a triple Salchow—what we called an edge jump because you didn't have the assistance of your blade's toe-pick, you took off from the back inside edge and landed on the opposite foot's back outside edge—followed by another one. A quadruple toe loop that I stumbled out of, and then did over and over again until I landed it. And then I went for a triple Lutz I was too burned out and exhausted to do, busting my ass hard on each landing. Falling and falling, one time after another and then another, my ass cheek *hurting* somewhere in the back of my head, but I wasn't focusing on it.

I had to land it.

I had to do it.

My hip ached. My wrist started hurting from trying to break my fall like a dumbass. The skin above my ankle began to chafe.

And I kept falling. Over and over again. I fell.

And the more I failed, the angrier I became with myself.

Fuck this. Fuck everything. Fuck *me.*

It was on another fall that went so bad, the back of my head grazed the ice that I finally lay there and closed my eyes, breathing hard, feeling like shit, anger burning through me so brightly I felt it everywhere. I made my hands into fists. And I gritted my teeth so hard my jaw ached.

I wasn't going to cry. I wasn't going to cry. *I wasn't going to cry.*

I loved my family. I loved figure skating.

And I sucked at loving both.

"Get up, Meatball."

I didn't think I'd ever opened my eyes faster than I did right then.

And when I did, a familiar face was there, hovering, staring down at me with two black eyebrows arched upward. In the time it took me to blink, there were fingers there too, halfway between the face and me, fingers wiggling in my direction. The eyebrows went up even further when I didn't say anything or move.

What was he doing here?

"Let's go," Ivan said as he looked at me with an expression I couldn't read on that face I had seen so much of already.

I didn't get up.

Ivan blinked.

I did too, swallowing hard as I did it, fire filling my throat.

With a sigh, Ivan reached into his pocket and then extended his hand out again, holding a Hershey's Kiss between his index and middle finger. He raised his eyebrows again as he gave the candy a shake between his fingers. Why the hell he was carrying around chocolate in his pocket was beyond me.

But I took it, keeping my eyes on him the entire time. I unwrapped it like a pro and popped it into my mouth. It only took about three seconds for the sweetness to soothe the pain in my throat, just a little, but it was something.

"You ready to get up now?" he asked after I'd had the chocolate in my mouth for a few seconds.

Shoving it to my cheek, I shook my head, not trusting my lips to form the right words and not really feeling like sacrificing the small bit of joy and comfort coating my tongue. At least not yet. My temples gave a throb that I hadn't even noticed before.

Ivan blinked down at me twice.

I still said nothing as the chocolate kept on melting inside my mouth.

"I'm not dealing with you if you get sick," he went on after another minute, crossing his arms over his chest as he did so, still watching me. Expecting something. I thought.

Still, I didn't say a word. I just kept sucking on the chocolate, ignoring the cold at my back that was finally beginning to sting.

"Jasmine, get off the ice."

I licked my lips as I stared up at him.

He sighed and tipped his head back to look at the rafters, probably taking in the banners with his name hanging from them and wondering where his life had gone wrong to the point where he was here at night, with me.

God. Did everyone think I was a piece of self-centered crap? Even him?

The throbbing at my head got worse when he sighed again.

"You have three seconds to get up or I'm dragging you out of here," he got out, still facing the ceiling and more than likely closing his eyes as he did it, if I knew him correctly.

It was my turn to blink. "I'd like to see you try."

But in the back of my head, I knew that if he said he'd drag me off the ice, he probably would.

Those blue-gray eyes narrowed on me, and he said, still speaking carefully, "All right. I won't drag you." Something about the expression on that classic face that had grown only the slightest brush of a shadow of facial hair on his cheeks, put me on edge, like I couldn't trust it. Like a reminder of what we had been like before. "But you have two seconds from now to get up."

The *or else* hung in the air.

The stinging on my back was getting sharper, genuinely hurting my back and ass, and honestly, I wanted to get up. I would have gotten up if I'd been by myself. Chances were, I would have been on my way to the changing room if I'd been alone.

But now I was going to have to get frostbite because I sure as hell wasn't going to do it since he'd asked.

And Ivan seemed to sense that because those glacier-colored eyes narrowed into slits.

Then he began counting.

"Two," Ivan started, not even giving me a warning.

I didn't move.

"One."

I still didn't move. Fuck it. I didn't give a shit.

His sigh was deep, deep, deep, and he even shook his head as he said, "Last chance."

I stared at him.

He stared back at me and finally shrugged. "You asked for it. Remember that."

This bastard was going to drag me off the ice? What the—

Ivan bent at the waist, his eyes intent on me, and just as he reached toward my head with one arm—and I tilted my mouth to the side to bite whatever I could reach if he decided to try and pull my hair—his palm shoved itself beneath my shoulders and the ice. His other arm went under my knees, and in a move that was so fast, I forgot this man had built up his life and accomplishments lifting women for a living, I went over his shoulder, ass in the air, head and arms dangling along his back.

This bitch.

Be better. Be better. Be better. Don't punch him in his giant balls. At least not yet.

"Ivan," I told him, sounding calmer than I felt, barely realizing he had put on his skates before coming out to hunt me down. He was skating toward the boards, and I didn't know where we were going. "Ivan, put me down right now, or I'm going to kick you in the face and not feel bad about it."

"Meatball," he said, just as calmly and quietly as I had been talking. "I'd like to see you try," the asshole claimed, mirroring my words right back at me just as what had to be his forearm locked down over my calves, holding them against his chest before I did what he figured I was capable of.

And he would be right.

"Ivan," I said again, still calm, part of me kind of hoping I was the kind of person who would yell and try to bite his ass so he'd put me down. But I'd promised. I'd promised to behave in public. So my voice was still nice and quiet as I said, "I swear to God, put me down this second."

His response? A soft "No."

"Ivan."

"No," he repeated, stepped off the ice, grabbing something out of my vision, and continuing walking... somewhere. I couldn't see. What I could see was that he didn't have his skate guards on either.

"I'm not playing with you right now," I let him know, beginning to get really mad.

"I'm not either," he replied, giving my calves a squeeze closer into him. "I gave you a chance. I gave you several chances, and you didn't want to listen or let this go the easy way, so don't get pissed off at me because you're stubborn."

My hands clenched from where they dangled, and I seriously considered biting his ass if I could reach it. Fuck it. He'd brought this on himself. I was more of a wedgie person than a biting-on-the-ass person, but I wasn't about to stick my hand in the back of his pants.

"I don't know what's wrong with you right now, but I drove all the way over here, so you're not going to act like a spoiled brat with me," he let me know before shifting me on his shoulder and huffing. "Jesus Christ, you're heavy."

"Fuck you," I spat, seriously talking myself out of biting him.

"Fuck you too," he replied, not missing a beat, not sounding at all angry or frustrated, which annoyed me even more.

"Put me down."

"No."

"I will kick you in the face."

"You make me bleed, and we'll have to take time off from practicing, and we both know you don't want to do that."

He had a point, damn it.

"I'm going to beat the shit out of you the first chance I get when the season is over," I hissed, arching my back for a moment when the blood rushing into my head started to make my nose sting.

"You can try," he replied.

"You're so lucky I don't want to make a scene," I pretty much growled.

His "I know" only annoyed me more as he took a turn down a hall.

Where were we going?

"Why are you even here?" I asked, trying to lift my upper body again to get a look at the hall we were in.

Ivan didn't say a word. He just kept walking down the hall, before turning down another hall that I'd never bothered going down because I'd never had any business going to it.

"Ivan."

Still nothing.

Fuck me. I didn't want to hurt him... because I didn't want to delay practices... so I couldn't kick my legs... and biting his ass was way more personal than necessary... so I reached toward his butt, which I belatedly realized was in a different pair of sweat pants than the ones he'd been wearing during our afternoon session, and reached for the curve I knew was laying beneath... and I pinched it. Hard.

He didn't even flinch.

So, I did it again. In a different spot.

And still no response.

What the fuck kind of cyborg was he? I'd pinched my brother half as hard, and he'd acted like I'd shot him.

Before I could figure out if he was an alien, he turned us to the left and stopped. I peeked around his leg to see that he was standing in front of a door, and at that point, was punching buttons on a numeric keypad above a doorknob. Where the hell were we?

"What is this?" I asked him.

He hit what I could only assume was "enter" just as he replied with, "My room."

His room?

And then, with his free hand, he turned the knob, shoved the door open, and took a step forward, his one and only free hand going to what had to be the light switch, because a split second later, everything was lit up. And by "everything" I meant the twenty-by-twenty-foot room with what looked like a kitchenette along one wall, a couch in the middle with a small coffee table in front of it, and who knew what else on the other side that I couldn't see from where I was dangling, arching my neck one way and then the other to get a look around.

"Since when do you have your own—*goddamn it! What the hell was that for?*" I cried out at the sudden sharp pain coming from my right ass cheek. "Did you just pinch me?" I cried, reaching back to cup my cheek over the spot that hurt like hell.

"That's for pinching me." Then the son of a bitch did it again, and I tried to kick my leg out, making me forget I hadn't wanted to hurt him. "And that's what you get for not paying attention," he answered easily, still standing there with me over his shoulder.

"For not paying attention?" I shouted again, rubbing my soon-to-be-bruised ass. "That fucking hurt, Ivan." Because it *had*. Jesus Christ, he was strong.

"You tried to hurt me too. I'm only giving you exactly what you planned on giving me." He had a point, but still. "If you paid more attention, you'd know I fall on my right cheek. I know you fall on your left one."

Shit.

He had another point. I had less sensation on my left cheek than I did my right from so many falls. I bet half the nerves on my ass were dead.

And it was annoying he knew that and used it against me.

And it was even more annoying that I'd tried pinching the butt cheek on him with the same trauma and failed, damn it.

"We're even," he said before going into a squat position, bending over and dropping me ass and back first onto the carpet floor, like I was a sack of worthless potatoes.

I glared at him.

Those pure black eyebrows of his went up. "You're lucky I'm in a good mood," he let me know right before he kneeled in front of me. Those intense eyes lingered on me for a moment before he glanced down and his hands went to my right skate. I jerked my leg toward me, but he didn't let that stop him. His fingers went to the laces of my boots, and he began plucking at the tight double knots I always made.

Some part of me wanted to ask him what the hell he was doing... but I didn't. I just sat there, with my ass hurting, and watched as he undid one set of laces, pulled the boot off my foot, and then did the same to the other. He didn't say a word and neither did I as he then sat down and undid his own skates, setting them beside mine. Ivan did glance at me as he got to his feet and headed toward the kitchen area, taking up an entire wall along the back of the room.

Rubbing my ass cheek, I sat there, wondering what the fuck was going on, and then getting onto my knees and looking around the room, taking in this place that I hadn't known existed. How long had it been here? Did anyone else know about it?

But I asked him the most important question bouncing around in my head, as I sat there. "What are you doing here?"

He was bent over, rummaging through what looked like a small fridge built into the cabinets when he answered, "I came to check on you."

What?

Ivan didn't look back at me as he stood up straight, holding a carton of almond milk in his hand as he kicked the door to the fridge closed. "Galina called Lee, who called me," he went on, like he was reading my mind.

Galina? Where the hell had Galina been? And why would she call Lee? I wondered before shoving the questions to the side and focusing.

"You didn't have to come," I blurted, wincing afterward at how much of an asshole I sounded like and kind of regretting it. Just a little.

My partner said nothing as he opened up more cabinets and started pulling things out of them.

I pinched the bridge of my nose with one hand while the other one went to my ass again to rub at the spot he'd pinched the shit out of. "I don't even know why she called. Everything was fine," I snapped, gritting my teeth at just how much my butt hurt.

His snicker was loud.

"What?"

He had his back to me as he said, "*Everything was fine. Sure, Jasmine. Keep telling yourself that.*"

I straightened on my spot on the floor and tried to tell myself to keep my attitude in check. *Be better.* I could be better. "It was fine."

Maybe not.

I could see him shake his head as he messed around with whatever he had taken out of the cabinets. "So you come back to practice after working out for hours, and instead, work on your jumps, falling and getting back up like you're possessed, and you're fine?" he threw back, messing with something on the countertop.

"Yes," I lied.

He snorted. "You're the worst liar I've ever met."

"I don't know what you're talking about," I replied, sounding awfully close to bitter but deciding to ignore it. I moved to get my legs under me and stood up.

Ivan sighed at the same time something opened, closed, and beeped.

"I'm fine," I kept going as I straightened and gave my ass cheek another rub, glancing at things around the room out of the corner of my eye.

He turned around and leaned against the counter behind him, raising his eyebrows, his expression... irritated. Really irritated. Huh. "What happened?" he asked.

I looked away, deciding to see the rest of the room. There were racks of clothes along the wall to the right, filled with costume after vaguely familiar costume. I had always wondered what he did with all of them. I had mine stuffed into every closet that had space at my mom's.

"Jasmine."

I ignored the frustration in his voice and kept on taking in the pale gray painted room, taking in how organized and clean it all was. That didn't surprise me. Ivan was meticulous about everything. His clothes, his hair, his technique, his car. Of course he wouldn't have a mess.

I couldn't say anything. I was almost a clean freak. *Almost.* I was definitely a time freak.

"Jasmine, tell me what's wrong."

I kept my eyes glued on his rows of costumes, kicking myself mentally in the ass for not checking to make sure Coach Lee or Galina hadn't been around when I'd first showed up. I hadn't even looked to see if their cars were in the lot. Rookie mistake.

"You can tell me anything. You know I know what this life is like," he murmured the words I hadn't expected from him. Words that cleaved deep into my gut.

Because he was right. If anyone did know, it was him. Of course he would. He might even know better than I did since he'd been doing it for longer.

Except, he'd done what he wanted to do, and kept on doing what he wanted to do.

While I hadn't.

There was a reason he had his name on banners all over the LC, and I didn't.

The microwave beeped, and I finally felt so defeated and... sad. Just so fucking sad, so fucking fast, it almost took my breath away. Standing with just one hip against the counter, he was holding a cup in his hand and a spoon in the other, stirring something. But he was looking at me expectantly. Waiting.

And it just made me sadder that I was this person he expected to fight him over everything.

Be better. It was never too late, was it?

I pinched my lips together for a moment and tried to wrangle it all in, my anger, this fucking sadness, my disappointment. And I thought I'd done a decent job as I said, almost weak, definitely weird, "I didn't know you had your own room." I swallowed. "Must be nice."

Did that sound as fake as I thought it did or...?

His face didn't change at all. Neither did that tone I didn't know what to think of. "I don't bring people here."

The "huh" out of my mouth sounded about as flat as I felt.

He kept on stirring, his eyes going nowhere. "It's my quiet place."

That had me flicking my gaze at him, surprised by his comment.

"It used to be a conference room and a storage closet, but I had it renovated a few years ago, when some fans snuck into the facility and went into the changing room while I was showering."

What?

"They took pictures of me. Georgiana"—the general manager—"had to call the police," he told me, his gaze steady on me even after he shrugged. "It had only been a matter of time anyway. Some nights back then, I was too tired to go home, so I'd stay here," he explained, catching me even more off guard. "I don't do that anymore."

I wondered why.

Then I remembered it wasn't any of my business. Friends, or whatever the hell we were, or not.

Ivan didn't say another word as he came toward me, the mug still in his hand, the spoon in his other. I didn't say anything either. I just watched him, trying to figure out what he was doing.

When he stopped directly in front of me, so close that for anyone else who wasn't used to the lack of personal space, would have been too close, I still said nothing.

He didn't sigh or make a face when he held out the cup toward me and kept it there just an inch or two away from my chest. The fact that I didn't ask him if he poisoned it popped into my head as quickly as it popped back out. I wasn't in the mood to be a pain in the ass. I really wasn't. Not anymore.

And that's how I knew there was something wrong with me.

I peeked inside of the mug, taking in the milky brown liquid inside... and then sniffed it. And I glanced back at him.

Ivan raised his eyebrow and moved it half an inch closer to me. "It's the packet stuff," he explained in a damn near murmur like he didn't want to say the words or something. "I don't have any marshmallows, if you like that kind of thing."

He...

He....

Oh, hell.

"And I made it with almond-coconut milk. You don't need the extra dairy," he kept going, still holding that damned mug half an inch from my chest as I stood there.

He'd made me hot chocolate.

Ivan had made me fucking hot chocolate. Without marshmallows according to him, but he wouldn't have known that I only treated myself to hot cocoa with marshmallows on very rare occasions.

How he knew—*why he even had the mix*—I couldn't handle. I just couldn't process it. It was like that moment when he and Lee had asked me to first partner up with him, like I was on drugs and didn't realize it.

Ivan Lukov, the greatest frenemy in my life after my siblings, had made me hot cocoa.

And suddenly, for some fucking reason that I would never, ever understand, even years from then, I officially felt like the biggest piece of shit on the planet. That was the last straw. It was in the record books.

My eyes began to sting almost instantly, and my throat suddenly felt drier than ever before.

He had come here because Coach Lee had called him.

Ivan had given me a Hershey's kiss.

He had dragged me to his room.

And then he'd made me hot cocoa.

My hand went up on its own, my mouth still staying shut, as I wrapped my fingers around the warm ceramic and took it away from him, glancing back and forth between the mug and that face that was so beautiful, so annoyingly perfect, it made my unclassicness difficult to appreciate for once. When he dropped his hand away, I brought the cup up to my mouth and took a sip, even as my eyes burned worse than before. It wasn't as sweet with the non-dairy milk he'd used, but it still tasted great.

And he was still standing there, watching me.

And I felt... I felt shame. I felt ashamed of myself for this small kindness he'd just paid me that he didn't have to. A small kindness I wasn't sure I'd do if we were in opposite situations, and that just made me feel worse, worse, worse. My throat grew tighter than before, and it was honestly like I'd swallowed a giant grapefruit.

"What happened?" he asked again, patience punctuating every letter out of his mouth.

I glanced away and then glanced back at him as I pressed my lips together and fought the softball-sized turd pressing down on my vocal chords. *You're a piece of shit, Jasmine*, some part of my brain whispered, and my eyes stung even more badly.

I didn't want to tell him. I didn't. I didn't want to say anything.

But...

You're an asshole, that voice reminded me. *A self-centered asshole.*

I turned away from him, taking a sip, the hot liquid soothing the tightness along my vocal chords, and then I said, sounding so fucking hoarse I almost stopped talking but didn't, "Do you ever feel guilty for making *this*," he knew what "this" was—it was everything, "a priority?"

Ivan made a noise that sounded like a thoughtful one, and I was almost tempted to turn around and see his facial expression before he replied, "Sometimes."

Sometimes. Sometimes was better than never.

You don't care about anyone or anything but figure skating, my ex-partner had said to me one day weeks before he'd jumped ship and abandoned me. I had ripped him a new one when he'd texted me the night before to say he thought he was coming down with a cold, one week before nationals. *You're so cold.*

But I wasn't cold. All I wanted was to win, and I'd always told myself there was nothing I wouldn't do for it. I didn't expect or want to be mediocre. When I wasn't feeling well, I sucked it up and still showed up. Was that so wrong?

Was it so wrong to love something you'd dedicated your life to that you wanted the best? No one ever became good at something without repeatedly working at it. Like Galina had told me once when she'd been really mad at me as a teenager, *natural talent only takes you so far, yozik.* And like with so many other things, she hadn't been wrong.

I had just made some stupid fucking decisions. Really stupid decisions that painted everything black.

"Do you?" Ivan asked when I didn't say anything else after his response.

Shit.

I took another sip of the warm drink and savored the taste, a lie at my chest, ready for us.... And I hated it. So I told him the truth, even though it felt like sandpaper. "I didn't. Not for a long time, but now...." Yes. *Yes*.

There was a pause. Then, "Because you started doing other things when you took the season off?"

Took the season off. That was the prettiest way of saying it.

"That's what started it," I admitted, keeping my gaze on the mug even as my eyes began to sting again. "Maybe that's why I see everything now better than I ever did before. I see how much I missed out on."

"Like what?" he asked gently, and I couldn't help but snicker.

"Everything. High school shit. Prom. Boyfriends." Love. "The only reason why I went to my sister's college graduation is because my mom made me go, you know. I was supposed to have practice that day, and I hadn't wanted to miss it. I'd thrown a fit." Acted like an asshole, but I was sure he could reach that conclusion all by himself. "I forget how obsessive I am."

I could hear the soft breath he let out. "You're not the only one. We're all obsessive in this sport," Ivan replied softly. "I've given up my whole life."

I shrugged my shoulders and swallowed hard, still not facing him. He was right. If I thought about it, I would realize, but it didn't make it any easier to swallow the truth.

I was obsessive. I had ignored my family for the last ten plus years. Nothing and no one else had mattered as much as figure skating had... at least on the outside. I had taken them for granted until I thought I had lost this sport. Nothing else had mattered as much as the chance to win *something*. To be someone. To make them proud. To make everything worth it.

But mostly, everything I had done had been for myself. At least at first. It had all been for me and how it made me feel. Good, strong, and powerful. Talented. Special. It had made up for all the other things I didn't have and wasn't any good at.

At least until I had gotten into my late teens, and then everything had gone to shit, and I became my own worst enemy. My own most critical judge. The one and only person who was guilty of sabotaging herself.

I spun the bracelet on my wrist and rubbed the pad of my finger over the inscription.

"I used to regret not going to school like everyone else," Ivan added almost hesitantly. "The only time I genuinely spent with other children was when I would visit my grandfather during the summer. My only friend for a long time was my partner, but even then, it wasn't really a friendship. The only reason I knew what a prom was, was because of television. I used to watch reality shows to know how to talk to people."

Something tickled at my eyeball, and I reached up to wipe at it with the tip of my index finger. It came away wet, but it didn't scare me or make me mad. I didn't feel weak.

I felt pathetic.

I felt like shit.

"Everyone, Jasmine, *everyone* that's an athlete—that's successful—has had to give up a lot. Some of us more than others. You're not the first person, and you're not the last person that sees that and feels bad about it," he started to say, his voice steady and even. "You don't get to become good at anything without sacrificing something to make time."

I didn't look at him as I pressed my middle finger against the same eye, feeling the wetness on there too. I opened my mouth and felt a choke in there, so I closed my lips. I wasn't going to cry in front of Ivan. I *wasn't*. When I opened them again. I made myself say, "I—" and my voice just... cracked. I pressed my lips together and closed my eyes and tried again. "Successful people, Ivan. It's worth it if you're successful, not if you're not."

And we both knew I wasn't. Everyone knew I wasn't. Not even a little bit.

More wetness formed at the corners of my eyes, and it took the pads of every other finger to dab the liquid away.

Everything had been for nothing, I had told myself a year ago when Paul had left. And it had cut me open.

And it did the same thing again right then.

Everything had been for nothing, and I couldn't justify all of my sacrifices anymore.

The sniffle that came out of me, embarrassed me. Humiliated me, but I couldn't do anything to stop it, even as my brain said, *Don't do it. Don't you fucking do it.* I was better than this. Stronger than this.

But I sniffled again anyway.

I wanted to walk out. I didn't want to talk about this anymore. But if I left, it would look like I was running away from Ivan. Running away period. And I didn't run away. Not ever.

Maybe turning away so you wouldn't see something wasn't exactly the same as running, but it really was at the end of the day.

And I wasn't my dad.

"I've never won anything," I said, fully aware my voice sounded watered down and lame, but what was I going to do? Hide it? What the hell did I have to be proud of? Of making my mom feel like she didn't want to bother me after she had been in an accident and had to go to the hospital? *You're a piece of shit, Jasmine.* I had no reason to hold on to my pride. None. And it wasn't like Ivan didn't know that. Like he wasn't aware of how much of a loser I'd turned into. How much of a loser I really was. That's probably why we were only in this together for a year. Why would he want to get stuck with *me?* Natural talent only took you so far. I was the fucking poster child for it. The poster child for being a letdown of a human being, daughter, sister, and friend.

And it burned me. Oh hell, it burned the fuck out of me so bad, I couldn't stop the words from coming out of my mouth. Little pieces of glass sharp along every jagged, broken edge. "So what's it all been for then? Second place? Sixth place?" I shook my head, bitterness swelling up inside of me, crowding out everything; everything, everything, everything. My pride, my talent, my love, fucking everything. "That doesn't seem worth it at all." I hadn't been worth it at all. Had I?

There was no response, but when there was it came in the shape of two big hands landing on my shoulders, curling around them.

My entire life had been for nothing. Every goal for nothing. Every broken dream and promise for nothing.

The hands on my shoulders squeezed, and I tried to shrug them off, but they didn't go anywhere. If anything, they got even tighter.

"Stop it," Ivan's demand was gruff in my ear. At the same time, I felt the heat and length of his body come up behind me.

"I'm a loser, Ivan," I spat and took a step forward, only to come up short when the hands on me kept me from getting an inch away. "I'm a loser, and I gave up so much of my life and so much of my time with the only people who have ever loved me, for nothing."

I was a failure. At everything. At every single fucking thing.

My chest *ached*. It hurt. And if I'd been dramatic, I would have thought it was breaking in half.

"Jasmine—" he started to say, but I shook my head and tried to shake his hands off again as my chest hurt even worse at how my mom had tried to play her accident off. Like she was okay with me not making her a priority.

Like my own mom thought she didn't matter to me.

My throat *burned*. My eyes burned. And I... I was a giant asshole. A loser.

And the only person I could blame was myself.

I almost didn't recognize my voice as I kept on talking for some fucking reason I would never understand. "My own family thinks they don't matter, and for what?" My voice cracked as anger and some other shit I didn't know how to classify swelled up inside of me. "For nothing! For not a single fucking thing! I'm twenty-six. I don't have a college degree. I have two hundred dollars in my bank account. I still live with my mom. I don't have any functional career skills besides wait-ressing. I'm not a national champion, a world champion, or an Olympic champion. My mom's gone nearly bankrupt for fucking *nothing*. My family has paid thousands of dollars going to competitions for me to come up in second place, third place, fourth place, sixth place. I don't own anything. I'm not anything—"

Was I dying?

Was this what having you heart broken felt like? Because if it was, I was sure fucking glad I'd never fallen in love before because *goddamn*. My God.

It felt like my organs were rotting away.

My mouth watered and my throat was sore, but by some

miracle, I didn't actually start bawling. But I felt like it. I was doing it on the inside. Crumbling. Falling apart. Feeling like a piece of worthless, worthless, worthless shit.

You can have all the talent in the world and still do nothing with it, my dad had told me once years ago, when he'd tried to convince me to go to college instead of pursuing figure skating full-time.

I screwed my eyes closed and held my breath as the pain in my chest got so bad, I wasn't sure I could breathe if I tried. And I sniffed. This tiny little sniff I only barely heard.

"Come here," was the soft whisper right by my ear as the hands on my shoulders tightened.

The "No" out of my mouth sounded like two rocks sliding against each other.

"Let me give you a hug." His voice sounded even closer, his body warmer.

Shame burned me inside out, and I tried to take another step forward, but the hands on me didn't let me go anywhere.

"Let me," he demanded, ignoring me.

I squeezed my eyes closed even more and said, before I could stop myself, "I don't want a fucking hug, Ivan. Okay?"

Why? Why did I do this to myself? Why did I do this to other people? All he was doing was trying to be nice and—

"Well, too fucking bad," Ivan replied a moment before the hands on my shoulders started to shift, to slide, going across my upper chest, right beneath my collarbones until his forearms were crossed over me in an X, and then Ivan was pulling me back—stumbling me back—until my upper back hit his chest, flesh to flesh.

And he hugged me. He hugged me so tight to him I couldn't breathe, and I hated myself. I hated myself for being a hypocrite. For not being nicer. For expecting the worst all the time. I hated myself for so many things, I wasn't sure I could count them all and survive.

And the arms around me somehow got even tighter, until every bone in my spine was curved into every bone in his upper body.

"You're the best figure skater I've ever seen," this man whispered directly into my ear, his hold the strongest thing I had ever felt in my life. "You are. The most athletic. The strongest. The toughest. The hardest working—"

I leaned forward to get away from him because I didn't want to hear this shit... but didn't go anywhere. "You know none of that fucking matters, Ivan. None of it means anything if you don't *win.*"

"Jasmine—"

Dropping my head forward, I squeezed my eyes even tighter because the burning in them only got worse. "You don't get it, Ivan. How could you? You don't lose. Everyone knows *you're* the best. Everyone loves you," I croaked out, not able to finish the words, not able to say *and no one loves me the same except the people I've let down over and over again.*

Warmth hit my cheek at the same time the arms around me swarmed me. Ivan whispered, his lips against my earlobe, "You're going to win. We're going to win—"

I choked.

"—and even if we don't, you're as far away from being a loser as anybody can get, so shut up. I'm sure your mom doesn't feel like it was worth nothing. I've seen her watching you before. I've seen you before. There's no way anyone would see you on the ice and think there was a price limit on it," he suggested.

I squeezed my eyes closed and held back the next choke crawling up my throat, and I felt like I was dying all over again. "Ivan..."

"Don't 'Ivan' me. We're going to win," he whispered into my ear. "Don't give me this bullshit about you being a loser either. I don't win every time. Nobody does. And yeah, it isn't fun, but only a quitter says things like that. A quitter gives up and really does make that kind of statement come true. You're only a loser if you give up. Are you a quitter now? After everything? After all those broken bones and falls, you're going to quit now?"

I didn't say anything.

"You giving up, Meatball?" he asked, rocking me back into him.

I said nothing.

"These young girls quit right after they win gold medals because they're scared of losing after that. You say nobody remembers second place, but no one remembers the girls that win once and disappear afterward either. The girl I know, the Jasmine I know, isn't scared of shit. She doesn't give up, and that's the girl people will always remember. The one who is there time after time. You'd win and keep trying to win afterward. That's the girl I know. The one I partnered up with. The one I think is the best—and you better not ever ask me to repeat that because I won't. I don't know what happened to you earlier, but whatever it was, you need to move past it. You need to remember what you're capable of. What you are. You make every sacrifice worth it. You make every penny worth it. Do you understand me?"

Understand him?

"Just let me go," I croaked. "Please." *Please.* Please. Out of my mouth. Jesus Christ.

He didn't. Of course he didn't. *"Do you understand me?"*

I dipped my chin and kept my mouth closed, my organs burning up and melting.

Ivan's sigh went over my ear, and he squeezed me in that

hug I hadn't wanted but didn't want to leave now. "Jasmine, you're not a loser." What had to be his chin touched my ear because it prickled. "Not years ago, not last week, not today, not tomorrow. Not ever. Winning isn't everything."

The snort out of me burned. It was so easy for him to say that. To think it.

And in that Ivan way, he knew what I was thinking because he said, "Some of the unhappiest times in my life have been after big wins. Your family loves you. All they want is for you to be happy."

"I know that," I whispered, hating how weak I sounded, but not able to do anything to change it.

I was miserable. More miserable than even after Paul left. More miserable than maybe after I realized my dad was moving away.

"You and me will give them that. Understand me?"

A sob tried to crawl out of my throat, but I kept it in, and I buried it. Buried it so deep I wasn't going to risk ruining this chance by replying. Because this was enough. This was too much.

And I was miserable.

"That night I had dinner at your house, the second thing your mom said to me was, *I can make things look like an accident*," he murmured, and I froze. "When I was leaving that night, your brother's husband told me that you're like his little sister and that he hoped I'd treat you with the same respect I would treat my little sister. And your sister Ruby randomly whispered that her husband was in the army for over ten years. I think she meant it as a threat.

"And both your brother and your sister said that you have experience digging holes to put bodies into," he finished, his voice still gentle. "They sounded proud of it. Real proud of it, Jasmine."

I blinked, and then I blinked some more. This... something, just barely replacing the burn going on inside of me. Not much, but it was enough for the weight on my chest to lift just enough for me to feel like maybe I could breathe again sometime soon. Maybe in a year. Maybe in two. Because that was my family.

And Ivan's next words wrecked some more of that feeling eating me up slowly.

"They understand, Jasmine," he kept going. "How can you think you haven't done anything when they care about you so much? They admire you. They were bragging about how tough you are. How resilient you are. There are girls at the rink who light up every single time you walk by. You've probably changed their lives and inspired them by showing up here day after day, staying true to yourself, not letting anybody talk you out of anything. Not even me. I don't know what you consider a loser, but those aren't the kind of traits that come to my mind when I think of with that word."

I ducked my head and bit my lip, my words lost, my mind too slow to process everything.

And then he finished me off.

"You and me, Meatball. We're going to win if that's what you need. Understand me?"

CHAPTER 12

"I THINK WE'RE DONE FOR THE DAY," COACH LEE CALLED OUT from her spot a couple feet away from where I'd landed after a throw.

Breathing in through my nose and out through my mouth, trying to keep from panting after a practice that had made me sweat so much the L and R on my hands had started to fade, I nodded. It was time. I was tired, and I knew Ivan was too. I'd felt how deep into his reserves he'd had to dig to throw me that last time.

Plus, it didn't help that I'd slept like shit. It also didn't help that we'd been so busy at the diner that morning that I hadn't gotten a chance to even take a break. I'd overdone it the night before. Inside and outside, and my body hadn't forgiven me for not treating it as well as I usually did.

I hadn't been able to stop thinking about my choices—about what I wanted to do and needed to do—and... if I was going to be honest with myself, I'd thought more about Ivan's kindness than I would have ever expected. He'd probably hugged me for ten minutes straight as I'd calmed down and slowly, in tiny bits and pieces, gotten grounded.

He hadn't asked what upset me. He hadn't teased me for it. At some point, he had just let me go while I finished drinking my hot cocoa and then taken the cup from me to wash and set beside the sink. Then he'd followed me to the empty changing room, waited for me to grab my things...

And he'd followed me home.

We hadn't said much to each other, and I wasn't sure if it was just because he knew I was in my head or if he didn't know what to think about me losing my shit. Honestly, I wasn't sure either. The one thing I did know was that if Ivan thought I was going to be embarrassed the next day, he had to have been real fucking surprised when I wasn't.

I could see it in his face every time he looked at me. Those crystal clear almost sky blue eyes roamed over my face every time we were in front of each other. For one tiny millisecond the first time I caught him watching me, I thought about looking away.

But I didn't. I refused to.

Because to do that would say I was ashamed that he'd found me like that, that he'd heard and watched me damn near cry, which was almost as bad. And one of the best lessons I'd ever learned figure skating was that when you fell, you got right back up and acted like nothing had happened to begin with. You made things important, or you didn't. And if you got up and smiled and held your head up high... you still had your dignity.

And I was going to squeeze the shit out of my dignity with both hands.

At least what was left of it.

We were friends. And sometimes friends lost their shit around each other. At least that's what I figured.

"Take it easy and get some rest, Jasmine," Coach Lee said as she skated toward me and gave me a serious, lingering look.

I forgot she had been the one Galina had called the night before. I only managed to nod. What else could I say or do?

"See you tomorrow bright and early," she finished, touching her fingertips to my shoulder for a brief moment before dropping them and skating away.

Planting my hands on my hips, I kept trying to catch my breath as I looked around the ice, taking in the six other people still practicing, taking advantage of the last few minutes before the private ice time was over and it opened up for group lessons. I spotted Galina almost immediately sitting at the same spot she used to sit in when it was me and her, her chin resting on the folded hands she had on the wall. Her gaze was on the teenager going through a sequence of arm movements a few feet away.

"Am I invited to dinner tonight?" Ivan's question came from behind me.

I blinked and turned to look at him over my shoulder. He had started off practice wearing a dark green fleece pullover, but had stripped it off about an hour ago, leaving him in fitted black sweatpants and a light gray long-sleeved shirt with patches of dark damp material along his chest and abs. Maybe I hadn't slept well, but from the lack of bags under his eyes, he hadn't had the same problem. His face was as clear and bright as always.

Lucky shit.

Breathing in through my nose, I pressed my lips together for a moment, and just as I was about to shrug, I nodded instead. I owed him that much. He deserved that much. "If you don't have anything else to do," I said, making sure my voice was nice and even.

Ivan nodded. "Not until later."

What did he have to do later? I wondered.

"I'll follow you home then," he said, sounding just like he always did... without the sarcasm. "If you can manage not to drive like a psycho, that would be nice."

And there we went.

"I drive the speed limit."

Those thick, dark eyelashes swung over his eyes. "Is that what you call going ten over?"

I made a face. "I've never gotten a ticket."

"Uh-huh."

I rolled my eyes and just barely managed not to shoot him a dirty look. "I'll wait for you by the front doors, sock boy."

One corner of his mouth twitched... but he dipped his chin.

He blinked at me.

And I blinked right back at him.

Then the other corner of his mouth twitched too.

"You suck," I said before I could stop myself.

"You suck more," he replied before starting to skate backward. "Meet you in ten."

I scrunched up my nose and made my way to get off the ice, getting to the opening at the wall right after Ivan. I put my skate guards on, watching him watch me as I did it, noticing out of my peripheral vision, the families beginning to show up and make their way to the stands.

But we didn't argue. I took off and headed toward the changing rooms, not wanting to be the last one to the front doors. I'd rather wait for him than him wait for me. It would probably be a good idea to text my mom before I left just so she'd know he was coming.

I hadn't seen her since the night before when she'd told me about her accident, and even though I wanted to talk to her about what she had implied, I didn't know what exactly to say. I wasn't positive what would be more effective than "I love you."

And she deserved so much more than that.

I rounded the first corner, where Ivan would turn to head to his special room, and headed straight instead. I spotted the two teenage girls standing outside the room immediately. It was the two girls who were always nice to me. Sure enough, just as I approached the door, they turned and gave me two shy smiles.

"Hi, Jasmine," one of them said while the other one squeaked, "Hi."

I thought about Ivan's words the night before and gave them both a little smile as I walked in front of them. "Hi." My hand went to the door to push it open... and I paused, before saying, "Have a good practice."

"Thank you!" the outgoing one basically shouted as I went in.

Just like every Saturday night, the changing room was full of teenage girls between the ages of thirteen and eighteen. They were talking so loud it made my ears hurt. I headed to my locker, casting a side glance around to see that they were all familiar faces with no names, and then I turned my back to them. It didn't take long to open my locker and take my boots off, pull out my bag and set my skates in their protective case before taking my phone out, wiggling my toes and rolling my achy ankles as I unlocked the phone screen.

I found my mom's name under messages and typed up a text as quickly as I could, making sure my words came out spelled correctly, while trying my best to ignore the girls' voices.

Bringing Lukov to dinner, I sent her before dropping my phone onto the empty bench beside me.

Pulling my socks off and then my wraps, I felt my phone vibrate and picked it up. It just said **OK. ;)**

I wasn't even going to touch that winky face. I set my phone back down and bent over to start going through my bag for my flip-flops when I stopped zoning the girls out for some reason and heard, "...*big hands and big feet.*"

"*How do you know that's true? There's a lot of guys with big hands and big feet that don't have bulges.*"

What the fuck were these kids doing talking about bulges?

"*Like who?*"

"*Like...*" The girl talking dropped her voice to a whisper, like I still couldn't hear her after she did it. Idiot. "*Ivan Lukov. I've never seen anything under his costumes, if you know what I mean.*"

The fuck were they bringing up Ivan for? And what were these little perverts even doing staring at his crotch? He'd been 99.99 percent naked in front of me, and I hadn't looked at it for more than the second it took to see he had it covered.

And why the hell were they bringing up him not having one? That didn't mean anything. Most guys taped it down, I thought. I'd asked Paul about it once, and he had just turned red and stuttered as he laughed, avoiding the question, like I didn't know he had a penis under his clothes. Another idiot.

"*His hands and his feet are huge,*" another girl tried to whisper, but she was even worse at it.

"*But has anyone even seen anything?*" one little shit asked before giggling.

I spun around on the bench seat as fast as I could and chose my words as best as I could. "Would you stop? You all want some guys talking about your... stuff behind your backs?"

Just like that, they all stopped talking and turned a shade of red that I'd thought only Ruby was capable of.

That's what I thought.

I made sure to look at each one of them before shaking my head and turning forward again. No one else said anything, and I didn't worry about them tattling on me, because what were they going to do? Admit they were talking about Ivan's crotch?

Slipping my flip-flops on and giving my toes another wiggle as I stretched my arches, I snatched up my keys and purse and got up, bending over to grab the handle of my duffel. I side-eyed the girls on the other side of the room who all looked like I'd kicked their puppy, and I didn't give a shit. I put the lock back on my locker and headed toward the door, yanking the door open a lot rougher than necessary.

God, what was wrong with teenagers? I couldn't remember talking about people's dicks when I was their age. Seventeen, okay. But fucking maybe fourteen?

"—ugly and fat in that leotard."

And there it was.

Children.

Thirteen, maybe fourteen-year-olds standing outside of the door. Two teens that looked a whole hell of a lot like the two that had been talking shit about me weeks ago.

And those two were standing in front of my two girls that always greeted me. The two sweet, but funny little girls that had just been grinning at me maybe five minutes ago but who currently had their backs to the wall and had glassy eyes that looked a whole hell of a lot like they were on the verge of tears.

Damn it.

Why did this have to happen to me?

I wanted to walk away. I really did. I'd already had my beef with these little shits, and I didn't want to get into it again and risk getting in trouble.

But...

My outgoing little buddy had tears in her eyes, and one of these fuckers had just called her or her friend fat and ugly, and I didn't play that bully game.

So, I stopped and made eye contact with my two friendly girls, raising an eyebrow. "You two okay?"

The more outgoing one of the two blinked away what had to be tears, and the action instantly made this strange feeling zip up my spine, and I narrowed my eyes as I glanced at the two mean girls that both looked like they regretted the decision they had made while I'd been in the changing room that had led them to this moment.

When neither one of the two nicer girls agreed that they were fine, the feeling in my spine intensified, and I recognized it for what it was: protectiveness. I hated bullies. I *really* hated bullies.

"Were they picking on you?" I asked slowly, calmly, keeping my focus on the two nice kids.

"We weren't doing anything," one of the little shits tried to argue.

I slid my gaze over to the one who had spoken and said, "I wasn't asking you." Then turning back to the one with the tears in her eyes, I asked again, "Were they picking on you?"

It took a swallow before I got a nod. From both of them. And that feeling in my spine only got stronger.

I bit the inside of my cheek before I asked, "Are you okay?"

Their little nods almost broke my heart.

But what they did manage to do successfully was focus on the two little shits as my best bitch expression came over my features as I said, slowly, slowly, slowly, wearing that smile that Jojo had called horrifying on more than one occasion, "If I ever, *ever* hear or see you picking on them—or anybody here—again, I'm going to make you both regret the day you decided to take lessons here, do you understand me?"

Neither one of them nodded or said yes, and that only made the tingle in my spine recharge. A better person would have added some inspirational shit. But that wasn't me.

I turned my attention to the two nicer girls. "You get picked on again, come tell me, okay? I'll deal with it for you. Tomorrow, next month or a year from now, don't be shy, as long as I'm here, I'll take care of it for you. Nobody deserves to be spoken to like that."

I would know. I'd been through it enough. In return, I got two blank looks, but whether it was in alarm or what, I had no idea, before both girls nodded, fast, fast, fast.

And I smiled at them, to tell them it was okay. I had their backs. Not everyone was terrible, but the bad ones made it easy to forget that. I should know.

But then I glanced back at the two little shits and let the smile fall away as I focused in on their petty-ass faces. "And you two, I catch you doing that again and I will open a can of whoop-ass on both your rude—"

"Jasmine!" I heard a familiar male voice yell from close, but not that close.

Sure enough, glancing up, I found Ivan down the hall, one hand against a wall. He was too far for me to see more of him, but I knew from the shape and length of that frame it was him. That, and I'd recognized that voice anywhere.

"Let's go, I'm hungry," he called for no reason, I thought, until it hit me.

He'd heard me. That's why he had yelled and stopped me from calling these girls motherfuckers like I had planned on.

It wouldn't have been a good idea, but, well, whatever. They deserved it.

"Don't be jerks," I pointed at the two rude shits, then

turned to the other girls and said, "and tell me if they pick on you again."

When I got two nods in response, I made sure to give the other pair a nasty look like I was onto them before heading down the hall toward Ivan, who was still standing there waiting, except I could see him shaking his head from a few feet away. The second I was close enough, I realized he was grinning. Those straight, bright white teeth were all out there as he asked, "Is today your day to pick on little kids?"

I rolled my eyes as I stepped in front of him, having to tilt my head back to look up at him. "Those are monsters, not kids."

Those eyes were focused on mine as his grin only grew and he said, "What I want to know is..."

I blinked, not sure what he was about to ask.

"What is a can of a whoop-ass and where can I get one?"

I didn't mean to smile, and I sure as hell didn't want to.

But I couldn't help it.

I smiled so wide my cheeks instantly hurt and said the only thing that came to mind, "You're an idiot."

AN HOUR LATER, I WAS HEADING DOWN THE STAIRS AT MY MOM'S house, trying to wring more water out of my hair so that it wouldn't soak into the light, tank dress I'd put on. I hated washing my hair every day—and my hair hated me washing it every day if how dry it was said anything—but with how much I was sweating with two-a-day practices, it just got way too greasy if I went longer than twenty-four hours without a wash. I was going through a bottle of conditioner every two weeks.

By the time I made it to the bottom landing, I could hear

the voices in the kitchen. When we'd pulled up to my house half an hour ago, there were Jonathan and Aaron's cars in the driveway. I hadn't asked what my sister or brother were up to, but I'd seen both of them a few days ago when they had dropped by randomly for dinner.

I'd only gotten a chance to give my mom a kiss to the right of her bruised and swollen nose before Jojo's dramatic ass had gone off with, *Jas, how could you not call and tell me about Mom's accident*? I almost threw her under the bus and said that she didn't want me to say anything... but I was no snitch. So I told him it was because I'd been too tired the night before to deal with his shit. That had gone about as well as I'd expected, and I ran up to get a shower five minutes later, watching Ivan shoot me a curious look that said he might have been putting the pieces together from what happened last night to what he was seeing on my mom's face.

And... I didn't care if he did.

Making my way across the living room toward the kitchen, the voices became clearer and louder. I recognized the sound of my sister and mom laughing... and thought I heard a light chuckle from Ivan mixed in there. Thinking about the moment in the hallway with the girls made me smile again, but I wiped it off. He really was an idiot.

"...did they make you tape everything up?" I heard Jojo ask.

Oh God.

"Jonathan," his husband hissed. "What does it matter?"

"Uh, I'm curious. I looked up the magazine this week. I didn't see a hint of balls or anything in those pictures, and it doesn't seem possible from the angles the pictures are taken at. I don't care how tight anybody's ball sacks are, it isn't physically possible for there not to be a tiny sign of nuts somewhere. Get what I'm saying?"

They were talking about the photo shoot for the Anatomy issue, and of course it would be Jojo asking that.

"Maybe I need to get that magazine when it comes out—" my mom started to say before Ruby and Jojo almost wailed, "Stop!" and "Nobody wants to hear that!"

"You two are so sensitive," my mom muttered, but didn't continue with her sentence. "I have eyes. You have eyes. The human body is a wonderful thing, isn't it, Ivan?"

There was no hesitation from Ivan when he responded with, "It is."

"I'm sure Grumpy looked beautiful."

But there was a pause before Ivan asked, "Who is Grumpy? Jasmine?"

"Yes."

No one said anything for a second before Jojo butted in. "She hated Snow White when she was a wittle baby."

"Why?"

It was my mom who answered. "Because she... what did she used to call her? A lazy fart that took advantage of men?"

Jojo burst out laughing in that way that made me smile. "She used to get so mad watching it. Remember? She would sit there in front of the television talking smack to herself. She hated it, but she'd still watch it over and over again anyway."

Then it was Ruby that started laughing. "She would walk around saying that Snow White wasn't that pretty, and even if she was, she needed to have a little respect for herself. She didn't even know what that meant, but she heard you, Mom, say that once and it stuck."

Then my mom started laughing. "That's why we started calling her Grumpy, because she said he was the only smart one of all the dwarves because he knew he had a reason to be in a bad mood. Work in the mine all day and then have to take care of some girl that didn't do anything." Her laugh went higher. "Oh, that girl. You can all blame yourselves for how she came out. She picked it up from you all. Ivan, it's their fault."

There was another moment and then, "She's my idol" from Ruby, which earned a husky laugh from what had to be Aaron.

"That's my girl," my mom echoed.

My nose itched, and my eyes might have begun stinging a little.

Okay, more than a little.

I had to blink and listen to them laugh while I got my shit together and felt that nice, warm feeling in my chest growing, growing, growing. It made me feel... better. Better than I'd felt the night before after Ivan had been so kind.

After a couple more swallows and blinks that made sure I was back to normal, I headed into the kitchen and found everyone except my mom's husband around the island. Ben was busy stirring what I knew was a giant pot of his awesome chili on the stove, with his back to the group. There was one seat empty between Ivan and my sister, and another seat open between Aaron and Jonathan.

I went for the one next to Ivan.

And for some reason I wasn't going to overthink, I snuck my hand from my side over to the thigh closest to mine and gave it a squeeze. Not a mean squeeze, just a normal one that wasn't too hard or too loose. Friends did that, didn't they?

"Jas," Ruby started to say as she leaned forward over the island and shot me a careful smile that made me wary. "I know you're really busy—"

Why did my stomach flip?

"—but remember we talked about you watching the kids for us a few weeks ago? Do you think you still can?" She smiled. "It's okay if you can't."

My stomach clenched. It was too soon. It was way too soon. But I could handle it. I would. I could be better.

"I didn't forget," I told her, trying to ignore the tension right around the center of my body. "I can watch them."

"Are you sure? Because—"

I tried to give her a smile. I tried to tell her that I loved her and that *yeah*, I loved her kids too. I'd do anything for them. But instead, I said as softly as I was capable of, "Yes. I'm positive. I can watch them."

"We can watch them too," Jojo piped up.

I shot him a look. "No. I can babysit them. Find your own niece and nephew."

Jojo rolled his eyes and turned back to Squirt. "I can watch them anytime you want, Rubes. They don't need Rosemary's Baby over there rubbing off on them."

"Do you really want Shrek Junior over here to be what Benny wakes up to?" I asked my sister, shooting my brother a look.

"I'm average height," Jojo claimed.

"Sure you are, boo-boo," I returned, smiling at him for real. "Either way, you didn't say you don't look like Shrek, so...."

Jonathan decided to scratch at his forehead. With his middle finger.

"Would you two stop?" Mom finally sighed.

"You don't really look like Shrek, Jojo," Ruby added. "More like Donkey, I think."

Jonathan just blinked over at her before sliding his eyes to me and saying, "You're the worst influence."

"Your mama."

My brother looked right at Ivan beside me, his middle finger going back up to his forehead—for me of course—and said, "Ivan, if you accidentally trip and fall doing a lift with her, none of us would blame you. Really."

The side of a thigh touched my knee, and a second later, so did the palm of a hand I knew very well. "I'll keep that in mind. Maybe during an exhibition after worlds," my partner offered.

And I couldn't even be mad or butt-hurt.

CHAPTER 13

"You don't have to come with me," I told Ivan as we got out of his car, subconsciously rubbing at the weird tingle in my throat that had been bothering me all day. I blamed it on leaving my water bottle in the car and not having a chance to run back out to grab it, or else face the wrath of Nancy Lee.

He huffed, and I swore to God he rolled his eyes. "I already said I would."

"I know that, smart-ass, but you can still back out. My sister or her husband can give me a ride later, if you want to leave," I suggested, waiting for him on the path up to my sister's house since the passenger side was closer to the curb.

Ivan shrugged and shook that black head of hair. "I'm not backing out. It's just... how long did you say it would be? Three hours?"

"Four hours," I corrected him.

He seemed to think about it as he came up beside me before tipping his head to the side, coming to whatever conclusion he had gotten to. "I've put up with you for four hours, this is just two kids, it can't be that hard."

Obviously this man had never babysat before if he thought

it wasn't that hard, but I wasn't about to tell him that. I was kind of looking forward to seeing him deal with a toddler and a baby. "All right, don't say I didn't give you an out."

Ivan scrunched up that perfect, symmetrical face as we stopped in front of the door. "Give me some credit, we're only babysitting. It isn't rocket science."

I nudged him with my elbow right before reaching up and knocking on the door.

He elbowed me right back.

How the hell had we gotten to this point?

My damn car hadn't started. *Again.* And my uncle hadn't answered his phone when I'd called, and I couldn't exactly afford to call a tow truck driver. There were plane tickets and hotel rooms I was trying to save up for, and groceries, insurance, an electric bill I paid as part of my "rent" and other random expenses I had every month. Right around the same time that I was debating who to call to come pick me up, came the obnoxious *tooooooooot* that lasted maybe ten seconds and made me jump when it had first rang through the air, coming from a classy black car. Following the toot was a driver side window being rolled down and a very familiar face peering out from over the edge of the glass.

"Car trouble again?" Ivan asked from his spot behind the wheel with his sunglasses covering his eyes.

I sighed, then I nodded.

"You need a new one."

I just looked at him. "Okay, I'll get on that."

He made a face right back. "Get in."

"I'm not going home," I told him.

Those black sunglasses were aimed right at me as his jaw did this tick thing. Then, "What? You got a hot date?"

"No, numbnuts. I'm babysitting tonight."

The expression on his face instantly changed, but I didn't think anything of it.

"I'm going to my sister's," I finished, reminding him about what Ruby and I had literally talked about in front of him a week ago.

Ivan shoved his glasses just above his eyes with the tip of his finger. "Get in then."

"It's further away than my mom's."

"How much further?" he asked slowly.

I told him what side of town, and watched as he made a face.

"How long are you supposed to babysit?"

"About four hours," I said, hearing the hesitation in my voice, mainly because I wondered where the fuck he was supposed to be going that he was worried about how long it would take.

Then he made a thoughtful face and said, "Okay. One second." He must have reached for his phone, because the next thing I knew, he was focusing on his lap and saying, "One more second."

Who was he texting? And what was he texting?

I'd barely started to wonder what, when he glanced back up and said, "Okay. If it's only four hours, I can drive you there and drop you off at home afterward."

Wait. Afterward?

"You're going to drive back and pick me up?" I asked with a frown.

He pinched his mouth in that way that used to drive me crazy because it looked like he thought I was an idiot. "No. That's the other side of town from where I live, genius. I'll babysit with you, and after that, I'll drive you back home... as long as it's only four hours. I need to be home after that."

What did he have to be home for? Was someone waiting for him? Did he... have a girlfriend?

"You getting in?" he kept going.

It wasn't any of my business. None.

Nope, none of my business.

If the swallow I took felt tight, I wasn't going to overthink it. "You can just drop me off and one of them can take me home after."

I didn't have to see his eyeballs to know he was rolling them. "Shut up and get in. I can take you as long as it doesn't run too late."

He had a girlfriend, didn't he?

"You don't need to stay—" I started to say before he cut me off.

"Get in, Meatball," he'd demanded, already rolling the window up.

And with a dirty look and a reminder that whatever he was doing afterward had nothing to do with me, I got in. And he drove us to my sister's, which was where we were, with me waiting on the paved sidewalk, arguing with Ivan after we'd bickered over whether he drove slow or I drove fast.

He drove slow.

That was how I found myself in front of Ruby's house with Ivan beside me.

"Coming!" I heard my sister call out from the other side of the door. All of a second later, the door opened and she was there, already beaming that great big smile that made me feel like I'd kill someone for her and eat their heart too. "Jas." She hesitated only a second before taking a step forward and wrapping her arms around me.

I hugged her back, deciding to keep my mouth shut about the pause she had taken before touching me. Had I ever not wanted her to hug me? I couldn't remember, and the possibility that I had once made her think twice about doing something like hug me, made my stomach tighten.

I could fix this. I could work on it.

Pulling back, I tipped my head toward Ivan at the same time her eyes strayed to him. "I brought reinforcements to take care of your gangsters."

My sister's face turned pink instantly, and she nodded tightly, her eyes shifting from me to him and back again. "Hi, Ivan," she managed to squeeze out.

Ivan smiled gently. Then, because he held his hand out toward her, and when she did the same, he took it and gave it a soft shake. "Nice to see you again, Squirt." He gave her a charming smile that made me uncomfortable for some reason. "You don't mind if I call you that, do you?"

My sister blinked, and so did I. But I knew her reaction wasn't because Ivan was handsome or anything like that. Her husband was smoking hot in a completely different but equal way as Ivan. And she was madly in love with him.

She was just shy.

And no one called her Squirt but family. At least as far I knew, not even Aaron called her that.

"I don't mind," she pretty much whispered, her eyes darting to me, and then back to him. "You're almost family now, right?"

Almost family? I shoved the idea aside just as Ivan nudged me, and I elbowed him right back.

"Come in," Ruby said, taking a step back. "We're ready to go. We're just doing dinner and going to a... eh, store afterward." By store, I'd bet my kidney she meant a comic book store, but I knew she wasn't admitting it because Ivan was right there. "We shouldn't be gone long."

I shrugged and stepped into the house I'd been in plenty of times over the last year since she'd moved back to Houston after spending the last four years living in Washington with her husband while he'd been in the army. He had rushed through a degree over the last few years, and gotten a job at a VA hospital doing.... Something with veterans. I was a shitty sister-in-law not to know what he did exactly. I really needed to ask Ruby. "It's fine. Do whatever you want. I don't have anything else to do besides go to sleep," I told her, purposely not mentioning that Ivan had to bounce after four hours to go do whatever it was he needed to do.

"Hey, Jasmine," a nice voice called out from down the hall a moment before the tall, blond man walked toward us.

"Hi, Aaron," I said, rocking on my heels. "Aaron, you remember Ivan."

The blond beefcake, who I swore could have had a successful career as a gigolo if he hadn't been in the military, held his hand out toward me, and I slapped his palm. He then turned to Ivan and held it out too, where Ivan shook it. "Nice seeing you again," my brother-in-law said, taking a step back to be side by side with my sister. "Thanks for babysitting."

I shrugged but Ivan said, "Sure."

"We'll get going so we can get back faster," Aaron let us know, leaning over to kiss my sister on the temple.

Ruby nodded. "You know where everything is. They're both upstairs right now. They've eaten. Benny's asleep on our bed. I didn't want to wake him up to move him. We're still working on his potty training..."

I waved her off. "Don't worry about it. I can handle it." I glanced at Ivan standing there and tried to imagine him changing a pull-up... and I came up with nothing. "We can handle it."

Maybe. At least I could.

With another kiss to the temple that Aaron gave Ruby, they filed out of the house, closing and locking the door behind them. The lock had barely been spun when there was a wail from upstairs.

"Let's get to work," I said, pointing at the stairs.

Ivan nodded, then followed me up the stairs of the nice, big four-bedroom house in the suburbs.

My sister's babies shared the same room. There were two cribs set up on opposite sides, one white, the other one wood tone. I headed straight to the white one, seeing the squirming, tiny body lying face down. Jessie was crying so loud I winced as I picked her up and brought her into my chest, cradling her. She was so small... and so damn loud.

I rocked her, whispering, "Shh, shh, shh," and bouncing her a little the way she liked, before turning to find Ivan standing in the doorway, grinning like an idiot. I blinked. "What?"

Jessie kept on wailing.

"You picked her up like it was nothing," he said, his eyes going from me to the baby and back again, like it was a miracle or something.

"She's just a baby, not a grenade," I told him, still whispering *shh, shh, shh,* and bouncing to try and calm my favorite little baby down. It always did the trick. I smiled down at the cute, pissed-off face.

"I didn't know you liked kids," Ivan murmured, coming to stand beside me, arching his neck to look at the child in my arms.

I smiled at Jess, knowing he couldn't see me, and wrinkled my nose. "I love kids."

His "Really?" didn't surprise me at all.

I bounced the baby a little more, her wailing toning down until it was just a whimper. *Bingo. Jasmine the Baby Whisperer.* "Oh yeah," I said softly, keeping my voice light. "I like kids. I just don't like adults."

"You don't like adults? I don't believe it." Ivan snorted, turning his neck to shoot me a smile before focusing back on the baby. His finger came up and touched one of Jessie's cheeks sweetly, probably taking in the softness if it was one of the first times he'd ever been up close and personal with a little human.

"Shut up."

I could hear him breathe gently. "She's so soft and little. Are they always this small?"

I watched her little face, knowing under her eyelids there were bright blue eyes that one day might come out the same shade as my mom's. "She came out almost seven pounds; that's pretty big for how small my sister is," I explained. "Benny is a big boy too, they get it from their dad." I dropped my head to give Jessie a kiss on the forehead as she gave a fussy baby cry. "Kids are innocent. They're sweet, they're honest. They're cute. They know right and wrong better than adults do. What isn't there to like?"

"They're loud."

I glanced at him out of the corner of my eye and cleared my throat, trying to ignore the tingle coming from it. "You're loud."

His gaze was already on me as he said, "They have tantrums sometimes."

I glanced up at the ceiling. "It still sounds like you're describing yourself."

Ivan laughed as quietly as possible. "They cry."

I made a face at him, that made him grin that white-white grin.

"Shut up. I don't ever cry," he whispered.

"Whining... crying... same thing."

"You're such a liar."

I shook my head and glanced down at Jessie, my little

niece. "I love babies, especially these babies. My babies," I whispered, moving her further up my arm. Jessie gave a whimper, and I moved her again to hold her up to get a whiff of her diaper. It smelled fine. She took after my sister, her poop reeked when it came out.

"Are these your only two?" Ivan asked out of the blue.

"No, I have another niece from my oldest brother. She's a teenager now."

"Are you close to her?"

I looked at Jessie again, thinking of all the ways I'd failed my other niece. I hadn't been in her life much. She had a favorite aunt, and it wasn't me. The only person I could blame was myself. "More now, but not enough. I was too young when she was born, and then once I wasn't... I didn't make time or enough of it, you know what I mean? She was a baby, and then she wasn't. It was too late by the time I realized it."

Of course he knew what I meant by time running out. I wasn't positive how. But he knew.

"Yeah, I know," he agreed. "That's part of it." Out of the corner of my eye, I could see him glance at me. "Don't hold onto that. It's pointless and you know it."

I shrugged. "You say it like it's easy, but you know it isn't. I shouldn't care that my oldest sister is her favorite, but it bugs me," I told him for some reason. "I'm a sore loser, that's probably it."

Something touched my shoulder, and I saw it was Ivan's hand. "You are a sore loser," he agreed.

The smile I gave him was a little one that I wasn't totally feeling.

"You'll probably be this one's favorite." He touched Jessie's cheek again.

"I'm working on it," I told him. "It's my goal. For once, I can be someone's favorite."

The way he turned his head slowly, made me cautious. Then he whispered, "What is that supposed to mean?"

I shrugged again, pushing that heavy feeling that had come out of nowhere off of me. I was going to fix things. I was going to be better. "Nothing. Just that I can be someone in my family's favorite, so I've chosen Jessie since I have a fresh slate."

His expression should have said something to me, but it didn't. "I still don't get what you mean by that. Explain."

I rolled my eyes. "What I said. My mom's favorite is my brother Jonathan. My dad's favorite is my sister Ruby."

"*What?*"

I shrugged. "They have favorites. Every parent does. Ruby's favorite person is my sister Tali. Tali's favorite is Ruby. Sebastian and Jojo's favorite is Ruby too. It's fine."

It wasn't that Ivan made a face—because he didn't—at least not a face that 99.99 percent of people would have noticed. But that was the thing. I was the .01 percent that *would*. Because I did. What he did, and I knew it was more of a reflex than something intentional, was flex his jaw muscles. It was quick. Just a quick flex that was the briefest, most insubstantial movement I had probably ever seen.

But I saw it.

"What?" I asked him, still making the same face.

He didn't look surprised at getting caught, and in that way that was all Ivan, he didn't bullshit me and lie. "Who's your favorite?" he asked me slowly, that gray-blue gaze intense.

I glanced at the baby in my arms and smiled down at the tiny face. "Both the babies."

Ivan swallowed so rough I noticed it, what I also noticed was how raggedy his voice sounded when he threw me another question. "In your family though, Meatball. In your immediate family, who is your favorite?"

I didn't even need to think about it. Not for a second. Not ever. I sure as hell didn't need to look at him as I answered. "All of them."

There was no disbelief to his tone when he threw my words back in my direction. "All of them?"

Giving the baby a kiss on the forehead, I said, "Yeah. All of them. I don't have a favorite."

He paused. Then he asked, "Why?"

The sting at my chest was so abrupt it almost took my breath away.

Almost.

What it did though, was hurt. Just a little. Just enough. But it did. It didn't matter how rare it happened, it always felt the same.

So I definitely didn't look at this man who I spent almost all day, every day with when I answered. "Because I love them all equally."

But this bastard didn't let it go. "Why?"

"What do you mean why? I just do," I said, still avoiding eye contact by trying to play it off like I hadn't already memorized the tiny face in my arms.

The thing about athletes—about people in general who have this *need* to win at anything and everything—is that they don't know the meaning of giving up... of letting things go. That concept is foreign to them. So why I expected the man who was even more of a sore loser than the biggest sore loser I knew—me—to let something it was clear he was hung up on, go, was beyond me.

So I shouldn't have been surprised when he kept going and asked the one question that I absolutely did not want to answer.

"But why, Jasmine?" He paused, letting the words really sink in. "Why do you love them all equally?"

The problem with hating lies was that when you wanted to fall into one, it hurt like a motherfucker to pick it up, hold it in your hands, and decide what to do with it... knowing either way it was going to ache. Maybe it made me a weak ass, but I acknowledged it and accepted it. So I told him the truth. "Because they all have good things about them, and bad things. I don't hold that stuff against them," I explained to him, not wanting to—definitely not wanting to—but having to. What was so wrong with the truth, except for the fact that it made me ache like crazy?

I glanced up at Ivan before I kept going, because I didn't want him to think I was embarrassed. I didn't want to make this seem like a bigger thing than what it was. Otherwise, he would take it to be more than it needed to, and I definitely didn't want that. So I told him. "I want them to know I love them just the way they are. I don't want any of them to feel bad thinking I like one more than the other."

And then it was out there. I couldn't take the words back.

The words hung in the air, in between Ivan and me, around and around and around and around, they were there.

He said nothing.

He didn't say a word for so long as he stood there, all long and perfect, staring at me with those blue eyes for so long that I wanted to fidget, but he was the last person in the world I wanted do that in front of, friends or not. He'd already seen me at my worst. He didn't need to see how talking about favorites really made me feel.

So instead, I rolled my eyes and asked, "How about you look at something else now? You're making me feel awkward."

What did this idiot respond with? "No."

I ignored him.

Luckily, it was right then that Benny waddled into the

room, his clothes rumpled, his face puffy and cute, and said, "I'm hungwy, Jazzy."

I jumped on that shit before it ran away and I got stuck talking about things I didn't want to think about more than I already had. "Okay, Benny." Then I looked at Ivan and asked, "You want the baby or the toddler?"

His face got alarmed so fast it made me snicker. "I need to take one?"

"What do you think I brought you for? *Yeah*."

Ivan blinked before his gaze slipped from Benny, who was still half asleep standing in the doorway, to Jessie's sleeping face. "They're both babies," he said, like it was news.

It was my turn to blink.

Ivan bit that pink lip of his and glanced at the little boy standing there, probably not even totally comprehending we weren't his parents. Then he decided. "I'll take the baby."

I didn't let the surprise show on my face. I thought for sure he'd take Benny instead of Jessie. "Okay. Here," I said, stepping in front of him, already holding my arms out.

His face *almost* made me laugh.

"I've never held a baby before," he muttered, his whole body tensing.

"You can do it."

That had him glancing up at me as he formed his arms into the same shape I had mine. "Of course I can."

I snickered, and that made him smile. It was pretty easy transferring the baby from my arms to his. He was a natural, slipping the crook of his elbow underneath her head and then bringing her in close to his body.

"She's so light," he commented the second she was fully in his arms.

"She's only a few months old," I told him, already turning to crouch down to Benny.

Ivan snickered. "That doesn't mean much. You're little too, but you're heavy as hell."

"Oh, shut up. I'm not that heavy." I turned to look at him over my shoulder as I extended my arms out to my nephew.

"You are. You're the heaviest partner I've ever had."

"It's all muscle."

"Is that what we're going to call it?"

I laughed as Benny came toward me, still rubbing at his face. "Okay, Tinkerbell, you aren't exactly light either," I threw out before wrapping my arms around my favorite three-year-old, picking him up.

Ivan laughed softly as he brought the baby up to his face the same way I had moments ago. "I'm not supposed to be. It's all muscle."

∾

"I DON'T KNOW WHY PEOPLE COMPLAIN SO MUCH. THIS IS EASY," Ivan said, holding the bottle to Jessie's mouth as she sucked hungrily at it.

I hated to admit how easy this baby shit was with Ivan. It probably shouldn't have been. But it was.

The second time Jessie had started wailing, this time in his arms, he'd kind of jumped a little, frowned, given me a panicked expression, and before I could tell him what to do, he'd started humming and rocking her all on his own. His *shh, shh, shh* sounding weird out of his mouth. I hadn't timed it or anything, but it felt like less than a minute later, her kitten cries had turned into whimpers, and a minute after that, she had completely stopped. I had almost called him a natural, but he didn't need that shit to go to his head. He already thought highly enough about himself.

And then he amazed me some more.

When she'd cried not too long after that, and I'd told him she probably needed a diaper change, all he had said was "Okay." So when I offered to change it, while he took Benny, he had said, "I can do it. Tell me what to do," and that had been it. He changed her diaper and only fake gagged twice.

He was infinitely patient. He didn't get tired. He didn't complain.

And it shouldn't have surprised me. It really shouldn't have. I'd seen him be patient, tireless, and complain-less, every day for weeks and weeks. He got it from figure skating. But I couldn't help but think that maybe I didn't know him as well as I thought I did.

"I've spent the night with them before. Do that and then tell me it's easy. I don't know how my sister isn't a walking zombie," I told him as I lay on the floor beside Benny, handing him blocks that he was making a castle out of. Or something that looked sort of like a castle.

"They wake up a lot, huh?"

"Yeah, especially when they're this young. Ruby and Aaron are both crazy patient; they're good parents."

"I could be a good dad," Ivan whispered, still feeding Jess.

I could have told him he'd be good at anything he wanted to be good at, but nah.

"Do you want to have kids?" he asked me out of the blue.

I handed Benny another block. "A long time from now, maybe."

"A long time... like how long?"

That had me glancing at Ivan over my shoulder. He had his entire attention on Jessie, and I was pretty sure he was smiling down at her. Huh. "My early thirties, maybe? I don't know. I might be okay with not having any either. I haven't really thought about it much, except for knowing I don't want to have them any time soon, you know what I mean?"

"Because of figure skating?"

"Why else? I barely have enough time now. I couldn't imagine trying to train and have kids. My baby daddy would have to be a rich, stay-at-home dad for that to work."

Ivan wrinkled his nose at my niece. "There are at least ten skaters I know with kids."

I rolled my eyes and poked Benny in the side when he held out his little hand for another block. That got me a toothy grin. "I'm not saying it's impossible. I just wouldn't want to do it any time soon. I don't want to half-ass or regret it. If they ever exist, I'd want them to be my priority. I wouldn't want them to think they were second best."

Because I knew what that felt like. And I'd already screwed up enough with making grown adults I loved think they weren't important. If I was going to do something, I wanted to do my best and give it everything.

All he said was, "Hmm."

A thought came into my head and made my stomach churn. "Why? Are you planning on having kids any time soon?"

"I wasn't," he answered immediately. "I like this baby though, and that one. Maybe I need to think about it."

I frowned, the feeling in my stomach getting more intense.

He kept blabbing. "I could start training my kids really young.... I could coach them. Hmm."

It was my turn to wrinkle my nose. "Three hours with two kids and now you want them?"

Ivan glanced down at me with a smirk. "With the right person. I'm not going to have them with just anybody and dilute my blood."

I rolled my eyes at this idiot, still ignoring that weird feeling in my belly that I wasn't going to acknowledge now or ever. "God forbid, you have kids with someone that's not perfect. Dumbass."

"Right?" He snorted, looking down at the baby before glancing back at me with a smile I wasn't a fan of. "They might come out short, with mean, squinty, little eyes, a big mouth, heavy bones, and a bad attitude."

I blinked. "I hope you get abducted by aliens."

Ivan laughed, and the sound of it made me smile. "You would miss me."

All I said, while shrugging was, "Meh. I know I'd get to see you again someday—"

He smiled.

"—in hell."

That wiped the look right off his face. "I'm a good person. People like me."

"Because they don't know you. If they did, somebody would have kicked your ass already."

"They'd try," he countered, and I couldn't help but laugh.

There was something wrong with us.

And I didn't hate it. Not even a little bit.

CHAPTER 14

"WHAT'S WRONG WITH YOU?" IVAN SNAPPED ABOUT FIVE seconds after coming out of a sit spin—the same sit spin I'd stumbled out of a second before, landing right on my ass. The same one I'd *kept* losing my balance on the last six times we'd done it. The same spin I could usually do over and over and over again, one variation after another, a flying sit spin, a death drop, with a twist.... It was usually no big deal.

Unless your entire body was burning up, every muscle between your knees and chin ached, and your head felt like it was about to explode.

On top of that, my throat was acting like I'd chewed on sandpaper, and just standing up in general was taking everything out of me.

I felt like *shit*.

Total, complete shit. I had all morning. I was pretty sure I'd woken up in the middle of the night—which I never did—because my head hurt and my throat had burned like I'd swallowed a glass of lava for shits and giggles.

But I hadn't told Ivan or Lee about it.

With only one full day left before we started working on

choreography, we didn't have time for me to be sick. Since the morning of the day Ivan and I had watched Ruby's kids, one thing after another had started acting up. My throat had started tingling, then tingling a little more. Another day my head began to feel weird. Then I started to get tired. Then everything started to ache, until *bam.* The fever came. And everything else decided to go full-fledged sick.

Ugh.

Flopping onto my back, the groan that came out of me was thanks to how bad my head was pounding. I couldn't remember the last time my balance had been so bad. Never?

"Are you hung over?" Ivan asked from wherever the hell he was.

I started to shake my head and immediately regretted it when the urge to throw up kicked me right in the gut. "No."

"You stayed up last night, didn't you?" he accused, the quiet swish of his blades on the ice telling me he was getting closer. "You can't be coming to practice exhausted."

Rolling over and then coming to my knees, all I had the energy to do was wiggle the fingers on one hand. "I didn't stay up, jackass."

He huffed, the black of his boots coming into view. "You're full of—" I saw his hand reaching for my upper arms too late. So late there was no way, no fucking way based on how shitty I felt, that I could have moved before he touched me. His hands grabbed me right above the elbows and just as quickly let them go.

I'd been so hot, I had taken off the pullover I had on over my tank top over an hour ago, leaving my arms exposed. If I could have stripped that off too, I would have.

Ivan's hands went to my forearms, gripped them for a second, and let them go too.

"Jasmine, what the fuck?" he hissed, his palms going to my

cheeks as I just waited there on my hands and knees because I had no energy left. If I could have laid down on the ice in a fetal position, I would have. He cupped my face for a moment, then moved his other hand upward to cover my forehead, cursing so creatively under his breath in Russian, I would've been impressed any other day. "You're burning up."

I groaned at the coolness of his hands on me and whispered, "No shit?"

He ignored my smart-ass comment and palmed the back of my neck, earning him a moan straight out of my mouth. Jesus, it felt good. Maybe I could lay on the ice for a minute.

"She's got a fever?" I faintly heard Coach Lee ask as I started lowering myself slowly down, hands to elbows, then elbows going wide until I was sprawled spread eagle on the ice, my cheek on it, arms and palms flat on it too.

It was cold as hell, but it felt amazing.

I could hear Ivan talking to Lee, their words becoming fainter and fainter by the second.

"Give me a minute," I said as loudly as I could, feeling the coldness on my lips and seriously feeling tempted to lick it.

I didn't. I wasn't sick enough to forget how dirty some people's blades were.

I heard something that sounded like "stubborn" above.

Turning my face to the other side, I let the cold kiss my cheek and sighed. A nap sounded so good. Right here. Right now.

"Never mind, five minutes please," I whispered numbly, trying to reach back toward my neck with one of my hands but too tired to even do that.

"Okay, all right, roll over, Jasmine," a feminine voice I was pretty sure belonged to Coach Lee said from somewhere over my head.

"No."

Three minutes. If I could just close my eyes for three minutes....

There was a sigh and then something that had to be fingers at one of my shoulders, pulling and yanking on me. I didn't fight it. I didn't move. But somehow, they rolled me over, and I just let them, flopping over almost painfully until I was on my back with the bright lights at the ceiling forcing me to close my eyes because they made my head worse. I had to grit my teeth to keep from moaning.

"Two minutes, please," I whispered, licking my lips.

"Two minutes my ass," Ivan replied a moment before something started forcing my shoulder upward, tunneling its way across and under my shoulder blades at the same time something else went beneath the backs of my knees, doing the same.

"Just a minute. Come on. I'll get up, promise," I got out as I felt myself being lifted. It wasn't like I could see. I still had my eyes closed and probably would until the lights weren't blinding me.

"I know there's a thermometer in the staff room," it sounded like Coach Lee said. "I'll get it."

"Meet you in my room," I heard Ivan respond, drawing me off the ice and into his chest.

Oh God. He was carrying me.

"Put me down. I'm fine," I croaked, feeling anything but fucking fine as a shiver raced across my arms and spine, making me shake.

"No," was the one and only thing that came out of his mouth.

"I am. I can get through practice...." I trailed off, squeezing my eyes closed as my headache got worse and the urge to throw up did too. "Fuck, Ivan. Put me down. I'm going to throw up."

"You're not going to throw up," he said, carrying me and skating at the same time from the movements of my side against his chest.

"I am."

"No, you're not."

"I don't want to throw up on you," I gasped, *this fucking close* to gagging as acid flowed around in my stomach.

"I don't care if you do, but I'm not putting you down. Suck it up or swallow it, Meatball," he said with all the comfort and care of my mom. Which was none.

My head *throbbed*. "I'm going—"

"You're not. Hold it in," this man—my partner—demanded, rocking me against him as he started walking and not skating.

"I'll feel better if I throw up," I whispered, the sound of my own voice irritating me. My throat irritating me even more. But I couldn't be sick. We didn't have time. "Let me, then we can get back to practice. I can take a Tylenol—"

"We're not practicing anymore today," he let me know in that annoying snobby voice. "Or tomorrow."

That had me groaning as I tried to lift my head, which was against his shoulder, and realized I couldn't even do that. I was *gone*. Jesus Christ. "We have to."

"No, we don't."

I swallowed and licked my dry lips, but it didn't do anything. "We can't take time off."

"Yes, we can."

"Ivan."

"Jasmine."

"Ivan," I basically moaned, not in the mood for this shit. My shit or his.

"We're not practicing anymore, so stop bringing it up."

We only had a day left. Choreography was supposed to

start *tomorrow*. I started trying to roll up, engaging ab muscles that had decided to take a vacation, and... couldn't. Oh my God, I couldn't do shit.

Ivan sighed. "I'll put you down in a minute. Quit squirming," he ordered, still carrying me, still walking effortlessly, his breathing steady and even as he held me up in his arms.

I was going to blame being dizzy and exhausted on why I did what he said. And why I let my head rest against that curve between his shoulder and neck. I didn't need to wrap my arms around his neck. There was no chance in hell he would drop me. This was nothing for him.

"Is your mom at work?" Ivan asked me quietly a moment later.

"No, she—she went on vacation with Ben to Hawaii," I replied, weakly, just faintly taking in how quickly I'd gone downhill. Another shiver slid through my whole body, and I shook even harder than I had any time before. *Damn it.* "I'm sorry, Ivan."

"For what?" he asked, tipping his head down to look at me from the way I felt his breath on my cheek.

I pressed my forehead against his cool neck and let out my own breath, dismissing the lines between his brows as aggravation, just noticing my shivering was going nonstop. "For getting sick. It's my fault. I never get sick." Another hard case of the shakes went straight from my shoulders down my spine.

"It's fine."

"It's not. We can't take the time off. Maybe I can take something, nap, and we can train again this evening," I offered, each word coming out longer and more drawn out than the last. "I'll stay as long as you want."

From the way his neck moved, he had to be shaking his head. "No."

"I'm sorry," I whispered. "I'm really sorry."

He didn't say a word. Didn't tell me it was fine. Didn't tell me to shut up again. And I was too wiped to argue with him more.

But it was in no time, that he was walking us into his room at the Lukov Complex and then gently—so, so gently—depositing me on the couch so I could lay across it. I shook again, hot and cold at the same time, my back hurting even more than it had a few seconds ago. Putting my hands up to cover my face, I held back a moan.

This was what dying felt like. It had to be.

"You're not dying, dumbass," Ivan said a second before something was laid over my body and two seconds before something cold and wet was draped over my forehead.

Did he just...

Yes, he had covered me with a blanket and put a wet towel on my forehead.

"Thanks," I had the clarity to say as I lay there, knowing I should wrap my head around what he'd done but feeling too much like shit to do so. Later, *later*, I could appreciate how nice he was being. But right then, it felt like my head was going to explode.

Ivan didn't reply, but I did hear some other noises going on in the background, and at some point later, maybe seconds, maybe minutes, there was movement by my feet. A few seconds after that, one of my skates came off and then the next. I didn't ask him to be careful with them. I didn't say anything.

Then he said, "Sit up, Meatball."

Obviously, he didn't feel bad enough for me to not call me that.

I did, or at least I tried to sit up, but my body wasn't functioning. It needed things: rest. Sleep. A good vomit. Some

Tylenol. A cold bath and then a hot one. All of those things in no particular order.

He made some sound that came out like a huff, then his hand went to the back of my neck, lifting it and my head higher.

And then he slipped onto the couch.

And laid my head back down... on his thigh.

"Drink this," he ordered as something smooth and hard touched my bottom lip.

I opened my eye to see him a holding a glass to my mouth. I reached toward it, weak, so damn weak, taking it from him because it was one thing to lay my head on his lap, but it was another thing to let him hold up a glass of water for me. I took a sip and then another one, my throat closing up around each drink in protest from how sore it felt.

"Swallow this too," he said afterward, holding up two white tablets in his hand.

I glanced at his beautiful, stupid face.

And he rolled his eyes. "It's not arsenic."

I still looked at him.

"I'm not going to poison you until after worlds, all right?" he added, not sounding anywhere near as much of a smart-ass as he usually did.

Closing both my eyes at once in a way I hoped he took as "okay," I opened my mouth and let him drop the tablets on my tongue, chasing them down with three painful gulps. Dropping my head back onto Ivan's thigh, I closed my eyes. "Thanks," I mumbled.

There was an "uh-huh" that I definitely heard in reply. What had to be fingers touched my hair, moving around my head. Gentle, gentle... until they started tugging.

"Oww," I hissed, opening an eye to find him hunched over

me, staring down with a frustrated expression, as he yanked on my hair again.

"What is this?" he hissed, pulling some more.

I flinched when he did it again. "A scrunchie?"

He pulled, but not tugging as many hairs out with that attempt. Just like a hundred. "It's so tight."

"No shit," I croaked, not sure if he even heard me.

He made a face and gave my hair one last tug before pulling the band—and another two hundred strands of hair—out, holding them up victoriously. "How do you not get headaches using this?" he asked, looking at the black elastic like it was some crazy shit he had never seen before.

How had he not seen a scrunchie before with the other women he'd been partnered up with over the years? Ugh. I'd worry about it later. "Sometimes I do," I whispered up to him. "I don't exactly have a choice."

He frowned at my explanation and then dropped his hand, making the band disappear for a moment before it was back and he was empty-handed. Closing my eyes once more, I felt his fingers go back to my hair and start stroking it away from my face and what had to be over his lap. It felt good, his thigh under my head, his fingers in my hair, and I couldn't help the sigh I let out as he did it.

I might have dozed off, but the next thing I knew, something was poking at my lips, and I opened my eyes to find my head still on Ivan and a big hand holding a thermometer right in my face. He raised his eyebrows expectantly, so I opened my mouth and let him put the blue stick in, closing my lips afterward.

"She needs to go to the doctor," Ivan claimed, looking over at where Coach Lee was sitting... which was on top of the coffee table, with a worried expression on her face. I hadn't heard her come in.

Then I processed the word Ivan had used: doctor.

"I agree," our coach replied, already digging into her pocket to take out her phone. "I'll call Dr. Deng and then the Simmons to reschedule."

Ivan glanced down and gave me a stern look. "Don't say you're sorry." Then, before I could get out a word, he told the other woman, "Tell her it's urgent. I'll take her as soon as she has an opening. And tell the Simmons to keep their schedules open. I'll make sure they're taken care of for their time."

She nodded, already pulling her phone to peck at the screen.

Meanwhile, I shook my head, waiting for the thermometer to beep so I could talk. Coach Lee was on hold when the device finally did. The display read 103.7. Great.

"No doctor," I said, to both of them when Ivan took the thermometer out of my hand to get a look at the reading.

Those blue eyes flicked toward me for all of two seconds before going back to the thermometer.

"Ivan, no doctor."

"You're going to the doctor," he let me know, his face tensing as he took in the number on the screen before saying to Lee, "Tell them her fever is almost 104."

I licked my lips uselessly and looked up at him, the whole hot-cold thing making me want to kick off the blanket on top of me but also drag it up higher to my neck. "No doctor." I swallowed, closed my eyes for a moment, and said, "Please."

Ivan's hand stroked my loose hair, and he gazed down at me. "Do you want to feel better or not?"

I tried to give him an ugly look but couldn't get my face to work. "No, I love feeling like shit and missing training and screwing everything up."

Both those thick eyebrows went up like "no shit."

"Forget about it. You're going to the doctor. If you need

medicine, you need it the sooner the better." He pursed his lips for a moment and then added, "So we can get back to the choreography. When you're ready."

This fucker. He knew exactly how to get me. Jesus.

"Look, I need today, tomorrow—"

"We're taking it off." He blinked. "Why don't you want to go to the doctor?" He squinted. "I swear, if you're scared of needles—"

I moaned and started to shake my head before stopping myself when the pain there triggered my nausea. "I'm not scared of needles, who do you think I am? You?" I whispered.

Coach Lee was talking quietly on the phone, but neither one of us was paying her any attention.

"All right. You're going to the doctor."

I closed my eyes and told him the truth because he'd get it out of me eventually and I wasn't in the mood for him to nag. "I don't have insurance. I can't afford a visit right now. Seriously, I'll be fine. Just give me a day. It'll pass. My immune system is usually great."

Ivan's lips moved. He blinked. He glanced up and then looked back down before shaking his head, his voice rising from a mutter. "You stubborn ass...."

"Fuck off," I whispered.

Ivan *hissed*, "You fuck off. I'll pay for your doctor's visit and medication. Don't be an idiot."

I closed my mouth and swallowed the ache in my throat and the painful stab in my chest at his choice of words. "I'm not an idiot. Call me whatever you want other than an idiot."

He either chose to ignore me or just didn't care. "You're an idiot, and we're going to the doctor. Don't let your pride get in the way of you getting better."

That's how bad I felt that I didn't even argue with him. He had a point, unfortunately. I just closed my eyes and said,

"Fine. But I'll pay you back." I swallowed. "It might take me a year."

Ivan muttered something under his breath that didn't sound very nice, but his palm stroked my hair some more, brushing through the strands like the last thing he wanted to do was hurt me. For once. It was nice.

"They can see her at noon," Coach Lee finally said. "We need to reduce her fever in the meantime. Did you give her a painkiller already?"

"Yes," the man whose thigh I had my head on replied.

They whispered some other words to each other, words too low for me to care about while I was debating if I could offer to pay Ivan to keep running his fingers through my hair, when I felt a tap to my cheek. "Hmm?"

"Time to get up," Ivan whispered. "You need a shower."

Get up? "No, thank you."

There was a pause and then, "I'm not asking. Get up."

"I don't want to get up," I whined.

"Okay," he agreed too easily. "I'll carry you in."

"No thanks."

His hand stroked over my head, then picked at the corner of the towel over my forehead and peeled it off, brushing his fingers over the skin there with those hands I knew so well that had never been so gentle before. His voice was low as he said, "I know you don't want to, and I know you feel bad, but you need to get up, little hedgehog. You need to cool down."

I groaned and ignored his h-word.

Ivan sighed, but his hand still petted my hair. "Come on. Get up for me."

"No."

There was a snicker and another stroke. "I wouldn't have thought you were a baby when you got sick," he said, sounding amused I thought but wasn't sure because I was too busy trying to zone out how shitty I felt.

"Uh-huh," I agreed, because my mom had always said the same thing. *What a crybaby.* I didn't get sick often. It wasn't like I tried to milk attention... even if she would have given it to me. But she was always more worried about my sister than me having a little cold or cough, and I'd never cared.

"Are you going to get up?" he asked, palming my forehead with a hiss I wasn't so sick to not know it meant my skin was hot.

"No," I said again, rolling onto my side so that my cheek was pressed to his thigh and my nose was at his hip. His crotch was *right there*, but his dick could have been out and I wouldn't have cared.

"You're not going to get up on your own?"

"No."

There was a pause and a definite sound of amusement when he finally grated out, "If you insist."

I insisted. I really insisted, especially as another shiver racked through my entire body, my spine aching in that way it only did after a bad season and real illness. I wasn't getting up.

But Ivan had other plans.

Plans that involved him sliding out from under me while I groaned in protest at the loss of the most uncomfortable pillow I'd ever laid my head on, but beggars can't be choosers so I'd take that hard thigh any day. Those plans were then followed up by two arms sliding into the same spots they'd been in minutes before: supporting my shoulder blades and the underside of my knees. Then, he lifted me and started walking, each step solid and balanced.

And I didn't argue. Not even a little bit.

It might shame me later that I didn't even try and help him with my weight to ease the load; instead I just lay there like a kid being carried to bed after a long car ride, with my head resting against his shoulder while I shivered some more. I could have walked, of course I could have. But I didn't fucking want to. Not when he was so willing to help me out.

And just feeling his warm, hard body against me made me feel a little better.

In no time at all, he opened a door I hadn't noticed before, leading us into a bathroom. It wasn't anything fancy, just a shower stall with a sink and toilet. Ivan squatted and slowly let me get to my feet, where a head rush made me dizzy.

"You need a cold shower," he said, stabilizing me with the arm around my shoulders.

"Ugh," I mumbled, closing my eyes. He was right. I knew from the rare times I'd seen other people with high fevers how dangerous it could be. I didn't need to lose any more brain cells. Another shiver tore through my body, and that had Ivan letting go of me and stepping around to turn the handle on the shower.

"Come on," he urged.

I tried lifting my arms but let them drop when they didn't move much more than an inch away from my body. Fuck. I was more exhausted than I could ever remember being before.

With a swallow, I opened my eyes again and thought, *Fuck it. I'll go in fully clothed.* I had a change of clothes in my bag. Lee or Ivan could grab it for me. Doing my best impersonation of every single member of my family on Christmas, I stumbled forward, squinting my eyes because the bright overhead light was goddamn blinding.

But two steps before just walking right into the stall with my socks still on, Ivan's arm went up, parallel to the floor, and blocked me from going any further. "What are you doing?" he asked.

I peeked at him. "Going in?"

"You're fully clothed."

"No energy to take my clothes off," I said, sounding hoarse.

I didn't miss the way he rolled his eyes. "I'll help you."

"Okay," I whispered, not thinking twice about it. Why would I? He'd had his hands all over my body daily, had already seen me basically naked, seen me half-dressed, and in skintight clothes. We were past being self-conscious.

He hesitated for a moment... and then smiled a little. He took a step to the side to stand in front of me, that funny, small smile on his face, and he reached for the bottom of my tank. And before either one of us could overthink it, he pulled it up over my head.

Unlike some other girls I knew with little to no chests in figure skating, I always wore a sports bra. I liked the support. They didn't need to be moving around the place when I was upside down, even if there was hardly anything that moved.

And if Ivan was surprised that I wasn't braless under my clothes, it didn't show on his face.

Then again, if he was, I barely had my eyes open so I might have missed it.

But his hands continued their path down until he got to the top of my tights, and taking a knee, he stripped those down my legs. Just as I was about to try and toe my socks off, still down there, he picked up one of my legs with one hand, and with the other, pulled off the thin socks and bandages I'd put on that morning, dragging the flat of his thumb over the arch before lowering my foot and picking the other one up. He did the same to it, his eyes lingering on my toes if I was seeing correctly, and if I'd had the energy, I would have scrunched up my sparkle pink nail polished toes. The fact that he glanced up at me and smiled, kind of threw me off, but I didn't let my thoughts linger there. My stomach gave a roll, and I just barely managed not to throw up the breakfast I'd forced down that morning.

Ivan snickered as he gave my heel a squeeze and dropped my foot. "In you go, champ."

~

I WAS DEAD ASLEEP WHEN SOMETHING—OR SOMEONE—HIT MY forehead. Hard.

Then that something—or someone—hit me three more times, one right after the other. It was the fact that there was a rhythm to it that had me snapping my eyes open.

Someone was knocking on my forehead.

And that someone was Ivan.

Ivan who was leaning over me, his fist held just a couple inches away from my face. He was smirking. At me.

"Wake up, *Outbreak* monkey. It's time for your next Tylenol."

I blinked. Then I looked at the ceiling behind him, trying to remember what the hell was happening. It was then, as I was wondering that, that my head reminded me it was still hurting. *Still hurting.* I shivered, a reminder that I'd had a fever. More than likely still had one if the tremor that went through my body meant anything.

I was sick. The doctor had said it was a virus. Ivan had driven me there, then afterward, taken me to the pharmacy, where I'd sat in the car, shaking from hot to cold, to buy a bottle of Tylenol because I couldn't remember how much I had. Then, he'd taken me home. Home to an empty house because my mom and Ben were gone, enjoying the beach and doing fun shit I would love to do.

Instead, I was in my room, under the covers, having my

forehead used as a bongo drum by someone who was clearly enjoying it.

"What time is it?" I asked, trying to scoot up toward the headboard while I blinked, just barely noticing how raspy and hoarse my voice sounded. It was even worse than it had been before.

"Time for you to take your Tylenol," he replied, shaking the fist he'd been using to knock on me.

I groaned and tried to roll to my side so I could go back to sleep, but he grabbed my shoulder and moved me back to lay the way I'd been.

"Two more and then you can go back to sleep," he tried to compromise with me.

"No."

Those glacier eyes stayed locked on me, his facial expression still a happier one than I ever would have bet on. His voice though, didn't sound so playful. "Take the pills, Jasmine."

I closed my eyes and moaned at how much my back and shoulders ached. "No."

I could see the sigh he let out in his shoulders. "Take the damn pills. Your fever still hasn't broken," he ordered, still holding on to my shoulder because he knew damn well the second I got a chance, I'd try to roll over again. Ugh. Was I that predictable?

"My throat hurts," I whispered, using that against him.

He sighed again, shaking his fist once more. "I'm not buying you children's Tylenol. Take the pills."

I closed one eye and left the other one open as I whispered, "I don't want to."

I'd swear on my life, Ivan flashed a smile so quick, it was there and then it was gone. Back to normal. Back to trying to boss me around for my own good. "You need them," he reminded me.

I just stared at him with my one eye.

"No?"

"No," I said, just barely loud enough for him to hear.

His jaw twitched, and his gaze narrowed. "Your mom warned me you're a pain in the ass when you're sick."

She would say exactly that, that didn't surprise me. I was a whiney little bitch when I was sick. It was true. So I didn't waste my words and throat on agreeing.

What I did wonder was... when the hell had he talked to my mom?

And just as soon as I wondered that, I decided I didn't give a shit.

Then it hit me. "I forgot to call—"

"Your mom called your boss for you," he cut me off. "Now take them."

"No."

"You want to play this game, we can play this game," he replied easily, making me suddenly wonder if I was screwing up. He kept going. "You're *going* to take them."

I swallowed and winced at the ache that answered that action.

The blink he gave me put me on edge instantly. Then his words confirmed that tiny worry he'd given me. His voice was low as he said, "You're going to take them, or I'm going to make you take them."

Ugh.

"Bitch," I whispered.

He beamed at me, literally *beamed*, fully aware that we both knew his threat wasn't in vain. Not at all. Not even a little bit. "You ready then?"

I opened my mouth, shooting him the nastiest look I was

capable of while basically looking like a baby bird, and watched as he moved his hand over my face and dropped the pills into my mouth a moment before handing over a glass of water. Three small sips later, I swallowed the medicine and handed the glass back over. He took it and set it on the night-stand, before turning to me from where he'd been sitting on the edge of my bed the whole time.

"You feeling any better?" he asked.

"Little," I whispered, because I was. Just a little. My headache wasn't *as* bad, and even though I knew I had a fever, I was pretty sure it had to have gone down some. At least that's what I hoped. I had to get better as soon as possible. That I hadn't forgotten.

Ivan gave me a microscopic smile, his fingers coming back to touch my forehead with the backs of them, gentle, gentle, gentle. "Your fever has gone down. It was down to 102 when I checked it an hour ago."

He'd checked it an hour ago? God, I was out of it.

Ivan flipped his hand over and touched my cheek with the tips of those cold fingers. "You want another wet towel for your head?"

"No," I answered before adding, "thank you."

That got me another little smile. "You want anything?"

"To feel better."

"You'll be better tomorrow," he said.

"I have to."

He rolled those bright blue eyes. "No, but you will," he claimed, scooting his hip further into the bed. "There's some soup for you downstairs."

I couldn't stop the frown from coming onto my face. "You made it?"

"Don't look at me like I'm trying to poison you. If I wanted to, I would have done it already." He grazed my forehead with the tip of his finger. "Your brother's husband brought it over."

Now that time, I did smile, thinking of sweet, wonderful James. "He makes the best soup."

"It smelled good. He wanted to see you, but you were sleeping."

I pulled the top of the comforter up, my muscles protesting that movement alone, but somehow I got it to go up the two inches to reach my chin. "He's the best."

That made him blink. "You think somebody's the best?"

"He is," I said. "My mom is too. So is my sister, Ruby. My sister Tali when she isn't having girl problems." I thought about it and swallowed again. "Lee's pretty cool. My brothers are too, I guess. Aaron's great. He can be on the list too."

Ivan made a noise, then scooted even further into the bed. I watched him and slid to the side to give him more room, wondering what the hell he was doing. His hand landed on the spot over the covers where my elbow was tucked inside, and he asked, almost hesitating, which wasn't at all like him, "And your dad?"

That's how crappy I felt that I couldn't even get mad at the mention of my dad's name. Or disappointed, which said something too. But I told him the truth. "Not to me."

I'd barely gotten the words out when his eyes sliced in my direction.

But he didn't ask why I thought that, and I was genuinely relieved. He was the last person I wanted to talk about. If not the last, then in the top three. Top four for sure.

"Anyone else on the list?" he asked after an awkward second while I'd been thinking about my dad.

"No."

I didn't miss the casual look he slipped me before mentioning, "I've won two gold medals."

"You don't say," I muttered sarcastically, watching him continue to shift on my mattress until his right side faced me.

"*Yeah*," he answered just as sarcastically. "Not one. Two. A few world championships too."

"What does that have to do with anything?" I croaked, my throat demanding water, as he then began to scoot backward until his spine met up with the headboard, just like mine had.

Ivan kicked his legs into the air, toeing off one fancy black leather boot after another, letting each thump to ground. "Some people think I'm the best."

"Who?" I snorted weakly as I watched him settle his legs onto the bed, crossing one ankle over the other, showing me the purple and pink striped socks he had on.

He angled his upper body just enough so he could watch me with both eyes, chin to his T-shirt-covered chest. "Lots of people."

I gasped, immediately regretting it because it made my throat ache. "I mean... I guess you're pretty cool too."

Those ebony eyebrows went up. "You guess?"

"I guess. Your skating is pretty good. And you've been really nice to me today. Yesterday. I don't even know what day it is," I mumbled. "You can be on the list too, if you're going to make it awkward."

"Don't sound so excited."

I laughed, wincing as I did it, and eyed the long body beside mine, the fingers knit on his chest that had at some point been running through my hair while I'd been at my worst. And without thinking about it, I scooted closer to him, wanting the touching again, wanting affection, lining up our hips and making my legs rest against the sides of his even under the covers. I swallowed, knowing somewhere inside of me he wouldn't tease me about wanting to be closer to him, and tipped my head to the side, resting it on his shoulder. We had been closer than this every hour of the day for the last two months. It didn't mean anything, I told myself. It didn't mean a single thing. And that's what I was going to go with, regardless of the knowledge that I had never, ever done something like this with bitch-ass Paul.

"You are the best," I told him, sounding about as weak as I felt, "at pairs skating."

Something landed softly on my head as he snickered, and I figured he was resting his head or cheek on top of mine. "Thanks for making sure to clarify that."

I laughed some more, the sting totally worth it. "You've been a good friend to me so far, but I really only have your sister to compare you to."

"Hmm," he sighed, shifting in his spot beside me, before slipping his arm over my shoulder unexpectedly. It wasn't like I was going to complain. It was warm and heavy, and I liked the way it made me feel: cocooned. Safe. I liked it a lot. "That's true."

"She used to let me borrow her clothes before she grew eight inches and left me behind. But she can't pick me up like you do."

His laugh was soft as he agreed. "You've got a point, Meat-ball. I'm easier to look at though."

I couldn't help the snort that I instantly regretted. "You're so annoying."

"You keep saying that."

I smiled against his shoulder and heard a huff of air that told me he was more than likely doing the same exact thing. "You don't have to stay, you know."

"I know. Your mom said your sister or brothers could come check on your grumpy ass until she gets back," he let me know.

I made a face. "She calls Tali throwing saltine crackers and

Gatorade into my room taking care of me. I'd rather be by myself."

"No Gatorade and no saltine crackers. That's the last thing you need," he said. "Sugar and pointless carbs won't do anything."

Leave it to Ivan to judge every ounce of nutrition that went into my mouth.

"Now I definitely can't leave you, if that's what will happen if I do," he whispered.

I snickered.

"I don't mind staying a little while longer, but I need to go home later, at least for an hour."

Somewhere in the back of my mind, I registered that he had to leave to go do something. Just like he had when he'd babysat Jessie and Benny with me, and just like when he'd eaten dinner at my mom's. But I didn't focus or question what and why he had to leave. I was too tired.

"You can go now if you want."

"No, it's only five, Meatball," he replied. "I've got hours. It's fine."

"I'm sure you have better things to do."

The arm over my shoulder went down, and Ivan's hand went to my shoulder, cupping it before going up and down my upper arm, one stroke up, one stroke down. "Be quiet and go back to sleep, all right?"

Sleep? It sounded wonderful. Just fucking awesome.

Without arguing, I closed my eyes, and asked with an exhale after I got a whiff of the light cologne he wore every day without fail, "Do you do this for all your partners? Or just the ones you're stuck with for a year?"

Beneath my cheek, his body tensed and stayed tense even as he answered. "Stop running your mouth and go back to sleep, would you?"

I moved my palm just enough so that it lay directly over the flat, solid slabs called his abs. I'd seen them a hundred times in glimpses here and there when he'd take off his sweater, or reach up to stretch or scratch his stomach... but I hadn't touched them. Not once in more than brushes. But they were just as hard as they looked.

"You really don't have to stay," I repeated myself again as exhaustion weighed heavy on my eyes, trying to give him an opening.

He sighed, and I sensed him shaking his head. "Nobody else is going to take as good care of you as I will." He had a point, didn't he? The faster I got better, the better it would be for him. For both of us.

If that was disappointment in my belly, I ignored it. It didn't matter. He was here now, doing what nobody else would want to do.

"Before you fall asleep again, where's your remote?" he asked.

Reaching behind me blindly, I grabbed the remote off the other nightstand and then dropped it on his stomach.

And I passed the fuck out.

SOMETHING WARM TOUCHED MY MOUTH LATER, AND I'D SWEAR I heard, "Drink it, baby," whispered to me.

And I drank it all. Whatever the hell it was.

I WOKE UP AT ONE POINT, SENSING MY HEAD ON SOMETHING hard, and peeked my eyes open enough to find that I had my head on a lap, my arm thrown over kneecaps. The television was on softly, and the comforter I'd crawled under had been kicked down to the bottom of the bed.

I was sweating. Hot. But somehow I managed to fall back asleep.

∾

"JASMINE," A FAMILIAR VOICE WHISPERED INTO MY EAR, STROKING my hair and then arm. "I need to go home."

I felt like shit. All I could do was mutter, "Okay."

Ivan's familiar hand stroked my hair, my arm, my wrist, lingering there. "Your cell is right next to you. Your mom said someone would come check on you. Call me if you need anything though, all right?"

"Uh-huh," was all I managed to get out before his fingers, or his hand, left my wrist.

"I'll be here in the morning," he said, something warm and damp touching my forehead so lightly and quickly, I thought I might have imagined it.

"Thanks," I whispered in my one moment of clarity, my throat parched.

"I left you water on both nightstands. Drink up."

Something else touched my forehead, and I sighed an, "Okay, Vanya." Then, I rolled over and went back to sleep.

CHAPTER 15

IT WAS THE POKE TO MY FOREHEAD THAT WOKE ME UP. THE "wakey, wakey," that came after it that got me to open my eyes and squint up at the finger hovering over my face. But it was the dryness coming from my throat and the dull pain from my head that had me shoving down the sheet I had pulled up to my neck. I had no clue where my comforter had gone.

Sitting with his butt halfway on the bed, with his hand above my face, was a clean, fresh-looking Ivan in a blue T-shirt that made his eyes look as if he had on colored contacts.

"What do you want?" I moaned, shuffling up the bed until my shoulder blades rested on the headboard.

He ignored my borderline rude words and smiled. "Get dressed. You need a shower and you need to get out of this room for a while."

I watched him the entire time I yawned, wincing at the soreness coming from my throat, and then reached over for the nearly empty glass of water that had been sitting on my nightstand since Ivan had left it there last night. Sipping what was left of the room-temperature water, I blinked at him and asked, "And that's why you had to wake me up? To tell me to shower?"

"And get you out of the house."

But I didn't want to leave the house. Much less my bed. And especially not to shower.

His fingertip came at my face so fast I didn't get a chance to move out of the way before he poked me on the forehead. "Get moving. Lacey isn't exactly patient."

"Who's Lacey?"

"You'll meet her in a minute. Hurry up. I'll get you another glass of water in the meantime." Ivan stood up and made a face. "Brush your teeth too."

For a second, I thought about blowing out a long breath of air just for his comment, but didn't have the energy... and he'd been nice to me for the most part. He'd at least gone totally out of his way since the day before.

I could keep my sick breath to myself this once, even though he was being an ass.

But the question remained... who the hell was Lacey and why did I have to meet her? Especially when I was sick. Just as I was about to open my mouth and argue with him, my head gave a throb to remind me my body was making up with this one virus, all the months and possibly years that had passed since the last time I'd been ill.

My whole body said, "fuck you," as I flipped the sheet to the side and swung my legs over the edge. I wasn't new to aches and pains, but there was a certain kind of hell that being sick put your body through. Everything from my eyeballs down to my toes ached and seemed to creak just from those movements, and I only barely held back a groan as I slowly stood up.

Ivan let out a "huh," maybe seeing my face or sensing the stiffness in my movement, but he didn't say anything else.

Just that was exhausting. "I don't feel like doing anything."

"I'm not going to make you do anything," Ivan returned. "I already said that you need to rest."

I eyeballed the jeans he had on. "Then... where are we going?"

His facial features didn't give anything away. "Nowhere bad."

I blinked.

"Do you trust—" He made a face. "Never mind. Just get dressed."

It said how tired and crappy I felt that I didn't argue or ask any more questions. I dragged my feet toward my dresser and pulled out underwear and a bra, becoming even more tired after that. Casting a side-look at Ivan, I found him still sitting on my bed... watching me. I sighed, and he raised his eyebrows again.

"I'll be back in ten," I basically whined, shuffling toward my door.

"Holler if you need me." There was a pause and then, "I've already seen you almost naked twice. It's no big deal."

I would have choked if I had the energy, but I didn't. I would have given him the finger too, but that didn't happen either. All I managed to do was grab my bathrobe from the hook behind the door. I headed, huffing and puffing, to the bathroom across the hall that I used to share with Ruby back when she had lived here. It took me longer than normal to shower, and it was only because my legs felt so damn prickly that I forced myself to shave. I didn't have the energy to put lotion on or anything. I just barely managed to pull on my underwear and my most comfortable bra.

I slipped on my robe and was just about to tie the sash on it when my arms gave up. I just held it together at my waist as I dragged myself back to my room, asking myself one more time: *Who the hell was Lacey?* And, where the hell were we going?

I had barely made it two steps into the room... barely seen Ivan sitting on the edge of my bed directly beside my nightstand... barely caught on to the fact that the top drawer of it was open... barely caught on to the fact he was holding white sheets of paper that *he shouldn't have seen* and *shouldn't have known existed*, when Ivan's head snapped up and I saw, *I saw*, his face was a color it shouldn't have been.

And then he lost it.

"What the hell is this?" he asked, shaking the papers in his hand, angrily, so angry, so fast, I really felt bad.

Only for a second. But it still happened.

The breath I hadn't realized I'd blown out of my lungs, came back in me before I managed to hiss out, "What the hell are you doing looking through my things?"

It was a sign of how angry he was that he didn't immediately have a comeback for me.

It was my fault. I knew he was nosey. I knew he was nosey because I was nosey. But *damn it!* Those papers had been in there safely for years.

Ivan ignored my question, crushing the sheets in his hand so tightly, they formed partial balls. "Who... who...?" he stuttered, another sign of how furious he was. Ivan never stuttered. Never faltered. *And even his neck was going red.*

He gave the papers another shake. *"Who did this?"*

I swallowed.

"Who sent this shit to you?"

"Ivan—"

He shook his head, the hand holding the papers dropping until his fist bumped against his thigh, his head cocked to the side in anger. In so much anger, I could almost taste it. "Don't 'Ivan' me. *Where did these come from?"*

Shit.

Shit, shit, *shit*.

I didn't even think I could try and play stupid and act like the notes I'd had hidden in my drawer were a joke—because my mom wouldn't look through my things, we were past that stage in my life. I knew Ivan too well. I knew he wouldn't drop this crap until I explained every detail.

And I couldn't say that I blamed him.

If I'd found pictures of naked men with his face taped to the bodies, with hearts glued to them, with arrows pointed at his genitals, connected to words like YUM and YES, I might laugh for a minute... and then worry like hell.

God, god, god, *goddammit.*

"Jasmine." He started to get revved up all over again, the red on his face and neck climbing to the tips of his ears. Good lord, I'd never seen him so pissed. I didn't even think he was capable of being so mad unless he was on the ice and something had gone wrong during a competition.

I held back my sigh, seriously regretting that I'd taken my hiding places for granted and hadn't shoved them into my underwear drawer... or somewhere else that was harder to find. I'd throw them away, but I wasn't an idiot, if anything ever happened, I needed proof.

Waving my hands, palms down, I tried to tell him in my softest voice, which probably wasn't as soft as it needed to be, "Calm down."

Yeah, that was the worst thing to do. He shook the fucking papers again. "Don't tell me to calm down!"

Oh fuck me.

"You have a fucking stalker, Jasmine!" he yelled again, making me thankful that my mom and Ben were gone.

I winced, trying to think of what to say and coming up with, "He hasn't threatened me...."

Ivan tipped his head back and made a noise I wasn't really sure what it was called. A growl? "*What the fuck?*"

I finally snapped. "Don't fucking yell at me!"

If looks could kill, I would have been dead, for real. "I'm going to yell at you when you've been getting things like this! Why didn't you tell me?"

Oh. My. God. I wasn't in the mood for this shit. Not ever and definitely not then. "I haven't told you because it's none of your business!"

"You're my business! So this is my business!"

"No, it's not!"

"Yes, it is!"

"No, it isn't! This has been happening since before we paired up."

And, I'd fucked up. I'd fucked up like I always did while speaking before thinking. For letting my mouth run away from me as far as it could.

Ivan's face literally went tomato red. So red, I was genuinely worried for his health. "I'm going to kill you," his voice dropped instantly. He stared at me, bug eyed. "I'm going to fucking kill you."

I couldn't even make a joke about it. "Just fucking stop, all right? I'm not in the mood."

Ivan shook his head and raised his fist, dropping the papers onto my perfectly made bed. "I don't give a single fuck right now that you're not in the mood, Jasmine," he stated, and before I could argue some more, he said in a tone I'd never heard from him, "How long has this been happening?"

I rolled my eyes and shrugged, so angry with myself for being so dumb. I knew better. I knew better. I should have planned for the worst, especially with this unrelenting, stubborn asshole. "Three years," I mumbled, so mad I could barely talk over the ache in my throat.

He closed those blue eyes and opened his mouth, shaking his head in the process. "Three years," he repeated the words roughly. "How many of these have you gotten?"

"I don't want to talk about it."

One ice blue eye opened and aimed itself right at me. "Too bad. How many of these have you gotten?"

I groaned, grunted, and tipped my own head back once more in frustration. There was no escaping it. Was there? Shit. "I don't know—" he started to cut me off, but I didn't let him. "No, seriously. I don't know. When I first started getting them, I threw the first few in the trash. My best guess is... twenty? Maybe?" More like thirty, but I sure as fuck wasn't going to admit that.

He was breathing so hard I almost didn't want to look at him, but I wasn't a little bitch. Especially not in this situation. "Does your family know?" he asked in a creepy, calm voice.

Could I have lied? No. This fucker knew my tells too well. "About a few of the ones in the past," I gritted out.

"What does that mean?" he demanded, still watching me with that one eye.

"They stopped coming in when I deleted my social media pages," I explained, wishing I didn't and wasn't. "They know about a few of the ones I got before that."

The other blue eye snapped open, and Ivan stared at me. "Are you still getting them?"

I moved my gaze away from him as I shrugged, so damn mad. "I don't know. I don't open my mail anymore."

I didn't. I didn't want to get distracted. I didn't want to over-think my situation.

So, I had decided to play the ignorant game. But I didn't admit that to him.

I also wasn't going to bring up the comments and private messages I had gotten.

The thought had barely occurred to me when Ivan's jaw went tight and he asked, "What about your Picturegram and Facebook? Have you gotten anything on there?"

Fuck me.

My face must have said everything because he dropped his head back and rolled it from side to side, breathing loudly the whole time.

"It's not—"

"Where's your phone?"

I blinked. "Why?"

"I want to see what you've been sent."

"It's none of your—"

It was his turn to blink at me after tilting his head forward. "Don't finish that sentence," he told me, slowly. "Let me see your phone. If there's nothing bad, it shouldn't be a big deal."

I hated it when he made a good point.

"Let me see it," Ivan repeated, using a tone of voice I hadn't heard from him before.

Damn it. There was no question he wasn't about to let this shit go. Ugh. "It's on the other nightstand," I muttered, pissed off at myself. "Let me see your phone then too." I don't know why the hell that sentence came out of my mouth, but it had.

He slid me another killing look before standing up, tossing his phone at me, and then crawling over my bed. "I already unlocked it," he let me know, angrily.

I shot him the same facial expression back, even though he couldn't see it. "My password is—"

"I know your password. I've seen you put it in," he muttered as his hand snatched my phone from the other nightstand.

"Fucking stalker."

He gave me *another* "I'm going to kill you" face but kept his mouth shut as he sat on the edge of my bed once more and started poking around on the screen.

Even though I was holding his phone in my hands, I watched him instead. Lines appeared on his forehead twice, his left hand went to the back of his head and stayed there. Then he started breathing hard.

Shit.

"What the hell is this shit?" he spat, looking down.

"Dick pics, messages from assholes...."

"This guy is jerking off."

"I didn't watch the fucking video, Ivan. Are you done now?" I hissed at him.

He stared at me for a moment then said, "Yes, I'm done." That pink mouth opened and then closed again. Ivan sputtered. *Sputtered.* His face went even redder, and then he said, "Get your shit together. You aren't staying here tonight."

It was my turn to sputter. "What?"

"You're not staying here tonight. You pack or I pack for you. Decide now."

"The hell you will, and the hell I'm going with you. I'm staying here," I told him.

He blinked. He blinked so steadily, it was kind of scary from how psychotic the movement was. I was pretty sure it reminded me of Hannibal in *Silence of the Lambs* when he'd had that face mask on that had given Ruby nightmares for months. Sebastian had bought me a similar one for Halloween one year after I'd begged.

"You're not staying here by yourself," Ivan claimed, snapping me out of my memory. "You either come with me or you're going to one of your brothers' houses. You choose. You were already going to spend the day at my place anyway."

"You're not the boss of me. You don't get to—"

The asshole cut me off. "You come with me or I'm calling

your brothers right now and telling them why you aren't staying here until your mom comes back."

That time, my mouth really did fall open. Until my mom got back? That was two weeks from then. And I told Ivan exactly that.

What did he do? He shrugged, tightness all over his shoulders and arms through the T-shirt he had on. "Choose, baby. Me or your brothers."

What in the hell? "No!"

"Yes!" he shouted back.

What the hell was happening? "No!"

He watched me, eerily still, barely breathing if he even was, before shrugging. "Fine."

And then he held up my phone. By the time I realized what he was doing, it was too late for me to snatch it back. I still rushed toward him anyway.

"Ivan!" I yelled, getting up to my tippy-toes as he stood and held it straight over his head, so tall I wasn't even close to reaching.

"You got three seconds, you hardheaded ass. Three seconds or I'm calling them, and if you kick me in the balls, I'll call *all of them*."

He would. He definitely would.

Idiot. Idiot. Idiot. *Fuck.*

Gritting my teeth, I held back the yell I really wanted to give him and spat, "Fine. *Fine.*" Dickhead. Ugh.

"What's it going to be?" he snapped, sounding maybe even angrier than me, if I thought about it.

But I didn't.

I held back the middle finger I wanted to give him and groaned, "You, ass. I'll stay with you." There was no way I'd stay with either of my brothers if I could help it. And just like that, I got mad all over again. "This is bullshit."

He snorted angrily. "Yeah, it's real bullshit that I give a shit about you. Suck it up and get your things, you've got a lot of explaining to do and you need to pack. I'm so mad at you, I don't want to look at you."

I could have fought him over it. Well, I could have tried. But if there was one thing in the world I'd learned over the last few months: Ivan wasn't the kind of man who didn't live up to his words. And if there was one other thing I'd learned over the course of that period too, it was that if I didn't agree to whatever bullshit he was threatening me with, I would probably regret it.

And luckily for him—and unluckily for me—both times I had spent the night at Jonathan and James' place, I'd learned that their walls were thin. Too thin. And apparently, James had a giant dick.

So, yeah, no thanks. I loved my brother and James, but there was some shit in the world, I just didn't need to know. Nope.

As for Sebastian, if he were to find out about the mail, I would never hear the end of it. Dealing with Ivan was one thing, but Jojo would call Tali and call Seb, and then I'd have three people breathing down my neck, calling me a fucking moron for keeping a secret.

No thanks.

I was going to have to go with the lesser evil... Ivan who was probably more evil than both my brothers, but definitely wasn't as evil as both my brothers and Tali.

Damn it.

"This is so damn stupid," I grumbled.

My partner shrugged, totally and completely unapologetic. "What's stupid is you not telling anyone about this. Get to packing, Meatball."

I whispered, "Dick," loud enough for him to hear.

If he did—and he had to—his face didn't register it. More than likely though, he just didn't give a shit. God. Was this what dealing with me was like?

Turning my back to the man standing right by my bed, I opened my closet to grab one of my bags. Going up to the tips of my toes, I tried to reach for it but couldn't. Without looking at Ivan again, I left my room and went to the hallway closet to grab the step stool from inside.

But by the time I made it back to my room, the bag I'd been reaching for had been set on my bed.

And Ivan was back to sitting on the mattress, facing the wall and staring at it with an expression so tight, the bones along his jaw had never looked more visible.

Fine. If he didn't want to talk to me, that wouldn't bother me at all. I didn't exactly want to talk to him either.

Sure, I hadn't been crazy about staying home alone to begin with while I was sick—I wasn't that stupid—but did he have to boss me around?

Neither one of us said a word as I pretty much grabbed anything that was black or white and stuffed it into my bag, making sure I packed a work uniform with me, just in case. Because just like taking time off to train, I couldn't take time off from work either. It didn't take me more than ten minutes to grab my clothes and toiletries and shove them all in my bag. Then I grabbed another set of clothes, threw them on, and slid into some flip-flops.

"Ready," I muttered, eyeing the man who hadn't moved from his spot on my bed.

He got up, still not looking at me, and walked right out of my room, pretending like he didn't see me.

Bitch.

I followed behind, flicking off the lights with a frustrated sigh. It was awkward and quiet, with Ivan going straight down the pathway while I set the alarm and locked the front door. How had I been so stupid to leave that crap in my nightstand? And why the hell did he have to go through my things anyway?

Damn it.

Damn it.

My head was pounding all over again, and I was back to being nauseous. I took my time turning around, and then sighed again as I did, looking for Ivan's car. I found Ivan.

But I didn't find his car.

Instead, he was standing beside a white minivan.

I blinked.

"You coming or are you going to make this difficult too?" he asked, his tone that shitty, condescending one.

I was too tired to hold up my middle finger, and I hoped he knew that. "Where's your car?"

His hand sliced to the side. To the minivan. He raised his eyebrows while he did it.

I blinked again.

That hand he had aimed didn't go anywhere.

"I'm serious."

"I am too. It's mine. Get in."

It... that... was his?

I didn't have anything against minivans. My mom had owned one back in the day before everyone but Rubes and I had moved out, but... Ivan? Why the fuck did Ivan have a minivan?

He couldn't have had a kid. He'd specifically said he didn't know what he was doing with Ruby's babies. I had known his parents for a long time, and neither one of them owned a minivan either.

So....

"Today."

I blinked and still didn't move. "What is that?" I asked slowly.

He rolled his eyes and opened the door. "It's a car."

"Whose?"

Climbing inside of it, he replied, "Mine."

"Why?"

Holding the door open, he answered, "It's fuel efficient, low to the ground, and has a lot of room." A flicker of a baby smile flashed across his face before it disappeared like he remembered that he was mad at me. "And it's a Honda. Get in."

He wasn't the only one who forgot he was mad. "It's... yours?"

"It's mine," he went on. "Get in. I'm not in the mood right now," he demanded before slamming the door shut *hard*.

What the hell did he have to be in a bad mood over? Ugh.

The van purred lightly as it started, and before I had a chance to blink, the driver side window was being rolled down, and Ivan repeated himself. "Today."

I scrunched up my nose and shot him a dirty look as I took in the Honda like it was some spaceship I had never seen before. Just as I opened my mouth to say something about him he couldn't hear or respond to, something inside the minivan's back window moved, and the next thing I knew, a brown head popped around the side... to rest on Ivan's shoulder. Two big eyes blinked at me. And I lost all my words again.

Ivan didn't even glance at the head on him before he flicked his fingers for me to come forward. "We're not going streaking, and I'm not dumping your body anywhere. Not yet at least. Get in. Even Russell's getting tired of waiting. They've been out here for half an hour waiting for you."

I opened my mouth, closed it, and then opened it again to get out, "You have a dog?"

He nodded, and the dog's head moved with his movement. "Russell. Come on. I'm not in the mood."

Who the hell was this person? *What* the hell was this person? Ivan didn't just have a dog but he had a goddamn minivan too? I'd only ever seen him in his Tesla. Not... *that*.

I wasn't even positive I'd ever seen dog hair on his clothes before.

Had I?

"We don't have all day. Get in before I put you in and someone calls the cops thinking I kidnapped you," he threw out, pulling his glasses over his eyes, jerky and pissed off. "If you get in right now, I'll think about forgiving you eventually."

As if being totally aware of what Ivan was saying, the dog licked his cheek and stared back at me with eyes that I was pretty positive were a golden hazel.

And then I heard a shrill little yip come from somewhere else inside the van, and Ivan turned his upper body in the opposite direction to look in the back seat and say, "Not right now, Lacey. We already talked about this." Then, like he hadn't just been having a conversation with what may or may not be a small dog based on the pitch of the bark, he turned back to face me and raised his eyebrows. "*Drama queen.* You ready?"

Ready.

Was I ready?

To get in a minivan with him and two dogs. Two dogs that I didn't know he had. One of those dogs that he talked to like he was arguing with a child. Both of them named human names.

Lacey. He'd warned me about Lacey.

I don't know what it said about me that I wanted to get in that van even as my energy continued to disappear by the second and my anger seemed to waver somewhere in between.

"I'm counting to four before I get out of this car and drag you by your underwear in here," Ivan called out.

I wrinkled my nose, and without totally accepting that I'd made a decision, I said, "You can try, but I'm not wearing any," a moment before I walked around the curved front of his hood and opened the passenger door. Cold air conditioning was the first thing that hit me. The second thing that hit me as I slid my butt onto the captain's chair was the fact that the brown snout that I'd seen above Ivan's shoulder a moment ago was now hovering over the headrest of the seat I was in.

The dog's eyes *were* hazel. Huh. And he looked... really interested and curious. About me.

"Hi," I whispered, mostly because my throat hurt after talking so loud and yelling at Ivan.

"He doesn't bite, but he drools," Ivan informed me. "You can pet him if you want."

The dog was still staring at me from two inches away. But Ivan was right; he didn't look even a little bit aggressive. He looked like he wanted me to pet him, and if the *thump, thump, thump* said anything, it was that he really wanted me to pet him.

So I did. I raised my hand with a closed fist and let him smell me. And when that went okay, I opened my hand and stroked the top of his head gently, and when that went fine, I drew my hand over the soft, soft fur on his ears.

Then he licked me.

And I couldn't help but smile, even as my head hurt and my throat ached and I felt like a complete asshole for getting caught.

Ivan didn't say another word as I stared at his dog with possibly the biggest, dumbest smile I'd had on my face in a really long time, but finally, after a few moments, he said, very calmly, very coolly, "Buckle up. I'm not getting a ticket for you."

I looked at his dog, Russell, one more time, stroked his ear, and then sat back in the seat and slipped the seat belt on. Just as soon as the metal clicked into place, the same yip I'd heard before I'd gotten into the car came through the van once more, and Ivan clearly groaned as he shifted the van into drive.

"Lacey, I swear to God, don't start," he tossed out over his shoulder.

He was already driving when I turned to glance into the second row, coming face to face with Russell once more before I moved and got a good look at the passenger making noises. Sure enough, Russell was standing in the sliver of space between the seats, but wedged in the corner of the second row... in a pink harness that was latched through the material of a seat belt, was a small, short-haired white dog with pointed ears and a snub nose.

"Is that...?" I started slowly, feeling like this was a dream, and if it wasn't a dream, I knew nothing about Ivan. Absolutely nothing. Everything I'd thought I'd known was a goddamn lie, and I wasn't sure how that made me feel. "Is that a French bulldog?"

We were already on the road and heading toward the nearest major freeway when Ivan nodded, his eyes on the rearview mirror. "Yes. The diva in the back is Lacey. She's in time-out. I should've left her at home, but she can't be in the car with anyone else other than Russ, and today's his day for a ride."

He'd just said his dog was in time-out, hadn't he?

Oh my God.

I almost couldn't get the question out, I was so torn up in this second life and second personality I had no idea this person I trained with six days a week was capable of. But somehow, I managed. "Why is she in time-out?" I practically whispered.

"She's been giving me a lot of sass this morning, picking on her sisters, trying to steal food, peeing on one of the beds because she got in trouble," he explained like it was the most natural thing in the world.

I didn't know what to say. The dog had been giving him sass, picking on her sisters, trying to steal food, and had peed out of revenge. Just like that. So I didn't say anything else. Because what the hell else was I supposed to do?

I didn't know this man. I didn't know this man at all, and it made me feel awful. More like shit than I already did.

How had I not known he had dogs? And more dogs from the sound of it, because how else would Lacey have *sisters?*

Damn. I didn't really know anything about Ivan.

But maybe no one did. Because there was no way the girls in the changing room would have avoided talking about his prissy white Frenchie if they knew about her. Hell, his fans would probably throw dog toys at him at the end of his programs if they did.

No one knew. There was no chance.

But here he was.

The sound of a low growl, so high in pitch but at the same time quiet, had me glancing over my shoulder to eye the white body in the second row of seats. She wasn't even looking at me; it honestly looked like she was glaring at the back of Ivan's seat. But it was the pink harness she had strapped to her chest and then secured by a seat belt that I couldn't get over.

And I was almost positive she had a lighter pink collar with rhinestones on it. At least I thought they were rhinestones.

Then it was my turn to glance at Ivan, knowing there was

no way I was about to let this go. "Your little dog has a seat belt on," I said, like he hadn't been the one to strap her in.

All he did was drop his chin a fraction of an inch, gaze focused ahead of him. "She moves around too much in the car. She doesn't know how to sit still." He glanced at me. "Like someone I know."

I ignored his comment and eyed the dog again. She was still glowering at Ivan's seat. I could feel the tension and drama coming off her.

Huh.

"I don't need her flying out of the windshield if we're in an accident either," he went on, oblivious to me sneaking peeks at his dog. "Russ only gets up when I'm not driving," Ivan continued explaining, easily. "He's a good boy."

That had me glancing at Russ, who I thought might have been a brown Lab but wasn't totally sure. He was lying on the floor in between the seats at that point with his head on top of his paws. His tail went *thump, thump*.

"I didn't see any signs of dogs at your house," Ivan commented out of the blue.

I shifted forward again to look out the windshield. "No. My mom's allergic." Then, without even meaning to, I said, "My sister used to have one."

"Which one? The ginger or Ruby?"

I glanced at him again. "Ruby," I answered him. "It was Aaron's dog. He passed away a couple of years ago." I had cried, but I'd never told anyone about that.

Ivan nodded slowly, as if that said everything. "Is she the youngest?" he asked, his tone still snobby.

"In my family?"

"Uh-huh," was his response as he steered us through traffic.

"No." Wasn't it obvious? "I am. She's five years older than me."

He swung his head around to give me a "you're full of shit" expression. "*She is?*"

I didn't even get offended. "Yeah."

"*You're* the baby?" he asked, sounding totally surprised.

"Why are you saying it like that? You're making me feel like I need to apply for an assisted living home or something."

"It's just...." He scrunched up his nose as he drove and even shook his head. "I don't know." He glanced at me and shook his head again.

I knew what he meant. It's what my mom and everyone had always said about me. Physically, I looked younger than Ruby, who still had a baby face like my mom's. But I had an *old, grumpy grandma soul.* "I get what you're trying to say."

From the way he was contorting his face, it was like he was still in denial. "You're really that much younger than her?"

Sliding my hands under my thighs, I held back a sigh as I leaned my head against the seat. "Yup. She had a heart condition for a long time. We were all really overprotective of her."

"I didn't know that. She's cute," he threw out suddenly, and my head did something straight out of the *Exorcist*. I swear to God my neck swiveled effortlessly, without a hitch, as I turned to glare at him.

"Don't look at my sister. She's married."

Ivan snickered. "I know. I've met her husband how many times now? All I said was that she's cute, not that I want to take her out on a date or anything."

"Great, she's too good for you," I threw back out, still staring at him.

That had him go, "Ha!"

"She is," I told him slowly, not letting his laugh get to me.

"You know, there are a lot of people in the world that

would think I'm too good for them," he said, his tone sounding... off.

I rolled my eyes and settled into the seat, crossing my arms over my chest. "Probably. But you wouldn't be good enough for my sister, hot shit. So reel the ego in a little."

"If I was interested in your sister like that—and I'm not, all I said was that she's cute, but there are a ton of cute girls in the world—"

"My sister is the prettiest. Both of them are. Don't compare them to the rest of the world's women."

Ivan snickered. "*All right.* Jesus. All I'm trying to say is that, if I was interested in one of your sisters—*and I'm not*, listen to me—you really wouldn't let me date them?"

This weird feeling I wasn't about to mull over made my stomach uncomfortable, but I ignored it. "Hell no."

His snicker made me smile from how insulted he was. "Are you serious?"

"*Yeah*," I emphasized.

"Why?"

"Where do you want me to start?"

There was a pause. "I'm a catch."

"A catch and release."

He groaned, and I couldn't help but look at him out of the corner of my eye. "Plenty of women would want to go out on a date with me. Do you know how many messages I get on Picturegram a week?"

"Teenagers who haven't grown up yet to realize how dumb they are don't count, and neither do elderly women with bad eyesight," I let him know.

Apparently, he was going to ignore my stipulations because he kept going. "I'm rich."

"So?"

"I'm not ugly."

"To your eyes."

Ivan snorted, and if the corner of his mouth tilted up into a partial smile, I was going to ignore it. "I have two gold medals."

I made a "pfft" noise as I angled my hips and upper body to watch Ivan. "One of those is a team gold, *and* what's-his-face has like twenty."

This man opened his mouth for a moment, on the verge of saying something, and then closed it before shrugging those shoulders he seemed to hold me above half the day. Lean, strong shoulders, so much stronger than anyone ever gave them credit for. I wasn't exactly light as a feather. I was heavy for my size, but it was all muscle. I was sure I did weigh more than most girls did in a smaller frame, and he always lifted me like it didn't matter.

His head ticked to the side, and his hands flexed on the steering wheel. And then he smirked, even though he was facing forward. "You've got a point," he conceded, not exactly sounding happy about it. "But how many do you have?"

What happened next, I would never have been able to predict. But it happened.

We both went "OOOOOOOOH" at the bullshit that came out of his mouth like we were in fifth grade and had made a really good "yo mama" joke.

We went "OOOOOOOOH" so deep and into it, totally unexpected, that it lasted maybe three seconds before we both burst out laughing, my head crying *no* at the movement and my back aching, but I did it anyway.

Was it fucked up of him to point out that I hadn't won any gold medals even fully aware it really chafed me? Duh. But this was Ivan. What the hell else would I expect?

Plus, it wasn't like I wouldn't have said the same exact thing if we were in opposite positions.

But it made me laugh. And it made him laugh.

And I still muttered, "Asshole," even as I laughed to myself, head pounding and all that mess, but smiling. "Eat shit."

"Got you," he chuckled, that mouth of his split wide into a smile so big it was like his face couldn't handle it.

"Shut up," I responded, shaking my head. "You're a pain in the ass."

He laughed. "That'll never get old."

"Fuck off."

"No thanks."

I couldn't help it, I laughed again, and then Ivan did too, but I caught him sneaking glances over in my direction twice, a smile pasted on that pale pink mouth. He did it again. Then again.

"What are you looking at?" I asked him, unsure why he kept glancing over and not liking it.

The smile on his face didn't go anywhere as he replied, "You."

"Why?" He looked at me every day.

"Because."

Was there something wrong with my face? "Because what?"

"It's rare you laugh."

If there had been any semblance of a smile left on my face, I wiped it clean. "I laugh."

"I've only seen it happen a few times."

I tried not to huff, but it still happened. He wasn't the first person to ever tell me that. "I don't laugh unless I find something funny, but I do. I laugh with my family all the time. I've laughed with Karina a million times. I'm just not going to pretend like I think something is funny if someone makes a shitty joke or says something stupid. I'm not fake." Did I sound crazy defensive or was I imagining it?

Ivan was still smiling as he said, "You're probably the least fake person I know, Meatball. Jesus. I like your laugh, even if it sounds a little scary."

I blinked. "Scary?"

"You sound like a psycho when you laugh, all heh, heh, heh, heh."

My spine went rigid, and it wasn't because of the fever still in my body. "What am I supposed to sound like? *Hehehe*?"

He was still grinning. "No. Your heh, heh is just like you, and don't ever laugh like that again. *That's* creepy. I might have nightmares tonight from it. God. You sound like a possessed doll or something laughing from a dark corner, waiting for me to go to sleep."

I couldn't help but laugh again, even though my head hurt.

Then he ruined it by glancing over his shoulder and wiping his expression clean. "I'm still pissed off at you by the way. Don't think I forgot."

I had forgotten.

I had forgotten I was mad at him and that what he'd done was total bullshit.

But now that he reminded me, I shifted away from him and shut my mouth. And when I set my forehead against the glass, thinking of how much I'd screwed up, I didn't mean to fall asleep, but it happened.

WE WERE SITTING BESIDE EACH OTHER AFTER EATING A DINNER we'd made after only exchanging three words the whole time.

Dinner. Is. Ready.

He'd woken me up when we'd gotten to his house—the absolute last house I ever would have imagined him living in —and he'd said maybe ten words to me. To top it off, he hadn't joked around once while saying any of them. Which was fine by me because I wasn't in the mood either.

Luckily, I'd been too busy taking in the ranch-style home to really care. A rich blue with white shutters, it was nothing like the loft-style or Mediterranean home I thought he would live in, in some glitzy neighborhood with a guard and a community center with a badass waterpark. *Nope.* As I looked around the property, all I saw was green grass and trees in the distance. Ivan had acreage. So much acreage I couldn't see another house anywhere or hear any voices in the distance.

"Don't freak out when I open the door," he muttered, sounding annoyed or frustrated, or probably both knowing him. And people thought I had a bad attitude.

I didn't ask him what there would be to be freaked out about as he got out of the van and went around to the sliding door of the passenger seat that was opening on its own. "Come, Russ," I heard him mutter before he whispered something that sounded like, "Lacey, be good," as he unclipped the little white dog from the seat belt, and she jumped off the seat and out of the car, running full speed toward the front of the house the second she could.

I got out too, grabbing my bag and damn near moaning at the weight before hefting it to the house, regretting that I didn't ask Ivan to help me. Not that he would in the mood he was in, but maybe.

I had just kept looking at the house, the three-car garage attached to it and the grass on top of more grass.

It was beautiful.

Not that I'd admit it to him, especially not right then.

"Don't freak out," he reminded me once more, a split second before I heard him unlock the door while I had my back to the front deck.

And then all hell broke loose.

What I'd learn about one minute later, was that five animals—three dogs, one pig, and a giant bunny—had come hauling ass out of the house like they'd broke out of jail. Two dogs were tied together, and the other had three legs but ran like hell, but they were there. Swarming me. Wagging tails as they joined up with Russ and little miss priss, Lacey. They were excited as fuck as they went around me, sniffing, sniffing everything and more, like they couldn't believe *I* was there.

One small pink pig stomped on my toes, and my heart gave this... this thing that I couldn't describe.

I didn't know what the hell happened to the bunny I had seen, but I was too busy taking in all the excited faces and excited tails.

And if anyone would have been surprised that I spent two hours outside playing with five dogs and a piglet, none of them would have been more surprised than me. Because I had felt like total shit not even ten seconds before, but it was like it all went away when they were shoving their faces against my legs and hands.

So hours later, when Ivan had come out of the house and told us all to come in, I hadn't complained too much, especially not when I noticed he was still in his little shit mood.

Still in his little shit mood, holding up the bunny I'd seen against his chest.

And I definitely didn't complain that he stayed in his little shit mood as he made his way to a kitchen my mom would have described as rustic.

Ivan had a whiteboard on his fridge with his lunch and dinner plans written on each. So, considering it was Saturday, he'd pulled out a package of chicken breasts and the meal on the fridge said CHICKEN, JASMINE RICE, BEETS, I figured that's what we were doing. I'd always expected him to have a chef or something, but I was coming to see that I didn't know him at all.

So I found the jasmine rice in a cupboard after searching through his crap—and eyeing a glass container he had on the counter filled with Hershey Kisses—and then found the right sized pot after he'd continued ignoring me as I looked for it. And we got to cooking. I let him make the beets because I wasn't sure what to do with them. Plus, I wasn't that great of a cook to begin with, mostly because I could have lived off baked meat seasoned with just salt and pepper, whatever grain I could make in a rice cooker, and steamed or baked vegetables for the rest of my life if it was up to me.

Just as I was measuring out a cup and a half of rice onto each plate—because Ivan had measurements on his whiteboard of how much of everything he wanted on his plate—his cell rang. He brushed by me to grab it off the counter and instantly answered, "Hello."

I finished measuring as I heard him keep talking, "Yes, she's here... Better but she's still sick..." Obviously I was the "she." I think. The question was, who the hell was he talking to? "Tomorrow?... It depends on what we'll have... That'll work... Okay. Sounds good. We'll see you tomorrow then... I love you too. Bye."

I told myself it wasn't any of my business who he talked to.

But if he left his phone lying around and I could figure out the password, I'd look at it.

Ivan didn't say anything to me about where we were going or what we were going to do, and I sure as hell wasn't about to ask, so I kept my mouth shut and stood back as Ivan finished putting the food on the plates and then later as we ate.

I had just finished swallowing the last bite of the lime chicken he had stir-fried in coconut oil when Ivan shoved his plate away and finally turned to me, looking just as pissed off as he had two hours ago. Even his stupid shoulders were rigid and tight.

I gave him a lazy look, expecting the worst.

So, because I was expecting him to give me hell, I wasn't anticipating what actually came out of his mouth.

"I want you to cancel your accounts again."

"What?"

He repeated himself. "I want you to cancel your accounts again. Having a few followers isn't worth you getting things like that in the mail."

What the hell was happening? "Ivan," I started to say, confused. "I don't know if they're still coming in the mail or not, but the private messages and comments are no—"

"We can delete the team one too. Lee will understand," he said, each word coming out angrier and angrier.

Well, I wasn't the kind of person to throw other people under the bus, *but*... "She knows about them. Or, she has an idea about them. We talked about it months ago."

Those bright blue eyes could have had lasers in them from how uncomfortable his gaze was making me feel. "What?"

"When I first agreed to be your partner, we talked about it. I didn't tell her much, I just kind of gave her an idea why I'd cancelled my accounts."

"Wait a second...."

I ignored him. "She told me to tell her if things started coming up again, but I didn't. I just stopped reading my mail to begin with."

He blinked. "You told her. But you didn't tell me." Why the hell were his words coming out all stiff and robotic?

"Yeah." Because I had. "I didn't think you needed to know."

Yeah, he was getting all pissed off again. "You thought I didn't need to know?"

"Yeah. I didn't. We weren't exactly talking then. It seemed

pointless. Why would you care?" I asked him with a shrug, not about to feel bad for doing what I'd done.

"Why would I care?" he murmured to himself, still trying to kill me with his eyes alone.

"Now, I get it. We're friends. We're partners. But chill. It's fine. I've never gotten aggressive messages or threats. It's always just... the pictures and those videos. I might not even be getting them anymore."

At some point while I'd been talking, he began to tip his head back to eye the ceiling. He wasn't looking at me as he said, still sounding like he was made of metal on metal, "Is that why you didn't want to do the TSN shoot?"

I didn't want to tell him, but I did. "Yes. That was the other part of it. I wasn't lying when I told you I didn't want you to make fun of me either."

His groan was basically a rumble as he continued to look at the beams across his high ceiling. He sighed. He sighed and he shook his head.

It was my turn to sigh. "Cut it out. It's all right. I knew what I was doing."

That had his chin dropping. "Yeah, being a stubborn ass, and it's not fucking all right."

I scoffed.

He stared at me.

Okay, maybe he had a point. "Look, I don't want anyone worrying. Everyone has enough stress in their lives, nobody needs me to add more to it. I can't... I won't stop living my life and wearing whatever I want to wear or don't want to wear because of other people being assholes. I hate that I let it bother me as much as I do and did, to begin with."

He kept on staring.

"If I need help, I'll ask."

The laugh that came out of him was a sharp one. A fake

one. One that said he knew I was full of multi-layered shit. "You could need a kidney replacement and not ask anyone you know for one, Jasmine." He shook his head, a frown crossing his mouth. "You think I don't know you?"

Well. Shit.

"You are so stubborn. So fucking stubborn it drives me *insane*. You know how many times I've wanted to choke you?" he asked, shaking his head in clear exasperation.

I blinked. "Probably half as many times as I've wanted to choke you out too."

He didn't take my joke. "What we have, it's more important than a marriage."

I rolled my eyes and let the m-word go.

"It is, and you know it is. I need you healthy, and I need you focused."

Something uneasy burned through my belly. "I get it, Ivan. Without me, you can't compete. Trust me, I get it. I know it. I'm not planning on screwing you over. I didn't mean to get sick and screw up starting our choreography. You know I'm sorry."

The look he gave me....

"You're my friend, Jasmine. Not just my fucking partner. Don't give me that bullshit."

I reeled back at his tone and watched his face get *furious*.

"I want you to be safe because you matter to me. You think I bring my partners to my house? You think I let them into my life? You think I spend time with their families? I don't, and I never have. I learned my lesson when I was a teenager and my partner tried to blackmail my family by saying they paid for us to win our junior events. That's why I do contracts now, to keep it professional. I don't ever want to be as unhappy as I was after my first partner did those things to my family and me. But you...."

Well... I hadn't known, had I?

And if I suddenly wanted to open two cans of whoop-ass on his bitch of a juniors partner, I would think about it later.

"You. Matter. To. Me. *You.* I couldn't forgive myself if something happened to you because of me," he kept going, his voice rising. "I've known you since you were a little kid, helping my sister off the ice when she fell. You didn't treat her different because of her last name like everyone else did. You didn't ask her about me. You and Karina just picked each other. I know the things you did for her, she told me. She told all of us about *Jasmine Santos who isn't scared of anybody.* About Jasmine *who doesn't like unicorns because she likes Pegasus, because they can fly.*

"I wanted *you* to be my partner for years, dumbass. When Karina had told me you were thinking about switching to pairs, I had thought you would say something to me, even in passing as a joke. I thought you would say you were going to kick my ass, and I had planned on talking to you over it. But you never did. The next thing I knew, you *had* a partner. Some dipshit that wasn't half as good as you."

Was I on imaginary drugs again?

"Do you remember that? Do you remember that I didn't talk to you for six months after that?" he asked me, his entire focus on *me.*

And I nodded because I did. I remembered how he'd come back at me with a vengeance out of the blue, talking so much shit over those next two years, I wasn't sure how my ears didn't bleed and how I managed not to key his car.

"You've been in my life for thirteen *years.* How could you not think I don't care about you? We fuck around with each other because we both like it. Because there's nobody else we can fuck around with that can handle it."

I mean... he was right. He drove me crazy, he always had,

but he was the only one I could talk to on that level. He had annoyed the shit out of me for years.

But...

But...

My mouth gaped open, and I was silent.

I—

He—

Well—

His hand went to take mine from where it was laying limply on the table because... I was shocked. Surprised. Totally and completely caught off fucking guard. "I don't want anything to happen to your stubborn, mouthy, mean ass. My partner or not my partner. Do we have that clear?"

What. The. Fuck?

"But I'm not letting you get away with this crap. I want you to be safe. I want you to be happy. But I'm not putting up with your secretive shit, or your bullshit, so you need to get used to it. You could have told me about your mom's accident. About the letters and the comments. You could have told me you weren't feeling well, Jasmine. But this ends now. This is the way it's going to be. Okay?"

Safe. Happy. Not putting up with my shit.

I didn't say a word, but he must have taken it as an agreement because he let go of my hand and sat up straight, ending the conversation with a look I wasn't sure what it meant.

"Now that that's over with, I'm going to take the dogs for a walk. Want to come? If you get too tired on the way, we can drag you back."

CHAPTER 16

"I don't know if this is a good idea."

Behind the wheel of his Tesla, Ivan shrugged a shoulder and spoke the second sentence he'd decided to deem me with all day. "You won't get anyone sick. Your contagious period is over already."

If he said so.

I'd spent most of the day sleeping on and off in the guest room that Ivan had dumped my stuff in the day before. I'd been so distracted by his pets, that I hadn't noticed when he'd gone back outside to grab the bag that I'd dropped on the ground.

After dinner, we had taken the dogs on a long walk. Apparently he had 103 acres forty minutes outside of the city, and he took the dogs—and the pig—on a walk every day he could. Twice a day, he had a woman named Ellie come by to feed all of them, give them their medications, and let them out to run around while he was at practice. With me.

Who the hell would have known?

I wanted to know what had made him get so many animals, but the truth was, I didn't know how to speak to him after the night before. No one had ever spoken to me like that before. At least no one that wasn't my mom.

He said he wanted me to be safe and happy. And that it had nothing to do with us being partners.

What did it have to do with? I wanted to know. But I was too scared to ask and find out because what if his answer ruined what we had built up?

I didn't think the truth was worth it.

So after a walk I'd bet was at least a mile long, I'd silently followed him to the living room and taken a seat on the opposite side of the couch from him, getting surrounded by Russ and an eight-year-old, three-legged Husky named Queen Victoria who had decided she liked me a lot. Ten minutes on the couch with a dog on my lap and one along my side, I passed the hell out and only woke up hours later when Ivan flicked me on the forehead and marched me half asleep to my room with his hand on the back of my neck.

And I hadn't been too half asleep to not remember that I'd crawled under the covers, and that it had been him who had dragged them up to my chin, then followed that up by palming my forehead before he'd turned off the light and left.

I slept in the next morning and didn't get up until almost noon, which said just how awful I felt. Ivan had been gone, but he'd left a note on the fridge that said he'd be at the LC and would be back around one, and that I shouldn't worry if a woman came into the house because it was the pet-walker/caretaker, Ellie, who usually came at seven in the morning. I'd been asleep, obviously.

So I took advantage of it. For the next hour, I snooped through his house and found more things about Ivan that surprised me.

The rabbit alone had a big, fancy play area and house in

one of the five bedrooms. It was honestly nicer than my own room.

He had four big dog beds and one small one in his giant master bedroom, and I was pretty sure they were custom Tempur-pedic mattresses. I'd sat down on one with Russ, who had been laying down outside of the room I was sleeping in with the Husky, Queen Victoria, and decided even their beds were more comfortable than the one I had back home.

Ivan kept a tube of lube in one of his nightstands—and my stomach had only given a dull pulse of dread that I pretended hadn't happened.

His house was immaculate.

There weren't any beauty products in his bathroom, which meant that perfect skin of his came naturally—total bullshit. But I did find a tin container of organic hair shit in one of the drawers.

I didn't find any condoms anywhere.

But I did find a room filled with trophies, plaques, and two gold medals.

He had a desktop computer with a password I couldn't break into.

The only pictures he had up were either of him with his family, candids of his pets, and his family in general. I happened to be in two of them.

It was all very interesting.

The one and only thing I wasn't totally surprised by was the fact that I was 99.9 percent sure Lacey, the white Frenchie, didn't like me. She watched me every time we made eye contact with each other and just glared the whole time. I liked her. She was smart to not be sure what to think of me.

By the time he got back home, I had already looked through his entire house. Opening up drawers and cabinets I had no business looking in, but not even feeling a little bit bad about it. He knew me well enough. He had to expect it. And if he didn't, then it was his fault for being so trusting.

My fever had kicked back in again at some point while I'd been snooping, and I headed back to the guest room to nap while he took the dogs—and the pig—out. It wasn't until almost six o'clock that something wet nudged at my face and woke me up. It was the pink pig sitting on my chest, with Ivan standing off to the side of the bed, watching me, while he held his huge bunny in one arm.

"What?" I croaked, reaching to stroke the piglet like I'd pet one a thousand times before and this was nothing new.

Those gray-blue eyes remained on my face as he said, "You almost look sweet when you're sleeping."

I blinked.

"I said almost."

Still petting the pig and not sure if I was doing it correctly, I gave Ivan a wary look as his own hand brushed through his bunny's coat. "Why are you standing there watching me, creep?"

Ivan's gaze had moved to the piggy when he replied, "I came to wake you up. We're going to dinner at my parents' house. Get dressed."

"I don't feel very good."

"All we're doing is eating. You can sit there for an hour. My mom has been worried about you."

Shit.

"I don't want to get them sick." Which was true. I didn't. The Lukovs had always been nothing but wonderful to me. Genuinely. They were rich—wealthy, if you wanted to be exact —and came from a bloodline that had probably married Russian royalty at some point, according to Karina, but they were some of the kindest and most well-mannered people I had ever met.

That and they gave me a huge discount on my LC fees. As in 90 percent off. All I'd had to pay for almost the last ten years was pretty much just my coaching and choreography fees. They'd insisted.

"They'll be fine," he said, still standing there, holding his rabbit like it was second nature. "And it's Father's Day. I want to see my dad."

It was Father's Day?

"What? You didn't know?" Ivan asked, reading my mind.

I'd been so busy over the last month and hadn't gotten a chance to watch any live television.... "No. I didn't."

His eyebrows bunched together. "You want to call your dad first?"

I didn't hesitate to shake my head, even though it still felt weak and wobbly. Heavy.

"You're sure?"

"I'm sure." It wasn't like he'd care if I contacted him or not. He probably wouldn't even notice.

But...

Be better.

Maybe that was the point. I could at least send him a text. Be better.

Remind him I was his, regardless of whether that disappointed him or not.

"I'll send him a text on the way," I told Ivan with a shrug. He was probably off with his step-kids doing something fun. This funny fucking feeling swam around in my stomach for a second, but I shoved it away. Far away. "I'll send my brother and Aaron one too."

"You'll come then?"

For Mr. Lukov, I would. Even though I still felt like a giant butthole. He'd said an hour. I could make it an hour at their house.

His nod took a moment, but it finally came at the same time his gaze shifted to me and the piggy that had walked up to cuddle against my neck, then he smiled. "She'll take a shower with you if you let her."

The little creature gave two soft snorts into my skin, and I felt my heart give this tiny tingle. "She will?"

He might have nodded, but all I heard was, "Uh-huh."

"Do you care?"

I glanced up that time to find his gaze hadn't moved anywhere. "No."

And just like that, despite feeling like I'd gotten half my energy sucked out of me and the headache that hadn't gone away, I sat up, kicked the sheet off my legs, set Charlotte back on the bed before I swung my legs to the side and got up.

"If your head still hurts, I left painkillers on the table beside your bed," Ivan let me know.

I managed a nod, then grabbed the pills, dropping them in my mouth and swallowing them with what was left of the water in the glass beside the bed. And it wasn't until I was swallowing them, that I realized he'd brought them to me.

I glanced at Ivan, who hadn't moved from his spot standing beside the bed with his rabbit, less than two feet away from me, and said, the words coming out easier than they ever had before, "Thank you."

He didn't look surprised... but he did just... look. As he held that freaking giant bunny.

One shower minus Charlotte, the most unenthusiastic three minutes of my life getting dressed, another glass of water, and a short drive later, we were pulling up to his parents' house. And I was ready to take another nap.

The house was in a gated community in south Houston set up on a couple of acres that separated each mansion from one another. The Lukovs lived in a six-thousand-square-foot stucco and tile-roofed monstrosity with an infinity pool that Karina and I had spent a lot of time in during our teenage years. Well, not a lot of time, but more than I spent just about anywhere else that wasn't school, the LC, or home.

Ivan pulled his car into the winding driveway leading to the back of the house and parked it just outside the over-sized four-car garage. I let out a tired breath as we got out and headed toward the back door that I'd always gone through in the past. Ivan opened it using a key, and I finally took the time to take in the button-down shirt he had on tucked into fitted gray pants that I had a feeling were custom-made, because there was no way his bubble butt could fit into anything that didn't stretch, and black leather shoes that almost looked like boots. Then I looked down at the fitted T-shirt and leggings I'd put on, and shrugged inside. The Lukovs had seen me in worse. They knew I wasn't feeling well. It wasn't like I was meeting my new boyfriend's parents.

Not that that had ever happened. I'd dated a little before I switched to pairs, but every guy I went out with turned out to be a dick by the second date. There had only been one guy I'd seen for a few months, but I couldn't remember what he looked like anymore.

"Hello?" Ivan called out the second he was inside the kitchen that the door led into.

I closed the door behind us, leaning against it for a moment when exhaustion hit me hard once more. The kitchen was the same as the last time I'd seen it, almost... a year ago. The last time I'd come over was for Karina's last birthday, and that had been right after Paul's bitch ass bailed on me. Then she had left for another year of medical school, and now we were here.

"Living room!" Mrs. Lukov's voice called out.

Ivan glanced at me over his shoulder and frowned. "You all right?"

I nodded, and even that seemed like it took too much energy.

He must have read it on my face because he frowned. "We should have stayed home."

"I'll be fine," I said, pushing away from the door.

He didn't look like he believed me, but he didn't say anything either as I walked toward him.

Instead, Ivan held out his hand, and I didn't think much of it as I slipped my hand into his and leaned into his side without thinking about it. I was used to it, I could tell myself. I was used to being right up against him. It felt more natural than it should have.

"You're feeling that bad again?" he asked gently, taking my weight without a complaint.

I shook my head against his shoulder. "Just tired."

His hand squeezed mine. "Want some more water?"

"I'm okay."

He "hmmed" before asking, "What hurts?"

I swallowed and closed my eyes for a moment. "Everything."

There was no hesitation as Ivan asked, "Want a hug? You liked that before."

I nodded.

Ivan was silent as he turned his body and wrapped those long, muscular arms around me, pulling me into his build so that my face went right for that space between his pectorals. My own sigh was instant. One of his hands went flat to my spine and started rubbing up and down the length of it before pausing at the highest point and then rubbing over one shoulder blade and then the other. Circle, circle, circle, easing the ache somehow like it was fucking magic.

"That feels nice," I whispered, trying to get closer into him.

Something about being sick just made me want to be held. And especially when it was Ivan. He was big enough to really hold me, and he wasn't squeamish or weird about affection or the contact. He was used to it too, I guess.

One of those big hands went to the back of my neck and started kneading the muscles there, and I swear to God, I moaned.

Ivan chuckled low into the top of my head. "That good?"

"So good," I whispered, pretty much leaning my entire weight into him. "I could fall asleep like this."

"I'll rub your back some more when we get back," he offered, one hand going to my neck, the other one still rubbing up and down both sections on either side of my spine.

"Promise?"

He chuckled some more. "Promise. But when I get sick, you're going to have to return the favor."

"Sure. Uh-huh."

"Promise?" the pain in the ass asked quietly, his tone pretty amused.

"Promise."

I sighed into his chest, taking a whiff of that subtle, sweet cologne he usually had on.

"My poor, poor Jasmine," came a familiar voice from somewhere close by.

I froze, realizing where the hell I was and what the hell Mrs. Lukov would see and think, and was about to take a step back when the arms around me grew tighter. So tight I knew there was no way I was about to get a chance to jump back like we'd gotten caught making out, when all he'd been doing was giving me a hug and rubbing my back. You know. Considering

I'd been butt fucking naked a few weeks ago in front of him and he'd had his hands *all* over the place.

But something about getting caught getting a hug from Ivan seemed even more vulnerable and personal than if we would have been kissing.

At least that's what I thought.

"She's not feeling well," Ivan murmured directly above my head, almost like he was talking into my hair.

"Are you taking your fever reducer?" Mrs. Lukov asked from somewhere behind me.

I still didn't move as I said, "Hi and yes. Ivan's been keeping me stocked on them."

How did she know I'd had a fever?

"Stop being greedy, Vanya, and let me give her a hug too," Mrs. Lukov demanded.

With one more squeeze around my body by those warm arms of his, he let me go, and I immediately felt heat rise to my face, and I prayed it came off more like I was overheated because of my fever—if I even still had one—and not because of getting caught getting affection from this woman's son. The second I was out of his hold, I turned around slowly and came face-to-face with Mrs. Lukov, who had apparently been standing directly behind me.

The older woman was already beaming at me. A little older than my mom, Mrs. Lukov looked liked a perfect mix of both her kids... except older. Jet black hair that she had been dying to her natural color for as long as I had known her, tall, slim, with pale skin and the brightest blue eyes that she had passed down to Ivan. She was almost as beautiful as my own mom.

She just wasn't nuts.

"You look terrible, Jasmine," Mrs. Lukov claimed, a moment before she wrapped her arms around me to pull me into a hug. At what I guessed was about five foot seven, she almost dwarfed me.

"I feel terrible," I told her honestly, hugging her back. "Thank you for inviting me. I hope I don't get you sick."

"Oh, shush. I've been telling Vanya to bring you by since he told me he's been having Saturday dinner with your family, but he pretends not to hear me," she claimed, rocking me from side to side. "I was so excited when he told me you were going to be his new partner. Petr and I had always thought it was only a matter of time."

Yeah, his parents were sweet. And a little naïve. But I liked them a lot.

"I had a dream once many years ago that both of you were on the stands winning a gold medal," she said, still rocking me like I was a baby, and I was eating that shit up because not even my own mom did that to me. "Maybe it was a sign, hmm?"

And I couldn't help how I tensed at the reminder of what I wouldn't get.

At least not with Ivan.

But I had known that coming into this, hadn't I? I didn't have a reason to be disappointed. Something was better than nothing. Hopefully we could take a stand together, only it wouldn't be for an Olympic medal.

But it would have to be enough.

"It would be nice," I told her, my voice sounding off and not from feeling bad. "I'm sure Ivan will look great with whoever is his partner then."

It was her turn to tense around me. I felt her head move but didn't hear anything come out of her mouth except a "Hmm" I didn't know what to do with.

And as much as I told myself to relax, I couldn't.

Because I wouldn't be the one standing beside Ivan when

he made it to the Olympics in two years, and I was going to have to be okay with that.

I just wasn't right then.

And from the weird vibe I had gotten for a moment from Mrs. Lukov, I didn't know what was going through her head.

What I did know was that what might have been a minute later, she patted my back and rubbed a circle a lot like the one Ivan had given me, before she said, "I know exactly what you need right now to get over this virus."

I'd had Mrs. Lukov's teas once years ago while I'd been on my period and had almost thrown up. She's sworn it would stop cramping. What it had done was killed my appetite.

"Fresh squeezed orange juice for the vitamin C—"

Oh, thank God. I relaxed in her arms then.

"And vodka. It will kill all the bad germs in you."

Then I tensed back up. "Ah—"

"Vanya said you weren't on antibiotics," she told me like I didn't know. "You don't have practice tomorrow. It will be good for you, Jasmine."

Where the hell was Ivan and why wasn't he telling her that I couldn't drink? I didn't *want* to. I didn't like the taste of vodka, but—

"Are you going to tell me no?" the older woman asked, but it came out more like a dare.

Did I have the balls to tell her no?

I couldn't begin to count the amount of times I had gotten into arguments with people. Couldn't begin to imagine ever putting a number on the amount of people I'd called bad names. It had been a long time since I cared what anyone other than my family thought, and even then, that pressure usually wasn't enough to keep me from doing something that would embarrass them.

If this was my mom, I wouldn't have a problem telling her no.

But she wasn't.

And from the tone of her voice, chances were that I'd hurt her feelings if I didn't do something she thought would help me.

Fuck.

"No, Mrs. Lukov," I said, a moment before Ivan kicked me in the calf.

I lifted my leg to try and donkey kick him back, but he was out of range.

"Excellent," the woman responded, pulling away from me with a smile on her face and two hands on my shoulders. "Vanya?" She looked around at the floor suddenly, like she remembered something and was confused. "No babies?"

Babies?

"I left them at home," Ivan replied.

Oh. *Oh.*

"You didn't bring my little Lacey?" Mrs. Lukov asked, disappointment dripping from her words.

"No, especially not Lacey."

Her shoulders dropped in definite disappointment, and she even frowned before glancing at me and shaking her head. "He always comes with at least two of his babies. Always. They make a mess, get hair everywhere, and now I miss them. Silly, isn't it, Jasmine?" She gave Ivan a tender look that only a loving mom was capable of. "Vanya and his rescues. Always taking the things other people don't want anymore, ever since he was a little boy."

Something weird happened in the upper half of my body, and I couldn't help but slide a look toward Ivan, who had leaned against the kitchen counter and crossed his arms over his chest while I'd been with his mom. His eyes met mine. And they didn't go anywhere.

"Next time I suppose. The soup is ready, let me make you something to drink, and we can eat!" Mrs. Lukov exclaimed.

~

I WOKE UP KNOWING I WASN'T IN MY BED.

I woke up knowing that mostly because there was no way I'd wake up in my bed naked.

And my room wasn't painted a royal blue.

But mostly, I didn't sleep topless ever. I didn't trust anyone in my family enough to not barge into my room while I was sleeping and do something to me. And I wasn't about to scar them for life by seeing parts of me that I would rather not see of theirs.

And as I blinked into the semi-dark room, something else confirmed I wasn't in my room or my house.

There was no way in any universe, or in any level of hell, that I'd wake up in my bed in only my underwear *with a fucking arm wrapped around my waist.*

I could have freaked out the second I realized the heavy weight draped over my hip and curled over my belly was covered with hair. I could have screamed when I felt the first puff of breath against the nape of my neck.

I could have done any and all of those things after I woke up.

But I didn't.

Mostly because *I knew that fucking royal blue.* I'd seen it when I'd been snooping the day before. And as I glanced down and squinted, *I knew the shade of skin color* resting against my belly. Lighter than mine. Dusted with dark hair. The forearm lined with ropey, lean muscles. If that wasn't enough, I would be able to recognize the fingers on my belly if I were blindfolded.

But even knowing all of that, I still couldn't help but turn into a mannequin as I lay there, without a top or a bra, and basically in the arms of the one and only man in the world who I would let touch me like this because I trusted him, even though I wouldn't tell him I did. Because I wasn't even sure when I'd started to trust him, but it had happened at some point. It had just snuck right up to me, and was there when I needed to think about it.

But what the fuck had happened?

"Morning, Meatball," the familiar voice whispered softly and roughly, the puffs of his breath touching my neck... along with what had to be his damp, soft lips as they formed the shape of every letter coming out of his mouth.

"Morning?" I asked, frowning in horror but not as much as I would have figured.

What the hell had happened? I tried to think.... But all my body could do was acknowledge the fact that I felt like shit and couldn't remember a single damn thing after we'd made it to his parents' house and his mom had started shoving borscht and what she refused to call screwdrivers, but was really a screwdriver, at me every chance my glass went empty, despite Ivan telling her to stop after the second one.

But like my own mom, nobody told Mrs. Lukov what to do. Especially not her son.

And after that, everything was a blur of nothing.

What in the fuck had happened? I wondered as Ivan sighed against my neck.

"Quit freaking out. You spilled Gatorade all over yourself getting out of the car and crawled into my bed halfway through the night."

Oh God. I groaned in horror. Seriously. Horror. Where the

hell had the Gatorade come from, and had I been that drunk that I'd spilled it on myself and decided the best thing to do was to strip down instead of shower? There was a reason I rarely drank, other than because of how high in calories some drinks were.

And Ivan must have known exactly that because he chuckled, his mouth landing on the nape of my neck. "I told you to go back to your bed, but you kept saying you were dying—"

I wanted to be surprised.

I wasn't.

"—then you kept saying '*I broke it,*' and I asked what you broke." His voice cut off at the same time those puffs of breath came in quicker and lighter against me.

Fucker.

He was laughing, half asleep and trying not to.

"And you said you broke your... your...," he managed to choke out, those puffs getting faster and faster, telling me he was laughing. Like the way his upper body was shaking didn't say exactly that and much better.

I groaned. "Shut up."

He was still shaking. "You kept insisting you broke your liver," he huffed out.

Fine. It did feel like I'd broken something. And broke it good. I couldn't remember *shit*. I'd drank more than I ever had. More than I might ever again. But how much vodka had Mrs. Lukov been slipping into my drink to begin with? It hadn't tasted like she'd put a lot into it but...

Fuck.

But Ivan kept right on going. "And you wanted me to take you to the hospital."

I groaned. I groaned on the inside.

"You said you wanted me to hold your liver together—"

Oh God.

"*Just for a little, Vanya, just a little,*" he choked out. "*I broke it.*"

I'd called him Vanya? Huh. I shoved that aside and focused on the most important part. "So you let me stay in your bed? Without a shirt on? So you could hold my liver together?"

The arm around me tightened. "You insisted."

"Without a bra."

"You came to me that way. What was I going to do? Force you to get dressed? You know how stubborn you are when you're not drunk."

"You could have gotten dressed."

"I was in my bed, comfortable, asleep. It was you that showed up."

I tipped my head to try and look at him over my shoulder before remembering I probably hadn't brushed my teeth. "Do you even have pants on?"

"No."

"You couldn't put any on?"

"And ruin how warm I was?"

"You could have put a shirt on me."

"And put my hands on you when you hadn't given me permission?"

I held my breath. Then I rolled my eyes as the pale hand on my belly made the slightest movement. "You idiot, your hands are on me right now."

His laugh was slow and awesome, unrepentant and all Ivan.

"Or put a shirt on yourself."

He paused. Then said, "Nah."

I was going to kill him.

"So you just thought it would be fine for both of us to be here?"

I felt rather than saw his shoulders shrug.

"Why didn't you get out of bed?"

He huffed. "Why would I? It's mine." His soft laugh curled over the back of my neck. "And it isn't like I haven't seen you naked—"

I groaned.

"And my job is to make sure you're fine."

That was one way of looking at it. If you tipped your head to the side and squinted. "Not when I don't have a shirt on."

"But I already did, remember?"

Did he have a point? Of course he did. Did I care? Of course I didn't.

"You let all your partners into your bed drunk and naked, you goddamn pervert?"

He stopped breathing and laughing behind me for a moment, but the tension eased out of him just as quickly and he said, "No. You let all your partners see you naked?"

"No." It was more like a "hell no," but my head was hurting so bad, I couldn't get it out.

Neither one of us said anything for a moment until Ivan decided to ask a question I didn't expect.

"Do you miss him?" Something bluntly touched my back, and I did my best to play it off like it was no big deal it was probably his dick covered in just underwear, when it absolutely was. Friends didn't touch other friends' penis, did they?

Friends with benefits do, a small voice in my head whispered before I made that bitch shut up and asked instead, "Who?"

There was a pause and then, "Paul."

That time I could get out "Hell no" real easy.

His maybe-dick was still touching me when he asked, "You're sure?"

"I'm positive." Then I couldn't help but glance over my shoulder to see him literally *there.* Right fucking there. Morning breath be damned. "Do you miss your old partners?"

I threw out the question like a complete moron, even as some part of my head warned me that was a stupid idea.

"Not even a little bit," he echoed.

Huh.

"Do you regret that Mindy took a year off and now you're stuck with me?" I asked another dumbass question, instantly regretting it.

He stared at me. He stared at me for so long, inches away from my face, while neither one of us had any clothes on, that I thought for sure he wouldn't respond. But he did, and his one word answer felt like so much more. "No."

No.

Okay.

Neither one of us said anything. Not for a minute and not for five based on the digital clock on the nightstand I could see over his shoulder.

The soft but hard organ that was more than likely poking at me seemed to move, and I swore my clit felt it. It was about time I gave it a rub, from the feel of it. I hadn't masturbated since the morning before I'd gotten sick, and that was almost a world record for me.

"Ivan?" I asked gently.

"Hmm?" He sounded all sleepy and lazy again.

"Are you going to move your dick or is that what kind of friends we're going to be?" I tried to joke.

His laugh was soft as he said, "That's what kind of friends we're going to be."

And if that was disappointment in my belly, I told myself I was just embarrassed that I'd crawled into his bed to begin with.

CHAPTER 17

SUMMER/FALL

Squirt: Dinner at Margot's at 7PM with Dad.
Seb: OK
Jojo: Works for me. Me and James will be there.
Tali: Sounds good.
Mom: Ben is coming with me.
Squirt: Okay, Mom.
Mom: I know you're making a face, Rubella. Don't.
Mom: I'm married. He knows it. He's married. I know it.
Squirt: I didn't say anything!
Mom: But I know you don't approve.
Squirt: -_-
Mom: I'll be on my best behavior.
Squirt: Promise? You won't antagonize him?
Mom: I promise. Not one word.
Squirt: You promised.
Squirt: Jas, you're coming, right?

I SIGHED AND RUBBED AT MY BROW BONE WITH THE BACK OF MY hand. I had known my dad had arrived a few days ago. I hadn't forgotten.

I just had chosen not to go over to Ruby's house, where he was staying, to say hi.

I'd been tired after our two-a-day practices, ballet, Pilates, workouts, runs, and work. With only two weeks left before our first competition, it was fucking *crunch time*. We were running out of it, and I was stressed as fuck. I had been for the last two-plus months. Because from the moment I had gotten over being sick and Ivan had finally "allowed" me to go home, we had gone straight into learning the choreography for our short program and free skate. We'd decided not to even bother focusing on the usual exhibition program most pairs teams put together for galas that took place after major competitions. Ivan and I had decided that between the three of us— Coach Lee included—we could put something together.

We had all smirked when he had decided on the music for it.

And while learning choreography was tiresome to begin with, it had been even harder on me than Ivan. Not that I told him that or let it show. Because I'd had to do the same thing I had from the beginning. I'd had to practice it five hundred times more when I *wasn't* with my coach or choreographer.

If any of them had thought it was strange that I'd brought my own camera and tripod to practices to film them, they hadn't said anything. Coach Lee already had her camera set up to tear apart things her eyes couldn't catch. My eyes needed that camera to track the moves and elements at night in my room or the living room. And during the week, I'd invite my mom or Tali or Jojo to come with me to the LC at damn near the middle of the night—from ten o'clock until midnight—to watch me and correct me while I did the programs so many times, my muscles were forced to memorize them.

For almost a month, I survived off three hours of sleep six days a week.

It had been hell. It had sucked. It had put me into a bad mood.

But I couldn't complain, and I wouldn't. Even if it meant I had to start putting on makeup before practices so that my dark circles weren't *that* obvious.

But I had survived June into July.

And I had survived the intensity of July into August and then into September as our movements were picked apart, rebuilt with repetition and a lot of fucking patience. Perfection was *hard*. But none of us expected or wanted any less.

So...

We kept going.

I made time for my family on Saturday nights, when Ivan usually joined me unless one of his "kids" was sick. And on those rare days when one of them didn't feel well, I'd drive out to see him on Sunday, and we'd hang out at his house and take them for a walk, or watch television on his big, comfortable couch. And twice, I'd brought Jessie and Benny along with me, and it had been just as fun, because Lacey might be a little sassy ass with a side-look that impressed the fuck out of me, but she loved kids.

I worked. I practiced. I trained. I did ballet with and without Ivan. I did Pilates without him, sometimes with my mom. I went for runs, sometimes with Jojo. I went rock climbing a few times with Tali. Ruby and Aaron came by for dinner randomly.

Every single minute of my life began to count. Measured, booked, and given away before the day had even started.

But I loved it. Valued it. All those squeezed-in moments were appreciated and necessary for me.

I was making things work. I was happy. The happiest.

So, the last thing I wanted or needed was to go see my dad.

But...

"What's that face for?" Ivan asked from where he dropped his bag beside me at the gymnastics facility we were going to be training at that afternoon, while we tried to work on doing a quad throw—because *fuck it, why not?* I had asked when Coach Lee brought up how easy our triple throws had become and how she thought we could add another rotation to the mix *easy, easy.* Only, at the gymnastics facility, we could try them without the fear of me busting my fucking head open on the ice. Apparently, they had found out thanks to my check-up, that I'd had five concussions already in my life and had to try to avoid getting another one. I'd offered to put on a bike helmet, but all I'd gotten were two blank stares.

Ivan was the only one who had gotten a middle finger in return though.

They hadn't appreciated my joke about us trying a Pamchenko while we were at it either.

So here we were.

I didn't put my phone away as I glanced over at him. He had on a thin white T-shirt that must have been ancient it was so threadbare, and faded black sweatpants I had never seen before, not even at his house when he *dressed down* in the same sweats he practiced in. And he looked great. I didn't know why that surprised me. "My dad is in town."

He blinked. "I thought your dad was a deadbeat."

The snicker that came out of me was more sad than funny. "No." I scrunched up my nose and looked away. He wasn't.

Ivan hummed thoughtfully, and I knew that never meant anything good. "I don't think you've ever mentioned him other than on Father's Day when you said you weren't going to call him. I figured...."

I glanced at my phone sitting on the floor and caught

myself shaking my leg. Months ago, I would have changed the subject. But Ivan had grown into... he'd grown into someone I didn't lie to. Not ever. Even knowing all that and accepting it, I still only told him a part of it. Telling him *everything* was too much. For me. I was happy. I didn't want to ruin it. "We're not close. He lives in California," I explained.

"So? He's a dick? Didn't pay child support every month?" he asked bluntly.

I shook my head, prying more honesty out of myself and realizing it wasn't as hard as I'd expected it to be. "No. He paid child support, came to visit a lot back in the day when Rubes, Seb, and Tali were still growing up. He still comes to visit once a year now. Calls on birthdays. Sends gift cards for Christmas...." While he spent it with his step-kids. But I didn't say that. What was the point?

Something funny came over his face, but he didn't say anything, and it only made me sigh. I could see him trying to figure out what my deal was. And he either got it out of me now, or he'd pester me over it for as long as it took to get it.

"He's just not very supportive of me figure skating, that's all." I shrugged. "You can guess how that makes me feel. Anyway, he's visiting and my family is doing a group dinner tonight with everyone, and I don't want to go."

He leaned forward and flicked me on the forehead. "Then don't. Say we have to practice."

I gave him a side-look but kept my hands to myself. "I used to do that to him every time he came to visit. For years."

"So?"

"I'm not trying to do that anymore," I repeated. "And I don't like the idea of running away from seeing my dad just because I don't want to hear him call me a disappointment."

Ivan's blink was slow. The tick that pulsed at his jaw, even slower, and he lowered his voice in a way that I hadn't heard since the morning over two months ago when he had sat beside me as I deleted my personal Picturegram account after the rude comments and messages had kept coming. When he had asked to go with me to check on my PO Box from then on, I hadn't even argued, but nothing must have come in because Ivan hadn't brought up creepy letters since. "He's called you that before?"

Shit.

"No, but some people are really good at sugarcoating what they really think." I sighed again and rubbed at my forehead one more time. Should I go? Should I lie and stay home or go do something with Ivan instead? I knew what I really wanted to do. It wasn't even a choice. But... *fuck.* "It'll be fine. I've grown up. I can keep my mouth shut and not argue with him for two hours."

At least that's what I was going to tell myself.

Ivan nudged my arm with the one he hugged me with several times a week, usually for no reason at all, but always when we nailed something or just had a great workout. "I'm free tonight."

I snorted. "You're free every night."

Because he was. Other than his family and me, the only other thing he spent his time on were his babies at home. He'd told me once that he'd been away so much growing up, that now he just liked being home as much as possible.

He nudged me again. "I can pinch you if you start to argue with him," he offered.

I couldn't help but give him a smile. "I'm sure you'd pinch me even if I didn't argue with him."

The smile that came over his features lit me up, and I bottled it up and set it aside for later, just like I always did. "You want me to clear my busy schedule with Lacey then?"

Oh, Lacey. The distrustful, grudge-holding, cute monster

had only just barely started letting me pet her. But only when she wanted. And only for a second. And not on her head. "You don't have to do that. I know you'd rather hang out with the crew at home."

"Yeah, because it's the only time people aren't looking at me and talking about me," he replied, the honesty in it catching me off guard. "But I don't like you dreading going to see your dad more." He gave me another one of those bright-ass smiles. "You know I'll keep you in check."

I snorted and rolled my eyes. "You can try."

Ivan leaned back on his hands, his grin widening. "Meatball, you know I can. I'm not scared of you. You like my face too much to punch it."

What an idiot. *An idiot.* And I only egged him on by snickering because I wasn't about to laugh and make it that much worse. "One of these days, I'm going to shove my foot up your ass so you can keep that in check."

He laughed, loud, grinning. "You can try."

I rolled my eyes and pretended like I didn't have a smirk on my face.

"Did you get your Anatomy issue already?" he asked suddenly.

I blinked. "It's out?"

Ivan nodded. "Yesterday," he replied, already reaching toward his bag and dragging it over. It only took him a moment to pull out a shiny black magazine with a familiar-looking football player on the cover and drop it on my lap. "Page 208."

Flipping through the magazine and catching bits and pieces of thighs, biceps and sculpted backs, I found the page and stared at the spread. I had thought for sure they would use one of the shots the photographer had taken of us doing a star lift, a move where Ivan had me over his head with his hand on my hip, while I looked like I was upside down in a split position. The photographer had shown it to us when we had wrapped up for the day.

But the magazine hadn't chosen that image.

Instead, it was the most perfect shot of us doing a death spiral that was in the issue. Well, a modified death spiral because instead of having my arm at my side, mostly parallel to the ice, I had it over my tits, covering the two pieces I wasn't about to show: my nipples. With Ivan in a pivot position, which basically looked like he was sitting in an imaginary chair with one leg slightly back so that his toe was anchored in the ice, one of his hands was holding one of my hands. In motion, he would have been spinning me around in a circle, with my body parallel to the ice, my head level with my knee, so I was inches from grazing the ice.

It was one of my favorite elements period.

But looking at us on the magazine... it was something else.

The lines of muscle at Ivan's thighs and calves were unbelievable. The arm holding mine was long and strong, his visible shoulder and neck were graceful as hell. Ivan looked amazing. A perfect physical example of all the things that made up figure skating: elegant, powerful, and limber.

And I looked pretty fucking good too. Jojo wouldn't be crying too much. The angle the picture was taken at mostly showed a whole lot of thigh, the profile of one butt cheek, and skin at my hips, some abs, ribs, and flesh all the way up to the hand holding Ivan's.

It *was* a work of art. A work of art that would be worth any shit I might get in the mail that Ivan was now screening for me. It was beautiful.

I was going to need to get a copy and frame it.

"What do you think?" the man beside me asked.

I was looking at the ridge of muscles that wrapped from his ribs around to his back as I answered, "It came out all right."

I couldn't even be surprised when he elbowed me in response.

∾

I HAD MADE A HORRIBLE MISTAKE.

A terrible, terrible mistake.

I should have stayed home. I should have gone to Ivan's. I should have stayed at the LC.

I should have done anything other than come to dinner with my family to see my dad.

Because it was easy to forget that love was complicated. That someone could love you and want the best for you, and at the same time, break you in half. There was such a thing as loving someone the wrong way. It was possible to love someone too much. Too forcefully.

And with me, my dad had mastered that shit.

I'd sat all the way on the other side of the table, trying my best not to bring any attention to myself after I'd given my dad his first hug in over a year. It had been awkward, for me at least. All of my siblings and even my mom had given him one, so I had too.

My goal had been to shut up as much as possible to prevent myself from saying anything that could trigger the f-word that came up way too often when we were around each other.

But it had come up, like it always did, no matter how much I didn't want it to.

And I had Ruby to thank for it.

Ruby who brought up my *awesome new partner*—who had taken a seat beside me and on the other side of Benny—and how we had several competitions coming up over the next seven months.

And just like that, without congratulating me on teaming up with the man he probably didn't know was a *gold medalist*, a *world champion*, who had fan pages and even an unauthorized biography written about him, my dad had just jumped right in to a conversation that had never, ever ended well between us.

He had leaned over the table, a good-looking man with skin and hair color the exact shade as mine, and asked with a condescending smile, "I'm happy for you, Jasmine, but what I want to know is, what are you going to do afterward?"

Goddammit.

Later, I'd tell myself I had tried. I had tried to play dumb and give him an out, even though I hated playing that game. I hated having to give him a chance.

"After the season?" I got myself to ask, hoping, *hoping* he wouldn't embarrass me or insult Ivan by not giving a shit he was figure skating in a body.

But like every other time, he either didn't give a shit or ignored the signals I could feel everyone giving him to shut the fuck up. "No, after you retire," he answered, a pleasant expression still on his seventy-year-old face. "Your mother told me you're still working at a diner. It's wonderful you're making your own money after all those years you used to say you couldn't because you *had to practice*," he chuckled.

Like I hadn't said that shit when I was sixteen and seventeen and eighteen, when I'd been struggling with school and trying to squeeze figure skating into every other minute of my life because I'd been killing it then. I had dominated the juniors scene then. I sure as fuck hadn't wanted to work because a part-time job would have meant the end of my dream.

My mom had always known that and understood.

But he hadn't.

And I had fucked up at eighteen and asked him for money, even though I knew better.

You're a little old for these skating things, Jasmine, no? Focus on school. Focus on something you will always be good at. These dreams, they waste a lot of time.

I wasn't a superstitious person. Not at all. But the season after that one had been the worst I ever had. And each one after that hadn't gotten much better.

Practices were good. Everything leading up to every event was great. But the moment it really mattered... I choked. I fucked up. I lost my confidence. Every time. Sometimes more than others, but always.

And I had never told anyone that I blamed it on my dad. *Focus on something you will always be good at.* Because according to him, I wouldn't always be good at the one thing in the world I was actually great at.

And his words then, at the restaurant surrounded by my family, were a fucking punch to the solar plexus I had no way of avoiding or handling.

And he'd kept right on going.

"But you can't work there, waitressing forever, and you can't skate for the rest of your life, you know," my dad said, still smiling like every one of his words weren't sending a hundred needles straight into my skin, each one going deeper and deeper by the second, so deep I wasn't sure how the fuck I would ever get them out.

I clenched my teeth together and looked down, forcing myself to keep my mouth shut.

To not tell my dad to fuck off.

To not blame him for all the damage his words and actions had done to me.

To not tell my dad that I had no idea what I would do after figure skating and somehow not admit that the lack of an answer—of even an idea—caused me to panic. I didn't even know what I would do a year from now when this was all over with Ivan, but I wasn't going to bring that shit up. Even Ivan hadn't brought it up in months. The last thing my dad needed to know was that Ivan didn't want me for longer than a year, even if he was my best friend and a person I enjoyed spending my time with.

My pride could only handle so much.

"I think, maybe, you should have gone to college like Ruby. She went to school and still did what she wanted to do," my dad kept talking, oblivious to the fact he was killing me inside and that my mom, who was sitting beside me, was gripping her knife for dear life. "It's never too late to go back and make something out of yourself. I've thought about going back to get my MBA, see?"

Make something out of myself. *Make something out of myself.*

I swallowed and fisted my fork tighter, stabbing my ravioli with a vengeance, and shoving it into my mouth before I could say something that I might regret.

But probably not.

Something touched me beneath the table, sliding over my knee and cupping it. I hadn't realized I was shaking my leg until he stopped it. Glancing out of the corner of my eye, I could see Ivan's arm partially hidden under the table. But what I could definitely see was the fact that he was side-eyeing me, his cheeks flushed.

Why were they pink?

"You have to focus on what will make you money when

you're older and can't get on the ice anymore," my dad kept going, oblivious.

I held my fork so hard, my fingers were going white around it. The hand on my knee cupped it even tighter before moving slightly above it, just on top of the knee cap, lining it. Did he have to say this stuff in front of someone who had dedicated his entire life to figure skating? It was one thing to insult me, but it was another thing to undermine all the hard work that Ivan had put in.

"You weren't so good in school, but I know you can do it," my dad kept talking, sounding so enthusiastic at the idea of me going back to school, it was that, that set me right off.

Jasmine doesn't have a learning disability, he had argued with my mom one day in the kitchen when I'd been maybe eight years old and I was supposed to be in bed but had snuck downstairs instead. *All she needs is to focus.*

Looking up at him, up at this man who I had loved and wanted to love me just as much for so long, all I felt was an anger that I hadn't come to grips with in the twenty-plus years since he'd divorced my mom and left. Left me. Left us. Just *left*. And I swallowed carefully, accepting that he didn't know me at all, and he never had. Maybe it was my fault. Maybe it was his.

But that didn't mean I was going to shut the hell up like I had promised everyone I would.

"No, I didn't do so great in school. I hated it," I told him slowly, watching every word out of my mouth. "I hated myself for hating it."

My dad's dark eyes flashed toward me in surprise. "Oh—"

"I have a learning disability, Dad. It was hard for me, and I didn't like it," I kept saying, keeping my eyes on him and ignoring the looks that I was sure my brothers and sisters were giving each other. "I didn't like having to go to... what did you call it? 'Get special treatment' to learn my ABCs while everyone else was already reading. I didn't like having to figure out different ways to learn how to spell because my brain had a hard time keeping track of letter sequences. I didn't like that I could never remember my locker combinations, so I'd have to write them on my hand every single day. I hated that people thought I was stupid."

Even from across the table, I could see his gulp. But he'd done this shit to himself. He had brought up something that everyone else except for Ivan and probably Aaron knew about. "But there are classes you can take, things you can do to help."

I kept my sigh inside of me, but I took it out on the fork I was still gripping the shit out of. "I know how to read and write. That's not it. *I learned how*. I don't like school, and I never will. I don't like people telling me what to do and what to learn. I'm not going to graduate with a college degree. Not tomorrow, not five years from now, not in fifty years."

Dad's expression faltered for a moment, his gaze going around the table like he was searching for something, and I didn't know what he thought he saw or why he decided to say the words that fell out of him a moment later, but he sealed his own deal in a voice that was too light. Too joking for a moment that to me, wasn't humorous at all. "Jasmine, those are the words of a quitter."

I heard my brother Jojo suck in a breath and heard Ivan's fork clink against the side of his plate. Mostly though, I heard the anger in me churning to his words. To his bullshit-ass assumptions. "You think I'm a quitter?" I asked him, fully aware I was giving him the same look I gave other people when I was three seconds away from losing my shit.

"Jas, we all know you aren't a quitter," Jojo chimed in quickly, finally.

We both ignored him.

"You don't want to finish school because it's hard for you.

Those are the words of a quitter," my father claimed, slashing my heart in half at the same time.

Had he not heard a single fucking thing I'd just said?

Beside me, Ivan cleared his throat, his fingers sliding up even higher on my thigh and squeezing me, not in anger but... in something else I couldn't place. And before I could open my mouth to defend myself, to yell at my dad that that wasn't the point at all, he beat me to it. "I know I'm not a member of this family, but I need to say something," my partner said calmly.

I didn't look at him. I couldn't. I was... I was so damn mad, *disappointed*, I wanted to throw up.

But Ivan kept going. "Mr. Santos, your daughter is the hardest working person I've ever met. She's persistent to a fault. Someone will tell her not to do something, and she only does it more. I don't think there's anyone in the world who has fallen more than her and gotten right back up, never complaining, never crying, never quitting. She'll cuss herself out, *but it's at herself*. She's smart, and she's relentless," he said calmly, his hand squeezing my leg tighter than before.

"She gets to the facility at four in the morning Monday through Friday and trains with me until eight. Then she goes to work, on her feet right after that until noon. She eats her two breakfasts and her lunch in her car, then comes inside and trains with me until four. Three days a week, she has three ballet lessons by herself and one with me for two hours each time. One day a week, she takes Pilates from six until seven. Four days out of the week, she goes for runs and works out after we train. She goes home, eats, spends some time with the rest of her family, and goes to bed by nine. Then she's up at three o'clock in the morning and does it all over again.

"And for months, she was going back to the facility to practice by herself from ten at night until midnight. Because she was too proud to tell me that she needed help. Then she would go home, sleep for three hours and do it all over again. Six days a week." The hand on my leg gripped the fuck out of it, not hard but... desperate. And Ivan kept talking. "If Jasmine wanted to go to school, she would graduate with honors. If she wanted to become a doctor, she would be a doctor. But she wanted to become a figure skater, and she is the best I have ever had as a partner. I think that if you're going to do something, you should be the best at it. And that's what Jasmine is. I understand school is important, but she has a gift. You should be proud of her for never giving up on her dreams. You should be proud of her for being true to herself."

Ivan paused and then said three words that slayed me. "I would be."

Fuck. *Fuck*.

I didn't even realize I had shoved my seat back until I was getting to my feet, dropping my napkin and fork and knives beside my plate. Something in my chest burned. Seared. Flayed me inside out.

How did Ivan know me so well and my own dad not?

How could Ivan know all these things about me, and my own dad be disappointed in who I was? I knew I wasn't book smart. When I'd been younger, I'd wished that I had been. Finishing high school had been hard enough for me, but it was because I hadn't given a shit about it, because I had loved this sport and wanted to be like the other girls who were homeschooled or had private tutors. I hadn't been lying when I said I hated school and had no interest in going back.

But it was hard enough to be a disappointment with the one thing I *was* good at, without being able to handle disappointing my own dad, simply by being me.

That burning sensation made its way up to my face, and I honestly felt like I couldn't breathe. It almost felt like I was drowning as I pushed past the people waiting by the hostess podium, shoving the door open as I tried to gulp for breath. My palms went up to cover my eyes as I sucked in air, trying so hard not to cry. Me. Cry. Over my dad. Over Ivan. Over the reminder that I was dumb and a failure, regardless of how I looked at it and how happy I was. It had all been too soon. Or maybe I was finally just acknowledging how much my dad's beliefs and desires and actions affected me.

But *goddamn*. It hurt. It sucked.

I could win every competition this season, and I would still be stupid, useless Jasmine to my dad. Disappointing, big-mouth Jasmine. Cold, pissed-off Jasmine with dreams that were a waste of time and money.

I hadn't been enough when he left, and I still wasn't enough for him now.

But I wanted to be. It was all I had ever wanted. I had wanted to be enough for my fucking dad. Even now after all this shit, I still just wanted him to *see me*. To *love me*. Like everyone else in the restaurant did.

I wanted to be enough just the way I was, without Ivan having to tell my dad all the things about me he should have known.

My palms grew wet, and I sucked in a breath that sounded like a sob but felt like a razor blade straight into my sternum.

The one man I wanted to appreciate me and respect me, didn't.

And the other man, the one whose appreciation and respect I had told myself for so long didn't matter, seemed to think the world of me.

Why didn't he know how hard I was willing to work every day for the things I wanted?

Digging the meat of my palms even tighter against my eyes, fully aware I was probably smudging my mascara and eyeliner but not giving a single shit, I sucked in a breath that probably could have been heard from down the block.

The doors beside me opened and I heard a "you should probably give her a minute," said by my brother, followed by the sound of the door closing.

I didn't sense someone close by until it was too late, and two arms wrapped themselves around my shoulders. It only took a single sniff to know who it was.

My choke reached down into my lungs, pretty much making my entire chest contract in a near hiccup. The arms hugging me pulled me into a chest I was too familiar with while I dropped my arms and let them hang loosely at my sides. And I let it happen. I let my face fall forward into the spot directly between pectoral muscles I'd seen countless times, and touched countless times, and admired more and more by the day, and I grit my teeth to keep from making anymore choking noises.

I failed.

The muttered "fuck" went in one ear and out the other. Followed by what must have been a cheek pressing against the top of my head. Ivan's voice came low, so low I barely heard him. "Why do you do this to yourself? Huh?" he asked me.

My chest stuttered, a hiccup, a compressed choke that hurt me more than I already was.

"You know how good you are. You know how rare that is. You know how much work you put in to everything. You know how strong you are," he whispered, his arms crossed over my shoulder blades. "Your dad doesn't know anything about figure skating, Jasmine. From the sound of it, he doesn't know you at all. You know better than to let what he thinks get to you. *You know better.*"

"I know," whispered into the bone directly between his

pecs, squeezing my eyes shut so that I wouldn't disgrace myself even more by bawling into him.

"You warned me, but I didn't believe you," he went on, some part of his face still pressed against the top of my head.

"I told you," I said, the miserable feeling inside of me growing by the second. "I told you. I didn't even want to come. I knew it was going to happen, but I'm stupid, and I hoped maybe this time would be different. Maybe I could shut up and he could pretend I wasn't there, like he always used to. Maybe this time he wouldn't criticize me and tell me all the different things I could be doing with my life, but no. It's my fault. I'm a fucking idiot. I don't even know why I still bother. I'm not going to be an engineer like Sebastian. I'm not going to use my GI bill to work in marketing. I'm not going to be a project manager like Tali, or even just be Ruby. I'm never going to live up to my brothers or my sisters. I never *have*—"

My voice broke. Totally just snapped in half.

And that was when the first wave of tears hit my eyes, and I gasped to keep them inside of me. To fucking keep them in because I wasn't going to do this. I wasn't going to fucking do it, especially not over my dad's comments.

But your body doesn't always listen to what you tell it. I was well aware of that. But it still felt like a betrayal when it didn't hold in the tears I was trying to keep a rein on.

And Ivan's arms tightened even more, pulling me in the millimeter left until we were plastered together from thighs to hips to chest.

"I was a mistake, you know? My parents had already been on the rocks, and then my mom got pregnant and my dad stuck around for another couple of years, hoping things would get better, but they didn't. And I wasn't enough for him to stick around, so he left. He just fucking left and came back once a year, and my brothers and sisters loved him, and he loved them, and—"

"You are not a fucking mistake, Jasmine," Ivan's voice shook into my ear and my shoulders went so tight, I started trembling. Me. Trembling.

And I cried. Because my dad had left when I was three, and instead of watching me grow up, instead of being there to try and teach me how to ride a bike like he'd taught all of my brothers and sisters, it had been my mom who had.

"Your parents splitting up had nothing to do with you, and your dad leaving is on him. It wasn't up to you to keep them together," he continued on, anger hanging onto the softness like a shield.

And I just kept on crying.

His arms were steel around me, his face and his mouth and his whole head over mine and to the side like he could block me and protect me.

"You're enough. You will always be enough. Hear me?"

But I kept on crying into him, his button-down shirt getting wet beneath my face, and I couldn't stop it. I couldn't help it. I cried like I hadn't cried... ever.

Because there were a million things wrong with me, and the one thing that wasn't, was one of the biggest things that disappointed my dad... and everyone else I loved.

Ivan cursed. He hugged me tighter. He cursed some more.

"Jasmine," he said. "Jasmine, stop. You're trembling," he let me know, as if I couldn't feel it for myself. "You said once in an interview that you skated because it made you feel special. But you'll always be special. Figure skating or not. Medals or not. Your family loves you. Galina loves you. You think Galina wastes her love on people who don't deserve it? Lee admires you so much she texts me in her car to tell me how good she thinks you are. You think she feels that way about just anybody? You have more heart in you than anybody I've ever met. Your dad loves you too in his own fucked-up way."

His head dipped down to my ear and he whispered, "And when we win a fucking gold medal, he's going to be watching you, thinking he couldn't be prouder of you. He's going to walk around telling everyone *his daughter* won a gold medal, and you're going to know you did it without him. That you did it when so many people didn't believe in you, even though those people don't matter. The ones that matter are the ones who have always known what you're capable of." He swallowed so loud I heard it. "I believe in you. In us. Regardless of what happens, you will always be the best partner I've ever had. You'll always be the hardest working person I've ever known. There will only ever be you."

I sobbed into him. These fucking tears just purging themselves from me. His affection, his words, his belief were just... too much. They were too everything.

And I was so greedy, I needed them. I needed them like I needed to breath.

"I'd give you every ribbon, trophy, medal, anything at my house or at the LC if it meant something," he told me. "I'll give you anything you want if you stop crying."

But I couldn't. And I didn't. Not for every medal in the world could I stop. Not for any and every figure skating honor I'd been dreaming about for half my life, could I have stopped.

I just kept on crying. For my dad. For my mom. For my siblings. For myself.

For not feeling good enough. For not feeling enough. For doing what I wanted to do despite all the noes and the eye rolls and all the things I'd had to give up along the way. All the things I'd lost that I might someday regret more than I already did.

But mostly, I cried because while I didn't care what most

people thought of me, I cared too much about the people whose opinion I did value.

Ivan held me and kept on hugging me the entire time I stood there, letting out things I didn't even know I had in me. It might have been a couple of minutes, but considering I'd only cried two other times in the last ten years at least, it was probably more like half an hour that we stood outside the restaurant, ignoring the people going in and out. Watching us or not watching us, who the fuck knew.

But he didn't go anywhere.

When the hiccups weren't so bad, when I finally began to wind down, and I felt like I could breathe again, one of the forearms draped horizontally across my spine moved. The flat of Ivan's hand went to the base of my spine and slid upward, making small circles there, one, two, three, four, five, before it made its trek back down and up.

I hated crying. But I didn't realize I hated being alone more.

And I wasn't going to overanalyze Ivan being the one bringing me comfort, being the one who understood me better than anyone else in that restaurant.

Slowly, and way more timidly than necessary when there was no sense of personal space between Ivan and me—when he'd seen more of me than any man and touched me more often than anyone else probably ever would, and hugged me more than anyone before him—I wrapped my own arms around his waist and hugged him back.

I didn't tell him thank you. I figured he would take my hug for what it was. A thank you and a thank you and a bigger thank you that was so large and pure, my mouth couldn't have done it any justice. It was always my mouth that got me into trouble, but actions couldn't lie.

In the middle of making a circle with his palm across my shoulder blades, Ivan said—not asked—"You're all right."

I nodded against him, the tip of my nose touching the lean, powerful pectoral muscle in front of it. Because I was all right. Because he'd been right about all the things he'd said. And a lot of me knowing I was going to be okay was because he believed in me. Ivan. Someone. Finally.

I sucked in a strangled breath, feeling shitty but not totally pathetic anymore. Some part of my brain tried to tell my nervous system that I should feel embarrassed, but I couldn't. Not even a little bit. I'd never thought my sister was weak because she cried over the most random shit.

My dad had hurt me.

And baby and adult Jasmine had never known what to do with that.

"You want to leave or you want to go back inside?" he whispered, still rubbing my back.

I didn't have to think about it as I stood there, not moving a muscle besides keeping my arms around the narrow waist in front of me. And when my voice came out hoarse and strangled, I sure as hell didn't let myself feel any shame. Maybe part of all this was my fault, but some of it was my dad's too. "Let's go back inside."

Ivan made this amused sound, his face still against the top of my head. "That's what I thought."

"It's already awkward in there, might as well make it more awkward," I said roughly, not totally feeling it.

The chest beneath my cheek shook, and the next thing I knew, Ivan was leaning back, those strong palms cupping my temples with those long fingers curling around the back of my head. He didn't blink. He didn't smile. He just looked me right in the eyes, his expression serious as fuck, and he said, "I might want to kick your ass sometimes, and I might tell you that you suck when you screw up and when you don't, but you know it's only because someone needs to keep you in check. But I meant what I said. You're the best partner I've ever had."

And a hint of a smile, tiny, tiny, tiny, stretched the corners of my mouth.

At least until he kept talking. "But I'm never going to admit that again, so you better remember it for a rainy day, Meatball."

And just like that, the tiny little baby smile on my face stopped in midgrow.

Ivan gave my head a gentle shake, his own mouth curling open, fully and totally. "And if your dad talks to you like that again, or says some shit like we aren't real athletes, we're going to have a problem. I was being nice because he's your dad."

I nodded, because it was the only thing I could do right then.

He dropped his hands, his eyes never straying from mine, and I dropped my arms too, leaving an inch of distance between us.

"I will always have your back, you know that," he stated, sincerity staining his tone.

I nodded again because it was the truth, but also because he had to know I had his back too. Always. Even in a year, when he was skating with someone else. Always.

I didn't have to say "let's go inside." This man knew my body language better than anyone already, so when we both turned toward the doors of the restaurant at the same time, it wasn't surprising. I wiped at my eyes as he opened the first door for me, and then the second one. Did I know I looked exactly like I'd been crying for close to half an hour? Yup.

And I didn't give a shit.

When the hostess started to beam at Ivan and me, and then abruptly stopped, I didn't avoid eye contact. I just looked at her. Chances were my makeup was running, my eyes had to be puffy and red, and my face might have been swollen too. But I kept on walking.

And when Ivan's hand slipped into mine, for all of two seconds, giving my palm a squeeze before sliding right back out like it hadn't been there to begin with, I swallowed and kept my head held up just as high.

Sure enough, the awkwardness at the table was noticeable even from a distance. The only person whose mouth was moving was my sister Ruby's, and from the expression on her face, it didn't even seem like she knew what she was talking about, but everyone else, including my dad seemed to be staring a hole directly into their plates. I wasn't surprised that it didn't make me feel good that I'd ruined dinner.

I hadn't meant to.

Sniffling before they could hear me, I got myself under control just as I reached my chair. "I'm back, bitches," I said in my fucked-up voice as I pulled my chair out.

Every set of eyes flicked up at me in surprise just as I plopped down into my seat, Ivan doing the same thing. "I made sure she only stole candy from kids and didn't try to beat them up," he said dryly, shoving his seat forward before picking up his napkin and dumping it on his lap. "Only one of them cried."

A smile twitched at my lips, even as my eyes felt dry and my face felt hot.

No one in my family said anything. Not for a minute. Maybe not even for two minutes.

Until...

"A wasp got you in both eyes too while you were out there, huh?" my brother Jonathan piped up, giving me an expression that wasn't totally a content one.

I blinked at him, ignoring the tightness in my chest, and

said, "After he stung you all over your face, from the looks of it."

Jonathan snickered, but it was half-hearted. "You look like a raccoon."

I sniffed and picked up my utensils, ignoring the look I could feel my dad giving me from his spot down the table. "At least Mom didn't find me in the trash."

My brother choked at the exact instant that a hand landed on my thigh for the second time that night and gave it a squeeze.

A throat cleared and a second later, my dad started to say, "Jasmine—"

But Ruby pretty much cut him off by shouting, "I'm pregnant!"

~

"DO YOU WANT ME TO DRIVE YOU HOME?" IVAN ASKED AS WE waited for the rest of my family to filter out of the restaurant.

My face was still puffy and tight, and I was sure I looked like a giant pile of shit, but I gazed right at that handsome face and shook my head. "No, that's stupid. I know it's past your bedtime and you need your beauty sleep. I can catch a ride with my mom."

The man who had been nothing but quiet the rest of dinner, nodded, not picking up on my jokes at all. Which said something. Said more than anything. He was still frustrated, but whether it was at me or my dad, I had no idea. Maybe I was imagining it too, thinking everything was always all about me.

Without thinking, I reached forward and took his hand, squeezing it tightly. "Thank you for coming, and for everything you said and did." I squeezed his much bigger hand once more. "You didn't have to—"

His eyes were on me, steady, steady, steady. "I did."

"No, you didn't."

"Yes." He squeezed my hand back. "I did."

I stared right into those eyes I couldn't tell were almost a sky blue in that moment, but knew in the bottom of my heart were. "If you have any family drama and I need to get involved, I'll be there."

What could have been considered a smile, creased his dimples and he shook his head. "No. No family drama. They're all supportive. But my grandpa would eat you up, you know." He paused and his dimples became that much more pronounced. "Ex-partners on the other hand... I'm lucky they signed confidentiality agreements. Save it up for them."

I blinked at him, taking in the explanation that didn't answer hardly anything, and I swallowed it for later, trying to cling onto the lightness of this conversation after earlier. "I've got you," I told him with a nod.

He squeezed my hand again.

At that moment, the doors behind him opened and I could hear my brother and James arguing, followed by my mom talking to my sister about how she shouldn't keep things from her mother. The hypocrite.

"I'll get going then," my partner—my friend—said, slipping his hand out of mine gently and effortlessly. "I'll see you tomorrow. Get some rest. Call if you need me."

I nodded, this... something... pressed right at the center of my chest.

And before I could think about what I was doing, I went up to my tiptoes and kissed what I could reach—Ivan's chin.

He looked down at me with an expression I had never seen before.

It pleased me. So, I smacked his hip and said, "Drive careful, Satan."

He blinked. Once. Twice. And then nodded, his eyes looking like they had glazed over for a moment before refocusing, and then just like that, he turned on his heel and headed toward his car, leaving me standing there, watching him... before something familiar hit my ass.

My brother.

An arm slipped around my waist, pulling me into a body only a few inches taller than me. Jonathan gave me a rough squeeze that banged me against him, before roughly whispering into my ear like his words embarrassed him, "Love you, Grumpy."

Letting my head drop to the side so that it rested against his, I put my own arm around the middle of him, around his ribs, and said, "Love you too, jackass."

He huffed but didn't let go of me. If anything, he held me closer to him and whispered, "I don't like my baby sister upset."

I groaned and tried to pull away.

He didn't let me. "My wittle, baby sister."

"If you say 'wittle' one more time...."

He laughed the lamest noise I had ever heard from him. "Love you, Grumps. And I'm proud of you. If I had kids and they grew up to be half as dedicated and hardworking as you, I couldn't ask for anything else."

I sighed and hugged him closer. "Love you too."

"Don't let Dad get to you, all right?" My big brother turned his head, gave me a sloppy kiss on the head, and let me go, just like that. So suddenly I almost fell over.

I could see my dad out of the corner of my eye talking to James and Sebastian, but while I didn't want to run away, I definitely didn't want to talk to him.

"Let's roll, Grumps," my mom said, slipping an arm through mine and dragging me forward in the same motion; her husband, Ben, following behind, an arm on my shoulder as he pushed me into the parking lot.

What was I going to say? No? Please stop?

My brother and sisters would only give me a tiny amount of shit for bailing without telling them bye, but they would understand why. Walking beside my mom, pretty much jogging, the three of us made it to Ben's BMW and got inside in record time, me slipping into the back seat while Ben got into the front and my mom in the passenger.

The second all three doors were slammed shut, my mom screamed.

Literally screamed so loud and for so long that Ben and I both covered our ears and looked at her like she was insane.

"I cannot stand your father!" she shouted the second her scream died down. "*What is wrong with him?*"

I looked in the rearview mirror at the same time Ben did, and we both raised our eyebrows at each other a moment before he started reversing out of the parking lot.

"I'm sorry, Jasmine, I'm so sorry," my mom apologized, turning around in her seat to look at me.

I still had my eyebrows up. "It's fine, Mom. Put your seat belt on."

She ignored me. "*God*, I want to light him on fire!"

That went dark real quick.

"You're sure you're okay?" she asked, still facing me. Her face this weird mixture of devastated and furious.

"Yeah, I'm fine." *Now.* "Put your seat belt on."

"Is he always like that?" Ben asked as he steered the car across the parking lot.

"An asshole?" my mom pitched in. "Yes, especially with the kids."

I loved how she called us her kids to a man that was only a few years older than my brother.

"But to tell you that you're quitter? He's lucky I promised Squirt I'd behave or I would've ripped him an asshole the size of my fist, and punched it."

If I wasn't supposed to smile to that, I wasn't sure how to make that happen.

"She was pinching me under the table," Ben let me know, like that would surprise me. It didn't.

That was my mom right there. My defender forever and ever.

"Sorry about that, Jas," my mom's fourth husband murmured.

"It's fine."

"It's not fine." Mom turned around to face me again. "You're a world-class athlete, and he makes it seem like you're some kind of... little girl that does it for fun on the weekends. And I just sat there, dying inside while my Grumpy went outside, upset."

"Mom—"

"I don't want to see him. I better not see him again while he's here. Better not see him again for another decade. Ruby can hang out with him after this. He better not expect you to see him."

"He never wants to spend time with me anyway, Mom. It isn't a big deal. Even dinner was a stretch, and I regret it. Obviously."

She blinked those big blue eyes at me that had the power to make men weak.

"I'm stressed. I don't know why I lost it. It's fine. I've made it this long only seeing him once a year for a day; I can go on with my life the same way. He's never been around anyway. And it isn't like he really cares or is going to lose any sleep over it. It's just me."

My mom just blinked some more.

I didn't like her looking at me so much, especially not when I knew I looked like shit. "Mom, seriously put your seat belt on."

She didn't move. Then she said, "Jas... you know your dad loves you, don't you?"

Where the hell had that come from?

"He doesn't love anyone else more than you," she kept going.

I *almost* snickered. Almost. But I managed just to look at her, not agreeing or disagreeing, because I didn't want to talk about this anymore. I didn't want to talk about him anymore.

And I didn't want any pity. At least any more.

My mom reached forward and tapped my chin. "He was being an asshole tonight, but he loves you in his own way. Not more or less than anybody else. He's just... wrong. Dumb. Close-minded."

That time, I couldn't hold back my eye roll as I leaned back against the seat. "Everyone knows Ruby is his favorite, Mom. It isn't a big deal. I've always known that."

Her frown was genuine. "Why would you think that?"

I snickered. "When was the last time he ever bought me a ticket to go see him? Every year, he gets Ruby tickets. He's gotten Tali and Jojo tickets too a few times. But me? When?"

She opened her mouth as if to argue, but I just shook my head.

"It's fine. It's really fine. I don't want to talk about it anymore. I'm okay with it all. I know he's closed-minded, and I know he thinks he loves me in his own way. But I'm done. If he can't accept me for who I am, I can't force him to, and I'm not going to change my dreams for him."

Her mouth opened slightly, just slightly, and she shook her head. "Oh, Jas...."

"I don't want to talk about it. I don't. Nothing is your fault. This is between him and me. We don't need to talk about it anymore," I said, closing my eyes and leaning back against the seat.

And we didn't.

But I still couldn't help but feel that sadness that somehow mixed up with determination as I sat there.

CHAPTER 18

"Can we talk?" my dad's voice came from behind me.

I froze as I leaned against the boards, waiting for Ivan and Coach Lee as they argued over whether we should change a jump or not. I hadn't cared whether we did or didn't; I was letting them go at it. I was too tired and too emotionally wrung out—seriously... exhausted from the night before—to bother putting up a fight. So I'd been waiting there, watching them, sipping on water from a comfortable distance away.

So I hadn't been paying attention. I hadn't spotted my dad inside the LC, or much less him managing to sneak up behind me.

"Jasmine, please," he pleaded quietly as I turned to blink at him over my shoulder. He was five foot seven max, with a slim, strong build that I knew I'd inherited. That dark hair, dark eyes, and skin that was a shade of olive that could have come from at least a dozen places in the world.

I looked like my dad. We shared all the same colors. The same structure.

But I got everything else from my mom... because he hadn't been around.

"Five minutes," he asked quietly, watching me patiently.

It had been hours since I'd seen him at the restaurant, and I knew his time in Houston was running out. Then it would be a year until I saw him again. Possibly even longer. It wouldn't be the first time he'd come to Houston and I hadn't seen him.

He'd never cried about it, and I had stopped long before I noticed it.

I wanted to tell him I had better things to do. I wanted to tell him to leave me alone. And maybe a few years ago, I would have done exactly that if he'd pulled some shit like he had in the restaurant, in front of Ivan and the rest of the family.

But if I'd learned anything over the last year and a half, it was the reality of how tough it was to live with your mistakes. I'd learned how hard it was to face them, and how much harder it was to own them. We all did things we regretted; we all said things we regretted, and guilt was a crushing weight on a person's soul.

And I wanted to be better. For me. Not for anyone else.

So I nodded and said nothing.

The deep breath he let out in relief, I didn't really eat up as much as I could have.

Making my way to the opening onto the ice, I put my skate guards on and glanced over my shoulder to try and get Ivan's attention. But he was still too busy talking to Coach Lee. On the floor, I headed toward the bleachers around the wall. Taking a seat in the middle of a bench, I stretched my legs out in front of me and faced the rink, watching my dad take a seat beside me but a few feet down.

On the ice, Ivan had turned around and was looking at us with a frown from his spot beside our coach.

He hadn't said a word during practice that morning, and I was grateful he decided not to bring up my dad, let alone me crying all over him. There was only so much my pride could take. Instead, Ivan acted like nothing different had happened, like everything was normal.

Worked for me.

"Jasmine," my dad said on an exhale.

I kept looking forward.

"You know that I love you, yes?"

Love was a weird word. What the hell *was* love? Everyone had such a different opinion on what it meant to them; it was hard to figure out how to use it. There was family love, friend love, romantic love....

Once, when I was younger, another skating mom had seen my mom smack me on the back of the head and had gotten really bent out of shape over it. But to me, that was how we were together. My mom had smacked me because I'd been a smart-ass and deserved it; I was hers and she loved me. Mostly though, my mom knew I didn't react to hisses and threats.

Galina had always been the same way with me. She taught me responsibility and accountability. She didn't take my back-talk. She'd smack me on the back of the head too.

But the thing was, I had never doubted that they wanted the best for me. I wanted honesty. I had needed them to love me more than my feelings, because I *wanted* to be better. I had wanted to be the best.

I had never wanted someone to baby me. I didn't need it; it made me uncomfortable. It made me feel weak.

Love to me was honesty. Being real. Knowing someone's best and worst. Love was a push that said someone believed in you when you didn't.

Love was effort and time. And while I'd laid in bed the night before, it had jumped out to me that maybe that was why I had taken things so badly months ago when my mom had made it seem like I loved figure skating more than her.

Because I knew what it was like to not be important to someone.

I had held this fucking grudge to my heart with duct tape and superglue, all the while being a massive hypocrite.

"Oh, Jasmine," my dad whispered, sounding pained when I didn't reply to his question. Out of the corner of my eye, I saw him reach for me, his hand covering mine.

I couldn't help but go stiff, and it was impossible to miss that my dad noticed and did the same.

"I do love you. I love you very much," he said softly. "You're my baby—"

I huffed, not letting myself suck in his claims of love.

"You *are* my baby," my dad insisted, his hand still resting on my own.

Technically, yes.

But I wasn't. And everyone knew that. He was just in denial, trying to make himself feel better.

"I want the best for you, Jasmine. I'm not going to say I'm sorry for it," he said after I didn't respond.

I still refused to look at him as I said, "I know you want the best for me. I get it. That's not the problem."

"Then what's the problem?"

On the ice, Ivan started doing really lazy laps, his gaze staying on my dad and me, no matter where he was. He was watching to make sure everything was fine. I didn't doubt that if I needed him, he'd skate over and butt in.

But I wasn't that kind of person. I had avoided dealing with this as long as I could. It was time though.

"The problem is that you don't know me, Dad."

He scoffed, and I turned my head just enough to finally look at him.

"You don't. I love you, but you don't know me or understand me. Not even a little bit. I don't know if it's because I'm a pain in the ass or if you just don't like me."

He blew out a breath of frustration that I was going to ignore. "Why would you think I don't like you?"

I blinked and tried to push away the gross, disappointed feeling in the middle of my belly. "Because you don't. How many times have we spent time together, just us two?"

My dad's mouth hung open for a moment before he closed it. "You were always busy. You're always busy now."

The answer was never. We'd never spent time together alone. He spent time with each of my brothers and each of my sisters, but never with me.

I was busy. But he'd never even *tried*. He'd never even come to the rink to sit at the bleachers and watch me practice, like everyone else had on multiple occasions. And if he'd ever even given a little bit of a shit, he would have.

So I controlled my breath, controlled my features and mouth so I could respond to him and not go off. "I am, but neither one of us made time for it. How many of my competitions have you gone to over the last... six years?"

For some reason, I didn't enjoy the look of discomfort that came over his face. "You stopped inviting me," he claimed.

Sadness that dwarfed every other sadness I had ever experienced in my life filled my entire body, but mostly the upper half of it.

"I stopped inviting you after you made me feel bad for asking you for money. I remember. You stopped going to any of my competitions before I was even nineteen. I remember you told me at the last one you went to, '*Maybe you should focus on school, no?*' Do you remember telling me that right after I'd won first place? Because I do," I reminded him, facing forward again to watch Ivan go into a shotgun spin that was half the speed he usually went at. The sadness in me grew stronger, thicker, and maybe in some way turned into resignation. Resignation that things had turned out this way and there was nothing I could do about it.

My dad said nothing.

"Do you know why I started figure skating?"

There was a pause and then, "It was a birthday party. Your mom made you go and you were mad because you didn't want to."

I blinked because that was exactly what had happened. I hardly knew the girl having the party, but she'd been a daughter of my mom's friend. It wasn't until she'd told me it was at a rink like in *The Mighty Ducks,* that I had agreed to go, still bitching the entire time.

At least until I'd gotten out on that ice and my body had just *known* what to do. "Like a duck in water," my mom had called from the sidelines.

"That's part of it, but not what I was asking," I said, my voice sounding as tired as I felt. Drained, just so damned drained. "I started because I loved it. From the first moment I got on the ice, it felt right. And once I didn't need to hold the walls anymore, it made me feel... free. It made me feel special. Everyone else that day could barely get around, but I picked up on it like this," I explained, snapping my fingers. "And the better I got, the more I loved it. Nothing had ever made me happier than figure skating. I felt like I belonged. Do you understand that?"

"Yes... but you could have played any sport."

"But I didn't *want* to. Mom had tried to get me into swimming, gymnastics, soccer, karate, but all I ever wanted was this. It's the only thing I'm good at, and you don't see that or get it. I work so hard. I bust my ass every day for this. I have to do something a thousand times to do it decently, not even well. I'm not a quitter. I've never been a quitter, and I'm never going to be a quitter. But you don't see that. You don't get it."

The man beside me let out an exasperated sigh as he tore his hand off mine and went to palm his forehead. "I've only wanted the best for my children, Jasmine. You included."

"I know that. But all I want is for you to be supportive of me. Not everyone can do what I do, Dad! It's hard. It's so hard—"

"I never said it wasn't hard."

I made my hand into a fist before shaking it out. Patience. *Be better.* "Yeah, but you basically say you aren't proud of me—"

"I never said that!"

"You don't have to say it when all you do is tell me all the different things I can do to be... better. To be more successful. I know I haven't lived up to my potential, I don't forget that, ever. Not for a minute. I put enough pressure on myself every day. Do you know how hard it is for me to know that you think I'm a disappointment too?"

Dad cursed and shook his head. "I don't think you're a disappointment!"

"Yeah, but you don't think I'm good enough. You don't think *I'm* enough. You don't want to spend time with me. You don't want to go to my competitions. I don't call you, but you don't call me either! All you ever do is tell me everything I can do different. Like if I don't go to college, that's it. I'm a failure. I'm not sorry, Dad. I'm not sorry I love this. But I am sorry I haven't been more successful. Maybe you'd be more proud of me if I'd won something big. Maybe then you would understand why I love this so much and then you'd be okay with it."

My dad cursed again, this time both of his hands going up to his face to scrub them.

But he didn't deny that he'd be more proud of me if I'd

won more. That maybe then he would be fine with it. That he would drop the college thing.

My head began to throb almost instantly, and I got up, knowing this was done and there was nothing else left to say. I didn't look at him exactly, but stood so that my side was to where he was sitting, my attention forward on one of the walls that had LUKOV COMPLEX painted on it. "I love you, Dad, but I can't change who I am and what I want out of my life. Yeah, I don't know what the hell I'm going to do when I can't compete anymore, but I'll figure it out. I'm not going to give up what I love just because I might not have it forever," I told him, sad and disappointed but a little relieved too.

By that point, my dad had his hands on his head and was taking turns sighing and mumbling under his breath.

I wanted to touch him, to tell him it was fine, but I couldn't. Not then.

"Have a safe trip back to California, and tell Anise and the kids I said hello," I told him, fisting my hand at my side.

He didn't look up, and I wasn't completely surprised. My mom had always said I got my ego from him. I didn't know him well enough to be sure. And that's just the way things were.

Feeling just a little sick, I made my way back toward the ice, debating whether or not to tell my mom about Dad showing up and trying to talk to me.

More than halfway around the wall, I heard the sound of blades on the ice get louder and then the sharp sound of them coming to a stop. There was only one person who sounded like that. So, I wasn't surprised when I heard, "Boo."

I turned around with just enough time to see something come flying at me. I caught the shiny thing instinctively and opened my palm to find a Hershey's kiss. I didn't look at Ivan as I undid the wrapper, stuck it in my mouth, and muttered, "Thank you."

"Uh-huh," he replied before going, "Want to get something to eat before ballet? I'll treat your broke ass."

I couldn't help the smirk I shot him even as I thought about how much better I would have wished the conversation with my dad would have gone, but I did control the nod I gave him afterward.

"Let's get this done, and then we can go."

"Okay."

He nodded, those blue eyes on me, and said, "Okay."

I was going to be all right.

I would.

But I had no idea how wrong I would be.

Getting back out on the ice, I couldn't shake off the uneasy feeling in my stomach that my dad gave me. Maybe if I won something this season, he would change his mind.

But if he couldn't, what was I going to do? Beg him to accept me? Fuck that.

"Let's go over that one part with the side-by-side triple-triple combo," Coach Lee called out as I met up with Ivan in front of her.

He smacked the back of his hand against my leg, and I smacked him right back.

I didn't need my dad to love me, I told myself. I didn't. I never had. I was going to do what I'd always wanted to do—*for me*. For my mom. For Sebastian, Tali, Jojo, and Rubes. I would.

"You sure you're good?" Ivan asked as we got into position.

I nodded at him, thinking about how I was going to do well for Ivan too.

"Positive?" he asked.

I nodded again. Everything was going to be fine... and if it wasn't, I would make the best out of it. I would know I had given it my all and some people just weren't meant for some things.

Ivan didn't look like he believed me exactly, but he nodded back. I didn't think about the combo we were going to do—two jumps with three revolutions each, back to back.

I was going to be fine. I wouldn't let myself be any less, especially not when the season was just about to start.

The music started a few beats before we were supposed to go into the jump. I could do this. Everything would be fine.

Ivan and I were going to do great. Be fine. Be awesome.

We started off in the same place in the music, a few seconds before the two jumps, with just enough time to gain the momentum to go into them.

The first triple toe loop went as well as it could have. The balance was right, the speed was right, and out of my peripheral vision, I saw Ivan in the exact spot he needed to be. Everything was going to be fine. This was what I'd been born to do. Digging my toe pick into the ice to go into the second triple toe loop of our jump combination, I had my opposite blade firmly on the ice, and I *went up* for another.

But I hadn't been focusing. Not enough. I took it for granted as I reminded myself that I could do this shit with my eyes closed.

That's when everything went wrong. My weight was off... I was too loose on my left side.... I hadn't put enough speed into it—thinking I was strong and it would be fine—but it wasn't. And the second I knew something was wrong, I tried to bail.

But I'd waited too long, when I tried to catch myself and land on my foot instead of just hitting the ice.

I felt it.

I knew the instant my blade grazed the surface that I had fucked up.

I knew the landing was going to be bad.

But there was no way to know just how bad. Not until the rest of my weight came down, and *then*, I realized how screwed up everything was, how off-center the rest of my body was. Later on, I could look back on the footage and see that it was just a giant clusterfuck. My foot was in the wrong position, my weight went in the opposite direction, and my ankle tried its best, but couldn't do the impossible.

I felt my foot give out under me. Felt my body try to compensate, but hit the ice because *holyfuckingshit*. Holy fucking shit. Holy fucking shit. *Holy fucking shit.*

It didn't hurt until I was already on my ass on the ice, clutching the area just above my ankle over the leather of the boot. There was so much adrenaline pumping through my body it was in shock. But I knew, I fucking knew something was wrong as the music for our set kept on playing in the background and I sat there, bad, bad pain shooting through my ankle.

Out of the corner of my eye, I could see where Ivan had stopped right after his landing, probably having gone into the next foot sequence before noticing I wasn't right beside him like I should have been. Like I was always supposed to be.

In my head, I could picture his face as he realized I wasn't next to him like we had practiced a thousand times in the past. I could picture his face as he realized I'd fucked up. I could picture his face looking back at me in confusion as to why I wasn't getting the fuck up to go after him, like I usually did when a jump went wrong and I didn't stick the landing.

But I'd fallen.

I wasn't in blinding pain, but I knew there was something wrong.

I knew there was something wrong, and I knew I needed to get up because we had a lot of work to do. We were supposed to work on nailing this shit. We were supposed to perfect all of this.

I needed to get up.

Get up, Jasmine. Get up. *Get up, get up, get up, get up. Suck it up and get up. Finish this.*

Still grabbing my ankle, that voice drove me to try and roll onto my opposite knee to get up. I had to get up. We had kinks to work out. Finger positions to perfect.

I could do this. I could get up. I had skated through bone bruises, hairline fractures, and minor sprains.

So I rolled to my knee, trying to listen to the music and figure out where we were so I could catch up. But just as I got to my knee and started to pull up the leg I'd landed badly on, pain like I had rarely in my life felt before slashed through me.

I opened my mouth... and nothing came out.

I didn't realize my arms had given out until the ice was on my face and there were some horrifying shouts coming from around me, and the next thing I knew, something was touching my shoulder, rolling me over so I could lay on my back. And the next thing I saw was Ivan on his knees beside me, his face pale and somehow red at the same fucking time. His eyes were huge. I think I would always remember that.

I couldn't get up. *I can't get up.*

And my ankle—

"Jesus Christ, Jasmine, *lay the fuck down!*" Ivan yelled into my face, sliding something around my shoulders, his chest pressed to my shoulder as I belatedly recognized that our music was still on. We had gone with *Van Helsing*. I'd been so excited even though I had played it cool. I had been so relieved that was the music Ivan had chosen. I had given him some shit over it, but only because it's what I did with him.

"Stop trying to get up!" the man beside me yelled again, his voice cracking, his face... frantic.

"Let me try," I managed to murmur. It felt like my brain had some kind of thirty-second delay behind what it wanted to say and what it actually said. I tried to roll over, I tried to move my leg, but the pain....

"Stop it, fucking stop it," he barked at me, his left hand coming down to cup my kneecap, stroking up my thigh.

His hand was shaking. Why was his hand shaking?

I can't get up. I can't get up.

"Jasmine, for the love of God, quit trying to get up," Ivan shouted at me, his hands going everywhere and nowhere, but I couldn't be sure because it felt like something was roaring in my ears, and the pain below my knee was getting worse, worse, worse.

"It's fine. Give me a minute," I blabbed, attempting to lift my bad leg only for him to hold it down, squeezing my thigh painfully.

"Stop it, Jasmine, fucking stop," he demanded, his hand above my knee. "*Nancy!*" my partner yelled somewhere, but I wasn't sure because I guess I had started staring at my leg....

I'd done something to my goddamn ankle.

I had done something to my fucking ankle.

No. No, no, no, no, *no.*

I didn't even realize I'd opened my mouth until Ivan whispered hoarsely into my ear, "Don't cry. Don't you dare fucking cry right now. Do you hear me? You are not going to cry on the ice, in public. Hold it in. Hold it in. Not one tear, Jasmine. Not a single tear. Do you hear me?"

I sucked in a breath, my eyes going glassy and everything going blurry.

Was I shaking?

Why did I feel like I was about to throw up?

"Don't you dare do it," he hissed again, the arm around my

shoulders tightening. "You don't want anyone to see you do this. Hold it, baby, just hold it...."

I didn't know what the hell he was saying or why he was saying it, but for some reason, I just held my breath. I held my breath as Coach Lee slid onto the ice on my other side, quickly flanked by a body shape I recognized as Galina's and another coach. They crowded me, surrounded me.

They asked questions, I tried to answer, but heard Ivan answer for me.

Because I couldn't breathe. I couldn't talk. I couldn't cry.

All I could do was stare in the general vicinity of where my white boot was, barely able to see shit, and think, think, think, think.

I fucked up.

I had fucked up.

I had fucking fucked up.

CHAPTER 19

"WHAT DO YOU THINK YOU'RE DOING?"

Stopping halfway into crunch number 108, I didn't need to look to my side to know who was standing there. I'd recognize that annoying, condescending, bossy voice in a crowd of a thousand. Only one person could aggravate me so easily by asking a question.

"Minding my own business. The one thing you don't know how to do," I muttered, rolling up the little bit I had left to keep my ab workout going.

"Jasmine," came Ivan's sharp tone again.

I ignored him. Going back up into another crunch, I watched out of the corner of my eye as he closed the door behind him.

I did another crunch just as he came walking toward me, those big feet in bright blue running shoes landing centimeters from my side.

I didn't look up at him, and I wasn't going to. I knew what he was looking at. It wasn't my body that was covered in sweat that he was eyeing, and it definitely wasn't the fact that I wore a pair of loose basketball shorts that belonged to my brother that were riding high up my thighs. The fact I only had a sports bra on had nothing to do with what he wanted to focus on either.

He was looking at the cast boot I had on my left foot. The left foot I had propped up on a pillow right beside my right one, which was planted flat on the floor, knee bent. The black boot that was a reminder, every single minute of my day, that I had fucked up and fucked up big-time.

I did four more crunches, staring straight up at the ceiling.

I swallowed so hard my throat hurt.

I had done the same thing so many times over the last two weeks, I was surprised I could still talk. Not that I'd been doing much talking since I'd been let out of urgent care. I hadn't been doing much of anything other than working out in my room, watching videotaped practices of Ivan and me *before*, and sleeping.

The tip of Ivan's shoe nudged my rib, and I ignored it.

"Jasmine."

"Ivan," I said, making my voice sound as uncompromising as his.

He nudged me again. And again, I did nothing.

He sighed. "Are you going to stop so we can talk or what?"

"I'd rather not," I answered, forcing myself to keep my gaze away from him.

I shouldn't have been surprised when he quickly dropped into a deep squat, hovering just to my side, so close there was no way to ignore him. Unfortunately. Because when I went up to do another crunch, his palm went to my forehead and gently pushed my head back down so that I lay there, on my back.

Looking around and past him, I focused on my ceiling fan.

"Meatball, that's enough," he said, his hand still on my face.

I waited a second and tried to go up into another crunch, but he must have been expecting it, because I couldn't even get an inch off the floor.

"*Enough,*" he repeated. "Stop. Talk to me."

Talk to him?

That had me flicking my gaze in his direction, taking in that face I hadn't seen in over two weeks. That face I had gotten used to seeing six days a week but had somehow become more like seven days a week from all the extra time we spent together. That face that the last time I had seen, had been beside me as I sat on an exam table, listening to the doctor tell me that, best-case scenario, I might be back on my feet in six weeks. *But no promises. Grade 2 sprains to your ATFL and your CFL are problematic,* the doctor had warned before dropping the recovery time period on me.

Eight weeks had never seemed so long before.

Especially when you couldn't forgive yourself for being a reckless moron.

It took everything in me to ask him, keeping my voice steady, "What do you want to talk about?"

He stared at me, those gray-blue eyes as intense as ever, and I watched his chest expand with a breath I knew was a steadying one. He was annoyed.

Tough shit for him, I was more annoyed than he was.

"I've tried calling you," he said, like I didn't know he'd called me at least six times every day for the last twelve days. Today alone, he'd called twice. And like every time my phone rang, I didn't pick up. I hadn't picked up. Not once. Not for anyone. Not for my siblings, not for my dad who had left moments before my fall, not Coach Lee, not Galina. Nobody.

I kept my gaze steady on him as I answered. "I haven't felt like talking. Nothing has changed. I don't get the boot off for another two days."

And then, after the doctor gave me the okay to take the boot off, I'd be replacing it with an Aircast air-stirrup ankle brace. The physical therapist I'd been driving myself to for the last nine days had been optimistic I was healing "*just fine.*"

But fine had never been good enough for me.

Especially not when it had been my own damn fault I was in this situation.

But Ivan blinked, and he sighed again, and I knew he was this fucking close to losing his shit. The thing was, I didn't care. What was he going to do? Yell at me? "I know nothing has changed, dumbass."

This asshole....

"Get your shit together. You're coming with me."

It was my turn to blink and then stare at him blankly. "What?"

A long index finger poked me right in the forehead. "Get your shit together. You're coming with me," he repeated, taking his time with every word. "You hurt your ankle, not your ears."

"I'm not going anywhere with you."

"Yes, you are."

"No, I'm not."

The smile that went over his mouth basically creeped me out and instantly made me wary. "You are."

I stared right at him, ignoring the weird sensation in my belly as I did.

That creepy smile didn't go anywhere. "You haven't left your room in two weeks other than to go to physical therapy."

I said nothing.

"It smells like you haven't showered in two weeks."

I had. Two days ago.

"Have you even been sleeping?" That finger gave my forehead another poke. "You look like shit."

It was that, that had me gritting out, "Yes, I've been sleeping." He didn't need to know not very well.

He didn't look like he believed me, but he still said, "You need to get out of here."

"Why?" I asked before I could stop myself, sounding just as angry as I felt.

"Because there's no point in you moping around in here, acting like *GI Jane* working out randomly, Jesus Christ, Jasmine."

That had me smacking his hand away from my face and sitting up straight, turning my upper body just enough so I could look him in the eye. "I'm not moping, ass. I've been working out. I can't just sit around and rest and totally let myself go."

"You're not working out so that you don't *let yourself go*. You're working out because you're pissed off and in a bad mood. You think I don't know you?"

I opened my mouth to say *no*, I wasn't working out for that reason, but he'd see right through my bullshit. Instead, I said, "I'm not in a bad mood. I haven't taken anything out on anybody. You can't call it being in a bad mood if I'm not being mean to other people."

"All right, then what do you call it when you're only being mean to yourself?"

I hated it when he asked me things I didn't know how to answer.

Ivan's face twisted up into this frustrated expression. "Your mom has invited you to do things with her, and you ignore her."

"I did not ignore her. I said no." I blinked and felt another wave of irritation. "Has she been snitching to you?" When? How?

"It's still rude and mean," he explained. "And your

brothers and sisters have tried calling, but you're ignoring their calls too. I bet Galina's called and you haven't answered her either."

It was true. It was all true. But I wasn't about to admit or deny it.

"You're not doing this shit to yourself, Jasmine," he let me know. Like he'd made this decision for me and I was going to fucking listen.

He could get the fuck out.

Something swelled up in me that almost took the breath right out of me. "I'm not doing anything to myself, Ivan. I'm minding my own business. Hanging out by myself. I don't see what's so wrong with that. I'm *healing. Resting.* Like everyone told me to do."

The blink he gave me made me feel bad. Really. But before I could apologize for snapping at him, he went back to frowning. "Don't get an attitude with me. We both know you're hiding, and I'm not letting you do it any longer. I was waiting, hoping you'd get out of this funk on your own, once you realized you didn't completely tear the ligaments or get a fracture like we had been worried about... but you're not, so I'm dragging you out of it if I have to. I'm done waiting for you to quit being a baby, and I'm not cutting you any slack, even if this is the first time you've pulled some shit like that."

It wasn't the first time I had pulled some shit like this. He hadn't seen me back when Paul had left. It had been just as bad, but this time felt worse than then.

I poked him in the forehead the same way he had me and said one thing. "No."

Ivan blinked those bright blue eyes, his eyelids hanging low over them, and he grit out, "Jasmine, you're about to get your ass up, get out of this house, and go to mine. You're either doing it on your own, or I'm doing it for you. You get to choose."

"I'm not leaving the house."

He shook his head. "You're leaving the house."

"I'm not leaving the house."

"Yes, you are. You choose. You do it or I do it."

I poked him in the forehead again. Twice. "No."

His nostrils flared. "I'm going to count to five, and you have to make a decision between now and then, or I'm choosing for you, and you know what I'm choosing."

"Ivan, I don't want to go with you."

"I don't give a shit. You could have left with anyone else in your family, but you didn't, so now you're coming with me."

Rage filled me in no time. Instantly, and I hissed, "No, I'm fucking not!"

Apparently, I wasn't the only one about to get pissed off, because he hissed back, "Yes, you fucking are!"

"I don't want to go with you, how hard is that for you to understand? *I don't want to be around anyone right now or anytime soon,*" I fucking snapped, sounding like so much of an asshole, it made me cringe on the inside.

His eyelids swung even lower over his eyes, so they were barely slits. "Why? Are you over me now?"

I jerked my head back. "Over you? What the hell are you talking about?"

That angular jaw of his went tight. "Are you over me? Are you pissed off at me and don't want to be my partner anymore?"

What in the fuck was he talking about? I gaped at him. Blinked. Then gaped a little more, because what the hell was wrong with him? "I don't understand what you're trying to say, Ivan."

His nostrils flared, and his eyes stayed just short of closing as he asked, "Do you not want to be my partner anymore?"

"Why would I not want to be your partner anymore?" I asked him, sounding angry.

"Because of what happened!" he shouted.

"Why would I not want to be your partner? Because I fell like a dumbass? How is that your fault, idiot?"

When his face had started turning pink, I had no idea. But by the time I realized it, it was all rosy. "Because I could tell you were distracted and didn't give you a chance to get focused. I landed too close to you."

Was he seriously blaming himself? "You didn't land that close to me, stupid."

He shot me a look that could have burned my eyebrows off. "I did, Jasmine. I landed way too close to you."

"Oh, shut up. No, you didn't. I landed wrong because *I* was distracted. Because I screwed up. That wasn't your fault."

He glared at me so hard, it made my blood pressure go up. Why would he think something so stupid? Why would he blame himself? How did that make any sense?

"You really thought I didn't want to see you because I blamed you?" I spat, looking at him like he was a jackass, because he was.

He still glared at me, telling me that answer was yes.

"You're so dumb."

"I'm dumb? Then why haven't you answered your phone?"

It was my turn to have my face close off, and I shut my mouth and shrugged my shoulders instead.

"No. You don't get to shrug at me and think that's enough of an answer. I've called you over and over again. I thought you were pissed off at me. I thought you didn't answer because you were mad at me, so now I want to know why you didn't other than you blaming yourself for being distracted."

I rolled my eyes and looked away, shaking my head. "It doesn't matter."

"It does matter. It matters a lot."

I lifted my shoulders again.

"Jasmine."

Why couldn't he just leave me alone?

"Jasmine."

Why would he think something so stupid?

"*Jasmine.*"

I grunted and turned back toward him, hissing, "Because what the hell would I tell you, Ivan? I'm sorry? I'm so fucking sorry? That I didn't mean to sprain my ankle and ruin *everything*?" I basically yelled at him. Horror filled me from the tip of my tongue down to the pit of my belly. Why was I yelling at him? And why the hell was I telling him this? Why didn't he already know it?

His mouth opened, and he looked at me like I'd punched him in the stomach. "Jasmine—"

"I'm sorry, Ivan," I croaked, horror and helplessness pulsing through my body. "I screwed up. I keep screwing up. I don't know why I'm yelling at you. You didn't do anything. It was me." My voice cracked, and I felt my hand fist. "I fucked up. It was my fault. Not yours."

I could feel a shout coming up, clogging my throat. Ripping me inside out. And I hated it. I didn't want it to come out.

"Stop it," he said, slowly, those eyes bouncing all over my face, something in them still looking like they were in shock. "Get your shit together. You're coming with me."

I looked into his eyes and sucked in a breath. "No."

"No. You want to make it up to me? Get your things for a few days and come with me. I'm not leaving here without you, and I will take you kicking and screaming. If you yell something about being kidnapped, I'll tell anyone who listens that you're on drugs."

I stared at him.

"You owe me the next six weeks, Jasmine. Get your shit together now. We're going."

"Ivan...."

He stared at me.

Anger and pain twisted my insides into a thousand knots. "I'm really sorry."

It was his throat bobbing that caught my attention. His response was a slow, "I know."

I had fucked up. It made my chest hurt. "I didn't mean to."

His throat bobbed again. "I know."

"I've landed that a thousand times."

Again. "I know, Jasmine."

"I don't know what happened."

If it wasn't for the breath on my chin, I wouldn't know he had let a long, low breath out. "I know you don't," he basically whispered, so at ease from how he'd just been speaking to me a second ago.

I almost choked. *Almost.* "I promise I'll do whatever I have to do to get better."

But it was Ivan who choked. Ivan who blinked, one, two, three, four, five times, fast, fast, fast. His eyelashes fluttered from how fast he'd done it. Like something got caught in his throat that he couldn't do anything about.

"Everything and anything. I swear. I know we'll have to skip most of the Discovery Series and the WHK, but maybe we can still do Skate North America—"

It was his hands that cut me off. Those hands that I was so familiar with, I could pick out from a crowd by touch. The hands that had held mine, held me, so many times I couldn't count.

But they had never held my face before. At least not the way he did right then. Because his palms went to my cheeks and he cupped them.

And then he cut me off.

With his mouth.

His lips pressed to mine. Surged to mine. Covered them. Hard.

And then he kissed my upper lip between his while I was still trying to figure out *what the fuck was happening.*

Ivan was kissing me.

Kissing *me.*

His mouth went to my eyes suddenly, and he pressed his lips from one of my eyelids to the other, quick, fluttering, so light I could barely feel it. One brow bone and then the other. And I just sat there.

I sat there and I didn't move away or push him away or tell him no.

His mouth went over my cheeks, warm and everything wonderful in the world. "You tried to get up," he said to me in a voice so low I barely understood his words. "You tried to get up and keep skating, and I swear I almost started crying right then."

He kissed one cheek and then the other, soft, his mouth brushing over the bridge of my nose as he moved around.

"Only you would sprain the shit out of your ankle and try to get up to keep going," he said to me, his voice hitching. "You kept saying, *I'm sorry, Ivan. I'm sorry, Ivan. I'm so sorry*, and I told you to shut up because if you kept saying it any more, I would have been the one...." His breath came out stuttered and choppy over my face, and his hands moved from my cheeks to cup my ears.

His mouth shifted over mine, grazing it, so light and sweet, something in me constricted.

Friends could kiss in relief. He wasn't shoving his tongue in my mouth or copping a feel. He was just happy I was fine. He was just kissing me because... why not?

He cared about me.

People had kissed for much less, knowing each other not even a little bit.

I let Ivan kiss the places he wanted to, telling myself it was fine, that he'd been scared for me, because he had been. He had. And with that one thought, all I could focus on at that point were his words. His hurt. All shit I had caused.

"I'm sorry. I'm so sorry," I repeated, because I was. I was so sad it hurt me that we were here. It hurt me that I had let him down. "You've only had to pull out of a few events before me, and now I'm making you do it. I'm sorry, Ivan. I didn't mean to fall."

Ivan's head shook in front of me. "Stop saying that."

"But I am," I whispered. "It's my fault."

"It was an accident," he finished for me, sharply. "There's nothing to be sorry about."

"But I ruined—"

"You didn't ruin anything. Shut the hell up," he said.

"We're out for six more weeks if everything goes well," I reminded him, like he didn't know.

"For two months total, Jasmine. Not the whole season. Not forever," he also said, like I didn't know that.

"But we've worked so hard—"

"Meatball, it doesn't matter."

I sucked in a breath at the reminder of how we were losing so much time out of the one and only year we had together. Eight less weeks that I'd get to be around this man who meant the world to me. Before he left me for someone else and I was on my own, the captain of my own destiny or whatever the hell it was called.

And I blinked.

"Don't start. It's only two months, and we were doing great. It was easy for us. Too easy." He pressed his warm cotton candy pink lips to mine like he'd done it a thousand times before and would do it a thousand times again. "If anyone can come back from this in six weeks, it's you."

It would be me. Of course it would. But I couldn't say the words then, as I stared into those eyes of his, our faces inches away from each other. All I could do was nod. And after a beat, then five, I said, "We'll win."

His gaze went even more intense as he said, with no hesitation, "You're goddamn right we will." He pressed his mouth, so quick, so hard against me, I didn't have a chance to react until he pulled back an inch and said, hoarsely, his fingers threading through the damp hair right above the nape of my neck, "I'll drag you back on the ice if I have to, Jasmine. I swear on my life."

Something about his words made me shake on the inside. Maybe it was the conviction. Maybe it was the anger. The passion. The reality that he wasn't leaving me any room to not do what he said.

Mostly though, it was something else completely.

I loved him.

I loved this man so much that losing him was going to break my cold, dead heart into so many pieces I was just going to have to stick them in the same box I kept my dreams and carry it around with me forever.

I didn't want someone to pat my cheek and tell me everything was going to be okay. I wanted this man who would never take my shit, who would never let me quit, and I had a feeling would never quit on me. Not ever. Not if I screamed, not if I kicked, not if I told him to go eat a thousand mounds of shit.

This was my partner. This was more than my partner. He was my other half.

And the only thing I could do to thank him for this gift he'd given me, this knowledge that he thought I was invincible, was to make sure we won.

I'd give him the thing he had wanted me for in the first place.

I'd give him my fucking all.

CHAPTER 20

FALL

IF I COULD DESCRIBE THE NEXT FOUR WEEKS OF MY LIFE WITH one conversation, it would have been like this:

Ivan: "Sit still."
Me: "No."
Ivan: "What do you think you're doing? Do you want to get healthy or what? *Stop walking around so much.*"
Me: [Trying to walk normal—but failing—across his living room with a new brace on] "Leave me alone."
Ivan: "I'm never going to leave you alone. Come sit your stubborn-ass back down, and I'll get you whatever you want."

CHAPTER 21

I WAS PRETTY POSITIVE I HADN'T IMAGINED THE WORDS COMING out of the wonderful doctor's mouth, but I needed to be sure.

"So... I'm cleared to skate again?" I asked her. Because I had to be sure. I needed to be sure.

The doctor nodded, smiling, looking at me like she understood how much was hanging in the balance and how much her words would mean to me. "You're as healed as you can be."

Excitement, relief, and nerves all barreled through me. But I had to ask. *Just one more time.* "For sure?"

The doctor's smile grew wider as her eyes slipped to the side briefly before saying, "Yes."

A hand landed my shoulder, rough, giving it a shake I could feel to my teeth, and I couldn't help but beaming up at Ivan. He already had his other hand at my side, and I smacked my palm against his, linking my fingers through his and giving him a shake. His head moved forward, his chin landing on my shoulder, cheek to cheek. His chest to part of my back.

"We've got this, Meatball," he said, hugging me, telling me with his body that we were going to be able to do Skate North America, the next competition we—he—had been invited to.

We were going to be able to do it.

We were going to get another chance.

CHAPTER 22

It was a good thing that no one had told me taking eight weeks off right at the beginning of the season was going to be easy, because it hadn't been.

It absolutely hadn't been.

The past two weeks had been the most exhausting two weeks of my life, and that included the month that I had been going back to the LC to work out until midnight. But this time, I hadn't been alone. I'd had my best friend with me the entire time.

And I had enjoyed every sweaty, grueling, frustrating, painful moment.

Especially right then, as I stared out the window of the van that had picked up Ivan, me, and six other pairs teams with their coaches, to take us to the facility where we would be competing at tomorrow. Relief like I didn't know I had in me, flooded my lungs, freeing them, as I took in the giant building with banners located around it. SKATE NORTH AMERICA, NOVEMBER 23-26. One of them even had Ivan—by himself—right after landing a jump the year before.

We were here and it was real.

We were ready.

Ivan had been quieter than normal over the last few days, while we'd done as many last-minute corrections as possible back at the LC. We had caught a flight to Lake Placid two days before, just in case the winter weather took a turn for the worst, but it hadn't. Skate North America only offered one day of official practice, so the past two days, we had just taken advantage of the giant conference room the WSU—World Skating Union—had booked for everyone with the same plans as us.

And when we hadn't been in the conference room, Ivan, Coach Lee, me, and the Simmons husband and wife team— our choreographers—had taken a taxi trip around, walked the downtown area, visited the Olympic museum, eaten lunch out, and then gone back to our rooms. At least until Ivan had showed up to my room to see what my view was like and we'd ended up ordering takeout and eating in there while we watched a show about cats from hell, and he'd told me about the three cats he'd had up until a year ago, when the last one had passed away from old age.

I didn't need to tell Ivan that this trip was different from every other trip I'd ever taken before, by myself and with Paul. But I thought he knew. I was excited—and I was nervous for the first time ever—but the excitement overwhelmed the rest.

And we were *here*. One step closer. One last thirty-minute practice away from the beginning of the end that I was trying so hard not to focus on.

We had just climbed out of the van when Ivan grabbed my hand out of the blue.

I glanced at him, not frowning but wondering what the hell he was doing. It wasn't like I minded it. I didn't. I grabbed his hand for random reasons every once in a while. But, I still didn't know why he was doing it. And it amped up my nerves a kick more.

"What is it?" I asked, when I took in the expression on his face as he turned his body to face mine.

Pulling my hand, he tugged me to the side to let the other teams we had ridden over with pass. We were all in Group B with practice times. Ivan's breath puffed white in the bitter New York air, and I shivered, trying to figure out what the hell was happening and why it had to be happening outside. Those bright blue eyes were focused on my face when the man who had driven me to every physical therapy appointment after he'd barged into my room so many weeks ago said, "I need you to promise me something."

This was going to be bad, wasn't it?

"It depends on what it is," I replied, worrying, trying to rack my brain for whatever the hell was so serious he wanted a promise out of me first.

That perfect face with its perfect skin and structure didn't sigh or give me an exasperated expression that he usually would have. "Promise me, Jasmine."

Shit.

"Not before you tell me what it is. I don't want to break my promise." I frowned, dread quickly filling my stomach cavity.

Chances were I would probably do whatever he asked but... what if he asked me not to fuck up. Or not to make a scene if he introduced me to the next partner he had lined up, if he didn't go back to Mindy. We hadn't talked about the future at all. Not once.

Shit.

Ivan's eyes roamed my face, slowly. His breathing slowed and his too-calm features, relaxed even more. Then, he sighed, glanced up at the sky for all of a moment and then back down at me with a swallow that made his Adam's apple bob. "Please, promise me. I'm not asking you for anything you aren't capable of."

I must have made a face, because he tugged at the hand he was still holding.

"Promise me, Meatball. You know you can trust me," he said, not making it a question but a well-known fact.

And he'd be right.

But still, I hated that he was trying to use that against me. I didn't want to break a promise to him. Not ever. But I also didn't want to do something I probably wasn't capable of... like smiling at the person he was going to replace me with in a few months. I glanced away, and it was probably my imagination that the air grew colder by the second. I shivered. "Fine, I promise. What is it?" I asked, hearing the attitude in my voice.

The smile he gave me in response, slow and smirkish, put me at ease a little, but just a little. "Promise me that if you see Paul and Mary, you won't try to start a fight with him—"

The fuck? That's what this was about? Paul and Mary?

Get the fuck out. I hadn't thought about either of those two assholes in months. Not since he'd talked me into doing the photo shoot.

My scoff was so loud, it genuinely aggravated my throat. "Oh come on, that's what you want me to promise you? You think I'm going to go out of my way to fight with him and risk getting in trouble?"

He blinked, and his hand gave mine a squeeze. "You didn't let me finish. I was going to say that you should save it up until after the competition, then go for it. We'll kill them with our scores, and then you can give the knockout punch."

I opened my mouth, and then I closed it.

Those gray-blue eyes lingered on my face even as his eyebrows went up, and he covered the top of my hand with his other one. "Is that a deal?"

I could only blink before I managed to get out, "What do you think?"

And his smile was just... ugh. "I think Mirror Lake across from the hotel is pretty convenient."

"You'll be my alibi?"

Ivan scrunched up his nose. "I know your sisters are here and all, but I thought you'd want me to help out. I'm stronger than they are. We wouldn't have to leave a trail."

What I wanted was him forever, but I'd take what I could get.

"Deal," I said.

He grinned. "One more thing."

Damn it.

"I want to know because you never told me, but what do you have against Mary McDonald?" he asked. "I want to know why we hate her."

Why we hate her. Ivan. Fucking Ivan. All I could do was shrug so that I wouldn't say anything else I had no business sharing. "When we were younger, before I was even in pairs, she used to talk shit about me behind my back. You can ask Karina. Mary didn't know Karina was my friend, and she talked about my weight, made some really racist, asshole comments about me being half-Filipino, and she was just a bitch in general."

Ivan blinked. "Did you say anything to her?" The question had just come out of his mouth when he snorted. "That's a stupid question. Of course you did."

I tugged on his hand. "You already know I did. I told her the next time she talked about me, I would open a can of whoop-ass on her."

∽

"*Son of a bitch!*" I hissed as I burned my scalp *again* trying to get my straightening iron as close to the roots as possible. Skate North America wasn't the most televised event in the season, but...

It didn't matter to me.

What did matter was getting my hair as straight as possible, even though it already was. Only, I couldn't see or reach the back of my head well. We had three hours before the event even started, and we weren't scheduled to skate until *almost* the end. But my makeup was on, so was the black long-sleeved lacy dress that Ruby had finished months ago, before I'd gotten injured.

Ivan had decided to go change in the men's restroom because he didn't want "any riots starting" if people saw him in his underwear.

The idiot.

And now I needed his help. He would help me straighten the rest of my hair. I knew he would.

But I was going to try and do as much as I could without hopefully burning myself for the sixth time. Turning back to one of the three illuminated mirrors in the room we were sharing with two of the teams we had worked out with at the same time the day before, I leaned into it and tried to angle my head as well as I could to catch a glimpse of what I was doing. I'd seen the other four people we were competing against—two teams that Ivan knew and had already said were nice—but they hadn't even changed yet.

I'd done two chunks of hair when the door opened, but I didn't think anything of it.

Until a voice I recognized spoke up.

And it wasn't Ivan's.

"Jasmine, I want to talk to you," the semi-familiar voice

requested as I turned to face him, instantly wondering where the hell Ivan was.

I'd made a promise to him.

I will not talk shit to Paul. I will not talk shit to Paul. I will not talk shit to Paul. He'd made me say it seven times total the day before when I'd sworn I'd seen him while we had been waiting for the van to pick us up following our practice session, because apparently, once you did something seven times you couldn't forget it.

I had promised him I wouldn't start anything or do anything. I was a lot of things, and half of them weren't good, but Ivan was.

And I wouldn't go back on my word. Especially not to him. Not after everything he had done for me.

But...

There was no way either one of us could have predicted that Paul would be dumb enough to try and come talk to me before our first skate—our short program. I had always thought I was the one who wasn't as smart as other people, but apparently, this guy I had spent three years of my life teamed up with was the real fucking idiot.

Keeping my gaze on my own reflection in the mirror, I set my straightening iron down on the counter and made my hand into a fist.

"Jasmine, please," the second man in my life to ever do shit to my heart kept going as I kept on looking at myself in the mirror.

I didn't think I looked that different from back when I was nineteen. My face was a little slimmer. My hair was longer, and I was more muscular. But on the inside... well, on the inside, I was definitely different.

Because nineteen-year-old Jasmine would have already

thrown her straightening iron at Paul and hoped it magically burned his balls through his costume.

"Jas, just... five minutes, please," my old partner basically pleaded from wherever he was out of the way from the mirror's reflection.

I fisted my hand tighter. Held my breath. Then I rolled my eyes because *fuck him*. Repeatedly. I hadn't given Paul a single thought in so long, I had genuinely forgotten how much I hated his ass.

But I remembered real quick. Real fucking quick.

You promised Vanya, that calm part of my brain reminded me.

And easily, so easily, I got myself under control... and I exhaled.

"You're just going to pretend I'm not here?" my ex asked, stepping so close behind me I could finally see him in the mirror. So close, I was pretty sure if I kicked out backward, I could easy-peasy kick him in the nuts.

You'd figure after three years together, he would know how dangerous of a position he was putting himself into.

Fucking idiot.

God, Ivan would know better.

Tall, slim, and brown-haired, he looked the exact same as he had almost two years ago, when he'd walked out of the LC and never came back.

Paul looked pale in the lights and the reflection. His hands were in front of him, and I could tell he was anxious.

Good.

"Look, all I want to do is talk."

I didn't mean to snort, but it happened just as I straightened. I was still so short, I had a clear view of me from the waist up. The front of the costume had a sweetheart-neckline in the center of my chest, the dark fabric covering everything important—no beads on mine or Ivan's costumes because they got caught on everything—with lace overlapping everything else, but ending a few inches above my wrist so that the lace wouldn't get in the way of my grip. I loved it. When Ruby had told me her idea for Dracula, I couldn't have picked a better costume design. Ivan had agreed.

Paul's dumbass took that sound for the opposite of what it was—an invitation—and kept on yapping his mouth. "After all the time we were together, you owe me, Jasmine."

And, there it was. The three words he had no business using. The same three words that just like *that* had me seeing red and hoping Ivan would forgive me for breaking my word to him.

But I could tell him that it was because of him, and because of what we'd agreed on, that I didn't punch my ex in the balls from the get-go. If that wasn't an achievement, I didn't know what was. He would get it.

That's what I was going to tell myself as I turned around slowly on the balls of my feet and looked up at the man who I had wasted so much of my time on. Tall but not as tall as Ivan, and with shoulders that weren't as broad, with light brown hair and an *almost* tan complexion, handsome, sure... he was just like how I remembered him. It had been almost two years, after all.

Little fucking bitch.

"I don't owe you shit," I said up to him, sounding so calm I was honest to God proud of myself.

This buttfuck sighed as he ran a hand through his short hair and said, "Give me a break, Jas. We have history—"

Yep, I went from seeing red to seeing fucking magenta. "Yeah, that history ended the day I heard about you pairing up with Mary from someone who had read an article about it online."

He flinched. Paul hesitated. Then he seemed to shake it off as he demanded, "What else was I supposed to do?" He shook his head, swallowed hard, and steeled his shoulders.

But it was pointless because he'd already pissed me off.

He wasn't about to try and guilt trip me or intimidate my ass. "You could have told me like a normal human being that respected the person who had stuck with them for three years?" I snapped, barely managing not to yell at the reminder of what he had done to me. "I tried calling you, Paul, calling you and calling you, and you not once picked up, you fucker," I spat. "You didn't have the balls to warn me or explain shit, not once over the last two years."

"It's not—"

I gave him a look that I knew was my crazy expression. "If you fucking say that's not what it's like, I will punch you right now, on the dick, as hard as I can."

He shut his mouth, because he knew I would.

But he'd broken this dam, and now he was going to have to live with it.

"I gave you three years of my life, Paul. Three. You were my partner, I would have done almost anything for you, and you treated me like a piece of shit. You just ran away and did what you wanted to do, without telling me. Don't tell me I owe you anything. I don't. I don't owe you a single fucking thing," I hissed at him, pointing my finger at him because there was no way I could keep my hand from doing *something* when all it really wanted to do was form a ball and break his nose or his dick.

"You make it seem like I could have just... told you. Like it would have been that easy," he replied, his hand still caught in his hair, his expression twisted.

I blinked. "Yeah, it would have been that easy. *Hey, Jasmine,*

I quit. I'm going to pair up with someone you can't stand. Good luck," I mocked, shaking my head. "Done."

His laughter held a sharp edge. "That's not how it would have gone, and you know it. You would've yelled at me, called me a quitter, a bitch, a pussy, all those things and more. You know you would have. You wouldn't have let me leave that easily."

You promised Ivan you wouldn't do this. You promised.

And I had.

And that's why I kept my hand at my side, *still.*

"Yeah, I would have. I would have done all of those things. We both know that. But you're an idiot for not understanding why. I would have given you a hard time because we were in it together. Because we were a team, and I wouldn't just give up on you like it was nothing. But you're a grown-ass man that makes his own decisions. I wouldn't have tied you up and forced you to stay. Give me a fucking break."

The moment the words were out of my mouth, I was genuinely surprised by them. I don't even think I had ever thought that way before. Much less felt that way.

But I had.

He'd hurt me, and I wanted him to know. I wanted him to know that I had cared about him. And I wasn't above wanting him to know that I would have fought for him.

But that was two years ago.

One year ago, I would have wanted to beat the shit out of him. I would have been too prideful to ever admit any of this. But I wasn't. Not anymore. At this point, all I wanted was to get this horrible guilt and anger I'd been suffering with off my chest. I wanted it out of my life. Out of me.

I wanted to move on. Maybe I already had. Mostly.

I still wanted to beat his ass, but I'd settle for making him regret the day he'd met me. The only way to do that was to kick the shit out of him and Mary on the ice. And I would. Ivan and I would.

"I cared about you too, Jasmine," he said, making me roll my eyes. "I still care about you. When I heard about your sprain, I was worried. I wanted to call you, but... I couldn't."

Yeah, he got another eye roll for that shitty lie. "*Okay.*"

"You don't understand...."

I raised my hands at my sides and let them fall right back down. "Okay, Paul. Tell me. Right now. What is it you want me to hear, huh? That you left me because you wanted a better chance at winning?"

This man gulped again, dragging his hand down his face and over the white and blue spandex bodysuit costume he had on. "Why do you always turn shit around? I miss you, Jas. I've picked up the phone to call you at least a dozen times...."

All I wanted was for him to shut. The. Fuck. Up.

"Honest to God, cross my heart and hope to die, I don't want to talk to you anymore. Or ever again. Whatever you thought you felt, whatever excuses you've talked yourself into believing to justify the way you treated me... live with it. Deal with it. If you know me half as well as you think you do, you know I'm not ever going to forgive you."

"Jasmine, I—"

"Nope. Don't even bother. If you see my mom, run the other way. If you see me, turn around and pretend that you don't," I said to him, sounding oddly calm. "I would have forgiven you if you'd talked to me first. I would have forgiven you for saying all that shit you did about finding a partner you can 'really work with.' And I could have forgiven you eventually for shoving me out of your life. But I'm not going to. I'm not that good of a person." I swept my eyes to the side, giving him my best blank expression and said, "You better go. I have shit to do, and I don't want you as an audience."

Paul Jones blinked. I'd swear maybe even his chin wobbled a little bit. But in that way that was his, he glanced away and sighed, pressing his lips together. "Jasmine, look—"

"Just go."

"I just want to tell you—"

"I don't care," I said, giving him my back again.

He was so full of shit. Ugh.

"Do you even know why I never called you back any of those times you'd leave me voice mails cussing me out right after? Or that time you called me drunk months later, yelling at me?"

"I don't know, and I don't really care," I told him, my voice even, almost robotic as I looked past him toward the door and prayed, *prayed* that Ivan was coming.

He frowned so deeply lines formed across his forehead. Those brown eyes sliced away from me before they came back. "Jasmine, it was because Ivan called me a week afterward and said he would 'fuck me up' if I ever contacted you again."

The hell did he just say?

"Stop looking at me like you think I'm lying. I'm not. He called me and said that if I knew what was good for me, I would leave you alone, but if I didn't, he was going to fuck me up so bad I would regret the day I ever decided to skate pairs."

Ivan.

Ivan had said that? Done that? But that had been a year before we'd paired up, weeks after we'd flipped each other off in a hallway, I was pretty sure.

Ivan had done *that*?

"I also said that I'd destroy you. You missed that part," a familiar voice piped up, making both of us turn to find Ivan peeking his head inside the room, the door barely cracked, hair perfectly gelled into place, his face shaved clean, everything about him bright and sparkling. And he was smiling. And holding red roses.

I loved him.

Goddamn I had no idea what the hell had happened or why it had happened, but I loved him so much in that moment, my heart could have burst.

"But Jasmine can too. She's so small and cute, it's deceiving how strong she is. And it's weird how mad she can get. She's like a little Gremlin; you better not put any water on her because she'll go crazy," he went on, smiling at me with affection as he stepped into the room fully, showing off his matching black costume. "But you should know that."

Paul looked between Ivan and me for a moment before taking a step to the side, away from me.

"I—"

"She's my partner now, Paulie, and she's going to keep being my partner. And you know what? I'm not real good with sharing, so it might be a good idea if you got out of here before all those things I had warned you about come true," Ivan cut him off, as he came to stand at my side.

Ivan didn't touch me. He didn't need to. I knew he was there, and he knew I knew that.

That was the thing with us. We understood each other. We knew the length and depth of our trust and loyalty. And that meant more than any empty-ass words ever would.

"Don't you have something you need to go do?" Ivan asked with a deceptively lazy blink.

Paul sighed, then took a step back. He glanced at me over his shoulder, his lingering look might have made me feel bad if I hadn't wanted to kill him, before he headed toward the exit. He'd barely opened the door when Ivan's fingers slipped through mine.

"You handled that better than I would have expected," he

said, not even lowering his voice considering Paul wasn't out of the room yet.

I peeked up at him. "You think?"

His nod was so enthusiastic, it made me almost laugh. "Yeah. Coach Lee and I thought you'd at least slap him."

"You told me not to." Damn it.

"No, I told you to wait until after this was over. I didn't think he'd actually come up to you and try and talk to you. He doesn't know you at all, does he?" Ivan snickered. "Dumbass. I bet he has no clue how close he was to dying. I could hear it in your voice, and once I saw your face, I was honestly worried you were going to do some *John Wick* shit with the comb I left on the counter."

I couldn't help but bust out laughing. I couldn't remember ever laughing before a competition. Ever. Not once.

The tug he gave my hand made me look at him as I kept on laughing.

"You good?" he asked, pressing our joined hands against his hip.

I nodded, and once I'd stopped laughing and still had a smile on my face, I narrowed my eyes on him. "Did you really call him and tell him not to contact me ever again?"

That was the thing about Ivan. He didn't bullshit. Not ever. I didn't think he was even capable of being embarrassed either. Because there was no hesitation as he responded. "Yes."

"Why?"

His body didn't move from its spot beside me, his hand didn't let go of mine either as he said, "Because Karina called and told me what happened. She asked if there was anything I could do. If I knew anyone else that you could pair up with."

This low-level hum began in my ears, but I made myself ask, "Then what happened?"

"I told her I didn't. Then I called him and told him how it was going to be, I was that pissed," he explained easily.

I felt like a dumb, pathetic girl asking for reassurances, but I didn't care enough to let it stop me. "You were mad for me?"

"No shit, Sherlock. The idea of you being upset over that waste of breath pissed me off. You deserved better." He smiled and pressed our hands tight against his side. "If you were going to cry for anyone, it was going to be me."

"You're an idiot."

"I know."

But then Ivan moved his body. He moved it to face mine, to stand in front of me, forcing me to tip my head back just enough so I could look at his eyes, the bouquet between us. Slowly, taking his time, his forehead dropped to mine. "Do you regret what happened?"

I looked right into those clear blue eyes and told him, "It was the best thing that could have happened to me."

"Me too, Jas."

And this... this thing that I knew was love bubbled up inside of me, and I knew it was a stupid idea. I knew I needed to shut the fuck up. But as I looked into those beautiful eyes and held that hand that had been there to hold me up so many times, I reminded myself that I was nobody's bitch.

Not even my own.

"Vanya," I started to say, oddly not nervous, so close his breath touched my lips. "I don't expect anything from you, and I don't want to make this weird, but I want you to know—"

His "Shut up" caught me off guard.

I blinked. "Don't tell me to shut up. I want to tell you something."

He suddenly dropped our hands, smiled, and took a step away. "I got something for you."

"You got me flowers?" I asked.

He shook his head as he set them on the counter beside me. "No, they're from Karina."

I smiled at the thought of her sending flowers. I'd have to send her a text later to say thank you.

"I did get you something, and someone else sent you something too."

I couldn't help but narrow my eyes. "Who?"

Ivan smiled. "Patty."

"Who is Patty?"

His smile drooped. "That teenager at the LC you stood up for. The one who looks just like you and is really outgoing?"

"Oh." Her. I hadn't realized we looked alike. "She sent me something?" Why?

"A card."

Huh. "She didn't have to do that."

"No, she didn't, but she found me the day before we left and begged me to give it to you," he said. "But I got you something too. It's not the souls of everyone that has ever pissed you off, but...."

That had me shutting my mouth. For all of a second.

"I was going to give it to you after, but I think I should give it to you now."

I pressed my lips together and asked slowly, "What is it?" as he turned to his giant rolling suitcase and dug his hand into large pocket on the outside of it.

"I thought we were past you thinking I'm going to randomly kill you."

"I don't think we'll ever be past that."

Ivan laughed with his back to me. "My plan is to kill you after worlds. Get it right."

"I'll write it down in my calendar then. Thank you for the warning."

His head shook as he yanked his hand out of the pocket,

holding something wrapped in tissue paper and something else in a white envelope.

"I was kind of expecting a scorpion, but I don't think you'd put your own life in danger to kill me."

"Shut up, I'll put the card here for you to read later," he murmured again, amusement in his voice as he turned to face me. "Let me see your hand."

I held out my right hand, but he smacked it gently down. So I raised the other one. I watched as he set the tissue-paper-wrapped thing on the counter and took my wrist with both of his big hands. He tugged the sleeve of my costume up about three inches on my forearm, exposing the bracelet I always wore. I had tightened the leather straps on it that morning so I could wear it under my costume, like I normally did.

I didn't think much of it until his thumb brushed over the slim metal plate held on by the leather straps I'd had to replace once a year since I'd originally gotten it made when I was twelve at a fair. *To Jasmine. From your best friend, Jasmine* was engraved on it. My mom had rolled her eyes when she'd paid for it. I'd showed her the documentary about another figure skater I admired who had worn the same thing. She had been amazing for her time, competitive and had never given a single fuck what other people thought about her. I thought she had been the shit, but mostly, she thought she was the shit.

It had always been my reminder that I had to believe in myself.

And I'd been wearing it proudly since.

But Ivan's fingers went to the straps I had just retied, and he began undoing the tiny knot with those long, graceful fingers. I wanted to ask him what the hell he was doing and why he was taking it off, but... I trusted him. So, I kept my mouth shut as he pulled it off and set it on the counter beside the tissue-wrapped whatever it was.

Okay.

He grabbed the thing off the counter in the same move and opened the tissue paper, pulling out something that looked almost identical. A sliver of metal with a leather band around it. Except the leather was bright pink.

"I don't want you to get nervous tonight," he started to say as he held the bracelet in one hand, his eyes on me.

I switched back and forth between looking at him and the thing in his hand. "I'm not nervous."

He snickered. "Fine, you're not nervous. But I want you to know that regardless of what happens today and tomorrow, it doesn't matter, Meatball."

And that had me snapping my head up to look him in the eye. The fuck was he talking about? "Of course it matters."

"No, it doesn't," he insisted. "It's just a competition. If we win or lose, it doesn't change anything."

What the hell did he mean by anything?

Ivan took my hand with the one not holding the bracelet and rubbed his thumb over the back of my wrist. "I'm not going to be mad. I'm not going to be disappointed. I hope you're not either."

I watched him carefully but didn't say anything.

His jaw moved, and his eyelids hung low over those spectacular eyes as he asked, "Will you?"

"Be disappointed if we don't win?"

I didn't like the nod he gave me.

But I thought about his words for one tiny moment. Would I be disappointed if I fucked up or if he fucked up and everything went to shit and we ended up in sixth place tonight and tomorrow? Would I be furious like I had been in the past?

"No." I wouldn't. "You'd be in sixth place with me. I

wouldn't be alone. If I'm going to fail, at least we'd do it together," I whispered, this funny fucking feeling going over my body.

It felt like... it felt like relief. Like acceptance. And it was the second single most beautiful thing I had ever felt in my life.

Second to loving this idiot and my family.

And that had to be the right fucking answer he was looking for because the smile that came over his face was the best one he'd ever shared with me yet. "Give me back your wrist, you little shit," he ordered, beaming that smile that I wished with all my heart was mine and only mine.

And except for his dogs and his pig and his bunny, it might very well be.

So I gave him my wrist.

And I watched as he tied the pink leather straps together, tight but not too tight, and left the bracelet up high on my arm like I'd had the other one, in the perfect spot to be hidden by the sleeve of my costume. He'd barely finished the knot when I brought my forearm to my face and read the tiny inscription on the metal.

To Meatball

From your best friend, Ivan

And in the time it took me to read the metal plate about four times, Ivan had already tied my bracelet to his own wrist.

But it didn't fit under his sleeve.

And when he smiled at me, I knew he didn't even care.

CHAPTER 23

"I don't usually give Ivan pep talks before he skates, Jasmine, but I can give you one if you need it," Coach Lee offered as we stood in the tunnel off to the side of the ice, as the team on the ice started their short program.

I didn't turn to look at her from my spot in front of Ivan and beside her. I was looking around at the crowd in the stands, keeping my breathing steady, my nerves in check. I felt calm. Calmer than I could ever remember. "I'm okay."

Because everything would be fine one way or the other. Like Ivan had said. It wasn't going to be the end of the world if things went to shit.

But I still hoped they didn't.

"Are you sure?" Coach Lee asked.

I didn't glance at her, knowing she was watching the pair performing too, as I shook my head and said, "Positive. Pep talks just psych me out." I did glance at her that time. "But thanks for offering."

The two hands that had been on my shoulders from the moment we'd come to wait for our turn, kneaded my traps loosely. Ivan's body was so close behind me, I could feel the heat radiating off him. We'd killed the last three hours, stretching and stretching more, then running through the program in the hall with headphones on, only doing a handful of lifts to gain confidence even though we'd done them a thousand times over the last eight months.

We were as good as we could be with everything that had happened before this.

We were going to try our best, and there was nothing more we could ask for.

"Your mom just waved at me," Ivan whispered into my ear before lifting a hand off my shoulder and more than likely waving it.

I had never looked for my family before I skated. It had always made me feel more pressure knowing they were there. I didn't even check my phone for hours before a competition. I wanted to be focused.

But the mention of my mom, who I hadn't seen since she'd arrived to Lake Placid the night before, had me looking up and around.

Ivan's hand went up beside my head, and he pointed to the right. Sure enough, I recognized the redhead standing, waving her arms over her head like a crazy person. I also recognized the dark-skinned man on one side of her, the other redhead on her other side, Sebastian's auburn hair, and—

There was a man his exact height standing beside him. Darker-haired, not as light-skinned. On the other side of that man was Jojo's unmistakable fat head and big ears, James's medium-brown hair, and a black-haired couple that had to be the Lukovs.

It was my dad.

It was my fucking dad sitting there.

"Your mom and Jonathan tried to talk him out of coming,

but he insisted he wouldn't bother you," Ivan whispered into my ear.

I swallowed. I swallowed because I had no idea how I felt about seeing him there. It wasn't excitement like it would have been a decade ago. But it was something. And I didn't think it was totally dread.

"You good?" he asked in his low voice.

Without realizing it, my hand went to the spot on my forearm where my bracelet was tied. My *new* bracelet. I touched it and the lacy-stretch material over it.

"I'm good," I said, as I went back to looking at my mom who had stopped waving her arms around in the middle of another team's program, finally. She was watching me and Ivan, and I could tell even from the distance that she was grinning.

I lifted my hand, the one with the bracelet, and waved it at her. Just a little, just for a second.

And she opened her mouth like she was screaming. She might have been, knowing her. But she looked so fucking excited—

I had to let my guilt go and try to focus on being better from now on. I had to.

The hand on my shoulder slid down to rest at the tops of my arms, and Ivan began moving his hands up and down my biceps and triceps.

The music ended a minute afterward, and we watched from our spot as the two figure skaters got off the ice, waving all over the arena before getting the hell out of the way while they waited for their scores to be called.

Coach Lee turned to us and raised her eyebrows at both Ivan and me, and said, "You're ready."

Not a question, but a statement.

Because we were.

"You've both exceeded my expectations for the season already. Ivan, remember to pace yourself after you come out of the triple-triple, and Jasmine..." She gave me a little smile then that I felt down to my bones. "Just be this you, okay?"

This me.

I didn't know what the hell she meant by that, but I nodded anyway.

This me.

"Let's get 'em, baby," Ivan whispered into my ear, with a squeeze to my upper arms.

I gave him a short nod. I zoned out the crowd cheering as the scores were called. Then we made our way toward the opening into the ice. The only person I was competing against that night was... myself. The person I had been with Paul. As long as I could do better than that version of me had... I couldn't ask for anything more.

It felt like a distant memory I could look back on later, me taking my skate guards off and handing them to Coach Lee before I got on the ice and waited alongside the wall as Ivan came on after me, doing the same. Coach Lee was right though, she wasn't much for pep talks or last-minute suggestions other than the ones she had just told us and the ones she had beat into us in past practices.

It honestly felt surreal standing out on the ice that night, listening to people cheering at Ivan and chanting his name like we were at a damn basketball game or something.

Ivan! Ivan! Ivan!

Lukov! Lukov! Lukov!

I'd heard it and witnessed it before from a distance—from the sidelines or the audience—but never while I was on the ice beside the man that these people were going fucking nuts for.

But as I stood there and listened, I could hear a small, tiny, itsy-bitsy hum in the crowd.

Jasmine! Jasmine! Jasmine!

And if it sounded exactly like a mash of all of my family members' voices... it was more than enough for me.

It was so much more than I deserved, but that familiar feeling I'd gotten earlier when Ivan had given me my bracelet and just minutes ago when Coach Lee had told me to be myself, it felt like home. It felt right. It felt an awful fucking lot like love.

Fingers squeezed the back of my neck, and I glanced up to see Ivan grinning down at me.

And I smiled back at him.

We turned around at the same time to face the center of the ice, and just like we had done without a single prompt or word every time before during practice, Ivan held out his hand to the side, between us, watching me. And I looked at him and put my hand in his. And we skated out toward the middle together, holding each other's hands as the crowd's chants turned into screams.

"Whatever happens, right?" I asked him as we skated to our starting point and stopped there.

Ivan didn't let go of my hand as he nodded and took a step back to get into place. *Whatever happens,* he mouthed to me. But then his lips kept forming words. Three words exactly. *I love you.*

If I'd had anything other than skates on, I would have tripped or fallen over or some shit like that.

I would have busted my goddamn ass and probably split my chin open.

But luckily, I was in the one thing I had more confidence in than tennis shoes or flip-flops. But that didn't stop me from having my entire body go tense as I stood there, knowing I needed to get into position but being too fucking dumbstruck to do anything other than hiss, *What?* Thinking I hadn't read his lips right.

Ivan stopped in front of me, a small smile on his face as he placed all of his arms and legs and fingers where they needed to be. *I love you,* he repeated like it was something he'd said a thousand times in the past. Like we weren't on the ice about to start our first short program in front of an audience that included more people than the other amateur figure skaters at the LC.

I blinked at him, trying to get my hands into position but not able to think about anything else besides the fucking *I love you* that had just come out of his lips. "Ivan," I started to say, forgetting that he couldn't hear me, swallowing hard and looking into his eyes as my hands and knees got into the place we had practiced so many times, getting into position because my mouth had stopped working but my brain hadn't.

The smile that came over his face was slow... and sweet.

And alarming.

"You suck, Meatball," he called out a second before I knew the music was about to start. *But I love you*, his lips formed.

My heart thumped. Thumped. Then thumped some more.

My world didn't tilt, my legs didn't give out from under me, but that feeling that had only intensified throughout the day, grew and grew and grew until it seemed to cover every inch of me, inside and out.

Ivan loved me.

Ivan fucking loved me.

And he didn't care if we won or lost.

And all I could do was get mad that he'd cut me off when I'd been about to tell him the same thing, and now he'd won.

"You couldn't have chosen a better time to say something?" I asked loudly, trying so hard not to move my lips.

I swore to God, this idiot puckered his lips and blew me a kiss so small there was no way that any of the cameras around the building could have caught it. *Nope,* he slipped out.

And then the music started.

He was so fucking lucky I could do our short program without thinking, because if we hadn't done it a thousand and a half times together, and I hadn't done it another five hundred times by myself, I would have screwed it up big-time.

And luckily for him, he was all business once the music started, and only sent me a wink and a smile once each during the entire two-minutes and forty seconds.

By some miracle, I managed to focus on what we had to do instead of the words that had come out of nowhere... at least until the second we hit our final poses and the music ended.

And then I remembered.

I remembered his *I love you,* and it pissed me off all over again.

Because. What. The. Fuck?

"You had to tell me right before we started?" I hissed, panting and out of breath.

His chest was puffing in and out as he gasped, "Uh-huh."

Uh-huh.

Just *uh-huh.*

"You—"

Before I could stop him, before I could realize what the hell he was doing, as we stood there, both panting, our faces inches apart, both high off adrenaline and power and something that I was 99 percent certain was love, he smiled that soft, slow smile.

He leaned forward, quick as lightning, and pecked me on the nose.

Ivan Lukov kissed me on the tip of my nose at the end of our short program.

And the fact that some of the audience made a soft coo, an "aww" that would have made me cringe under most circumstances, didn't even register to me.

It didn't register to me because I was too focused on the fact that he'd even done it to begin with. Let alone on television. Let alone three minutes after he told me he loved me.

"What is wrong with you?" I hissed a second before stepping out of our finishing poses to go into a bow.

He didn't let my tone stop him from flashing me that slow, slick grin as he got into place at my side. "You."

"Bitch," I whispered just as I bowed. I'd never liked curtsies. They felt too fake.

"Loser," he said while we rolled up.

"Why would you do that?" I asked, barely able to get the sentence out as we turned to the other side of the arena to do the same.

His hand slipped into mine, linking our fingers together as we bowed in that direction next. "Because I wanted to, Meatball." He squeezed my hand as we stood straight up and waved to the people throwing stuffed animals and flowers out onto the ice. I'd never seen so many for me before. Never. "Smile. We did it," he said, still breathing hard.

I smiled, but because I wanted to.

"Stop looking at me like you want to kill me. We can talk about this later. Don't be awkward," he murmured, pulling my hand once we were standing straight up again. "We both know you love me."

I wanted to deny it. I really did. Mostly because I hated the fact that he sounded so smug.

But we both knew I'd be lying.

Maybe I'd never said the words, but he knew. Like he'd known about my learning disability but never said anything.

Like he knew chocolate was my weakness and fed it to me when I needed it most.

It was my turn to pull at his hand as I tried to lead him off the ice, whispering, angrily, "Don't sound so smug about it."

"Too bad," he whispered.

Squirt: JASMINE, YOU WERE AMAZING
Squirt: Omg! Omg! Omg!
Squirt: You looked like a queen out there.
Squirt: You flew!
Squirt: You were a totally different skater.
Squirt: OMG.
Squirt: I cried.
Squirt: I wish I could have been there.
Squirt: I'm going to nationals. Aaron can stay with the kids. I'm not missing it.

FRESHLY SHOWERED AND STILL ON A HIGH EVEN FOUR HOURS later, I sat there on my bed and looked over the messages my sister had sent. I couldn't help but smile. Hitting the icon to call her, I leaned back and lay on the bed as I listened to the dial tone.

On the third ring, my sister answered. "JASMINE! YOU WERE THE BEST I'VE EVER SEEN!"

"Thanks, Rubes," I replied, feeling awkward saying "thank you," but what else could I say?

"Aaron and I were losing our minds! Even Benny was watching it and asked if that was Aunt Jazzy on the TV," she went on. "I'm so proud of you, Jas. I'm so freaking proud of you. I don't know what you did, but I've never seen you skate like that. I'm tearing up right now thinking about it."

Now that had me holding back a groan. "Don't cry."

"I'm so happy though," she squeaked, genuinely sounding like she was on the verge of tears.

"Me too," I told her, staring up at the ceiling with a smile on my face. "I don't think I've ever been so happy to be in second place after the short program."

Because Ivan and I had gotten second place. And it was only second by less than a point. That was... nothing.

Nothing because our long program was our strongest. At least I thought it was. Going with dark movies as our theme had been the best thing we could have done while most of the other pairs skaters performed to love songs and shit like that. Paul and I had done that back in the day, but I guess it wasn't believable because I was a shit liar and there had definitely been no love—and in the long run, no respect—in our relationship.

So Ivan and I were more than likely going to surprise the shit out of everyone when we did our exhibition skate to "A Whole New World" from the Aladdin soundtrack because... why not?

It was weird how things like that worked out.

"Well, you looked beautiful, and so did Ivan, and *I couldn't be any happier*," she choked.

"Stop crying," I told her with a laugh.

"I can't. I already watched your program five times in a row. We recorded it. Even Aaron's dad called to tell me you were the best one out there."

How the hell did Aaron's dad know to watch? I didn't ask, but I did wonder.

"Did you get to see the family after?" she asked, going right on into another subject.

And then, I did wince. To myself. "Yeah. We ate at the resort we're staying at." All of us had. *All of us.*

Ruby hesitated and asked the question I knew she had to be wondering about. She had to have known our dad had come. "How did it go with dad?" she asked, and I could hear the tension in her tone.

I closed my eyes and blew out a breath. "Fine."

"Fine you didn't fight with him but you wanted to? Or fine as in you hugged and everything was okay?"

Shit. "Fine as in... we gave each other a hug and he sat all the way on the other end of the table and didn't say anything to me." And I'd been fine with it. I really had. Relieved, honestly. I'd been so excited about the scores, I hadn't wanted him to ruin it.

And didn't that suck fucking ass that I expected my dad to ruin something I'd worked so hard for?

"Oh, Jas," Ruby sighed softly.

"It was fine."

"I don't want to argue with you, okay?"

Oh God. Here we went.

"Dad loves you. He wants the best for you."

I said nothing.

"He's... old-fashioned."

Is that what we were going to call it?

"You should forgive him. He's trying. He knows he's messed up, but none of us are perfect," Ruby kept going, only slightly making me feel guilty.

And I meant slightly. Because how many times had I done something to even Ruby to make her hesitate around me?

But...

"I know that, Rubes. I get it, but do you know how hard it is to listen to him talk about figure skating like it's some rec sport I do just for fun on the weekends? Do you know what it's like for him to.... what's that word?... belittle my dreams? To hear him say I'm better off doing something I hate?" I asked her, not getting at all riled up. Not feeling anything, honestly.

I could hear her breathing on the other line. Then she said, "Yeah, Jas. I do know. I know exactly what that's like, and I understand. I know it's not fun."

My body went instantly on high alert. "Who did that to you?"

"Mom. Dad. Both of them."

I tried to think but couldn't come up with any memory of that. "When?"

"After I graduated high school. You were too young to care or remember, but it happened."

What the hell?

"I wanted to go to school for costume design, and both of them—mom included—pretty much said how pointless that would be. For three months, they were on my case about going to school for something I could have as a backup. *As a real job*," she kept going, not sounding insulted or anything, but more resigned.

And that made me sad, because as far as I could remember, Ruby had loved designing and making costumes. Always. It was her passion in life. Her version of me figure skating.

I couldn't see her doing anything else.

And I'd always wondered why she'd studied accounting, gotten a degree, and then never did anything with it.

"But I'm not you," she said, still in that resigned voice. "Mom didn't believe in my dream like she did in yours."

"Rubes," I started, suddenly feeling terrible, because how the hell must that have been? Her seeing my mom supporting the shit out of me while telling her she couldn't do what she loved? I'd had no idea. No clue.

"It's okay, Jas. It worked out for the best. I'm only telling you because I want you to know that Mom and Dad aren't perfect. That you aren't the only one that's been told your dreams are pointless, but the difference is that you never let anybody talk you out of it. You didn't let anyone make you do something you didn't want to do, and I wish I could have done the same," Ruby finished.

I was stunned. Honestly, surprised out of my mind.

Because that was a load of shit.

"The only reason I even studied accounting was because I wanted to make them happy. Mom was even trying to talk me into taking a job where she works up until a few years ago. Anyway, all I'm trying to tell you is to... be open-minded. To forgive him. You don't have to do it today or tomorrow, but give him a chance. I don't think he ever knew what to do with you when you were little. You were so opinionated, and I think you reminded him too much of Mom, but I don't know."

"Huh" was the only thing I managed to get out as I thought her words over.

Had I been that much of a shit as a kid that he didn't know what to do with me? I had a faint memory of telling him that I hated him. Kicking him in the shin. Crying. Not wanting to go spend time with him when he'd come to visit. But I'd had to have been really small. Maybe four. Maybe five at the most. Right after he'd left.

Huh.

"I don't want to talk about it anymore. I don't want to ruin your high. So, tell me about that cute kiss Ivan gave you. When are you two going to get married, win all the awards ever, and have kids that are prodigies at every sport they ever play?"

I choked. "What the fuck are you talking about, Rubes? *Are you drinking while you're expecting my next niece?*"

Ruby laughed. "No! I would never do that!"

"It seems like it just now."

"No! I'm asking you a serious question. You two are so perfect for each other it gave me a toothache. No lie. Ask Aaron."

I rolled my eyes and shook my head at the ceiling, thinking again, *finally*, about the words Ivan had said to me while we'd been on the ice. *I love you.* He loved me. And he knew I loved him back.

And we hadn't talked about it since we'd gotten off the ice to get hugs and pats on the back from Coach Lee. I'd spotted Galina in the stands as we'd made our way to wait for our scores and had nodded at her, getting a nod in return, which from her was basically an I love you.

Everything after that had been a crazy mess of changing, interviews, and rushing out to have a late dinner because we'd all been starving.

Ivan hadn't even walked me back to my hotel room. He'd been too busy in the lobby talking to another pairs skater that he seemed to be friendly with from Canada. So....

"*Darn it!* Jessie is crying. I need to go. Good luck tomorrow, but I know you won't need it! Love you!"

"Love you too," I said into the phone.

"Bye! You were amazing!" my sister called out before hanging up on me without giving me a chance to say bye in return.

I'd barely dropped my phone on my bed when a knock came from my door.

"Who is it?" I called out, sitting up on the edge.

"Who else would it be?" Ivan's voice answered on the other side of the door.

I rolled my eyes and got to my feet, heading to the door so I could undo the bolt and the lock. I took my time opening it, to find Ivan standing there, his eyebrows up, still dressed in the clothes we'd gone to eat dinner in. A charcoal gray button-up shirt, black dress pants that he'd confirmed were tailored just for him because his glutes and quads were too big in comparison to his narrow waist, and those black fancy lace-up boots I'd seen him wear a few times by that point.

"You want to let me in?" he asked.

I shook my head and got a smile as I stepped aside, watching him as he came in and immediately went to sit on the edge of my bed, bending over to mess around with the laces of his shoes. I locked the door again and went to take a seat beside him, taking him in as he toed off one boot and then the other with a sigh.

"I'm exhausted," he admitted as he stretched his legs out.

"Me too," I replied, taking in his black and purple striped socks. "I just got off the phone with Ruby, and I was deciding if I was tired enough to go to sleep or not. I can't seem to wind down yet."

Cocking his chin, he turned to give me a smile right before slipping an arm over my shoulders, pulling me into his side. "How'd that go?"

"Fine. She said that was the best she's ever seen me skate. Then she gave me a lecture on my dad, but it was fine," I told him, not in the mood to go over those details again.

Ivan nodded like he understood. "That was the best you've ever skated though. I've already had at least twenty people come up to me and tell me how good you were." He blinked. "It didn't make me jealous. Don't worry."

"I wasn't," I said, dryly.

He pulled me in even tighter to his side, his hand going to my upper arm and rubbing up and down there. "You were amazing, Meatball. You really were... but don't expect me to admit that to you again anytime soon."

I pressed my head into his shoulder and smiled, glad he couldn't see it. "You were pretty fucking amazing too."

"I know. But I'm old news. Everyone is used to it."

I snorted. "You conceited shit."

His response? "It's the truth."

How the hell could I have fallen in love with this arrogant ass? Of all the billions and billions of people on the planet, *this* was who I fell in love with? This guy?

"But now everyone wants a piece of the Jasmine Pie, and I've got to tell them all to turn around and walk away," he let me know, reminding me again about the one topic we hadn't talked about in months.

The one I had purposely ignored.

But...

"Ivan," I started to say, knowing the last thing I wanted to do was ruin this moment, but also wanting an answer. Wanting to know just what the hell was going to happen so I could plan, even if everything hanging in the balance wasn't for months away. But I didn't want to run from this anymore. I wasn't going to be a pussy.

"Hmm?" he asked, still rubbing my arm up and down.

I held my breath and got my words together before spilling them out. "Whenever you and Coach Lee get around to finding me another partner—"

His hand stopped moving, and I felt him turn his upper body to look down at me. "What?"

It made me a coward for sure, but I kept my head on his shoulder, even knowing he had his total attention on me. "When worlds are over and you try to find me someone else to—"

"*Jasmine.*"

Now that tone had me glancing up at him to give him a crazy look, and the expression I faced was another version of crazy. "What?"

He blinked. "You think I'm going to find you another partner?"

It was my turn to blink. "Well, yeah. That was the deal, wasn't it?"

One eyebrow went up.

So, I made mine go up too.

"*I'm not going to find you another partner*," he said, his face and voice both telling me he was insulted. But I didn't get why. "Why the hell would I do that?"

"Umm, because that was the deal. Because you were the one that said like a hundred times that we were only pairing up for a year." I almost added "dumbass," but managed not to.

He blinked. Both of his eyebrows went up. Then he blinked some more. "You're not dumb, so I know that's not the problem," he said, taking his time with his words as his eyes narrowed. "But let's think about this, genius. Tell me if I'm wrong at any point."

I narrowed my eyes at him.

"You're the best partner I've ever had," he started. "There's no comparison. Am I right?"

I nodded because, yeah, I fucking was.

"You're my best friend."

He'd never called me that before, but I nodded at that too.

"You're my sister's friend."

I lifted a shoulder because he was right.

"If I had to choose anyone to help me bury a body, eat dinner with, or watch television with, it would be you, every time for everything."

My heart squeezed, squeezed, squeezed.

"I made up Mindy taking the season off when really our agreement had ended, and I hadn't planned on going back to skate with her. Because even though you drove me crazy, I wanted to skate with you."

What? Just... *what?*

"My family loves you."

I didn't know... anything.

I looked at him, watching as he tipped his head closer to mine and said, "And I love you."

He'd said it again.

"I love you so much I spend all day with you, and it still isn't enough for me," he kept going.

I stopped breathing.

"I love you so much, if I can't skate with you, I don't want to skate with anyone else."

Holy. Fuck.

"I love you so fucking much, Jasmine, that if I broke my ankle during a program, I would get up and finish it for you, to get you what you've always wanted."

It was love. All I could feel was love.

I was going to cry. I was going to fucking cry. Right. Then.

"You mean so much to me that that's why whatever happens doesn't really matter to me. Not like it used to. Not like it ever will again," he finished, pressing his forehead against mine, his eyes intense and heartbreaking. "You're not ever going to be anyone else's partner. Not while I'm alive, Meatball. I will drag your stubborn, beautiful ass kicking and screaming back to me because nobody else will ever be good enough for you."

I blinked. I blinked so fast I knew I was about two point five seconds away from losing my shit.

And then Ivan ended me. He ended every worry I'd ever had about there being someone after him. He did it right there with the tip of his nose touching my own and his forehead against mine too.

"Because I'm okay with you having ten other people be

your favorite. But you're always going to be my favorite person," he finished. "Always. No matter what."

I blinked so fast, I couldn't help but let my eyes fill up with tears. "I... I'm not good...."

His smile was so gentle, so sweet, it took half my soul with it. "I know," he whispered before he wrapped his arms around me and hugged me, the bottom of his chin going to the top of my head.

And he hugged me, and then hugged me for even longer, even as tears slipped out of my eyes and wet his shirt.

And while I was leaning almost all of my weight against him, he lowered us onto our sides and kept on holding me, pulling me so I was halfway on top of him, my head on his chest, one of my hands gripping his ribs, a leg over his own. We stayed like that until the tears stopped leaking out of my eyes, and I could take deep breaths again.

He brushed his hand down my hair, almost absently.

I had thought earlier that night had been one of the best moments of my life, but *this* was. This was, and I loved Ivan so much, I didn't think it was possible to love him any more. Everything he had said to me, I felt the exact same way about, except I would have skated with someone else if he'd truly wanted to go back to his old partner, but I would have done it as a tribute to him, for all the ways he had changed me and my life.

I wanted to give him all the shit and all the shit I couldn't forever and always, because he'd given me everything.

Neither one of us said anything for a long, long time as we lay there.

Not when his hands made longer strokes along my hair, not when his hand drifted to my shoulder and gave it a squeeze. Or when his palm moved down my arm, gentle,

gentle, gentle, his fingertips almost tickling me as he touched the thigh I had over him.

I wouldn't have moved away for all the money in the whole world. Not for all the awards and all the medals either. Not for fucking anything.

What Ivan did was move his fingertips across my thigh and then, *then* to my knee. It took everything in me not to react as all but one of his fingertips disappeared, and that one sole, lonely pad began making circles over my kneecap. So light, so soft, it felt like a feather.

I stayed right there.

His fingertip made wider and wider circles, dipping down to the sensitive skin at the crease behind my knee before making its way back upward again to my quads, making that track-like pattern one more time. Then that fingertip made a trail down my bare shin and calf, making a circle around the muscle I used and overused. Then he made another one.

I'd never been happier that from the moment Mom had given me permission to shave—right after I'd hit puberty and hair had grown in with *everywhere*—that she'd stressed how important it was to do it every day. And moisturize. Because if you asked my mom, moisturizing was one of the most important parts of the day. Just like brushing your teeth. Or wiping your ass after using the bathroom. I was so damn thankful I'd shaved after coming back to my room following dinner.

One fingertip turned into four. Then the length of four fingers. Then an entire palm. All covering my calf. Then my shin. Up and down.

"How's your skin so smooth?" His question was low, almost distracted if I hadn't known any better.

"Coconut oil," I answered, hitching my leg up higher so that it was closer to him.

"Coconut oil?" He spread his fingers wide to wrap around the entire width of my lower leg.

"Uh-huh," I answered, swallowing hard at the feel of his warm skin on mine.

If he noticed me moving it closer to him, he didn't comment on it.

"You know, Jasmine," he said, sounding almost distracted, "these things are so strong—"

"Things?" I almost panted out.

"Legs," he clarified, still touching my skin. "*Legs,*" he emphasized. "They're all muscle. I didn't think—" He made a noise in the back of his throat as his palm swept up over my knee to land on the top of my thigh. "—they would be so soft."

"You know how many bruises I get," I managed to get out, "how many cuts and scars... it helps... heal."

I swallowed. Gulped.

Ivan dragged his hand higher up my thigh, so high the fingers snuck beneath the hem of my shorts, his hands practically spanning the length of my entire thigh. It wasn't like I had long legs or anything, and I was grateful. Because he could touch more. Touch everything.

And I wanted him to.

"Jesus," he almost hissed, moving his hand around, fingertips so deep into my sleep shorts, the tips touched the very top of my ass. He made a little line over the skin there, grazing my crack, and I couldn't help but flex everything from my ankle up. "*Are you not wearing any underwear?*"

I didn't know what it was that had me tipping my head up, my nose touching his throat, when I whispered, "I'm wearing some."

He hummed, walking his fingers another inch higher into my shorts. God, I'd never been ungrateful for the fact he had such big hands, and I especially wasn't cursing it right then.

Because his fingers kept moving... but instead of going back in the direction of my back, they moved to the side... then back again... lower... reaching another crease... then again to the side...

And I sucked in a breath as those fingers found my underwear.

Specifically, the strip of my underwear that went right up between my ass cheeks.

It was then, as his fingers made contact with my thong, that he slung another arm around my lower back, and with a strength I was totally aware of, that I knew so well, he pulled me over his lap so that I was straddling him. The arm around my back crushed my lower body against his.

And I felt it. All long and thick and hard.

Jesus.

"Ivan—"

He cut me off with his mouth then. Those pink lips sealed over mine, slanted, wet, taking mine completely and totally. His tongue darted against mine, needy. Thirsty. He pressed our mouths together like they were meant to be like that. His fingers trailed up the sliver of fabric between my ass cheeks, touching over places on my body that I was shy with. That anybody would be shy with.

Most anybody.

Those fingertips went up, up, grazing over the triangle at the top of my thong. I slanted my mouth to the side, touching my tongue against his as he pulled at the triangle and let it go, letting it snap against my skin with a hoarse groan that I felt everywhere. "Only you would wear this fucking underwear under these shorts," he groaned, grabbing a handful of ass cheek and squeezing it almost hard enough to hurt.

Almost.

I moved my mouth just enough so that I could aim it toward his neck, biting it instantly.

And Ivan, fucking Ivan, groaned, tipping his head back to give me more room. So I opened my mouth wider and took more of his neck into my mouth, the skin soft and just a little salty and smelling like that clean, expensive cologne I knew he wore on a daily basis.

"Jesus, Jas," he hissed when my teeth turned into my tongue and lips, sucking on his skin a lot harder than I knew I should.

The hips beneath mine rolled, curled and fucking humped into mine, and they did it twice more when I sucked on the skin even harder, dragging my tongue across his throat.

"You taste so damn good," I moaned, sucking on him harder.

He let out a wild groan, his hips moving beneath mine, his arms restless, wrapping low around my back, bringing our fronts together, tight. Flush. My breasts smashed against the hard surface of his chest.

"Damn," Ivan hissed. His chin still tilted up, still giving me access to that beautiful, long throat as his lower body moved, gaining friction between the material of his pants, the anaconda I couldn't wrap my head around under them, and the thin, stretchy material covering the part of me that wanted him to fill it like I needed painkillers on a regular basis.

A new curse straight out of that wonderful mouth lit up my spine, my fingertips, my knees, and everything in between.

The trail of curse words had me pulling back, sitting my ass against his thighs, right by his knees, settling all my weight there while I sat up straight, and with a talent that would have impressed the best stripper in Vegas, I yanked my shirt over my head, leaving me in one of those lacy bras with no underwires that were one of the only good things about being either the smallest B-cup in the world or the largest A-cup.

Ivan groaned. *He groaned.* Leaning back against the bed, he let a noise out that I'd never heard before, the arms around my waist loosening until his palms were curled around my ribs, my waist, his thumbs parallel to my belly button. They went up, going over each ridge of every rib, taking his time, until the webbing between his index fingers and thumbs were set beneath the slight curves at the bottom of my breasts.

"Damn," he murmured, still holding the weight up. "Jasmine." Leaning forward, quick, quick, quick, he lowered his head. I knew what he was doing before he did it. I could have moved... if I was insane.

So I let him. I let him lean in my direction and suck a nipple and almost all of my breast into his mouth, bra and all.

And then it was me grinding against him. I moved, dragged, and humped against him, letting his hard dick drag across my clit.

One of those big hands slid down my ribcage to my hip and around to my ass again. Palming it, he squeezed the cheek, cupping most of it. Then letting the pressure go and just holding it instead, lightly, more of a caress than anything else. His moan was low, and I had to drag my mouth to his lips and take the top one between mine.

The one hand under my breast moved, and Ivan pulled the material covering it down, jerking it low, exposing it. Me.

I sucked in a breath, remembering... remembering....

"Beautiful, so fucking... beautiful," he whispered, hoarse, his lips hovering over my chest.

"You used to—"

"Shut up," he huffed, then latched onto my nipple again. Bare that time.

I let out a cry. A moan. All I could do was arch into his

mouth, wanting him to never let go. To never move. To do that forever.

And he did.

Pulling down the other cup, he took that nipple into his mouth too. The hand on my ass cupped all of it, trying to mold it with his fingers but....

"This fucking ass," he hissed. "I've been dreaming of this ass for so long," he claimed. "Perfect, perfect...."

What I hadn't gotten uptown, I'd gotten downtown. Exercise on top of it had molded it into something I was pretty proud of. Maybe I wasn't beautiful. Maybe I wasn't sexy. I got enough shit about it every time I got online. But this fucking body, I had busted my ass for, and I wasn't ashamed of it. Not even my unremarkable chest. But at least it was small, and tight and gravity hadn't gotten to it yet.

Ivan moved his face so that his cheek rested against the top of my breast, and he rubbed his cheek over the skin, then moved his face so that his opposite cheek rested above the other one. He nuzzled. He scraped that bristly cheek from one side of my chest to the other, down the center, and under it, his nose brushing against the lace still over me and around the curve of my breast. His hands guided me backward a little, but held me up so I was arched in midair. Then that cheek went across the center of my stomach, his lips brushing my belly button, his hair grazing my nipples.

Each of them. Over and over again with each of his movements over my skin.

His tongue darted out and dipped into my belly button. And all I could do was give him more.... More, more, more. Please, please.

"Ivan," I pretty much whimpered.

"Shh," he whispered back, dragging his lips straight up my sternum as he sat me back down on his lap, his mouth still moving until it reached the notch at my throat. Those long fingers that knew me so well made their way to the middle of my back and then up, pulling my bra along with it.

I kissed him, and he kissed me back. My hands went to his shoulders and gripped them, hard. We moved against each other, his hands going down, pulling my shorts and underwear down my hips until I had to get up to jerk them the rest of the way down and off my ankles.

It wasn't until then that I realized I was naked. Standing in front of him. Totally, completely naked.

But when I glanced up at his face, those cool blue-gray eyes were slits, and his cheeks were pink, and he looked....

Ivan sat up and undid the buttons on his shirt, shrugging it off with jerky and unsure movements, like he wasn't used to getting undressed so fast. And then he was up, a foot away from me, and in a move that was familiar, he undid his belt and then jerked his pants and boxer briefs down to his knees and kicked them off.

And *goddamn*.

Mother of God.

Holy shit.

Jesus H. Christ.

I'd seen Ivan with clothes on before. Not just for a second but for minutes. Hours. I'd seen him.

But nothing could have prepared me for the sight of Ivan naked the way he was without a sock. He was hard. Hard everywhere. From the tendons at his throat to the pectoral muscles that were pretty much rocks, to his eight-pack abs, and those thighs that could have had a song written about them....

But it was the hard, long, fat thing pointing at me that had stopped my breathing.

How the hell was it possible for someone to be that

damn perfect? Why? What kind of bullshit was this that someone so long and lean had that monster between his legs?

"I hate you," I whispered.

And Ivan laughed. Laughed. "You love me."

I didn't look at his face. I wouldn't.

But what I did look at was his hand rising, curling around the shaft trying to point toward his belly button, bobbing. He moved his hand down to the root, flanked by thick, curly black hair, and then up, toward the big, pink and purple mushroom tip that was so wet it dripped....

"I'm on birth control," I told him with a swallow. "And I'm not ovulating for another week."

It was only because he tipped his chin down that I knew he heard me, but he was so busy just looking at me, I would have thought he hadn't.

But he had.

Because in a movement so easy and effortless, he took a step forward toward me and wrapped his hands around my upper thighs, hauling me up. My body went high, my thighs instinctively went around his waist, his hands clutching me perfectly. I licked my hand, reached between us, and wrapped my fingers around the cock that made my mouth water. And I moved my hand up and down, taking in the smooth skin and what might have been the hardest muscle in his whole body. Then I pointed that pink-purple head right between my legs, and in that way that we read each other's minds, he lowered me down.

Down, down, inch after three inches, five inches, slowly, until I was seated on him. Completely.

Stuffed. Full. I'd never tell Ivan, but it hurt. At first.

I sucked in a breath.

And so did he, following it with a groan.

Then I followed it with a sound I wouldn't call a whimper but someone else might.

Those big hands slowly moved my body up and down on him. An inch, then down. Two, then back down to the root. Over and over again. Until it wasn't a fight, but a glide.

"Jesus Christ," Ivan chanted over and over again. His whole body tight, strained. Shoulders and biceps that could do this movement a hundred times when it wasn't sexual, tight and shaking. He was trembling. His breathing, the breathing of an athlete, was ragged. His hands moved, and he slipped a forearm under my ass while the other one went around the middle of my back and guided me up and down, my nipples brushing against his chest. "I love you, Jasmine," he said, the movement going faster. "I love you, I love you, I love you," he repeated.

And all I could do was close my eyes, close my eyes and wrap my arms around his neck and hold on for dear life, the words there, between us. My mouth found his and we kissed as he kept moving me up and down. Taking more, taking less, taking it all.

"Love you," I whispered, shaking on his dick as the hint of an orgasm tingled along my lower stomach.

He smiled. More than smiled. He lit up. And his hips powered up into me. Gripping me tighter. Closer. His hand went between us and circled my clit. It didn't take more than a few circles of his thumb, our bodies covered in sweat, before I came. I cried into his shoulder, coming around him, clinging onto him for dear fucking life.

His moans were so husky and rough, I almost couldn't hear his choked groan as he came moments later. He pulsed inside of me, gasping. I clung to him and he held me tight to him.

We were both covered in sweat. Out of breath and trying

not to be, but failing miserably. I gasped, and then I gasped again, shaking some more.

"God help me," he moaned.

I trembled. I panted. I could have been dying, but it would have been worth every second.

Holding me, Ivan walked us toward the bed and slowly lowered me onto it. His body came over mine, covering me. With his arms straight, legs bracketing mine, his smile was lopsided as he panted, "Practice makes perfect, Jas."

Fuck.

I tried breathing out of my nose as I raised my eyebrows at him, his dick resting against my thigh, still half hard. "That wasn't already perfect?"

"It was," he said, hovering over me. "But I want to practice anyway."

I couldn't help but laugh, loud, so loud it kind of freaked me out.

But what didn't freak me out was the giant smile that Ivan gave me from above. "Over and over again."

"Who says I want to do it again?"

His hand went over the side of my head, his fingers brushing my temple. "You came all over me," he said like I didn't know that. "We do everything good together. You know that."

I did know that, but he didn't need to.

"We're the best team. We do what we have to do to be the best," he said as he lowered his weight to really cover me, his thighs were spread wide on top of mine, the tops of his feet touching the inside of my calves, his forearms on either side of my face.

"And this will help our skating?" I asked him.

He kissed my cheek and then the other one. "It's not going to hurt it."

I laughed again and curled up to plant a kiss on his chin that made him blink slowly.

"I love the way you smile," he said with a dreamy, sleepy expression. "I want to tell you to do it more often, but I don't."

I took in every inch of that flawless face. "Why?"

He didn't even have his eyes open as he responded. "Because you don't give it to everyone." His cheek rested against mine, that sweaty chest did the same as he said, "And I don't plan on sharing you."

CHAPTER 24

"ONE MINUTE."

Shaking my shoulders out, I took a deep breath in, let it out, and then did it all over again. It was easy to zone out the audience cheering for the pair on the ice who had literally just finished seconds ago. It was even easier to ignore the flowers and stuffed animals raining down from the crowd.

I was strong. I was smart. I could do anything.

I wasn't weak or unprepared.

The world wouldn't end if I blew it.

I could do this.

I was always going to be able to do this. Maybe I hadn't exactly been born for it, but I'd made it mine. I had taken it for my own, and it would always be mine.

Four minutes and some seconds to show off a lifetime of hard work. No big deal.

"It's time," Coach Lee's voice spoke almost directly into my ear, her hand coming to land lightly on my shoulder.

I nodded, shooting her a look out of the corner of my eye before she let go and took a step to the side, to do the same to Ivan, who was standing a foot away, shaking out his hands and thighs. I noticed him glancing at her, the same way I had, nodding, the same as me too.

And then he glanced over his shoulder at me.

Those bright blue-gray eyes landed directly into mine, and we didn't need to nod or do anything. We just smiled at each other. Our own little secret. Our own thing.

We'd woken up this morning in my room, with me drooling on his hand and his leg thrown over one of mine, and it had been the best morning of both of our lives. He'd told me so, and I'd just known. Then he'd pinched the shit out of my ass cheek, and it was like it was supposed to be between us. Perfect.

We were going to do this.

We had this.

The smile that crept over his lips and cheek muscles was lazy... almost filthy... a fucking promise of what was for sure going to happen tonight regardless of anything else.

It was his trustful smile. The one he shared with me. It was mine.

And it zinged its way up my spine, this warm, comforting thing that told me he was as confident as I was. That we had this. But we had this together.

So I couldn't help but smile right back at him, wider than before. It wasn't anything big, but it was his and only his.

And he knew it was because his smile grew even wider.

I rolled my eyes as I looked away and stepped toward the ice, my heartbeat nice and even, my head calm and controlled. At the wall, I stood to the left to let the last skater off the ice and looked up. I'd already clocked my family when we'd first gotten to the tunnel, and they were still there. Each and every one of them holding up a sign, even my dad.

THAT'S MY SISTER.
GO JASMINE!
JASMINE!
WE LOVE YOU, JASMINE
JASMINE SANTOS 4 EVER
GET IT GIRL
YOU'RE AMAZING, JASMINE

But it was the NEVER GIVE UP, JASMINE that had me squinting. Because it was my dad holding it. He wasn't jumping up and down like the rest of them, but he was smiling. He wasn't embarrassed. He wasn't bored.

But he was there. And that was more than I could have wanted or expected.

And it was what I needed. Another little piece of glue to my mind and my heart.

I let myself think for a second about the card I'd read that morning, lying in bed beside Ivan. The card from the nice girl at the LC.

Good luck, Jasmine!

You're going to do great. Thanx for being so cool. I hope one day I can be like you.

Love, Patty

And I knew I could do this.

Once, when I'd been maybe fifteen or sixteen, Galina had told me that to win, I would have to be prepared to fail. Have to be okay with the idea of failing. And I had never completely understood what she meant by that then, because who the hell wanted to lose? I got her message now, and it had only taken me a decade to.

I took a step onto the ice and glided off just a couple feet away to give Ivan room to do the same. He followed after me, stopping just two feet away from me as the announcer called out our names.

That was when I looked over my shoulder at the man in the brown and gold costume that my sister had created, and found him already looking at me, with a smirk aimed right at me.

He looked happy.

And for the first time, I felt happy as I stood there, not nervous, not overwhelmed. I just felt happy. Ready.

So I smirked back at him.

We both seemed to let out a breath of air at the same time.

Just like that, Ivan extended his hand out at his side toward me. He watched my face as I gave him my own hand, draping my palm over his, both of us curling our fingers around the other's.

He mouthed *I love you,* and I winked at him. Then, we skated toward the center of the ice, hand in hand, stopping in the spot we needed. Ivan got into position at the same time I did, both of us never looking anywhere else. If the crowd went quiet, I had no idea because I was zoning them out just as Ivan's face came to pause an inch away from mine.

"You suck," he whispered, his breath against my cheek.

I just barely held back a smile as I said, "You suck even more."

A second, a split fucking second before the music started, he whispered, "Let's do it."

And we did.

EPILOGUE

"Look at the height on that!"

"I haven't seen a twist like that since the 2018 Lukov team!" the announcer on the television claimed.

Ivan and I both snorted at the same time.

I didn't need to look at him to know he was rolling his eyes. Because I was too.

"That was clearly at least half a foot shorter than ours used to be," Ivan muttered beside me.

I snorted again, keeping my eyes glued to the television.

"I was thinking more like a whole foot," my mom, who loved coming over so much she was on steady allergy medication, agreed from her spot on the other side of the couch.

"Mark needs to retire from being a commentator. I've thought he's needed glasses for at least the last three seasons, easy," Jojo claimed from where he was lying on the floor, his head propped up on one hand while the other one held a bottle to Elena's mouth.

"Jonathan, that's not nice," James said to him. I didn't need to look to know he was shaking his head.

All of our eyes were on the television as the Canadian

team on the screen moved around the ice effortlessly, their movements a perfectly measured amount of strength, grace, and beauty. I wasn't hating on them. They *were* good.

But not as good as we used to be.

"*That was amazing!*" the commentator on the screen cooed in excitement.

"Now he's just throwing words out to hear his own voice," I muttered, shaking my head.

The man beside me made a noise that had me glancing at him out of the corner of my eye. He had his head cocked to look at me, a smirk I knew like the back of my hand pasted on that mouth that had stayed just as annoying and wonderful as it had been even over the years. "Your spins were cleaner and faster than hers are."

I nodded, still looking at him, ignoring the huge television mounted to the wall, showing the 2026 Olympics. "You made it look more effortless too. And clearly, you're stronger than he is."

He snorted and leaned closer to whisper into my ear, "Clearly. Your butt still looks better than hers."

I snickered, and he smiled. We were already plastered at our sides, perfectly lined up from hip to thigh. His arm was pressed to mine. Ivan slipped it out and raised it, throwing it over my shoulder and hugging me to him even more than he already had. I lifted my legs and draped them over his lap, earning me a kiss on the cheek before we both faced the screen again just in time for the announcer to whisper, "*Incredible!*"

There were so many groans in the room, I couldn't count them.

I wouldn't use the word amazing, but....

"I bet you two could still win if you competed," Jojo muttered.

I nodded, watching as the couple did a death spiral that I bet Ivan and I could still do faster. It wasn't like we trained anymore, but a lot of mornings, before the rink was filled with young, hopeful figure skaters, he'd take my hand and we'd go through reserved versions of our old programs. We'd laugh through half of it, replacing triples with doubles most days, but every once in a while, we'd catch each other's eye and know we were thinking the same thing. And we'd do a triple toe. Or a triple toe loop. Rarely, on really, really good days, we'd do a triple Lutz. Just to know we could still do it.

And then, the kids would show up, and we'd get to work. Coaching. Ivan had several boys, and I had a few girls.

We had talked about coaching a pairs team... but only if and when we found the right team. We just hadn't yet.

It had been four years since we had retired, and it still didn't feel like enough time had passed.

Four years since Ivan had a surgery to fuse his spine. A surgery that had been so dangerous I had thrown up twice in the waiting room. Four years since the doctor had said it would be reckless for him to continue to skate pairs.

And four years since Ivan had looked at me and said, "Find another partner. You don't have to retire because I am."

What a fucking idiot. Some shit never changed. Like there was anyone else I would ever want to partner with.

It had been five years since we had won our last—and third—world championship.

Eight years since we'd won our second world championship.

Eight years since we'd won *two* gold medals. One in pairs and another in the team skate. Making Ivan the most decorated U.S. figure skater in history.

Nine years since we'd won our first world championship, and the first of three national championships.

Most importantly, it had been nine years since we'd gotten married. Nine years and three months from the moment he had said, panting and red-faced, out on the ice at the end of our long program while the crowd went fucking nuts, "I think you should marry me, Meatball."

I'd only made him ask three times. And when we got married in the same nondenominational church that Jojo had married James, it had been the greatest moment of my entire life.

And then Danny, Tati, and Elena had happened.

"Daddy," a little voice said from the floor. "That double Axel was sloppy, right?"

"Very sloppy," Ivan lied, giving my shoulder a squeeze.

"You'll tell me if I'm sloppy, right?"

I glanced at Ivan and raised my eyebrows, watching as he made a face at me because we both knew the truth. Him telling his little baby she did something wrong? Get real.

"I'll tell you if you're sloppy," a seven-year-old voice came up from the direction of the floor too. "You were yesterday."

"No, I wasn't!" the six-year-old shouted, sitting up so I could see her dark head for the first time since we'd all—three dogs and two pigs included— taken over the living room to watch the short program part of the night.

"Yeah, you were!" Danny claimed, still out of view. "I watched you!"

And either like she wanted to join in or if she was going to eventually be the mediator between her brother and sister, Elena gave a cry from where she was lying with my brother.

And just like that, the argument ended. There was a long, drawn-out sigh, and then another long, drawn-out sigh, and then the six-year-old laid back down beside her older brother.

The silence lasted maybe ten seconds before I heard them start bickering back and forth with each other.

God, they were nightmares. They were exactly the kind of argumentative, bossy, stubborn, strong-willed kids that I used to think were adorable, when they were really a pain in the ass.

But I loved them so much; they were worth the two seasons that Ivan and I had taken off to have them. Danny would never know he'd been conceived on accident the night we won our second world championship... but he definitely knew that once I'd found out I was pregnant, I had thought it was the best news of my life. Ivan and I had created a life. Something that was both of us on one of the best nights of our lives.

And twelve months later, when I ended up getting pregnant again, we had done it on purpose.

It had only taken me years to figure out I could make everything work with the right person. And this idiot beside me who hugged me and grabbed my ass at least a dozen times at the LC randomly throughout the day, who took care of me and motivated me and wanted the best for me every single day of my life, was it.

And like he knew exactly what I was thinking, Ivan leaned over and kissed my temple, squeezing me to him even tighter.

"*Mom*, Danny just flicked me on the forehead!" Tati wailed, totally blowing it out of proportion. Probably. "I'm gonna kick his b-u-t-t!"

"What's a b-u-t-t?" Danny asked a moment later.

My mom turned around from where she was sitting next to Ben and shot me a smug look. And I knew exactly what she was thinking.

I was going to pay for all my sins with these three.

And I wasn't even dreading it.

ACKNOWLEDGMENTS

A book is never written without a lot of love and attention from an army of people.

First, a massive thank you to all of my readers. I wouldn't be writing this right now if it wasn't for your support. I say it every time, but you guys are seriously the absolute best. Thank you for sticking with me and just being awesome in general.

To the greatest reading group in the history of the Internet, my Slow Burners, thank you for your patience and love. To my pre-readers/friends for putting up with me and the horrible drafts I send you. Ryn, I can't thank you enough for not just being a good friend but for also helping me out with this freaking blurb. To my new friend Amy who kept me company so many nights doing writing sprints and for letting me vent randomly, this book would have taken me way longer to finish (and it would have been less fun).

Eva, Eva, Eva. The list of all the shit you do for me is endless.

You're a wonderful friend and every book is so much more special thanks to your eagle eye and honesty and your constant reassurances that you love it. I can't thank you enough for everything. (Especially for putting up with me.)

Thank you to Letitia Hasser at RBA Designs for bringing to life my vague ideas for book covers. Jeff Senter at Indie Formatting Services for always being so great. Virginia and Jenny at Hot Tree Editing for your kindness with edits. Lauren Abramo and Kemi Faderin at Dystel & Goderich for all those foreign rights we've been selling.

A great big thank you to the greatest family I could ever ask for: Mom, Dad, Ale, Raul, Eddie, Isaac, Kaitlyn, my Letchford family, and the rest of my Zapata/Navarro family.

Last but not least, Chris, Dor and Kai. Every book is for you, my loves.

ABOUT THE AUTHOR

Mariana Zapata lives in a small town in Colorado with her husband and two oversized children—her beloved Great Danes, Dorian and Kaiser. When she's not writing, she's reading, spending time outside, forcing kisses on her boys, harassing her family, or pretending to write.

www.marianazapata.com
Mailing List (New Release Information Only)

facebook.com/marianazapatawrites

twitter.com/marianazapata_

instagram.com/marianazapata

ALSO AVAILABLE

CPSIA information can be obtained
at www.ICGtesting.com
Printed in the USA
LVHW03s0904280618
582081LV00003BA/543/P